P9-BNC-474

THE SAILOR
FROM GIBRALTAR

NOVELS BY MARGUERITE DURAS AVAILABLE IN
PANTHEON MODERN WRITERS EDITIONS:

The Ravishing of Lol Stein
The Sailor from Gibraltar

OTHER BOOKS BY MARGUERITE DURAS:

Novels:

The Lover
The Sea Wall
Moderato Cantabile
10:30 on a Summer Night
The Afternoon of Mr. Andesmas
The Square
The Malady of Death

Screenplays:

Hiroshima, Mon Amour
India Song

Autobiography:

The War

MARGUERITE DURAS

. . . .

THE SAILOR FROM GIBRALTAR

TRANSLATED FROM THE FRENCH
BY BARBARA BRAY

PANTHEON BOOKS, NEW YORK

TO DIONYS

All rights reserved under International and Pan-
American Copyright Conventions. Published in
the United States by Pantheon Books, a division
of Random House, Inc., New York. Originally
published in France as *Le Marin de Gibraltar*
by Librairie Gallimard. Copyright © 1952 by
Librairie Gallimard. This translation first
published in |Great Britain by |Calder & Boyars,
Ltd., London, in 1966, and in the United States
by Grove Press, Inc., in 1967.

Library of Congress Cataloging-in-Publication Data

Duras, Marguerite.
The sailor from Gibraltar.
Translation of: Le marin de Gibraltar.
I. Title.
PQ2607.U8245M313   1986   843'.912   85-43440
ISBN 0-394-74451-9

Manufactured in the United States of America

First American Paperback Edition

PART ONE

WE'd seen Milan and Genoa and been in Pisa two days when I decided we'd go on to Florence. Jacqueline made no objection. She never made any objection.

It was the second year after the war. All the trains were crowded. Packed, no matter what time of the day, no matter where you were going. Travelling had become a sort of sport; we were getting quite good at it. But this time, in Pisa, when we got to the station the ticket office was closed, they just weren't accepting any more passengers. We thought we'd go by coach. But they weren't issuing any more tickets for those either. Still, I swore I'd get to Florence that day. I was always like that when I travelled, always had to be going further on, and that day the very idea of having to wait till tomorrow to see Florence was unendurable. I probably couldn't have said why, what revelation or respite I expected to find there. Although that was the only sort of thing I could get worked up about any more, I never bothered to analyze my feelings. After we'd drawn a blank at the coach-terminus I made enquiries, and was told that there were some workers who went back to Florence every Saturday evening at about six. They kept their vans parked in front of the station. Sometimes they gave people lifts.

We went back to the station. It was five o'clock, so we had an hour to wait. I sat down on my case, Jacqueline on hers. The station and the square in front of it had been bombed, and you could see the trains arriving and departing from outside, through the holes in the walls. Passengers streamed by us in hundreds, sweating and exhausted. It seemed to me they were all coming from or going to Florence; I stared at them enviously. It was hot. The leaves on the few trees left in the square were all shrivelled up in the sun and

7

the smoke from the trains, and there was hardly any shade. But all I thought of was those vans going to Florence, I didn't care how hot it was. After about half an hour Jacqueline said she was thirsty and would like a glass of lemonade, we'd got plenty of time. I told her to go and have one on her own, I didn't want to miss the workmen. She didn't go, she bought a couple of ices instead. We had to eat them fast because they melted in our hands, but they were too sweet and only made us more thirsty. It was August 11th. The Italians we'd met had told us it would soon be the hottest time of the year, which generally came around the 15th. Jacqueline reminded me of this.

'This is nothing to what it'll be like in Florence,' she said.

I didn't answer. Nine times out of ten I didn't answer her. The summer tormented me. Perhaps because I despaired of ever finding a means of making my life accord with it. It annoyed me to hear her talk about it in that tone.

At last the workers arrived, in groups. They were stone-masons employed in the reconstruction of Pisa. Some were still in their working clothes. The first group started to run over to a little covered van not far from us.

Jacqueline hurried over to the man who was getting into the driver's seat. She thought a woman would have more chance of getting round him. She explained to him in Italian – she had done a two-month course in Assimil in preparation for our holiday ; so had I, for that matter – that we were French and in difficulties about transport, that we wanted to get to Florence, and that we'd be very grateful if he would be so kind as to take us in his van. He agreed at once. I sat beside him so as to see the road better. Jacqueline got in the back. At the Colonial Ministry I always sat nearer the window than she did. It had become such an established thing that she'd even stopped minding about it. Or so I thought. At any rate she climbed meekly into the back. The van was covered in and it was thirty-six degrees in the shade that afternoon; but it was taken for granted that she didn't feel the heat. In

8

a few minutes the van was full and we started off. It was six o'clock. You could hardly get out of the town for the bicycles. The driver kept on swearing and cursing at the cyclists, who just rode on two or three abreast without paying the slightest attention to his horn. The first thing he told me was that he'd spent a couple of years in France as a child, and for my benefit he lost his temper in French. And in no uncertain manner. It wasn't long before he moved on to other subjects than the cyclists. There was no work to be had in Florence, you had to come all this way, fifty miles, to find it. Everything was difficult for the workers, you could hardly call their life an existence at all. The cost of living was high, wages were low. It couldn't go on like that much longer, things would have to change. The first thing that needed to be altered was the government – it would have to be thrown out, the present president would have to be got rid of. He expatiated a bit about the president: every time he uttered his unworthy name he waved his arms about in impotent rage and only took hold of the wheel again with reluctance and just before it was too late. The van lurched about all over the road, the wind got under the roof and the tarpaulin kept cracking like a whip. But no one inside seemed worried. I told myself it must be like this every Saturday, every week the driver must get worked up like this about the cyclists coming out of Pisa. I wasn't afraid. I'd been too afraid of not being able to set out for Florence that day to be afraid of anything else, even of not getting there. I just sat and listened to the driver, dazed with satisfaction.

Soon after we'd left Pisa, before we got to Cascina, muffled squeaks started to come out of the back. It was Jacqueline. The men must be making up to her a bit boldly, there was no mistaking that laughter. The driver heard it too. He looked embarrassed.

'If you like,' he said, 'your wife can come and sit beside me.'

'It doesn't matter.'

9

He looked at me in astonishment, then grinned.

'We're very jealous in Italy. I suppose it's different in France?'

'I suppose so.'

'They had a few before we left. It's pay-day today, that's why. Are you sure you don't mind?'

He was amused.

'It's only natural,' I said. 'One woman in with a lot of men, especially if they've had a few drinks.'

'It's nice not to be jealous. I couldn't be like that myself though.'

The men in the back were laughing, and Jacqueline let out a sharper cry than before. The driver looked at me in growing amazement.

'We lead a narrow life,' I said, 'we never see anybody. So I'm quite pleased when other people . . . You see what I mean.'

'I suppose you've been married a long time, eh?'

'We've known each other a long time, yes, but we're not married. We're going to be. She's very keen on it, won't be happy till we are married.'

We both laughed.

'A lot of women are like that about getting married,' he said.

Usually people who were happy, or even just placid, got on my nerves. But I didn't mind him.

'Love's just like everything else,' he said. 'It can't last for ever.'

'She's nice,' I said.

'Yes,' he laughed. 'I can see that.'

When we'd passed Cascina the road became much emptier. He was in a conversational mood. He started off by asking me the usual questions.

'This your first visit to Italy?'

'Yes.'

'How long have you been here?'

'A fortnight.'

'Well, how do you like the Italians?'

He asked this in a challenging tone, with a touch of childish arrogance, and awaited my answer with an inscrutable expression on his face, pretending to concentrate on the road.

'I couldn't really say yet,' I said. 'I don't know any. But it seems to me it would be difficult not to like them.'

He smiled.

'Not to like the Italians,' I said, 'would be not to like the human race.'

He relaxed completely now.

'They said some pretty nasty things about us during the war.'

'People will believe anything when there's a war on.'

I was tired. He didn't realize it at once.

'And Pisa – Pisa's a fine town, isn't it?'

'Oh yes,' I said, 'splendid.'

'It's a good thing the square wasn't hit.'

'Oh yes.'

He turned and looked at me. He saw I was making an effort to keep up the conversation.

'You're tired,' he said.

'A bit.'

'It's the heat,' he said, 'and travelling.'

'That's it,' I said.

But he still felt like talking himself. He went on chatting about his own concerns and I didn't have to put in an answer for about twenty minutes. He told me he'd been interested in politics since the liberation, and especially since he'd been a member of a factory committee in Piedmont. That was the best time of his life. When the committees were abolished he'd come back to Tuscany in disgust. But he missed Milan: it was a place with some life in it, Milan. He had a good deal to say about the factory committees, and about what the English had done.

'It was disgraceful, what they did there. Don't you agree?'

He obviously cared. I agreed that it was disgraceful. Then he started talking about himself again. Now he was a stone-mason in Pisa. There was a lot of building going on there. The van belonged to him. He'd got it at the liberation and he'd hung on to it. As he spoke, and as we drove through the villages, he slowed down so that I could see the churches, the buildings, the inscriptions chalked up on the walls: 'Viva il partito communista' and an upside down W followed by 'Il Re'. I looked at them so attentively that he slowed down for each one.

We reached Pontedera, and he started again about his van. He was not altogether easy in his mind about the way he had acquired it.

'I ought really to have given it back to my comrades on the committee, I suppose, but there it is, I didn't.'

He could see I had no strong views on the subject.

'I ought to have, but I couldn't. I'd been driving it for two months, so I just couldn't.'

'Most people would have done the same,' I said.

'I thought, I'll never have another van all my life. Things can happen like that, you know, you can't stop yourself, you even steal. Well, I stole this car, I admit. But I just can't be sorry I did it.'

It was just an old wreck, as I could see, couldn't do more than sixty kilometres an hour, but still he was glad to have it. He was mad about cars. Besides, if the valves were properly re-bored, she'd go up to eighty. But he never had time to get them done. Still, she was a boon to him. Because of her he was able to go to a little fishing port on the Mediterranean for week-ends during the spring and summer; he could take a few friends with him too. It was much cheaper than going by train. I asked him where it was. A place called Rocca, he told me. He had relations there. It wasn't far. It was difficult to get there every week because of the petrol rationing, but he could manage once a fortnight. He'd been there the previous week. Oh, it was only a tiny little place. The last time there had been some rich American woman there, and no one could make out what she could want in a place like that. At least, people said she was an American. She had a lovely yacht anchored just off-shore. He'd seen her bathing: a marvellous woman. It just showed you couldn't afford to generalize about anything. Until then he'd believed people when they said American women were not so beautiful as Italians. But there was no doubt about it, this one was so beautiful he couldn't remember ever seeing anyone to surpass her. He didn't say she was pretty or attractive, simply that she was beautiful. He said it seriously, in Italian: 'Bellissima.' and he added: 'E sola.'

Then he talked about Rocca. Why didn't I go there myself if I had time? You couldn't get a proper idea of Italy if you only went to the big towns. You ought to go to a village or two, to the country. And Rocca was just the place for seeing how the ordinary Italians, the poor people, lived. They'd been through such a lot, they'd worked harder than anyone, and just you see how kind they are. He knew them well – his parents were peasants – but although he didn't share their ignorance any longer, that only made him love them more. The fact that he'd left them behind made him feel rather as if they belonged to him. He spoke of them with pride, as if he was talking about something wonderful. Yes, if I had the time, I must certainly go to Rocca. There was only one small hotel but we would be very comfortable there.

'The sea's on one side,' he told me, 'and the river's on the other. If the sea's too rough, or too hot, or if you just want a change, you can bathe in the river. It's always cool in the river, and the hotel's just beside it.'

He went on telling me about the river and the hotel and the mountains that overhung the valley and the underwater fishing.

'You can't imagine what it's like till you've done it. The first time you're scared, then you can't live without it. It's so beautiful, the colours, the fish swimming right under your belly. So peaceful you can't imagine.'

He told me about the municipal dances and the fruit that grew round about – lemons the size of oranges.

We got to San Romano in the Arno Valley. The sky was lurid. There was no more sun on the road, but it lingered for a moment on the tops of the hills, planted with olives the whole way up. The houses were pretty, the same colour as the earth. Even the smallest had cypresses growing beside them. A revoltingly charming landscape.

'Do you come from this part of Tuscany?' I asked him.

'From the Arno valley, yes,' he said, 'but from the other side of Florence. But my family live at Rocca now. My father likes the sea.'

The sun disappeared behind the hills, and now the valley drew its light from the Arno. The smooth, shiny surface of the little river, its many gentle curves, its greenish colour, made it look like a sleepy animal. It flowed happily along, safe between its steep banks.

'How beautiful the river looks,' I said.

Without noticing, he began to use the familiar form of address.

'And what do you do?' he asked.

'I'm in the Colonial Ministry,' I told him. 'Registry section.'

'Do you like the work?'

'Loathe it.'

'What do you do?'

'Copy out birth and death certificates.'

'I see,' he said. 'Have you been doing it long?'

'Eight years.'

After a moment he said, 'I wouldn't be able to stick that myself.'

'No,' I said, 'you wouldn't.'

'Being a mason's hard enough – cold in the winter, hot in the summer. But copying things out all the time – I couldn't. It's a good thing some people can, mind you – but me, no, I couldn't.'

'I can't either,' I said.

'But you do?'

'Yes. At first I thought it would kill me, but I do it, you know how it is.'

'And do you still think that?'

'That it could kill someone? Yes, but someone else, not me any more.'

'It must be awful, always copying things,' he said slowly.

'You can't imagine,' I said.

I probably said it as if I was joking. It must have sounded either as if it wasn't as bad as all that, or as if that was just my way of talking about my personal affairs.

'The sort of work people do is very important,' he said. 'You can't just do any old thing.'

'But somebody has to do it,' I said. 'Why not me?'

'No,' he said. 'Why should it be you?'

'I tried to do something else but I could never find anything.'

'Sometimes,' he said, 'it's better just to die of hunger. In your place I'd rather have died of hunger.'

'There's always that fear of being out of work. And then you feel ashamed, somehow, I don't know.'

'Still, there are some things it's more shameful to do than not to do.'

'I'd have liked to be a racing cyclist, an explorer, something impossible. And I ended up in the Ministry. My father was a colonial civil servant so it was quite easy for me to get in. The first year you don't really believe it, you think of it as a joke. The next year you say to yourself it can't last. Then it's the third year and there you are.'

He was pleased I'd started to talk. I went on.

'I was happy during the war. I was in a signals company. I learned to climb telegraph poles. It was dangerous – I could have fallen off or electrocuted myself. But I was happy. I couldn't even stop on Sundays – I used to climb trees.'

We laughed.

'When the time came to retreat I was at the top of a

15

telegraph pole. The others went off without me, but in the wrong direction. When I got down there was no one there, so I went off on my own. But I was lucky – I went in the right direction.'

He laughed heartily.

'The war! You couldn't help laughing sometimes during the war.' Then, after a moment, 'What about later, during the resistance?'

'I was with the Ministry in Vichy.'

He was silent, as if that called for further explanation.

'I made false certificates for Jews who were in hiding, especially death certificates, of course.'

'Ah, I see. And didn't you ever have any trouble?'

'No, never. But after the war I was demoted for having been three years at Vichy.'

'Couldn't those Jews you helped have said something?'

I laughed.

'I couldn't trace any of them.'

'Yes, but still. . . Do you just let people do what they like with you?'

He looked at me again. He thought I was lying.

'I didn't look very hard. Even if I hadn't been demoted I'd still have been in the registry section, so. . .'

'Yes, but still . . . .' he repeated.

He didn't believe me.

'It's true,' I said. I smiled at him. 'There's no reaon why I should lie to you.'

'I believe you,' he said at last.

I started to laugh.

'Usually I lie quite a lot. But not today. Some days are just like that.'

'Everybody tells lies,' he said after a moment's hesitation.

'I tell lies to everybody,' I said. 'To her, to my bosses. I got into the habit at the office because I often arrive late. I can't very well say I detest the work, so I say I've got liver trouble.'

He laughed, but not very heartily.

'You can't call that lying,' he said.

'You have to talk about something sometimes, after all, and my liver's the subject I'm best on. Every day I describe the tricks it plays me. At the Ministry, instead of saying good morning to me they say "How's your liver?" '

'And does *she* believe you?'

'I don't know, she never talks about it.'

He thought for a minute.

'And are you interested in politics?'

'I used to be when I was a student.'

'But not any more?'

'Gradually less and less, and now not at all.'

'You were a communist, were you?'

'Yes.'

He was silent.

'I started too soon,' I said. 'You know, you get tired. . .'

'Oh, I understand,' he answered gently.

There was another long silence, then he said suddenly:

'Come to Rocca for the week-end.'

My whole life was swallowed up in the registry section. Beside that calamity, what were three days at Rocca? But I understood what he meant – that life was so hard sometimes, as he himself well knew, that one ought to go to Rocca now and again to remind oneself that it could occasionally be less so.

'Why not?' I said.

'I love the place, I don't know why,' he said.

We got to Empoli.

'They make glass here,' he told me.

I said I was enjoying myself. He didn't speak for a bit. He was thinking about something else, me I think. After Empoli it got cooler again. We'd left the Arno behind now, but I didn't mind. I was happy: I wasn't wasting time. He looked at me and listened, and I could see I was the best travelling companion he'd had for a long time. We could be

17

friends. I was doing well. It wasn't usual for me to be happy. It exhausted me, I took a week to get over it, it affected me worse than going out and getting drunk.

'Go to Rocca,' he repeated. 'You'll see.'

'I've still got ten days,' I said. 'Why not?'

The van was now going as fast as it could – sixty kilometres an hour. It wasn't hot now, at least not if you weren't under the tarpaulin. With the dusk there came a cool breeze that must have been blowing from where the storm had already burst – it smelled damp.

We went on talking, about him, work, wages, his life, life in general. We wondered about what made a man happy – work or love or whatever.

'You said you hadn't got any friends,' he said. 'I don't understand that. People always ought to have friends, oughtn't they?'

'I ask nothing better,' I said, 'but I can't stand the people I work with at the Ministry, and she doesn't know anybody apart from them.'

'What about you?'

'Only some old friends from the university. I never see them now.'

'That's queer,' he said. He spoke kindly, his mistrust of me had almost gone. 'I should have thought people could always find friends.'

'I had plenty during the war,' I said. 'But now it seems as difficult to find a friend as to find . . . I don't know what.'

'A woman?'

'Almost,' I said, laughing.

'Yes, but still,' he said.

He thought for a moment.

'Of course,' he said, 'it's easier for us than for you. In Italy it's quite simple, everybody knows everybody else.'

'Not in France,' I said. 'There it takes time. Everybody calls everybody else monsieur. And then, when you're copying you can't talk to anyone.'

'Yes. At least we can speak whenever we feel like it. It's like – what's it like, now? – it's like during the war still, rather. You have to fight for wages and to get enough to eat. So having friends is quite easy.'

'I wouldn't mind killing my colleagues,' I said, 'but don't ask me to talk to them.'

'Perhaps when you're feeling too fed up,' he said, 'it's like that – you can't find friends.'

'Perhaps,' I said.

'Of course,' he said, 'nobody can expect to escape trouble. That's just life. But for every day to be so rotten, into the bargain, that you can't make friends – no, that's too much.'

Then he added:

'I can't stand it when I haven't got any friends. It makes me miserable.'

I didn't answer. He seemed to regret what he'd just said. But suddenly he said very gently:

'If you ask me, I think you ought to leave that job.'

'I expect I shall one day,' I answered.

He evidently thought I wasn't taking it seriously enough.

'I know it's nothing to do with me,' he said, 'but I do think you ought to leave that job.'

Then, after a moment:

'You've got stuck, haven't you?'

'I've been meaning to leave my job for eight years now,' I said. 'But I'll do it one day.'

'I meant you ought to do it soon,' he said.

'You may be right,' I said after a moment.

I found the coolness of the breeze extremely pleasant. He didn't seem to feel it as much as I did.

'Why are you saying this to me?' I asked.

'But you've been waiting for somebody to say it to you, haven't you?' he said softly. Then he repeated:

'You've got stuck. Anybody would tell you the same.'

He hesitated for a moment, then said in the tone of somebody who feels he must bring himself to speak:

19

'It's the same with the girl,' he said. 'What are you supposed to be doing with her?'

'I hesitated for a long time. But now I think, why not? She's keen on it, and there she is in the same office as me, wanting me to marry her all day under my very eyes – you know how it is.'

He didn't answer.

'You get so that you don't want to get out of the mess you're in any more, you say to yourself if that's how it is you'll make a life for yourself in it up to the neck.'

He didn't laugh.

'No,' he said, displeased by my cynicism, 'you mustn't say that.'

'Most people would do the same as me,' I said. 'I haven't any real reason for not marrying her.'

'What's she like?'

'As you see,' I said, 'always contented and cheerful. An optimist.'

'I see,' he said, and grimaced. 'I'm not very keen on women who are always cheerful. They're . . .'

'Tiring,' I said.

'That's it, tiring.' He turned to me and smiled.

'I wonder,' I said, 'if it's worth hankering after big things, life with a capital L. Perhaps three or four little things, conditions that might be fulfilled any time . . .'

He turned to me and smiled again.

'Yes, you need the little things,' he said. 'But in life, just being contented isn't enough. Now and again you need something more, don't you?'

'What?'

'Happiness. That's what love's for, isn't it?'

'I don't know,' I said.

'Of course you know.'

I didn't answer.

'Come to Rocca,' he said. 'If you come on Saturday I'll be there. We'll go underwater fishing together.'

20

We didn't talk about ourselves any more. We got to Lastra and left the Arno valley.

'Another fourteen kilometers,' he said.

He lowered the windscreen and the wind blew full in our faces.

'That's nice,' I said.

'It's always like this when we get past Lastra, I don't know why.'

The wind made it seem as if we were going much faster. We hardly spoke any more, we'd have had to put up the windscreen and the breeze was far too pleasant. Every so often he would shout:

'Another half an hour,' or 'Another twenty minutes,' or 'Fifteen minutes more and then you'll see it.'

He meant Florence, but he might have meant something else, some unknown happiness. I was enjoying it so much, sitting there beside him in the wind, that I could happily have sat there another hour. But he was so impatient for me to get there that his enthusiasm prevailed. I suddenly became as impatient as he was for us to get to Florence.

'Another seven kilometres,' he cried, 'and you'll see it down there, when we get to the top of the hill.'

It must have been about the hundredth time he had made the journey between Pisa and Florence.

'Look,' he shouted, 'down there.'

The city sparkled below us like a sky full of stars, and slowly, down the winding road, we descended into its depths.

But I was thinking of something else. I was wondering whether the answer mightn't be to go like this from one town to the other and be satisfied with the friends one happened to make on the way, like him; whether a woman mightn't be, in certain cases, superfluous.

When we got there we all had a glass of white wine together in a café near the station. Jacqueline climbed out of the back of the van dishevelled but not unduly molested. She probably looked quite pretty to other people. I thought she looked in good form; she was in a very good temper.

When we were in the café he began to talk to me about Rocca again. I looked at him while he was speaking – in the van I'd only been able to see his profile. I saw that all the other workmen looked alike, but he was different. Was it because it had given me so much pleasure to talk to him? Suddenly I felt a bit intimidated. He repeated that I ought to go to Rocca even if it was only to have a rest. The really hot weather would soon be here. And what was a week? We could bathe together in the Magra and if we had time he knew a good place to go underwater fishing – his cousin would lend me some goggles. Would I go, then? I said yes. Jacqueline smiled, she didn't believe it. He didn't ask her to go to Rocca.

Those few days were the hottest of the year in Florence. I'd been hot before – I was born and brought up in the tropics, in the colonies, and I'd read about such things too. But it was in Florence, during those interminable days, that I learned what heat really was. It was an event in itself. Nothing else happened – it was hot, that was all. For four days the town was consumed by a quiet conflagration, without flames, without cries from the victims. The inhabitants, tortured almost as much as they had ever been by wars or plagues, had no other thought but simple survival. Not only was it more than human flesh and blood could bear, it was more than any flesh and blood could bear: a chimpanzee died at the zoo. Even the fish were dying of suffocation – the Arno reeked of them, there were pieces about it in the papers. The tar on the roads melted. I don't imagine that anyone made love, or any child was conceived there in those few days. In that heat nobody could have written a line except in the papers, and they talked of nothing else. The dogs had to wait for more auspicious weather to copulate, murderers had to put off their crimes, lovers neglected each other. The intellect didn't seem to exist any longer; reason was crushed and could attach no meaning to anything. Personality became a relative and, to all intents and purposes, empty notion. It was worse than military service, worse even than God himself could have intended. Everybody in the town was reduced to the same limited vocabulary: for five days no one said anything but 'I'm thirsty. It can't go on like this.' It didn't last, it couldn't last, there was no precedent for its lasting more than a few days. On the night of the fourth day there was a storm. It was time. Everyone in the town went back to his usual devices. Except me. I was still on holiday.

Those five days were all more or less alike to me. I spent the whole time in a cafeteria. Jacqueline went to see all the sights. She got very thin, but she went through with it to the bitter end. I think she must have seen all the palaces and museums and monuments that it's possible to see in a week. I don't know what she was thinking about, but in the cafeteria, drinking my iced coffees and *crèmes de menthe* and eating ice-cream, I was thinking about the Magra. Whatever she was thinking about it wasn't the Magra, but something very different – perhaps the very opposite of the Magra. While I, all day long, I repeated to myself, the Magra's always cool, even on the hottest day, always cool. The sea wasn't enough for me now, I had to have a river, water flowing in shadow.

The first day I went from our hotel to the cafeteria. I intended to have an iced coffee and then go for a walk round the town. I stopped there the whole morning – Jacqueline found me there at mid-day, drinking my sixth beer. She was furious. What was the point of being in Florence for the first time in your life and spending the whole morning in a café? 'This afternoon,' I said, 'I'll try this afternoon.' It was understood that we'd each go about on our own and just meet for meals. So after lunch she went off again. I went back to the cafeteria, which was near the restaurant. The time went quickly. At seven o'clock in the evening I was still

23

there. Jacqueline found me drinking a *crème de menthe* this time. She was furious again. 'If I move it'll kill me,' I told her. I was sure of it, but I thought it would be better the next day.

It wasn't better the next day, though I made the effort. After breakfast, an hour after Jacqueline had set off, I left the cafeteria (I'd looked in there to begin with) and set off down the via Tornabuoni. Where was the Arno? I asked a tourist the way, and he pointed it out to me directly. To tell the truth, what I really wanted to see were the dead fish floating on the surface. I got there and saw them from the bank. The papers exaggerated. They were there all right, but not nearly as many as they said. I was disappointed. As for the river itself, it hadn't got much in common now with the one I'd seen on the way from Pisa, in short with the Arno of my youth. A rotten sell, I thought to myself, a mere trickle, and full of dead fish into the bargain. I reminded myself half-heartedly that it was the Arno, but it was no use, it wouldn't work. I left. The streets were crowded, but mostly with tourists. They all looked extremely hot. There were two or three streams of people coming away from the river. I joined one of them, not having any particular object of my own, and came out in a square. I recognized it. Where had I seen it before then? It was on a post-card, of course – I was in the Piazza della Signoria. I stood still, looking into the square. Well, there it is, I said to myself. The sun was blazing down on it; the mere idea of crossing it finished me. Still, now that I was there, I should have to cross it. There were all the tourists crossing it – one just had to. There were hundreds of them crossing it, even women and children. Were they so different from me? I'll do it, I said to myself. But before I knew where I was I was sitting on one of the steps of the Galeria. I waited. My shirt got gradually damper and damper and stuck to my back. My jacket got gradually damper and damper and stuck to my shirt. Inside the jacket and the shirt, I thought about them, I couldn't think about

24

anything else. The air over the square was shimmering as over a cauldron. I'll do it, I said to myself again. But then a workman came up to the Galeria, stopped a few yards away from me, took a large wrench out of his tool-bag, and opened a water-tap just beneath where I was sitting. The gutter filled up right to the brim. I watched it, and was seized by a sort of mad fascination. The water spurted out of the tap in a shining jet. I wanted to clap my mouth to the opening and let myself be filled up like the gutter. But fortunately the dead fish rose to the surface in my memory. Perhaps the water came from the Arno. I didn't drink, but I thought of the Magra all the more. Ever since I'd been here every object, every hour, made it seem more desirable to me. I could tell that it only needed a little more, a very little more, to make me go to Rocca. I was slowly getting to the point. But the little more that was needed was not to be added that day. The square was not enough. In any case I didn't give it time. After I'd seen the water in the gutter, I gave up the idea of crossing the square. I got up and went away. Through the narrow streets I made my way back to the cafeteria. I didn't have to say a word, just by looking at me the waiter understood.

'What Monsieur needs is a large iced *crème de menthe*,' he said.

I drained it straight off. Then I flopped back in my chair and sweated until it was time to meet Jacqueline.

That was the only walk I took in Florence – the only time, that is, I made an effort to see the sights. After that I didn't stir from the café for another two days.

The only person I could bear near me was the waiter there; that was why I kept going back. I used to watch him serving from ten in the morning till midday, and then from three till seven. He used to look after me. Every so often he'd bring me the papers. Sometimes he spoke to me. 'The heat!' he'd say. Or: 'Iced coffee is the best in this weather. It quenches your thirst and gives you energy.' I listened to

what he said and drank whatever he advised. He enjoyed
taking care of me.

Sitting there in the café, with the waiter, downing a pint
of something or another every hour, life still seemed bearable – worth the trouble of living, I mean. The trick was to
stay still. I didn't feel I had anything in common with the
tourists. They apparently didn't need to drink all that much.
I idly imagined them as made out of some special spongy
tissue, like cacti, which without their knowing it had con-
ditioned them for their vocation as tourists.

I drank, read, sweated, and every so often went and sat
somewhere else, changing from inside the café to the terrasse.
And of course I watched what was going on in the street. I
noticed that the swarm of tourists thinned out about midday,
and grew dense again about five. There were thousands of
them, braving the heat. Even with their special tissues they
were heroes, the only ones in the place, the heroes of tourism.
I was its shame. I was disgracing myself. Once I said to the
waiter: 'I shan't have seen anything of Florence. How awful
of me.' He only laughed and said it was a question of temperament not free-will – some people could and some couldn't.
He was sure about it, he'd seen plenty of heat-waves. He
added kindly that mine was one of the most typical cases
he'd ever seen. I was so pleased with this explanation I
repeated it word for word to Jacqueline the same evening.

About four o'clock a water-cart used to go by. Steam rose
from the road after it had passed, steam and a thousand and
one different smells. I inhaled them slowly: they were good,
and soothing to the conscience. They made me feel that I
was in Florence after all, in a sort of way.

I only saw Jacqueline at meals. I hadn't got anything to
say to her. She'd got plenty to say to me though. Naturally.
She told me all she'd seen and done during the morning or
the afternoon. She'd stopped asking me to make an effort,
but she kept on praising the wonders of Florence in the
belief that this was a more effective method of persuading

me to see them. She never stopped praising them. She kept babbling away about things that were so beautiful, no but really so beautiful, that I couldn't not go and see them — it was implied that my honour, my status as an educated man, perhaps even greater things were involved. I didn't listen to her. I just let her babble on as much as she liked. I was putting up with quite a lot of things then, from her and from life. In fact, I was tired by life, one of those whose tragedy it was never to have encountered a pessimism equal to their own. Such men always let the others talk away as much as they like, but it doesn't do to take it for granted. For three days I let her talk twice a day, at lunch and at dinner. And then came the third day.

On the third day, instead of meeting her at the hotel at seven, as arranged, I stayed on at the cafeteria. I thought to myself, if I'm not at the hotel she'll come and look for me here. Usually, even if only with a bad grace, I kept our appointments. That day I couldn't see that it was necessary any more. At seven-thirty, as I expected, she turned up at the cafeteria.

'You do take advantage, don't you,' she said quietly.

She seemed quite happy.

'You think I take advantage?'

'Yes, a bit,' she said, still without rancour.

She didn't want to go on about it. I noticed that she'd made up and changed her dress. She'd been sightseeing since nine that morning.

'Been anywhere?' she asked.

'No,' I said. 'Nowhere.'

'One can get used to anything, even the heat,' she said. 'All you need to do is make a bit of effort . . .'

For three years she'd been telling me every day to make a bit of effort. The time had gone quickly.

'You've got thin,' I said.

'That won't do me any harm,' she said, smiling. 'It'll soon come back.'

'You oughtn't to tire yourself out like that.'

'I can't help myself.'

'That's not true,' I said.

She looked at me in astonishment, and flushed.

'You are in a bad temper,' she said.

'I know I'm wrong. Since you're in Florence you might as well get all you can out of it.'

'What about you? What's the point of saying that to me?'

'I don't want to.'

'You really do like to be different, don't you?'

'No. It's just that I don't feel like it.'

'You don't mean to say you don't like Florence?'

'I've no opinion on the subject.'

She was silent for a moment.

'I saw the Giottos today,' she said.

'It's all one to me,' I answered.

She looked at me in surprise but decided not to take any notice.

'To think he only lived in thirteen hundred, before even, my goodness. . . .'

She went on about Giotto. I watched her talking, and she seemed pleased at this – perhaps she thought I was listening, she was quite capable of it. I hadn't looked at her properly for I don't know how long; months.

We went out of the cafeteria. She was still talking about Giotto. She took my arm. As usual. The street closed round me. The café suddenly seemed like an island in the midst of an ocean.

For the first time since I'd been living with her I felt . . . ashamed, yes ashamed at feeling her arm in mine.

There is such a thing as a last straw. Even if it's impossible to say by what fantastically complicated labyrinths it arrives, that's no reason for refusing to believe in it. And not only must you believe in it, but sometimes, I think, you just have to let it break your back. I let it break mine while she was talking about Giotto.

28

The next day, although it was already established that we didn't go about together, I told her I wasn't coming with her 'today either.' She looked surprised, but let it go and went off without me. I got up late, had a bath, and went straight to the cafeteria. I'd decided what I was going to do. I was going to try to find the man who'd driven us from Pisa. There wasn't much opportunity to talk to the waiter, and when there was we only spoke about either the heat or what it was best to drink to keep cool. In the end even he seemed to notice it was rather a case of out of the frying-pan into the fire. And then I was getting rather tired of seeing him rush about from one table to another without stopping. After hoping for two days that he might find a quarter of an hour to have a drink with me, I realized that it was impossible. So then I thought of the man who'd driven the van. After a couple of coffees I made my second excursion into the town. I went in the direction of the station, looking for the bar where we'd had a drink together the evening we arrived. I hadn't been able to muster the effort to see the sights, but I mustered the effort for him, to find him. I was so hot I thought once or twice it would kill me. But I kept on. I found the bar. I managed to explain what I wanted, but they told me that unfortunately all the men were in Pisa again – it was only Wednesday and they wouldn't be back until Saturday. In fact they couldn't tell me any more than I already knew. Had I forgotten it then? I don't think so. No, I was just pretending to forget it, hoping for the impossible, trying to provoke the unjust fate that I wanted to believe was inflicted on me alone. I succeeded. I was in despair at what they told me. I stood at the entrance to the bar again, convinced that there wasn't anyone in the whole of Florence with whom I could simply have a chat over a granita. Even the man with the van wasn't there. There wasn't anybody in Florence except tourists and Jacqueline. I didn't doubt that there must be some people like me somewhere, people with time to waste, people who didn't want to keep rushing about, but where were they? And did I really want to find them? No. No, what I wanted was to be alone in the town with no one but her. And so I was. For five days and five nights.

I lost all my freedom. She occupied every thought, claimed all my days and all my nights. A black wedge driven into my heart.

I was the son of a colonial civil servant, district officer of a province in Madagascar as big as the Dordogne. Every morning he reviewed his staff, and as they hadn't any guns to inspect he inspected their ears. He was as mad about hygiene as he was about patriotism. He made it compulsory for the pupils to sing the Marseillaise at the beginning of term in every school under his jurisdiction. He went into ecstasies every time the population had to be vaccinated, but when his house-boy was ill he sent him away to die. Every so often he would get an order to recruit five hundred men to work on the white plantations. Then he was in his glory. He'd set off with a band of soldiers and police, surround the villages, and hunt the inhabitants out with rifles. Then when he'd got them all herded into cattle-trucks bound for the plantations, which were sometimes over five hundred miles away, he would come home tired but happy, and say: 'It was hard work. They ought not to teach them French history. The Revolution is still at the root of a lot of our trouble.' This imbecile was in charge of a district of ninety thousand souls, over whom he exercised almost dictatorial powers. And until I was sixteen he was my only teacher. So I knew very well what it was to keep someone under constant surveillance, guarding every second, watching every movement. I knew very well what it was to wish every day for that person's death – when I was fifteen my favourite dream, the only thing that restored the world to a semblance of its original innocence, had been to imagine my father shot dead by one of his native recruits. I knew the peculiar madness that can almost seize you just at the sight of the knives on the dinner-table. I knew what it was to watch from behind a bush and faint at the sight of my father inspecting his servants' ears. But in Florence, during the heat-wave, I didn't remember all these childish things.

All day, sitting in the cafeteria, I would think about her, the girl I was imprisoned with in Florence.

I waited for her for hours, just like someone madly in love.

The mere sight of her satisfied me and made up for all the waiting. She was not only the subject of my unhappiness, but also a perfect image, a photograph of it. Her smile, her walk, the very dress she wore made me overcome all my past uncertainties. I was seeing things clearly at last, I thought.

She had never touched a rifle, never inspected the ears of anybody whatsoever, but so what? At breakfast she dipped her croissant in her coffee – that was enough for me. I yelled at her to stop. She stopped and looked at me in amazement. I apologized. She said no more about it. And then she was short – that was enough for me too. She wore a dress. She was a woman – that was enough for me. Even her simplest gestures, her most harmless words, dumbfounded me. When she said pass the salt please I was dazed by the towering significance of the words. Nothing escaped me, nothing she did during those five days was lost on me. I was just making up the account. In five days I was looking at her for three years.

I discovered a lot of things. I discovered that it wasn't just that she was on the one hand a woman and on the other alive, or again that she wasn't my type. No, there was something else: it was that she belonged to a particular category – she was an optimist. I meditated endlessly on optimists: their distinguishing characteristic is that they wear you out. They usually enjoy excellent health, nothing ever gets them down, they're full of energy. They are very keen on the human race. They love it, they find it noble, it's their main preoccupation. There is said to be a certain species of red ants, in Mexico I think, that can devour a corpse, bones and all, in next to no time. She looked so sweet, with little teeth like a child's. But she had been my ant for two years. All that time she had done my washing and looked after me scrupulously. She had the gracefulness of an ant as well, and you could just as easily have crushed her between your fingers. She'd always been a most exemplary ant. Alone and unaided she could make you forswear optimism for ever, so depressing did all its cere-monies appear, so deceitful all its works, so crushing its tyranny. Alone and unaided she could make you deny optimism and all its works until your dying gasp. And I lived with her for two years.

So it was in Florence that I discovered that she surpassed all my hopes.

The unquenchable source of – what shall I call it – my new passion for her was of course the heat. She would say, 'I love the heat,' or 'Everything's so interesting I forget how hot it is.' I discovered that it wasn't true, it wasn't possible for a human being to like that heat, it was just the lie she'd always told, the optimist's lie. And things only interested her because she had made up her mind that they should, because she'd banished out of her life those liberties that make one's moods liable to change and therefore dangerous. If she had ever allowed herself to doubt that the heat was a good thing sooner or later she would have come to doubt the rest – to doubt, for instance, whether her hopes concerning me were as sound as she liked to think. I discovered that she would allow any sort of doubt you liked except that doubt which she considered 'wicked.' Finally I discovered, I the champion liar, that small as her lies were, or seemed, they were in a different class altogether from mine.

'This heat's even killing the fishes,' I'd say to her.

She'd laugh. I didn't go on about it, of course. I discovered too that despite all the time we'd lived together she was still more of a stranger to me than, say, the dead fishes in the Arno, which at least poisoned the air quite openly. She never went to see them. She said she couldn't stand their mar-

vellous sultry stench. I sniffed it up like a bunch of roses. I
saw that we'd never even agreed about the weather. Every
kind of weather has its own attraction, she said; she wouldn't
say she preferred one to another. Whereas I – for some kinds
of weather I had an insurmountable horror. I discovered also
that even in my very hostility she had always seen fresh
reasons to hope, and saw them still. We're not married yet,
she used to say jokingly.

I found out other little things as well. For instance that
she'd never shown anyone either forbearance or curiosity,
and nobody had ever really touched her. I was the only
person she had ever preferred or been indulgent to. She said
that humanity was good, she professed to believe in it without reserve and to live for its advancement. But she had
never been moved by the distress of a single individual, only
by the sorrows of mankind as a whole. I remembered that she
had always liked to talk about those, and that she always had
a perfectly clear and unwavering picture of what needed to be
done about them. She had always preferred gym displays to
crimes; love she took to be a gentle pleasure, and it always
left her satisfied and smiling, as unmoved by that as she was
by crime. Everybody liked her at the Ministry; chirping
away like a nightingale, she grew more and more popular as
time went on. She was one of those well-known secret
optimists, of whom people say they would make any man
happy, they are so kind, so understanding. I discovered that
it was after she came that my suffering reached its peak. For
I definitely had nothing whatever in common with nightin-
gales or the paeans of nature, and I was the only one who
knew that she would never make anybody happy.

I wasn't bored any longer. I delved indefatigably into her,
and from this ant's existence, so agitated and so fragile, I
brought up tons of discoveries. To my dazzled eyes they
seemed like gold.

Once, slightly ashamed of all these riches, I tried to put up
a struggle. She came into the cafeteria. I tried to tell myself

33

that it wasn't so bad as all that, that her dress suited her, that lots of people would have been touched to see her braving the heat with her little *Guide Bleu*, that lots of people would even be glad of her, and there was no real reason why I shouldn't be. Then she came up to the table and said hello, and her optimism burst out again like a ripe fruit. I could no more avoid seeing it than I could avoid seeing the dead fish that had risen up from the depths of the Arno. I went back once more to them, to the fish that had been killed by the heat.

The most fruitful times were at night, when we were in bed. I was no longer capable of making allowances for the heat of the city on the one hand and hers on the other. With her I was no longer capable of making allowances for anything, of telling myself that anybody else would have been just as insufferable as she was, in bed on nights like that. No, I was sure there were some whose sleeping bodies would have given out a warmth that was bearable, fraternal. The warmth her body gave out seemed to me to betray her for what she was, to be an unmistakeable and obscene denunciation of her optimism. These nights brought marvellous visions. They were among the best nights of my life. I hardly slept. I kept starting awake – it seemed to me that her very presence woke me – and I would watch her for hours, in the dark, sleeping her indefensible sleep. Then when I couldn't look at this wonderful spectacle any longer I would lie down again. And it was then, every night, that the vision of a river appeared to me. It was broad, cold, without a trace of the feminine. I called it, whispering, the Magra. The very name refreshed my heart. We were alone, the driver and I. No one in the whole landscape but we two. She – she had vanished entirely out of my life. We walked along by the river. He had plenty of time. It was Saturday, a long Saturday. The sky was cloudy. Every now and then we'd put on our underwater goggles and dive, not in the sea, in the river, and swim side by side in that strange, green, darkly phosphorescent

34

universe, among the weeds and the fishes. Then we'd come out again. Then dive again. We didn't speak to each other, we didn't talk at all. We had no need of anything. This dream Saturday lasted three nights, endless, inexhaustible. My desire to be with him, on the river-bank or in the river, was so great it extinguished all other desires. I didn't think once of a woman. I couldn't have imagined any woman with me in that river.

But with daylight the river disappeared out of my life. Her presence, the woman's, leapt at my throat. I didn't have time to imagine anything on my own account.

It ended quite quickly, before the end of the heat-wave; suddenly, one afternoon.

She'd asked me to go with her to the museum at San Marco, a thing she'd not done ever since we'd been here. Since I'd had this new passion for her I'd been kind. I said I'd go. I was so preoccupied with her that when I wasn't with her I was at a loss. And a museum in Florence struck me as one of the best possible places, together with sports grounds, for spying on her, catching her red-handed in her optimism. So I accepted eagerly, and we went. It was the hottest day of the whole heat-wave. The tar on the roads was almost liquid. Moving about was like those nightmares where you have to force your way through air like treacle. Your temples thudded, your lungs burned, many fishes died. It was that day that the chimpanzee gave up the ghost. She trotted along, pleased as Punch, a little way in front of me, as if to guide me and keep up my enthusiasm. Slut, I thought to myself. She thought she had won, and kept turning round to see if I was still following. I felt I was approaching my boldest deeds yet – I didn't go into detail about what they would be. Anything might happen. At last anything may happen, I thought. I'd just wait and see. That was what I'd decided. And then what? I didn't know. I was inspired, with a thousand and one vague plans whose very indeterminateness seemed sacred. That they were so vague and so many

35

did not make them seem any less important. On the contrary: it was because they were so vague and so many that they seemed so important. But the slut, the slut, I kept repeating to myself. I walked, head high, towards the museum, and just to see her, through the trickles of sweat running down over my eyes, walking along in front of me so sweetly, filled me with *joie de vivre*, the joy of knowing that I was going to live.

We arrived at the museum.

It wasn't like any I had seen before. It was an old one-storey house, built for the summer and painted dull pink, which looked out not on the town but on an inner garden surrounded by an open arcade paved with red stones. Although that day I was at the height of my passion I stopped in my tracks as soon as I saw the house. It seemed to me very beautiful. It was simple in form – just a hollow square. I didn't think I'd ever seen such a beautiful house. It had a special sort of beauty. Nobody had intended it; it was beautiful naturally, so to speak, and simply because, looking at it, you could see quite clearly why it had been built. Why? Because the people that built it had a deep knowledge, and perhaps experience, of summer. Probably some people would have preferred other kinds of houses, more welcoming, more ornate, looking out over mountains or the sea instead of just turned in upon itself. But they would have been wrong. Because, coming out of this one, you must come upon the town as out of no other, as if out of the sea into the warm air, dazzled. The shadow it cast was so intense it looked like a river passing beneath. It was as if the Magra flowed by the garden. Coming out of the sun into that shadow I was taken aback.

'Come on then,' said Jacqueline.

I followed her. She asked a guide where the Annunciation was. Once, when I was about twelve, when my father was on leave and we spent a couple of months in Britanny, I'd had a reproduction of the angel hanging over my bed. Now I had

36

a vague desire to see what it was like in real life, so to speak. We were told that the picture was in a room near the entrance. We went straight there. It was the only picture in the room. A dozen or so tourists were standing looking at it in silence. Although there were three benches placed opposite, none of them had sat down. After a moment's hesitation, I did. Then Jacqueline sat down beside me. I recognized the angel. I'd seen other reproductions besides the one in Britanny, but that was the only one I could really remember. I recognized the angel as well as if I'd slept beside him the night before.

'Isn't it lovely?' whispered Jacqueline.

Although this observation was by no means unexpected, its effect upon me was. It had no effect upon me at all. I was resting as I sat and looked at the picture. For the last four nights, since I'd been dreaming of the river, I'd had practically no sleep, and I suddenly noticed that I was fantastically tired. My hands, resting on my knees, felt like lead. The light that came in through the door was green, as in a painting, reflecting the green of the grass. The picture, the tourists and I basked in this painted light. It was very, very restful.

'Especially the angel,' whispered Jacqueline.

I now saw that the other reproductions that I'd seen since didn't give such a good idea of the picture as the one in Britanny. I recognized the woman too. I was so young when I first saw the angel that I couldn't remember whether I liked him at first or not. But I knew I'd always rather disliked the woman. Is he telling her that her son is going to be murdered?

'Isn't it lovely?' said Jacqueline again.

I remembered that often, during those holidays, I wondered whom he could be leaning towards like that.

'Of course, she's lovely too,' said Jacqueline.

I suddenly thought I'd tell her I knew this angel, the swine, had known him since I was a little boy. It was an entirely insignificant detail that I could have told anyone; it

37

wouldn't have taught her anything about me that she didn't know, it wouldn't have committed me in any way. Yes, I'll tell her, I thought. But – whether it was because I was tired I don't know – I couldn't. It wasn't so much I myself who couldn't tell her as my lips. They opened, and then sort of stuck and shut up like a clam. Nothing came out. Something wrong here, I thought, slightly anxious.

'But especially the angel,' Jacqueline said again.

I tried again, but in vain. I simply couldn't bring myself to tell her a simple little thing like that, that the angel was as familiar to me as an old school-friend. It was quite clear: I was a man who'd conducted his life in such a way that not only had he nobody to whom he could say such a thing, but he couldn't even manage simply to utter it. And yet it was quite an easy thing to say: When I was small I had a reproduction of that angel for a couple of months. Or, Seeing that angel's like meeting an old friend, because once, in Britanny, I had a reproduction of it hanging over my bed. To say that might present a problem to a dog or to a fish, but I was a man. It wasn't natural. There were a thousand and one ways of saying it, but I couldn't find one way of saying it to *her*. I could have said to him, Do you remember? But what would be the point? He wouldn't remember anything, and I couldn't stand there talking to myself. The sun shone right on the picture now, making the colours blaze. Couldn't I just keep the fact that I knew it to myself?

It seemed to me not; or rather that the time had come for me to tell it to someone.

It was a thing I'd have liked to say. Not of any importance, of course, but suddenly something I found it difficult to do without. So I made another discovery – this time one that concerned only myself (one discovers what one can, at whatever age one can, and at whatever opportunity): that there was no reason why everyone should go on in ignorance of the fact that I had known that angel when I was a child, in Britanny, and no reason why I should keep quiet about it

38

any longer. The thing had to be said. The formulation of it trembled within me, with all the shamelessness of happiness. I was amazed.

I stayed sitting on the bench for a long time, probably longer than the picture was worth, over half an hour. Of course the angel was still there. I looked at him mechanically, without seeing him, my attention concentrated on the relief that had come with my discovery. It was a great relief. My feebleness was leaving me. I sat motionless and let it go. I was like a man who has been dying for a long time to relieve himself, and finally does it. When a man relieves himself he's always very careful to do it as well as possible, to the very last drop. So was I. I was relieving myself of my feebleness to the last drop. Then it was done, and I was at peace. The woman beside me slowly recovered her natural mystery. I no longer wished her the slightest harm. In short, in half an hour I grew up. And that's not entirely a figure of speech. And having grown up I began to see the angel again.

In profile. He was still only a painting, and indifferent. He was looking at the woman. She too was only a painting, and looked only at him. After half an hour Jacqueline whispered:

'There's all the rest to see and the museums don't stay open very late.'

I realized at last that she only said that because she didn't know I knew the angel, and she didn't know only because I hadn't told her, and for no other reason. But I didn't tell her, nor did I stir from where I was sitting. I'd have needed more time for that. The angel was still resplendent in the sun. You couldn't have said whether it was a man or a woman – it could be whichever you chose. On his back he bore the wonderful warm wings of untruth. I'd have liked to see him better – if he could have turned his head and looked at me, for example. After gazing at the picture all this time, steeping myself in it, such a thing didn't seem impossible. Once I even thought I saw him wink. Probably it was only refraction in the light from the lawn – it only happened once. Ever since he'd been there, imprisoned in that painting, he'd never looked at a single tourist, he'd only paid attention to the charge he was entrusted with. From all eternity he was only interested in the woman. Besides, the other half of his face didn't exist. If he had turned his head to look at me he would have revealed an exceedingly thin countenance with only one eye. It was a work of art. Whether it was beautiful or not I didn't know, but it was a work of art. One shouldn't always look at them too long. In four hundred years had he ever so much as winked at anybody? I couldn't take him away, or burn him, or embrace him, or gouge his eyes out, or kiss him, or spit in his face, or speak to him. What good would it do me to keep on looking at him? What I had to do was get up from the bench and get on with my life. And what good had it done me to look at the other, also in profile, while he drove his van like a maniac and told me to be happy? I'd dreamed of him every night, and now he was as fixed in his stonemasonry at Pisa as this one was in his picture. I suddenly felt a great pain in my chest, over the stomach. I recognized it. I'd cried twice before in my life, once in Paris and once in Vichy, both times because of the registry. He's the angel, I said to myself, that driver, that traitor. But why was I crying? The pain got worse: it was as if there were flames in my chest and throat, and I knew I could only get rid of them in tears. But still I asked myself why I was crying. I was hoping that if I could find the reason for this strange desire I should abolish it and the pain would end. But soon the fire was in my head, and I couldn't look for reasons any more. I could only say to myself, well, if you want to as much as all that, go ahead and cry. You'll find out why afterwards. If you try to stifle it you're not being honest with yourself. You never have been honest with yourself, and it's time you started, understand?

The words seemed to fall on me and submerge me like a huge, terrifying wave. I couldn't escape.

Everyone has his own way of weeping. For me the room

was filled with a sort of dull moan, like that of a calf that wants to go back to its shed, that has had enough of grazing and would like to see its cow of a mother again. I didn't shed a single tear, but the noise was all the louder. In the calm that immediately followed I, together with everyone else, heard the words: 'So much for the registry.'

It was I who had spoken them, obviously, but they made me jump. They made Jacqueline jump too, and all the tourists. Jacqueline recovered very quickly, more quickly than the tourists. The pain disappeared.

'You certainly like to be different from everybody else,' she said.

Although this was not the way I usually behaved she didn't ask any questions. But she took my arm and dragged me out of the room as hastily as if the Annunciation threatened my reason.

I had no difficulty in following her. I could now, because this time, I was sure, it was settled, I should never go back to the registry any more. She would, but not I. It was all quite clear. Because I'd become honest – suddenly or not, what did it matter? didn't one go mad suddenly too? – and because to stay on in the registry and with her – I couldn't dissociate the two – was dishonest, I could no longer stay on in the registry or with her. I wouldn't have treated anybody like that, not anybody, not even her. By what aberration had I treated myself so badly?

The pictures went past me one after the other. I walked gingerly, like a robot, afraid of disturbing the sense of calm and security I'd been filled with since my groan and the declaration that followed. It was all quite simple – I didn't even feel hot any more. For the first time for a long time – I believe since I'd escaped from the Germans – I felt a certain amount of respect for myself. At first I'd suffered, suffered even more than I'd suspected; because I'd cried, how could I doubt it? Then I'd spoken, not only without intending to but without even noticing it, or hardly. So as I knew very

41

well that I wasn't mad, and that Annunciations are not as frequent as all that, the strange things that had been happening to me rather impressed me. What element in me was it that had taken my personal affairs in hand so effectively, and without my knowledge? I say effectively because although to throw up a safe job doesn't sound much, even when it's the meanest of jobs, a second grade clerk in the Colonial Ministry, I knew very well, especially after eight years, that it called for heroism, no less. I'd tried to do it myself a hundred times without ever succeeding. What was it in me that had brought it off now, for heaven's sake? I couldn't say, and there seemed more point in trying to carry out its instructions than in wasting time trying to identify it. Its instructions suited me very well. Whether I knew its name or not, it was the part of me I knew best that would never go back any more to the registry.

Jacqueline didn't notice – at least I don't think so – that I was not looking at any of the frescoes. She still walked ahead and I followed. She stopped in front of each one. 'Look,' she'd say, turning to me, 'isn't it beautiful?' She said each one was either beautiful, or lovely, or remarkable, or terrific. I just looked at them, and sometimes at her. Even the day before to hear her talk like that would have made me run out of the place. Now I looked at her with curiosity, because only an hour before I would have willingly killed her. Now I hadn't the least wish to do so. There was no question of it. I was even touched by the innocence that had never suspected my evil intentions. All that had to be done was to restore her to the rest of the world, the optimists and the others, just as you would throw a fish back into the sea.

During the days that followed I began to think about her honestly, as you may imagine. I wished her well. But the good I wished her was a particular good that I couldn't avoid doing her. I was going to leave her, and for a while at least she was going to doubt herself, and to doubt whether human happiness was as easy to attain as she had hitherto supposed; perhaps there would be something of this good left for her later on. That was all I could do for her.

The day after the events in the museum I said to her:

'Ever since we've been here we've never looked at the town in the same way. You walk around and I sit still. Let's do the same thing for once. Let's go to the cafeteria.'

I hauled her off to my cafeteria and talked to her for a while. You have to waste a bit of time, I told her, otherwise you waste it all. It was difficult to explain, but true. I agreed that I wasted too much time; but she didn't waste enough. I told her that I'd brought her to the cafeteria to tell her this, which I thought was very important. As she was bound, within the week, to waste a lot of time crying, I told myself it might be a consolation to her to remember these fine words. She looked frightened, suddenly, and I could see she didn't believe a word of what I was saying and wondered what was happening. But I didn't bother about that: I was honestly doing what I thought I ought to do.

The day after I took her to the cafeteria again.

This time I talked to her about Rocca. I told her I couldn't stand the heat in Florence any more, that the driver of the van had told me a lot about Rocca, and that I'd decided to go there. If she didn't want to go there she could stay in Florence. Just as she liked. As for me, it was settled, I was going to Rocca. She looked the same as she had the day before, questioning and perhaps even a bit alarmed. It must have been at least a year since I'd talked to her in such a friendly way and for so long. But alarmed or not, she tried to dissuade me. We only had four days left – was it worth leaving Florence and making an additional journey? I said yes, I thought it was worth it. But why the sea? she went on. Isn't the sea the same everywhere? We can see it again in France. I said I didn't agree, the sea wasn't the same everywhere, and, again, that she could stay in Florence if she liked, but I was going to see the sea at Rocca. She didn't answer. I stopped talking, and our old familiar silence reassured her a little. It was only that evening, in the room, that she told me she would go to Rocca too. She told me she wasn't going for the sea, but to be with me. It was my turn not to answer. I didn't think she'd be in the way at Rocca. In fact I believed it would be easier, once we were there, to break my plans to her. She would go and bathe in the sea, which is what one usually does at the seaside, and I would go and bathe in the Magra. If necessary I would stay in the Magra for three days and nights waiting for her to take the train. It seemed to me more natural to wait in a river than in a hotel room; probably that was because of the heat. And then everyone has his own ideas about the best and least painful method of parting from someone. I saw myself waiting in the Magra for her to catch her train. I could already see myself hidden in its gentle waters more safely than in the strongest refuge. I could imagine myself being brave there. But not in a hotel room.

On our last night in Florence, the fifth of the heat-wave, there was a storm. From nine o'clock till midnight a scorching wind blew over the city and the sky was torn by flashes of lightning. The thunder was deafening. The streets were deserted. The cafeterias closed earlier than usual. The rain was a long time coming. Some said it wouldn't come till the next day. But it started to come down at midnight, in buckets, like a mill-race. I hadn't slept, I was waiting for it. When it started I got up and went over to the window to watch. Waterspouts were breaking all over Tuscany and over the fish that had died from the heat. On the other side of the street, then all over the town, lights began to appear at the windows. People were getting up to watch the rain. Jacqueline got up too. She came over and stood beside me at the window. But she didn't talk about the rain.

'It'll be cooler now,' she said softly. 'Why don't we stay in Florence?'

Then I told her what I hadn't told her in the cafeteria.

'I have to go to Rocca.'

'I don't understand,' she said after a moment.

'I don't know very well myself yet,' I said, 'but when we're there I'll know, and then I'll tell you.'

'Are you sure you'll know better when we're there?'

'Certain,' I said.

'You always have such funny ideas' – she tried to smile – 'and I always go wherever you do.'

'You're sweet,' I said.

She didn't answer, didn't press the matter. She stayed at the window a little while longer, then suddenly, as if she couldn't bear the sight any longer, she rushed over to the bed. I didn't move. She asked me to go back with her.

'Come to bed,' she said.

I didn't answer, I acted as if I hadn't heard. I hadn't touched her for days and days. In the first place because I couldn't, and then because since that day at the museum I knew I was not so strong as most, and had made up my mind to reserve my strength for the days ahead.

'Aren't you coming to bed?' she said.

'I'm watching the rain.'

'Are you going to watch it for long?'

'I want to watch it a bit longer.'

She didn't ask any more. She had begun to suffer. A forgotten freshness rose up out of the depths of the night, and men were astonished, after having despaired of it so long, that they could still rejoice at it.

I stayed at the window for a long while. I started to think about her, then finally I thought again about Rocca. I thought about the river again, and then again about him, by the river or in it, with me. Shoals of fish fled before us like flashes of light. The sky was still cloudy. I calculated that it was Thursday. He would arrive at Rocca on Saturday, in two days' time. A long time. If he'd been in Florence we would have gone out together in the rain. Over by the station there were cafeterias that stayed open all night. The waiter in the cafeteria where I went had told me. I'd asked him. We could

45

have drunk and talked together. But he wasn't there, I had to wait till Saturday. I had to be patient. I stayed at the window for a long while, the longest time I've ever stayed by a window in my life, smoking, thinking about the river and about him, and, for the first time, about what I would actually do once I'd left the Ministry.

It wasn't easy to get to Rocca. We had to go to Sarzana first and take a bus from there. The first part of the journey was very uncomfortable. The heat-wave was over, but the trains were still stiflingly hot. Jacqueline got a seat an hour after we left Florence. I stood up the whole way. She didn't come and stand with me once. I don't think she even looked out of the window much either.

We got to Sarzana at five in the afternoon. The bus wasn't due till seven. I went for a walk round the town, and Jacqueline, still silent, came with me. We met practically only women in the streets. All the men worked in the dockyards at La Spezia and when we arrived they hadn't got home yet. It was a small town with narrow streets and no trees. The houses were poor and stood wide open, huddled˙ together like one single dwelling, giving each other the necessary shade. Life was difficult there. But the sea was only a few kilometres away – you could smell it in the air – like an inexhaustible reservoir of happiness. It only took half an hour to walk round the town. Then I suggested we had something to drink while we waited for the bus. Jacqueline agreed, and I chose a cafeteria on the main square near the bus and tram station.

We stayed there an hour drinking coffee and beer, and still not talking. The square was drenched in sun and full of children.

About half-past six trams began to arrive from La Spezia, full of men. The trams were old and rusted by the sea air. The children stopped playing and the women came out of their houses to watch them go past. For half an hour the square

46

was full of shouts and greetings and laughter, and the enormous clatter of the trams.

'We've got four days' holiday left,' said Jacqueline.

She complained of the noise the trams made. She had a headache, and took an aspirin.

The bus arrived at the same time as the last tram, and it too was incredibly old. We were the only passengers to get on there. It followed the road to La Spezia for a few kilometres, then, when it came to a river, the Magra, it turned towards the sea. The road grew rough and narrow. But that didn't matter – it ran along by the river. The river was wide and calm; on the right bank there was a chain of hills with walled villages on their summits, and on the left the great plain of Rocca planted with olive trees.

It was a long journey. The sun set about half an hour after we turned towards the sea, and when we arrived it was already dark. The bus stopped in front of the trattoria which, as I already knew, overlooked the river. I stood for some moments looking at it in the darkness. I'd been thinking and thinking about it for six days and nights, more than I'd ever thought about anything in my life, perhaps more than I'd ever thought about anybody, up till then. And this was the place I'd appointed for talking to Jacqueline, for waiting for her train to go, for starting a new life. In short, for ten years I had been waiting to arrive on the banks of that river. I felt tired just to look at it, as tired as if I'd had to perform some titanic labour to get there.

An old man welcomed us. He told us his name was Eolo. Like the wind? I asked. Like the wind, he said. He spoke French. I told him the place had been recommended to me by a young man whose name I didn't know, a stonemason who worked in Pisa, with a green van, who came to spend every other week-end with his uncle at Rocca . . . He thought for a bit, then knew exactly who I meant. He served us a meal of ham and pasta outside, apologizing for not having anything else left to offer. All the other guests had already dined, he said, and were taking a stroll either towards the sea or along by the river. Most of them were waiting for the dance to begin. We didn't answer, and he said no more. But all through our meal he stood there watching us, probably a bit intrigued by our exhausted appearance and our silence. As soon as we'd finished dinner I asked him for a room and a bottle of beer. I was so tired, I said, I'd prefer to drink it in bed. He thought we wanted a room for two. I didn't say anything. We followed him up. The room was small and had no running water. There was a mosquito-net over the bed. When he'd gone downstairs Jacqueline said:

'It might still have been better if we'd stayed in Florence.'

Did she really think that, or was she only trying to make me tell her why I'd come to this village tucked away here by the sea? I don't know, I didn't want to find out. I said I thought we were right to come. She saw I was very tired and that I found it hard, painful even, to speak, so she left me alone. I drank my beer. I hadn't even the energy to wash before I lay down on the bed, and fell asleep almost at once.

It must have been about two hours later when I woke up. I'd got into the habit of doing that practically every night since the heat-wave. I used to wake up with a start several times during the night, and each time I would feel as if I'd slept for a long time, too long even, yet strangely refreshed. It was difficult, sometimes impossible, to go to sleep again. There was still some beer left in the bottle. I drank it and then got up and went over to the window, as I'd got into the habit of doing. Across the river the dance was at its height. The sound of dance-music played through a loudspeaker floated into the room. I didn't feel in the least tired now. You couldn't see the moon, but you knew it must be there, behind the mountain: it was lighter now than when we arrived. The room looked out on to the sea on one side and the river on the other. You could see the place better from the first floor, especially the mouth of the river. A little to the left of it lay the white form of a boat. There was a faint light over the deck. It was the American woman's yacht. The sea was calm, but it looked rough beside the perfectly smooth surface of the river. A bright band of spray showed where the two met. I'd always loved that sort of landscape – geographical, you might call it, with its capes and deltas and tributaries, and above all the mouths of rivers, the meetings of rivers with the sea. All the villages along the coast were lit up. I looked at my watch. It wasn't quite eleven o'clock.

I went back to bed. It was hotter under the mosquito-net than by the window. A mosquito got in at the same time as I did. He hadn't told me there were mosquitoes. I'd never slept in a mosquito-net since the time I'd lived in the colonies. There must be millions of them. The river. There must be swarms of them along its banks. It was all one to me. Jacqueline was fast asleep, turned towards me. When she was asleep she looked very small, smaller even than in real life. Her breath fanned my arm rhythmically. I shut my eyes and tried to go to sleep again. The mosquito woke up. With that added to everything else I knew I shouldn't get back to sleep. And I couldn't switch the light on to try to kill it without the risk of waking Jacqueline. The idea of being awake with her in the middle of the night, in the same bed, would have been enough to make me run away that night, from shame and perhaps even from fear as well. The idea of her and me together during those two years, the picture of the couple we had formed, frightened me.

I was free to choose – I could say it was either her, or the mosquito, or the dance that prevented me from going to sleep again. I chose the dance. From a distance like that, in a room where you had been woken up alone in the darkness, you could imagine it to be a big dance with lots of women, where everyone was having a marvellous time. I couldn't hear the mosquito or Jacqueline's breathing any more, only the sound of the pick-up, the sound of the dance. I didn't move. I concentrated all my strength on trying to go to sleep again, on trying not to hear the pick-up, on forcing myself to think of unimportant matters, not about him, especially not about him or about the river. I tried for almost an hour. And it was while I was trying to think about nothing, or about unimportant matters, or what day of the week it was, that the torture began. You may begin by counting sheep, but you never know where it will end. I've always had a curious aptitude for arithmetic. Once I'd started I went on to calculate other things besides sheep. How many days were there left before the end of the holidays, before Jacqueline's departure? How much money had I got left? How many months, or weeks, or days, could I make it last? How many years exactly had I spent with Jacqueline? And at the Ministry? In that stinking office? Eight years three months and six days. With Jacqueline, two years three months and two days. They were playing a samba, the one I had heard when I was standing by the window. How many years had I still got to do before I could draw a pension? Twelve. A bit more than I'd done already, half as much again. My forehead began to run with sweat. How much pension had I a right to at that moment, proportionate to the time I'd served? I wasn't sure – probably a bit less than half of the full pension. Ought I to ask for it or just let it go? Ought I to bother about such things at my age? How old was I? I suddenly remembered that three days ago, in Florence, in the middle of the heat-wave, I was thirty-two. I found myself staring my birthday in the face. A number appeared to me in letters of fire, then fell on me like a thunderbolt. The samba came back again. No, I decided, I'm not going to ask for a pension proportionate to my years of service. I would celebrate my birthday by scorning to ask the colonial administration for anything whatsoever, and by putting right out of my mind all such worries and calculations, according to which it was obviously too late to undertake anything, even just leaving Paris, Jacqueline, and the registry section. The tune came to an end. I heard applause, Then it began again. And for me too. Again I was seized on by those hellish calculations. My mind foundered among insoluble problems. Given the average length of a human life, could one give up a pension proportionate to a tenth of that length? In other words, could one afford to work, or rather live, for eight years for nothing? Especially when one was over thirty? I was covered in sweat, but I couldn't decide whether one could or not. Who could have solved that kind of problem anyway? What figures and what pension could ever make up for the eight years I'd endured in the registry? None, of course. But was that any reason for not trying to compensate myself just a little? For throwing away what could at least keep me in *apéritifs* and cigarettes?

It went on for a long time, nearly all the time I lay awake. Then I thought of a solution. I got up quietly so as not to wake Jacqueline, dressed in the dark, and went down. It was cool. In front of the trattoria the river stretched out below the fields of olives. On the other bank you could see the dance-floor all lit up. You could see others lit up here and there all over the plain. Everywhere people were dancing. In summer, by the sea, people went to bed late. They were right. I stood without moving on the river bank and looked across at the dance. My calculations had gone right out of my head and all I thought of now was the dance. It shone like fire. When people are alone in the midst of lights and music, they want to meet someone else as alone as they are. It's very difficult to bear. I was surprised to notice the signs of physical desire. I didn't especially want a woman. Was it the dance music? a reaction to the idea of my birthday? the proportional pension taking its revenge? But I'd forgotten about my birthday and the pension. Besides, my previous birthdays had never had that effect on me, and as for my proportional pension – I laughed – that would be more likely to produce the opposite effect. So what could it be? Just the desire to meet someone? talk to someone? Was it despair at not meeting anyone? I settled on that explanation. Besides, it wasn't really important. I walked about for a quarter of an hour or so, still

51

looking over at the dance, still in the same condition. Then, just as I had resigned myself to the fact that this evening there was nothing for it but patience, I found myself face to face with old Eolo.

'Good-evening, monsieur,' he said.

He was walking along by the river, smoking. I was glad to have met him. I'd never liked old people and talking to them had always got on my nerves, but that evening I could have talked to a centenarian. To a lunatic even.

'It's hot,' he said. 'I suppose you felt hot with the mosquito-net?'

'Yes,' I said. 'It's hard to sleep when it's as hot as this.'

'The mosquito-nets make it worse. I sleep without anything over me. The mosquitoes aren't interested in my old carcass any more.'

I could see his face quite clearly in the light reflected from the surface of the river. It was a mass of fine wrinkles. When he laughed his cheeks puffed out and his eyes lit up and he looked like a rather wicked old baby.

'I can't understand why they don't spray round the foot of the mountain with D.D.T. They've been saying they're going to come and do it for three years.'

It didn't matter what he said. I must have looked at him as if he was going to tell me something of the utmost importance. He looked slightly surprised.

'It's not only the mosquitoes,' I said. 'The music kept me awake too.'

'Yes,' he said. 'It takes more than one night to get used to it. You'll have got used to it by tomorrow.'

'I'm sure,' I said.

'And you can't stop them from dancing, can you?'

'Oh no,' I said, 'you can't do that.'

'But you soon get used to both of them, the music and the mosquitoes – you'll see.'

'I expect so,' I said. 'Anyway the mosquitoes are nothing like as bad as in the colonies.'

52

'Is that where you come from?'

'I was born and brought up there.'

'My wife's brother lived in Tunisia – he was a grocer in Tunis.'

We talked about the colonies for a little while. Then he went back to the mosquitoes. He was a bit obsessed, and started to get worked up.

'A single mosquito,' I said, 'can ruin a whole night.'

'And do you think they don't know that at Sarzana? Of course they know. But there aren't any mosquitoes at Sarzana, so they just conveniently forget.'

'And yet it's so easy – all you need is a dose of D.D.T.'

'That town council at Sarzana – they're no good for anything.'

'We came through there on our way here. Pretty little place.'

'I don't know about pretty,' he said angrily. 'All I know is they only think about themselves.'

'Still, I did think it was a pretty little place.'

He melted a bit.

'Did you really? That's funny, people don't usually. But I have to admit it's a good place for shopping. A boat goes from here once a week, up the river.'

This was a good subject. If I played my cards right I ought to be able to keep him for a good while longer.

'Is there much traffic on the Magra?' I asked.

'Still quite a lot,' he said. 'All the peaches that are grown in the plain are sent by river – they don't get damaged so much that way as by rail or road.'

'Where are they sent to?'

He pointed to a distant light along the coast.

'There. To Viareggio. And there –', he pointed to another light in the opposite direction, 'that's La Spezia. The best ones go by river. The ones they use for jam they send by bus.'

We talked about peaches, and fruit in general.

'I understand this is a very good area for fruit,' I said.

'Yes, they grow very fine fruit here. But the peaches in Piedmont are better than ours. Our real speciality is marble.'

It was the young man I told you about who told me. His father lives round here somewhere, I don't know exactly where.'

'At Marina di Carrare,' he said. 'Three kilometres from here along the shore. It's the port for marble. Nothing but boats in and out all the time.'

'He said his cousin lived here too,' I said. 'He goes underwater fishing.'

'His cousin lives here,' he said, 'but not by the sea, on the other side, by the river. He sells fruit. But the village where he lives isn't very pretty. Marina di Carrare now, that's a very pretty place.'

'He's supposed to be coming on Saturday', I said. 'We're supposed to be going underwater fishing together in the river.'

'I don't know what's got into them this year with their underwater fishing', he said. 'They're all going underwater fishing.'

'You can't imagine what it's like if you've never done it', I told him. 'It's beautiful – the most wonderful colours. The fish swim right under you. And you can't imagine how peaceful it is.'

'Oh, I see you do it too.'

'No, I never have yet', I said, 'I'm going to on Saturday with him. But everyone says it's like that.'

We hadn't much more to say to each other. He started to talk about marble again.

'At Marina di Carrare', he said, 'you'll see all the marble lying round the port, waiting to be taken away.'

'He didn't say anything about the marble', I answered, automatically. 'It's dear, isn't it, Carrara marble?'

So we talked about marble.

'It's the transport that makes it dear. It's heavy and fragile at the same time. But it's not dear here, of course. Here on the plain everyone's buried in marble, even the poor.'

54

He smiled, and I smiled back: we were both thinking about the same thing. 'Here even the kitchen sinks are made of marble.'

Leading on from the way the marble was sent all over the world, I made him talk about his own travels. He'd never been to Rome, only to Milan. It was then that he'd seen the peaches from Piedmont. But his wife knew Rome. She had been there once.

'She went to give her wedding ring to the Duce, like all the other women in Italy. She might just as well have kept it, for all the good it did us.'

He liked the French. He'd got to know some of them in 1917. He thought they looked down on the Italians.

'People will believe anything when there's a war on,' I said. But he thought they were right.

'After all,' he said, 'they made us bomb you. You can't expect anyone to forget a thing like that.'

It obviously still hurt him to remember. I changed the subject. What was he doing, walking about here so late?

'The dancing keeps me awake,' he said. 'Whenever they have a dance I go for a walk. And then I can keep an eye out for my youngest daughter, too – Carla. She's only sixteen, we had her very late. If I were to go to bed she'd slip out to the dance.'

It was clear he was very fond of Carla. He smiled when he spoke of her.

'She's only sixteen. I have to keep an eye on her still, or she might get into trouble.'

'But you could let her go just now and again,' I said. 'How do you expect to get her married if you never let her go dancing?'

'People have plenty of chances to see her during the day,' he said. 'She goes to the well ten times for every five she needs to – and I don't stop her. And then, what about my other daughters? – they've been going dancing for three years now and they're not married yet.'

55

He didn't know how he was going to get them married off, especially the eldest. To my surprise, when he talked to me about his daughters I noticed the same signs as before. I felt a flash of uneasiness. Would I ever know what I really wanted? What I really needed?

'Oh, I get quite a few offers for them from time to time,' he said. 'But people are poor, so they're afraid of marriage. Wages are very low in Italy.'

Then he added, 'And besides, they all want to marry Carla.'

I was hardly listening to him now; I was looking over at the dance. Perhaps that was what I had to do, after all – go to the dance.

'I think,' went on Eolo, 'I think it's because she doesn't think about marriage, only about dancing. Her sisters are thinking about marriage all the time. And men always know.'

'Yes,' I said. 'Always.'

'And it's not only the men,' he said. 'Carla's everybody's favourite.'

He told me about the American woman, and how she liked Carla better than his other daughters too.

'I've already heard about this American,' I said, 'from the chap that drove the van. Do you know her too?'

Of course he knew her. She had her meals at the trattoria. She liked his wife's cooking – and though he said it himself, it was the best cooking in the whole district. I'd see her the next day in the trattoria. He didn't say anything about her being beautiful, probably because he no longer took any interest in such things, perhaps because failing eyesight made it impossible for him to judge. But he told me that she was very nice, and very rich. And that she was alone. She had come here for a rest. He told me she had a yacht moored just off the beach. Yes, I'd seen it. A fine yacht it was, with a crew of seven. She wasn't travelling just for pleasure. They said she was trying to find someone, some man, that she'd known a long time ago. Funny sort of man. Funny sort of story. But people said anything . . . She was certainly very nice.

'And just as simple and natural as Carla. They get on very well. Sometimes she goes with her to the well.'

Every now and again she would have dinner with some of the crew from the yacht. He'd never seen a thing like that before. They addressed her quite familiarly, called her by her Christian name.

'And she's all on her own?' I said. 'Are you sure she hasn't got a man with her? Everyone says how beautiful she is.'

'She can't have a man with her if she's looking for the other one, can she?'

'I meant while she's waiting for him,' I said. 'If she spends her whole life looking for him . . .'

He seemed to find it embarrassing to talk about such things.

'Well, she hasn't exactly got a man with her – I mean, not always the same one. That's quite certain. But my wife – you know what women are – she says she isn't quite alone, she does have some men now and again.'

'Women are good at seeing these things.'

'She says you can see straight away she's a woman who can't do without men. She doesn't say it maliciously – on the contrary, she likes the American very much, just as if she were poor.'

'You can usually see these things,' I said. 'In short, she's a woman who's not too hard to please.'

'Yes, I suppose you could say that,' he answered with a sidelong glance. 'A woman who's not too hard to please. My wife says that when they're at sea she makes do with the sailors.'

'I see,' I said. 'It's certainly a curious story.'

We hadn't any more to say to each other. He told me I ought to go to the dance – he could take me across in his boat if I liked. I accepted. He started to talk to me again about the dance and about his daughters. I'd see his daughters there, he said, with a smile that I took to be a friendly warning. Anyway, he added, even if they don't ever

57

find husbands at these dances at least they enjoy themselves, and that's always something in this hard life. And after all – he got slightly angry – why shouldn't they find husbands the same as everybody else? Who organized the dances, I asked. The council of Sarzana, he told me; it was the one good thing they did. The workers from La Spezia came, and it was usually them that the local girls married. He left me on the bank. I offered him a cigarette, and he went off again to keep an eye on his Carla.

The dance-floor was near the river, raised on piles and surrounded by a trellised enclosure hung with Chinese lanterns. Some people were dancing outside too, on a little plot of ground opposite the entrance. I hesitated for a moment, then, as there wasn't a chair free outside, I went up. I looked round to see if there was a face there I recognized – you never knew, he might have come from Pisa earlier this week. But no. He hadn't come earlier. There was no one there who looked even the slightest bit like him. Once again I was overwhelmed with fatigue. I sat down at a table with four glasses of lemonade on it, and waited for the dance to end so that I could introduce myself to some girl. There were plenty of girls there, enough for twenty men alone and in my condition, I needed to find someone to talk to again quickly. The dance – a samba, I think – ended, but straight away they started to play another. No one sat down. I promised myself I would speak to some girl at the end of this dance. I had to. And it had to be a girl. It was true I already had one girl, alone in the room on the other side of the river, but she wouldn't do any more. She wasn't all that different from the woman I would be going up to and speaking to at any moment, except that for some mysterious reason she wouldn't do any more. It was at Vichy that she'd joined the Ministry and I first met her. I watched her out of the corner of my eye for three days. Then I had an idea, the sort of idea I used to have sometimes in those days. I said to myself, Seeing I've

58

been waiting for six years to get out of this hole and I'm far too big a coward to do it on my own, what I'll do is rape this clerk. She'll yell, somebody will hear, and I'll be sacked. One Saturday afternoon when we were the only two on duty I did it. But I made a hash of it. She must have been waiting a long time for a man. At first it was just a habit we got into on Saturday afternoons, then suddenly two years had gone by. I no longer had the slightest desire for her. I'd never really managed to like her. I know I was just like everyone else, capable of loving anybody. And yet I could never manage to see her as belonging to the rest of the world, and so love her too. I suppose there's nothing you can do about injustices like that except accept them. Tomorrow I was going to make her suffer. She would cry. I could foretell that as surely as that the sun would rise. And I was as incapable of preventing it as I was of loving her. Her tears would lend her a new charm, perhaps the only one she would ever have had for me. I would have to be careful. The women dancing recalled her to me with renewed force. She was alone in the room, asleep, or awake and wondering where I was, I didn't know which. I'd let her come to Rocca, and I hadn't said anything to her yet, for four days, about my decision. Was it because I was in doubt about it? No, I was sure not. Tomorrow she would cry—I knew she would, however I spoke to her. She would completely refuse to accept what I said. She would go away drenched in tears, and I would stay on. Our relationship would be an illusory one right up to the last. I suddenly felt sorry – just a mad whim, no doubt – for not having brought her to the dance. Who knows, when you're dancing perhaps you can talk better, understand one another better. I would have held her tight: 'I'm staying in Rocca, I can't go on. We must separate, you know it as well as I do. We didn't belong together, we were starving in the midst of the world's plenty. Why were we so hard on ourselves? Don't cry. Look how I'm holding you in my arms. I could almost love you. And that miracle is simply because we're going to part. Try to under-

59

stand how necessary it is. And then at last we'll understand each other – just like everybody else does.'

I repeated these fine phrases to myself with so much conviction I no longer saw the girls at the dance. But I knew all the time that face to face with her, her eyes dimmed with idiotic tears, I wouldn't say them. It was as if, for me, the thing was settled, and the words came to me as certain visions do before the irreducible injustice of life, and of death.

The samba ended.

Four girls came and sat down at my table. I chose one of them; she looked at me swiftly. The music began again – a blues this time, badly played. I asked her to dance. But there was a question I had to ask her.

'You don't happen to be the daughter of a man called Eolo, by any chance, who keeps the little hotel on the other side of the river?'

She wasn't.

'I'm glad I found you,' I said. 'I'm all alone.'

She looked flattered. I was the only Frenchman there.

'I saw as soon as you came in that you were looking for a girl to spend the evening with,' she said.

I didn't deny it.

'I'm alone. I only got here today.'

'I see. In Italy all on your own?'

'Yes,' I said.

More alone than if she hadn't been there on the other side of the river, alone too in the room. More alone than she. Probably more alone than if I'd loved her. It's never natural to part from anyone, no matter who. I'd lived through days of horror with her. I knew nobody would ever replace her, and that in spite of, and in the face of everything, the abstract and desolate couple we formed, in other words our error, was henceforward a true one.

'I don't like being alone, myself,' said the girl.

'Well, I'm not alone in the ordinary sense. I've got someone with me. At the moment she's asleep at the hotel. We're going to separate.'

The dance ended. We sat down together near the bar. She looked serious.

'That's always painful,' she said.

She was dying to ask questions but decided it was better to wait for me to speak. Probably one of those girls who have a passion for that sort of thing.

'She's very nice,' I told her. 'Pretty too. I haven't anything really serious against her. We just don't suit each other, that's all. It happens every day.'

When he goes back to Pisa, I thought, I'll stay on in Rocca at old Eolo's. I'll go to Sarzana and watch the trams go by. That was what I'd do to begin with, for the first few days. I didn't want to look any farther ahead. It was the height of summer, I couldn't go away. I couldn't go back to France until the summer was over. For the moment what I needed was a torrid heat that would pin me to the spot and overcome my last remaining doubts. The doubt as to whether I should write and ask for my proportional pension, for example. It was a difficult letter to write and here the sun, the summer and the river would put me off writing it. Anywhere else I couldn't be sure that I might not write it one fine evening. Two days from now we'd go underwater fishing. We'd fish for two days. Then I'd wait for him until next Saturday. I knew old Eolo in Rocca. I must stay there where I knew someone, I mustn't be alone again, ever. Never that horror again, or anything might happen. I knew myself very well – I was weak, capable of any cowardice you could think of.

'You don't say very much,' said the girl.

'Well, of course,' I said, 'all this gets me down a bit.'

'I understand. Does she know you're going to leave her?'

'I told her, once. But probably she didn't believe me.'

In Rocca, in summer. The summer would help me a lot. I mistrusted myself like the plague. My reputation for being erratic and irresponsible would come in useful at last.

'It's always like that,' said the girl. 'You don't want to

believe it. Perhaps you've often said it to her and never had the courage to do it.'

I found it quite natural to talk to her about it. Everyone was welcome to have an opinion about what was happening to me and about the difficult situation I was in. Besides I hadn't got anything else to talk to anyone about, even a woman, except what was happening to me.

'No,' I said. 'I've thought about it for two years, ever since I've known her, but this is the first time I've told her.'

'In that case she ought to believe it.'

'She doesn't.'

She thought. Love stories were what interested her more than anything else in the world.

'Well, what else can she believe?'

'She thinks it's just talk.'

She thought again.

'Perhaps you won't do it after all,' she said. 'After all, she must know you.'

'Won't do what?'

'Leave her.'

'Well, until it actually happens, of course, you can't tell. But I think I shall.'

She didn't say anything for some time, but she looked at me closely.

'It's funny,' she said at last. 'Because you're not as sure as you say you are, I believe you might do it.'

'I believe so too. I don't quite know why, but I do. And yet I've never made any decisions like this before, serious decisions – I've never been able to.'

'To begin with,' she went on, pursuing her own train of thought, 'you know you can never be sure of doing a thing you've said you're going to do. And then you're so calm. You see, you'll do it.'

'I think so. After all, it's quite easy. To begin with, she'll pack her things and I'll watch her pack, and then she'll get on the train and I'll watch it go. I don't even have to raise my little finger. I've only got to keep saying to myself, don't do anything, don't do anything. That's all.'

She could see it all – me in the room, the cases, the train, everything. At last she said:

'You can't stay in the room while she packs. Oh no. You'll have to go out while she packs.'

'You're right,' I said. 'The packing's awful. Besides, people pack very quickly when they're angry.'

'Yes,' she said, 'and sometimes you don't really mean to go, you only do it to frighten the other person. Every woman must have done it like that at least once in her life. You just do it so that the other person should stop you.'

'She's brave, though. She'll really mean it.'

'I can see the sort of person she is,' she said after a silence.

'I won't be in the room with her,' I said. 'You're right. I'd thought I'd go and bathe in the Magra, just float there, waiting – for three days if necessary, if she waits for three days in the hope that I'll go with her.'

She smiled.

'You certainly do need to get away from her.'

She would probably have liked to go on talking about it, but she saw that I was suddenly less eager to.

'Shall we dance?' she said.

She got up and I followed her. She danced well. We danced for a while without speaking, then she began again.

'It's funny,' she said, 'I'm always for the men and against the women in that sort of thing, I don't know why. Perhaps it's because women never want to give men up whether they're good or bad. They don't know how to want to change.'

'I've led her an awful life,' I said. 'I haven't been at all nice to her.'

'And she must be very serious,' she said. 'And I'm sure she'd never deceive you. They're the worst of all, the serious ones. They're not really women at all.'

She said she was thirsty and we ought to have a drink. We stopped dancing. The chianti they gave us at the bar was

63

warm, but she didn't seem to notice. She liked drinking.

I looked at her properly for the first time. She had an ordinary enough face with rather indeterminate features, a vigorous body and a splendid bosom. She must have been about twenty-five. After we'd drunk the chianti we danced again.

'And what about you?' I asked.

'I work in a shop,' she said, 'in Sarzana. I come here in the evening to dance. I was married to a sailor. It was all over a long time ago, but in Italy you can't get divorced. It costs an awful lot, you have to go to Switzerland. I tried to save up for it for three years, but I gave up. It would have taken fifteen years. I just take life as it comes.'

Our table was taken. We stood up with the others, near the pick-up. They were playing the famous samba. Did she like the tune? Yes, she did. It was popular all over northern Italy that year, everyone was singing it. I liked her. I asked her her name.

'Candida,' she said. 'Hardly appropriate.' She laughed.

'Have you got lots of lovers?'

'Enough. I shall always work in a shop and be married to that sailor, and so . . . The only thing I regret is not having any children.'

'And when there's one you like better than the others, do you keep him?'

'I do all I can.'

'Do you cry? Do you implore?'

'I cry, I implore,' she said, laughing. 'But sometimes *he* does.'

'I'm sure,' I said.

We danced and chatted for another hour and then, in the middle of a dance, I took her outside.

When I left her the moon had gone down and it was quite dark. She had half fallen asleep on the bank of the river.

'I go to bed late,' she said, 'and I get up early, and I work all day long. So I get sleepy.'

'I have to go back,' I said. 'You mustn't go to sleep.'

She said she had her bicycle with her and would ride back. I said I'd try to see her again, and she agreed and gave me her address in Sarzana.

I went over on the ferry. Eolo was still walking about. He would have liked to have another chat, but I was tired. I asked if he could let me have a single room. He didn't seem unduly surprised. I had to pass Jacqueline's room. There was no light showing under the door. She was still asleep.

I didn't wake till late the next day. Jacqueline was waiting for me outside. What had happened to me, she asked. Eolo had told her I'd changed my room during the night. I gave her a brief explanation. It was the heat, I said; impossible to breathe two in a room, I couldn't sleep. She seemed to be satisfied. We had breakfast together. She seemed changed, almost good-humoured. Perhaps after all it wasn't such a bad idea to have come; we could have a rest. I didn't comment on the irony of it all. I told her I was going for a swim in the Magra. What an idea, she said, when the sea was only a stone's throw away. I didn't ask her to come with me. She went off to the beach, making me promise to join her there after my swim. I promised.

It was almost as hot as it had been in Florence. But here it didn't matter. I stayed in the water a long time. Eolo had lent me a boat and every so often I came out and lay down in it in the sun. Then I dived in again, or else rowed for a bit. But it was exhausting, the current was so strong. Still, once I managed to get to the other bank without drifting too far downstream. I recognized the dance-floor, completely deserted now, and a little further on the place where Candida and I had been. There weren't very many houses looking directly on the river – it was mostly orchards enclosed by fences. Each one had its own little private landing-stage, with boats that the peasants were loading with fruit. The traffic on the river increased as the morning wore on. Most of the loaded boats were going downstream towards the sea; their cargoes were covered with tarpaulins against the sun. The Magra must be as splendid a river as he had said. Its waters were clear, and so warm you could have gone to sleep in them. But no doubt after a week working on the top of new buildings in Pisa in the blazing sun he appreciated it even more than I did. I wasn't resting from anything except an unsatisfactory past, and lies, and mistakes. Just staying out of the water for a while was enough to make the past turn my stomach again, and to make me doubt the future. But in the water I forgot it all, everything seemed easier, I could imagine futures that might be acceptable, even happy. It had done me good to go to the dance. I ought to keep on. With other friends than him, and other girls. Candida's freshness had taken my breath away, she had been astonished herself. She had said: But you must leave her, you must let her go. She was right. I ought to keep on telling myself over and over again that one couldn't, oughtn't to live as I had up till then. I ought to keep this simple decision, this practical method, in front of me, and not let myself depart from it for any consideration whatsoever. You had to come to that sooner or later in life. And Italy ought to be the easiest place to find people ready to talk to you, to pass the time with you, to waste it with you. As I swam I repeated this credo over and over to myself, and swore quite coolly and rationally that if I did not succeed in starting a new life I would kill myself. It wasn't difficult: I just made a simple choice between two images – to see myself getting into the train, or to see myself dead. I chose to see myself dead. The eyes of the one getting into the train were more frightening than the closed eyes of the one that was dead. Once I'd made this promise to myself, the river became one of the most delightful things in the world, like sleep, or wine, or like his friendship.

It was time to join Jacqueline on the beach. Perhaps I would have broken my appointment yet again if I hadn't suddenly remembered the American woman. I had a wish, just a slight wish, to see her. Ten days before I would have tried to dismiss it, but now I no longer wanted to. Of course there was no question of my getting to know her, I just wanted to see her. It wasn't so much what I had been told about her beauty as the little I had heard about the life she led. And I'd always loved ships. Even if I didn't see her I should see her yacht. Everybody would be on the beach now. I wanted to put off remembering that I had to talk to Jacqueline.

I took the boat back to Eolo and set out for the beach.

I saw at once that she wasn't there. As everyone except Eolo had said that she was very beautiful it was easy to tell that none of the women on the beach was her. There were only a few people bathing, mostly guests from the hotel that I'd already seen that morning at breakfast. But her yacht was anchored about two hundred yards from the mouth of the river, exactly opposite where the people were bathing. As soon as Jacqueline saw me coming she ran over to me.

'Was it all right? Did you have a good swim?'

'Yes thanks.'

She smiled, and then repeated practically word for word what she'd told me that morning, how she'd looked for me last night all over the hotel, how I'd got up an hour after she did, how old Eolo had said I'd been and asked him for another room in the middle of the night (he hadn't told her I'd gone to the dance), how she didn't like to wake me up, and so on and so forth. She hadn't talked so much for three days. Must be the bathe, I thought. I was sorry I'd brought her to Rocca. About the room, I told her now what I hadn't told her that morning – that the thought of its being my birthday had kept me awake, and that sometimes a person needed to be alone on such occasions. 'My poor darling,' she cried, 'and I forgot all about it!' The bathe, the bathe. I had to talk to her that very day. I remember she was wearing a blue swim-suit, a bit shapeless and faded, which she'd worn at La Baule the year before. Was it the heat she had braved so stubbornly in Florence? – she seemed to me thin and tired in spite of her good humour.

'Come in for a swim,' she said.

I'd walked in the open all the way there, but my bathe in the Magra had been so long and so refreshing that I could still bear the sun on the beach. No, I wouldn't go in just yet. She went and resumed a game of ball that she'd left to come and meet me. She was playing with a young man; she called out and laughed and went to great trouble to make me think she was enjoying herself. She played badly and kept looking at me. I gazed into the distance, my eyes half-closed, but I could see her just the same. It was only when she had her back to me that I dared to look at the yacht. It was dazzlingly white. It was impossible to look at it for long: it stung the eyes like a whip. But I looked at it as long as my eyes would let me, until I couldn't see it any more. I wouldn't shut them till then. And then I took it with me into the darkness. It filled me with a sort of crushing torpor. It was a thirty-six metre yacht with two decks. Its gangways were painted green. It was rigged for a calm sea. It was really so painful to look at I felt as if I were crying. But I'd probably ruined my sight, my life, sufficiently up till then to enjoy that sort of sensation. Every so often men could be seen on the yacht, coming and going between the gangways and the foredeck. It wasn't flying any flag, which is very unusual. Was it just carelessness? On the side, in red letters, was written the name: *Gibraltar*. Jacqueline ran to and fro between me and the ship, but suddenly she didn't bother me any more. But how pitiless that whiteness was. Moored there motionless in the blue sea, the ship had the calm arrogance of a solitary rock. And I'd been told she lived on it always, the whole year round. But I still couldn't see a woman's shape among the sailors.

The yacht threw no shadow. The heat was terrible. It must be almost noon. Jacqueline stopped playing. She said she'd had enough, and dived into the sea. Then I remembered the

68

promise I'd made to myself in the river; but it was the last time I ever did. Was it the sun? – it was so soon afterwards, yet I'd forgotten all about talking to Jacqueline, and all I could think of was going back to the hotel for an apéritif. I'll have one with old Eolo, I thought. As soon as it occurred to me it struck me as the best idea I'd had for a long time. I thought for a good while about what apéritif I fancied, going over them all in my mind with great seriousness. Finally I hesitated between pastis and *fine à l'eau*. Pastis was the best drink to put inside one in that sun. *Fine à l'eau* was more for the evening. You could only really watch pastis clouding, turning iridescent, turning milky, in the sun. *Fine à l'eau* was splendid, but it always seemed rather a pity to spoil the brandy with the water. Whereas you couldn't drink pastis without it. I'd treat myself to one and drink my own health. But while I was still only thinking about the pastis I had a strange idea. About the brass. Why shouldn't I clean the brass on that ship? I drove the thought away and concentrated on the pastis again. Anyone who hasn't longed for a pastis after a bathe in the Mediterranean doesn't know what a bathe in the Mediterranean is. And did I know how to clean brass? Everybody knows how to do that. No, anyone who hasn't experienced that longing for a pastis, in the sun, after a bathe, has never felt the immortality of his body's mortality. But then suddenly I felt uneasy. I'd never really liked pastis. I'd tried it two or three times, but it had never given me much pleasure. I'd always preferred *fine à l'eau*. What was the matter with me, wanting a pastis when the last time I tasted it I didn't like it? Again I asked myself what was happening to me. Perhaps I'd got a touch of the sun, I thought, trying to find an explanation for this new penchant and the exaggerated new pleasure I expected to get from it. I twisted my head about in all directions to cool it and try to puzzle things out. How does one tell if one's going mad from sunstroke? Apart from the longing for the pastis – and the brass – there was nothing abnormal about me; I felt fine. You must calm down,

I told myself. I stretched out on the sand again. But Jacqueline had just come out of the water, alarmed by my strange attitude. She came over and asked me the same question as I'd asked myself.

'What's the matter with you now?'

'Nothing,' I said. 'The sun's a bit too much for me. I think I'll go and have a pastis.'

'But you don't like pastis!' She was becoming agressive. 'Are you going to start on apéritifs again?'

'The first man of the modern age,' I said, 'was the one who first felt the need of something like an apéritif.'

She looked at me.

'What's the matter with you?' she said again.

'The man who came back from hunting one fine morning, full of health and strength, and who just as he was going into his happy little hearth and home lifted up his head and sniffed the verdant air of the forests and the rivers and wondered what it was that was missing. He had his wife and child and everything. But what he was longing for was an apéritif. Before they were invented. He was the real Adam, the first real traitor to God and brother of us all.'

I stopped, exhausted.

'Did you bring me to Rocca to tell me that?' She checked herself. 'You ought not to stay out in the sun.'

'It wasn't the apple on the tree that the serpent meant. It was the rotten one lying on the ground. Our Adam, the real Adam, bent down and smelt the rotten apple, and liked it. In the wormy, acid, bulbous fermentation of the apple of Calvados he discovered alcohol. He needed it because he was intelligent.'

'Listen,' pleaded Jacqueline, 'you really ought to just take a dip in the water.'

'Do you really think so?' I asked.

I ran to the sea, dived in, and came straight out again. I still wanted the pastis. I didn't say anything about it to Jacqueline.

'Better?' she asked.

'I'm all right,' I said. 'I was just joking, that's all.'

'You don't often do that,' she said. 'I was worried. Everyone says how dangerous the sun is.'

And then she added, as if apologetically:

'And I was just going to ask you to come and sunbathe over there on the other side of the reeds.'

I said I'd come. I got up, still wet, and we clambered along the dunes where the reeds grew. They were dry and black and so thick they even shut out the sound of the sea. Jacqueline spread her towel out in a clear space and took off her swimsuit. I lay down some distance away. I was still thinking of the pastis so as not to think of the brass. Or at least that's what I thought I was trying not to think of.

'What's been the matter with you these last few days?' said Jacqueline. 'Are you cross with me or something?'

'It's not that,' I said. 'It's just that I think we ought to part.'

Above us, to the left, the white slopes of the mountains of Carrara sparkled in the sun. On the other side, on the hills, the villages looked very dark in contrast, buried in their walls and vines and fig-trees.

She still didn't answer. I thought that perhaps the dust that rose in the streets of Sarzana, and that had looked so white, was marble dust.

'I don't understand,' she said at last.

I too waited a moment before replying.

'Yes, you do.'

When she's gone, I thought, I'll go for a walk among the quarries.

'But why do you suddenly say that, all of a sudden like that?'

'It isn't all of a sudden. I told you in Florence, in the museum.'

'Don't let's talk about the museum,' she said bitterly. 'Anyway you were only talking about the Ministry then.'

'Yes,' I said, 'but it all comes to the same thing. I'm going to stay in Italy.'

'But why?' she cried, frightened.

Perhaps he'd come with me to the quarries.

'I don't love you. You know that.'

I heard a sob. One sob. She didn't answer.

'You don't love me either,' I said, with what gentleness I could muster.

'I can't believe it,' she said at last. 'What have I done?'

'Nothing. I don't know.'

'I can't believe it,' she cried. 'You must explain.'

'We don't love each other,' I said. 'You can't explain that.'

The heat was getting unbearable.

'So what's going to happen then?' she cried.

'I'm going to stay in Italy,' I said.

She paused a moment, then said as if it were a simple statement:

'You're mad.'

Then she went on in a different tone, cynical now:

'And might one be allowed to inquire what you're going to do in Italy?'

'Anything. For the moment I'll stay here. After that I don't know.'

'And what about me?'

'You'll go back,' I said.

She changed and became aggressive again.

'I don't believe a word you're saying.'

'You must.'

Suddenly she started to cry, not angrily, but as if she'd expected this to happen for a long time.

There was no wind, the reeds blocked it. I was sweating all over, between the folds of my eyelids, at the roots of my hair.

'It's impossible to believe a liar,' she said, still weeping. 'I can't believe you.'

'I don't lie nearly as much as I used to,' I said. 'And why should I be lying now?'

72

She wasn't listening.

'A liar, that's what you are – a liar.'

'I know,' I said. 'But why should I be lying now?'

She still wasn't listening. She was crying.

'You've become nothing but a liar,' she said, sobbing. 'I've ruined my life for a liar.'

There was nothing I could say to her. All I could do was wait. I hadn't been able to see the yacht since we'd come behind the reeds. I wanted to see it. It gave me strength and hope. I had the feeling it was going to sail away at any moment.

'With a liar – and a coward,' she added after a moment, 'there's never any proof. That's the best of it.' She spoke spitefully.

I kept raising myself, little by little, imperceptibly, and I saw it again, still dazzling white, there on the sea. Between it and me, about ten yards away from where we were, a woman was sunbathing. I realized at once that it was her, the American.

'You can say what you like,' said Jacqueline, 'I know you'll come back to Paris. You're too much of a coward – I know you . . .'

I didn't answer. I was incapable of it. I was looking at the woman. She hadn't seen us. She was lying with her head resting on her hand. Her other hand lay still between her breasts. Her legs had fallen a little apart, abandoned, as in sleep. It was if she didn't mind the heat of the sun at all.

'What's the matter with you now?' asked Jacqueline.

'Nothing,' I said at last. 'If you like we can go back and have a pernod together.'

Probably I seemed rather absent. She got angry.

'You don't like pernod,' she said. 'Don't tell any more lies, *please.*'

She opened her eyes and looked in our direction, but she didn't see us. I was afraid she might hear us, and lowered my voice.

'I really do want one,' I said. 'It surprises me too.'

Her anger melted away again.

'I've got some lemons,' she said, quite gently. 'Lie down. You can't just leave me like that without telling me anything. We must have a talk.'

'I don't think we ought to talk any more,' I said. 'In a minute we'll have an apéritif together. That's better than talking.'

'Lie down, can't you?' she said. 'What are you doing?'

Had she noticed that I wasn't looking directly at the sea?

'Go on, lie down,' she cried. 'I tell you I've got some lemons. I'll cut one up for you.'

Her face lay so calm among her loose hair that from a little further away than where I was one might have thought she was really asleep. But her hand rose from her breast and came down again on her closed eyes. Was she beautiful? I couldn't see her properly. She was turned towards the sea. But yes, she was very beautiful.

'Are you listening to what I'm saying?' said Jacqueline.

As I still didn't move, she got up to see what it was I could be looking at like that. She held her bathing-cap in her hand with two freshly cut halves of lemon in it. She saw her. She dropped her cap, and the two pieces of lemon rolled out on to the ground. She didn't say a word. She didn't even pick up the lemon. She lay down again. I lay down again almost immediately after she did. I didn't have anything to say to her, everything had just happened without me. I picked up the piece of lemon that had fallen nearest me and pressed it to my mouth. We were silent. Over our heads, above the awfulness of life, the sun went on shining, blazing.

'Were you looking at her?' Jacqueline asked at last. Her voice was different; slow.

'Yes,' I said.

'While I was talking to you, you were looking at her?'

'You weren't talking to me, you were talking to yourself.'

She picked up her towel and covered herself.

74

'I'm too hot,' she wailed.

It wasn't true, but what else could she do? I felt a vague friendliness towards her because of it. She looked as if she was cold. I didn't dare look at her, but I could see she was trembling. I tried to think of something to say to her, but I couldn't yet. The air was heavy, poisoned with the presence of the woman, and I could no longer think of anything but her. And Jacqueline knew, she must know that something was making me suffer. It was just that I couldn't get up and go on looking at her. I had been able to look at this other woman while she suffered. She knew now that I hadn't been lying. So did I; better than ever. This knowledge was all that joined us together now. Now she was sinking in her own pain, going down like a torpedoed ship in the sea, and we both looked on at it without being able to do anything to stop it. And for at least several minutes the sun shone implacably down on the truth about our lives – shone and blazed down so fiercely that it was painful to endure. And yet Jacqueline, who had nothing on under her towel, trembled more and more. I still couldn't do anything for her. I couldn't help it – I just didn't feel anything. The only pain I felt was that of not being able to sit up. All I could do for her was keep on enduring the burning sun.

'Are you going to stay here?' she asked at last.

'I expect so,' I said.

She suddenly got angry again, but this time it hardly meant anything.

'That only goes to show,' she said with a sneer.

'Don't get excited,' I said. 'Try to keep calm and understand.'

'My poor darling,' she laughed derisively again. 'My poor darling.'

'I thought I'd already told you I was going to stay on here.'

She'd stopped listening again, and begun to repeat what she'd said before.

'Your being a coward has its advantages. I don't believe what you say. Even if you think you're sure, I know you're not capable of doing it.'

'I think I shall do it,' I said.

I must have said it with conviction. Her anger vanished.

'If it's just the Ministry,' she said suddenly, 'I could leave, we could do something else.'

'No,' I said. 'You won't leave the Ministry.'

'But supposing I did?'

'I shall still stay here. Whatever you say and whatever you do. I can't go on.'

Again she started to cry.

The woman stood up. She was wearing a green swimsuit. Her long body stood out over our heads against the sky. She walked towards the sea.

As soon as she saw her Jacqueline stopped crying and didn't say any more. I couldn't bear the burning of the sun any longer. I realized I had been enduring it partly so as to see her stand up and walk there in front of me.

'Come on, let's go in for a swim.'

She kept on pleading, her voice broken.

'Don't you want to talk any more?'

'No, there's no point.'

I put on my trunks.

'Come in and have a swim,' I said again, as nicely as I could. 'That's the best thing for us to do.'

Was it the way I said it? She started to cry again, but not angrily now. I put my hands on her shoulders.

'You'll see, in a week you'll suddenly start to think that perhaps I was right. And then, gradually, you'll be really happy – you'll see. You weren't really happy with me.'

'You disgust me,' she said. She moved away. 'Leave me alone.'

'You weren't happy. Understand that at least – you weren't happy.'

We came out from the reeds. I can remember it all quite

clearly. On the beach a few guests from the hotel were still playing ball. Their shouts varied according to whether one of them caught the ball or missed it. I'd heard them while we were behind the reeds. Sometimes, too, they shouted because the sand burned the soles of their feet and they couldn't stand still. Two young women, stretched out under a tent, congratulated or reproached them on the way they played. We ran towards the sea: the sand burned our feet too. As we passed the players I caught their ball in mid-flight and threw it back to them. After the sun the sea felt icy – it took your breath away. It was almost as calm as the river, but very small waves thudded regularly against the shore. A little while after we had passed them, the players stopped and followed us into the sea. There was no one left on the beach. I floated. Beside me, Jacqueline practised her crawl. I remember thinking she wouldn't suffer long if she was practising her crawl. She kicked furiously, disturbing the slumber of the sea. Everybody else was just floating. The yacht was there, anchored between us and the horizon. Between us and it the woman was swimming. I thought again about the brass – in other words, about the future. I wasn't afraid any more; I would stay on at Rocca. I had really come to a decision. I had come to it just that moment. All previous decisions seemed unimportant.

When we got back to the trattoria I ordered a pastis. Eolo said you couldn't get it in Italy, but that he kept a few bottles for his French customers. I invited him to have one with me. We sat down at a table on the terrasse. Jacqueline, who usually drank only fruit juice, ordered a Cinzano. A little while after we'd sat down, but after I'd finished my pastis, the woman arrived.

'L'Americana,' Eolo whispered to me.

I whispered back that I'd already seen her sunbathing on the beach. Heh, heh, he laughed, his old eyelids crinkling. Jacqueline didn't hear. She was staring wide-eyed at the woman, obviously unable to prevent herself. I drank my second pastis. She was sitting at the other end of the terrasse and smoking as she drank a glass of wine that Carla had brought her. Now I could see her properly. Nobody would have known her. I didn't know her. Till then I'd never thought, I could never· have suspected, that she could exist. Now I learned that she did. When I'd finished the second pastis I felt rather drunk.

'I'd like another,' I said to Eolo.

She turned towards us slightly when she heard us speak French, then looked away again.

'It's strong stuff, you know, pastis,' said Eolo.

She hadn't yet noticed that I existed.

'I know,' I said.

The last few days I'd probably started to take life rather solemnly. I stopped doing so at that moment.

'Three,' said Eolo, 'that's a bit . . .'

'You don't understand,' I said.

He laughed. No, he didn't understand. Jacqueline looked at me in alarm.

'Anyone not liking pastis?' he asked, laughing.

'No,' I said.

He looked at me, still laughing. I think she did too, but at that moment I wasn't watching her. Jacqueline let out a faint cry.

'What then?' said Eolo. 'Understand what?'

Jacqueline turned her head away, and her eyes filled with tears. Everybody must have heard her cry out except Eolo.

'Nothing,' I said. 'Understand what an apéritif really is.'

He told Carla to bring me another pastis. She brought it. Then, of course, we had to talk about something.

'You've got enough grapes there for the whole season,' I said.

Eolo looked up at the trellis. She looked up too, automatically.

'Yes,' said Eolo. 'There's plenty up there.'

The bunches were enormous, and there were many of them. The sun, shining down on the trellis, was filtered through a mass of green grapes. She was flooded in grape-coloured light. She was wearing a black cotton pullover and black trousers rolled up to the knee.

'I've never seen so many,' I said.

Jacqueline was still staring at her rather wildly, but she seemed not to notice. She seemed quite at ease with herself; it was strange.

'They're still green,' said Eolo, 'even when they're ripe. You have to taste them to see if they're ripe.'

'That's strange,' I said. I laughed. I felt that I was beginning to get drunk in earnest. Eolo hadn't noticed yet, but Jacqueline had. As for the other, she could hardly be interested.

'It's the same as with people,' I said.

'What?' said Eolo.

'Some stay green all their lives.'

'Young, you mean,' said Eolo.

'No,' I said. 'Mugs.'

'What does that mean in Italian?' said Eolo.

I explained.

Don't get excited, I told myself. But it was very difficult. I wanted to laugh – there are moments like that.

'I'm the only one who eats them,' said Eolo. 'My daughters don't like them. But there are far too many for me alone. Even the guests always say they're too sour.'

'But they're very beautiful,' I said.

Carla was leaning in the doorway listening to her father. She looked at him with a mixture of affection and impatience. I saw that. I was trying to look less at the other.

'Even Carla doesn't like them,' Eolo went on. No one was listening to him. 'She says they make her feel cold.'

It wasn't any use. I had to look at her.

It was like a momentous duty. I'd wasted so much time not knowing she existed.

'Don't you really like them?' she asked Carla.

79

In her voice was the same sweetness as in her eyes. She wasn't American. Even when she spoke Italian she had a French accent.

'I eat them to please him,' said Carla, 'but I don't really like them.'

No one except me noticed that I didn't particularly displease her. Perhaps Jacqueline did.

'My wife likes them,' went on Eolo. 'We planted the vine when we got married. Thirty years ago.'

The guests were coming back now. Two people came in from shooting. They asked Eolo for two chiantis, and he told Carla to bring them.

'Every year,' said Carla as she served the drinks, 'it's the same old story with the grapes. Ever since we were little he's made us eat them.'

'You're never satisfied,' she said to Carla.

'It's not that,' said Carla. 'But what's the point of forcing us?'

She didn't answer. It looked as if the conversation had come to an end. But no. Eolo didn't take much interest now except in things like the grapes, but he took a good deal of interest in those.

'It was a neighbour that gave me the stock,' he said. 'He gave me the wrong one, but when I noticed, seven years afterwards, it was too late – I hadn't the heart to dig it up again.'

'Once you've planted something . . .' I said.

'Yes,' said Eolo, 'you can't help feeling it's worthwhile.'

Every time I heard my own voice I wanted to laugh. This time I restrained myself. Jacqueline was still suffering.

'And what about the grapes you buy in Sarzana every Saturday? Do you like those?' she asked Carla.

'Of course. I choose them for myself,' said Carla.

She blushed. She must have told the American her secrets.

'I could do with another drink,' I said.

'No,' said Jacqueline quietly.

'No,' I said.

80

'There's no other vine that grows the way this one does,' went on Eolo, engrossed in his subject. 'This terrasse is famous all over the district.'

Only Carla was really listening to him.

'If the grapes are there you have to eat them,' I said.

'I'm the only one who does,' said Carla.

'You're never satisfied,' she said to her again. 'Never.'

'You always say that,' said Carla.

'When I think,' said Eolo, 'that this poor old vine has gone on producing grapes for thirty years just to have them thrown away. I eat as many as I can, but I can't eat them all.'

Carla had finished serving the apéritifs. She leaned in the doorway again, waiting for her mother to call her to serve the lunch. She was near the American's table. Eolo was a bit drunk too by now.

'No,' he said, 'I can't eat them all.'

'Here we go again,' said Carla. 'Every year it's the same.'

She didn't mind anyone being interested in her. I could see that already. And that whenever she spoke she blushed. But I also saw that I didn't exactly displease her.

'There are some things you can never get used to,' I said.

'I eat so many of them,' said Eolo, 'that every year I have colic for a fortnight. Every year.'

'There he goes,' said Carla, 'talking about colic just before everybody sits down to lunch.'

'But I'll tell you what I think,' said Eolo. 'I think it's one of those colics that are good for your health.'

'That's how he behaves in front of guests,' said Carla.

'You have to talk about something,' I said.

I laughed. So did she. It was getting more and more difficult not to look at her. Jacqueline wasn't listening – she was just looking from one to the other of us. She was very pale.

'Every year he nearly kills himself because of those grapes. He loses half a stone in a fortnight. One of these days he'll go too far.'

'The colic does me good,' said Eolo, 'brings down my blood

pressure. Besides, I can't just let them all go to waste. I can't.'

'Of course not,' I said.

'If we left him to himself,' said Carla, 'he'd kill himself. He eats them when nobody's looking.'

'You ought to leave him alone,' I said.

'What, to risk his life?' said Carla.

'Yes,' I said.

Eolo looked at me in surprise. I was almost completely drunk. I imagine Jacqueline must have been looking at me pretty grimly. Nobody said anything for a moment. Eolo looked at the empty glasses in front of me. Then I heard her ask Carla, in the tone of someone trying to change the subject:

'Did you go to the dance yesterday evening?'

'What?' said Carla. 'With him walking up and down outside the house all night?'

'There's another one tonight,' she said.

She looked at me, but so rapidly that only I saw.

'Yes,' said Carla, 'I know.'

Eolo was paying some attention to what they were saying. I didn't want to laugh any more.

'If I took you would he let you go?' she asked.

'I don't think so,' said Carla, looking at her father.

Eolo started to laugh.

'No,' he said. 'I've already told you. Not with you.'

I suddenly became very careful. My heart was beating loudly.

'I could take her to the dance,' I said.

Jacqueline was wild with anger, but she must now be suffering less. I'd done all I could. Carla looked at me in great astonishment, Eolo, I think, with less.

'What?' said Eolo. 'Just like that?'

'I'd like to,' I said.

Jacqueline gave another almost inaudible groan.

'I don't know,' said Eolo. 'I'll let you know this evening.'

'I can never do anything,' cried Carla. 'You let my

82

sisters do anything they like.'

She must already know how attractive her lack of sophistication was, and she exaggerated it a little. She looked at her father resentfully.

'You'll see,' she said to Carla softly. 'He'll let you go, you'll see.'

She stroked Carla's hair. Carla didn't relent. She still stared at her father resentfully.

'And this evening,' she said, 'he'll say he doesn't want me to.'

'Just for an hour,' I said. 'She'll only dance with me.'

'I don't know,' said Eolo. 'I'll let you know this evening.'

'You see what he's like!' cried Carla.

Her mother called her. Lunch was ready. Carla got up, scraping her chair on the floor, and disappeared inside. While she was gone no one had anything to say. Then she came back, followed by her sisters, all carrying great steaming dishes. The smell of fish cooked in saffron spread over the terrasse. Lunch began.

It lasted a long time. Carla waited at table. Eolo had gone back to the kitchen to help his wife, so there was no one left for me to talk to. And I was racked by the desire to talk. To talk? No, to shout, rather. To shout the need I felt to go away on a ship. It was an obsession that seized me at the beginning of the meal; it was my way of being drunk that day. Three times, unable to bear it, I got up to go out. Three times a glance from Jacqueline made me sit down again. I think she must have looked at the two of us quite a lot. I didn't look at her – I still vaguely realized that in my condition it would be dangerous. And I was fully occupied in trying not to shout. I ate little and drank a lot of wine. Glass after glass, as if it was water. I was drunk. If I had cried out I shouldn't have been able to produce anything but inarticulate noises like 'yacht', which out of context wouldn't have told anyone anything about my plans, but would have spoiled any slight chance I might have of realizing them.

83

It was the last meal Jacqueline and I had together. She spent it looking at me with insuperable disgust. If I remember rightly, she didn't eat much either. I must have taken her appetite away. We didn't speak either: she looked at me, and I drank. But as she was sitting with her back towards the rest of the terrasse, she could laugh derisively at every glass of wine I drank. It happened fairly often. But I was so drunk I took it in good part, more as a proof of complicity than of hostility. In any case, the more I drank the more easily I took everything. By the time we'd got to the cheese, and my tenth glass of wine, I no longer had any doubt that I would go away on the yacht. It seemed the easiest thing in the world, I'd only have to ask when I was sober. Everyone must understand, I thought, how much I needed to go away on a ship. All I could think of was going away on a ship – that ship. I had to. It was something I could no longer do without. I could see it in my mind's eye, white, on the surface of the sea. The Ministry was a thing of the past. I was drunk not only with wine but also with prudence. Up to a point I realized this: ask her when you're sober; not now, when you're sober, I kept saying to myself, in so many words. As if she was aware of my little stratagem, Jacqueline laughed quietly, scornfully. The smile I gave her in return was friendly, understanding even. But I must have gone a bit too far: towards the end of the meal she picked up a glass and threw it in my direction. It fell on the floor. I mildly picked up the pieces. I must have made an enormous effort not to fall flat on my face. It took a long time. When I sat up again my head was spinning and I no longer knew what was the best thing to do – shout out straight away and call everyone on the terrasse to witness that she had to take me on on her yacht, or go up to my room. I pondered as carefully as I could. Sleeping it off, asked Jacqueline, after all that wine? No, I said; after all that life. I was pleased with my joke and started to laugh, but her eyes were so frightening I decided there and then to go up to my room. I stood up, aimed at the passage between the tables and made a dash for it. I negotiated the terrasse with the utmost seriousness. Her table was at the other end, by the door into the hotel. Don't be a mug, don't be a mug, I said to myself as I went past her, don't spoil your one chance, don't be a mug. And I succeeded in making it without looking at her. If I'd looked at her her encouraging expression would probably have made me shout so loud I'd have frightened everybody off the terrasse.

I found myself on the stairs of the hotel, very pleased with myself.

It couldn't have been very long after I got to my room, ten minutes perhaps, when Jacqueline came in. But I think I must have slept for those ten minutes, knocked sideways by the pastis and the wine, because I have the impression that she woke me up. She came in without knocking, shut the door behind her quietly without turning round, and, bent double like a woman in a film staggering with a bullet in her stomach to make her last confession to the police, went over and leaned against the mantelpiece.

'Swine,' she said quietly.

As soon as she said it I felt sleepy again.

'Swine. Swine. Swine.'

She was perfectly justified, I thought. She went off like a gun – opened her mouth, and out came the words as regular as bullets. It did her a lot of good.

'Swine. Swine.'

After she'd said it as many times as was necessary she suddenly grew calm. Her eyes dimmed with tears and she said:

'As if all that about the grapes deceived anyone. Fool.'

'Don't get excited,' I said, just for something to say.

'As if everyone couldn't see you wanted to impress her. Lousy swine.'

I'd never seen her like this. She was a different woman. And of course, now, she'd given up hope.

'And in front of me,' she shouted. 'In front of me!'

'Don't get excited,' I said again.

'And everybody else laughing up their bloody sleeves at you.'

Then she added, almost laughing:

'And her laughing up her bloody sleeve as well.'

I didn't feel drunk any more; she'd sobered me. I listened to her with interest. She noticed.

'What are you hoping for, you poor fish?'

She hesitated, then, as in the end people can't resist delivering a fatal blow:

'Have you looked at yourself in the glass?'

I felt a faint inclination to get up and look at myself in the mirror over the mantelpiece. But I was too sleepy. I made shift with running my fingers over my face to feel what it was like. It struck me that I wasn't putting up a bad show.

'It's not a question of looks,' I said, feeling a bit shaken nevertheless.

'What is it a question of then, you lousy swine? Tell me, what is it a question of?'

I'd been speaking mildly and my tone exasperated her even more than what I actually said.

'What I want,' I said, 'is to go away on her yacht.'

'Go on her yacht? What would you do on her yacht?'

'I don't know – anything.'

'You can't even keep a lousy file properly – what the hell could you do on a yacht?' she shouted.

'I don't know,' I said again. 'Anything.'

'And why should she take you? What for? What does she ever take men on her yacht for, except to go to bed with them when she feels like it?'

'You exaggerate,' I said. 'It isn't only for that.'

'Do you think anybody else but me would take on a mug like you? You've looked at yourself, have you? You know what you look like, do you?'

She'd made her point. I got up and went to look at myself in the glass. As I looked I must unconsciously have put on an ingratiating expression.

'Swine!' she yelled.

They must have heard her all over the hotel.

'I'm a bit drunk,' I said. 'Sorry.'

I didn't feel so sleepy now. She was transfigured with rage. Her face seemed vaguely fraternal.

'You're going to come back with me,' she went on yelling, 'yes, you are.'

Had she started to believe again that it was possible? I felt a terrific need to do something amusing. But I stopped her.

'No,' I said. 'I'm staying. Whatever you say. Whatever you do.'

Her anger subsided. She looked at me mournfully, distantly – she'd expected it. Then, after a silence, she said, to herself:

'Two years I drag you about with me. Make you go to the office. Make you eat. Do your washing. You didn't even notice when your shirts were dirty.'

I sat up and listened to her, but she didn't notice.

'Didn't I eat?'

'It's only thanks to me you didn't get consumption.'

'And is that true about the shirts?'

'Everyone noticed it except you. And on Saturday, instead of going to the cinema . . .'

She couldn't go on. She buried her face in her hands and wept.

'. . . I stayed at home and washed them . . .'

And now it was my turn to suffer.

'You shouldn't have,' I said.

'What? I suppose I should have just let you get consumption?'

'Yes,' I said, 'I think that would have been better. Or else you could have sent my shirts to the laundry. That's what made you think you loved me.'

She wasn't listening.

'Two years,' she said. 'Two years down the drain living with a rotten swine.'

'Not really wasted,' I said. 'People always say that, but it's not true.'

87

'Two years gained perhaps, then?'

'People always waste a lot of time,' I said. 'It's inevitable. If they started regretting things like that they'd all cut their throats.'

She thought for a moment. Her face was sad. She'd not only given up hope; she wasn't even angry any more. I couldn't bear this silence. I spoke.

'Every holiday,' I said, 'I've hoped there'd be a miracle, that somehow I'd find the strength not to go back to the Ministry. You know it.'

She looked up.

'Is that true?' she said, quite sincerely. 'Am I and the Ministry one and the same thing for you?'

'No,' I said. 'It's my life and the Ministry that are one and the same. What was wrong with you, as far as I was concerned, was that the Ministry didn't worry you. You can't know what it was like for me.'

'You can take an interest in anything if you try,' she said, 'even in the Ministry. Look at you – the mug to end all mugs, the feeblest drip in the whole place – I managed to take an interest in you for two whole years.'

She said it with great conviction but with hardly any malice.

'Was I really the biggest drip in the whole place?'

'So they said.'

'I still can't understand how you managed it,' I said.

I was as sincere as she was, and she saw this. She didn't answer.

'Come and sit on the bed,' I said gently, 'and tell me how you managed it'.

She didn't move from the mantelpiece.

'I don't know,' she said at last, perfectly naturally.

'I never thought,' I said. 'You must be very strong.'

She looked at me suspiciously for a moment, but she could see I was trying to be friendly.

'Oh no,' she said, and hesitated. 'I was used to you, that's all, and then I hoped . . .'

'What?'

'I hoped you'd change.'

She waited a moment, then asked, still quite naturally:

'And that miracle you were talking about – is that woman it?'

'No. It's that I've made up my mind to leave the Ministry. I made up my mind in Florence, before I'd met her.'

'But as soon as you saw her you felt more certain?'

'I don't know whether I could have felt more certain. Perhaps – it's difficult to say. She's there with her ship, and I just think there's the ghost of a chance that she'll take me on.'

'Men who rely on women to solve their problems are swine,' she said.

'Some people think so,' I said. 'I've always thought it a bit silly. Why *do* people say that?'

'Swine and cowards,' she went on, not listening to me. 'They're not really men at all.'

'Perhaps,' I said, after a moment's silence. 'It's all the same to me.'

'Any man would understand.'

'When I made up my mind to stay we were still in Florence, I hadn't even met her.'

'So you'll scrub the decks, then?'

'I'm not so ambitious as I used to be.'

She collapsed on the bed, exhausted. Then, slowly, emphasizing each word:

'I'd never have believed you'd sink so low,' she said.

I couldn't sit up any longer. I lay down again.

'I was at my worst when I was at the Ministry,' I said at last. 'You're right, I was a swine, even to you. I was unhappy.'

'And do you think I was happy?'

'You weren't so unhappy as I was. If you'd been very unhappy you wouldn't have been able to wash my shirts.'

'And you think you'll be happy scrubbing decks?'

'I don't know. At least on a ship there aren't any papers or files.'

89

'You poor fish,' she said, 'believing in happiness. It's the same as with everything else – you just don't understand.'

'You often talk about the happiness of the human race,' I said.

'I believe in happiness,' she said.

'Yes,' I said, 'but in happiness through work and dignity.'

She sat up, as sure of herself and as unwavering as ever. I didn't feel like answering her any more, like saying anything to her at all. She made as if to go, then stopped and said in a tired voice:

'I suppose it's this tart's money that's done the trick?'

'Perhaps,' I said. 'Yes, that must be it.'

She went towards the door again, then stopped a second time. Her face was without expression, but streaming with tears.

'So it's really true? It's all over?'

'You'll be happy,' I said.

But I'd lost heart. I didn't believe any more that she would be happy; and besides it was all one to me whether she was or not.

'In that case,' she said, 'I'll catch the evening train.'

I didn't answer. She hesitated, then:

'Is it true about the yacht?' she said. 'Do you really think you'll go?'

'One chance in a thousand,' I said.

'And supposing she won't have you?'

'It's all one to me.'

Her hand was on the door-knob. I just stared at the unmoving hand that couldn't make up its mind.

'Will you come to the station with me?'

'No!' I shouted. 'No! Clear out, for Christ's sake!'

She looked at me dully.

'Pitiful,' she said, and went out.

I waited for a little, long enough for a door to slam in the silence of the hotel. It slammed, loudly. I got up, took my shoes off, and went downstairs. When I got to the back door I

90

put my shoes on again and went out. It must have been about two o'clock. Everyone was taking a siesta. The countryside was deserted; it was the hottest time of the day. I went along by the river, walking away from the sea, towards the gardens and the olive groves. I was still very drunk, as I had been all the time we were talking. Only one clear idea remained in the darkness of my mind: to get away as far as possible from the hotel. My undoing had been so total that I couldn't properly visualize its dimensions. I was a free man, unencumbered by any woman, with no other obligation than to try to be happy. But if you'd asked this free man why he had decided to leave the Ministry he wouldn't have been able to tell you. I'd broken with the world of happiness through dignity and work, because I hadn't been able to convince them all of my own unhappiness. In short, my fate now depended on myself alone, and henceforward concerned nobody but me. The heat made the wine go to my head again, and I felt myself getting drunk once more. Once I stopped and made a conscientious effort to bring it all up. But I couldn't. I've never been able to vomit, or to moderate my desires – it's something that's always been missing from my education and has got me into no end of trouble. I tried again, but it was no good. So I dragged myself on a bit further. I walked with difficulty, very slowly: the free man was as heavy as a corpse. The wine was circulating right through my body, mingled with my blood, and I had to drag it along with me, on and on, until I could eject it. I had to wait. Wait until I could piss the wine, wait for the train to leave, wait until I was ready to bear my freedom. For what I was drunk with was the wine of freedom. I could hear my heart pumping it right down to my burning feet.

I walked for a long time, perhaps an hour, I don't know, all the while among the olives so as not be seen. Then, when I turned round and couldn't see the hotel any more, I stopped. There was a plane tree a few yards away from the river. I lay down in its shade. I was as heavy as a corpse, the corpse of someone who'd died in the world of happiness through freedom and work. But the shade of the plane tree was just the thing for corpses like me. I fell asleep.

When I woke, even the shadow of the plane tree had deserted me and stood a few yards away, hostile, engrossed in its own imperturbable movement. I must have been right in the sun for one of the two hours I'd been asleep. I wasn't drunk any more. I wondered what time it was and whether her train had left. I'd forgotten the woman, the yacht, freedom. I could only think of the one who had gone, or was going. The thought was unrelievedly awful. I tried to think of all the good reasons for leaving her that I'd had as recently as that morning, but even when I succeeded in formulating them as clearly as before they were no help to me before the horror of that departure.

I know I experienced every aspect of that horror.

I wasn't wearing a watch. I still waited. It still seemed too early for her to have left. So I waited, on and on. The sun went down, and still I waited. Then when I'd quite given up hope of hearing it, I heard it: the whistle of a little village station, shrill and sad. There was only one train in the evening from Sarzana to Florence. I couldn't be mistaken, it must be it, hers. I got up and went back to the hotel.

Eolo came up to me in the passage.

'The signora has gone,' he said.

'We'd made up our minds to part,' I said. 'But I preferred not to go to the station.'

'I see,' said Eolo after a moment. 'It was painful to see her.'

'Did she leave any message?'

'She said to tell you she'd taken the evening train, that's all.'

I hurried up to my room. I think I was crying even before I got to the bed. Then at last I wept all the tears I hadn't been able to shed before because I wasn't free; ten years' tears.

When Eolo knocked at my door it was very late. He

opened it slightly and put his head round into the room. He smiled. I was lying down. I told him to come in.

'Everyone's at dinner,' he said. 'It's late.'

'I'm not hungry,' I said. 'It won't do me any harm to go without dinner.'

He came over, smiled, and sat down on the end of the bed.

'Life's not easy,' he said.

I offered him a cigarette, and lit one for myself. I realized I hadn't smoked since midday.

'It must be very hot on the trains,' I said.

'Trains are cheerful places in Italy,' he said. 'People all talk to each other and the time goes quickly.'

He hadn't anything more to say to me. He waited.

'I don't really quite know why I did it,' I said. 'It's a bit as if I'd killed her, for no reason at all.'

'She's young,' he said. 'You haven't killed her. You didn't look as if you really got on together.'

'We didn't understand one another,' I said, 'that was it. We didn't understand one another in the least. But that's no excuse.'

'I realized it yesterday evening when you came out of the room. Perhaps even as soon as you arrived.'

I felt sick. I didn't want to talk any more. I wanted to sleep.

'Come and have dinner,' said Eolo.

'I'm tired.'

He cudgelled his brains, thought of something, and gave me a broad grin.

'I'll lend you Carla to take to the dance,' he said. 'Now come on.'

I smiled at him. Anybody would have.

'I'd completely forgotten,' I said.

'I've told her. She's waiting.'

'But just the same,' I said, 'I'm tired.'

He spoke slowly:

'She's young, you know, that's what really counts. And

she's healthy – she'll be all right. You ought to go to the dance. By the time it's over the train will have got to France.'

'I'll come down,' I said.

He got up quickly and left me. I waited long enough for him to tell Carla; combed my hair, washed my face, and went down.

The terrasse was full of guests, more than at lunch-time, probably people going to the dance and starting the evening with a good dinner. She was there. She saw that I was alone and very late, but didn't appear to be surprised. Soon after I came in Carla followed. She blushed and smiled. I made an effort and managed to give her a knowing smile in return. The table was still set for two. Carla hadn't been told.

'Isn't the signora coming down for dinner?' she asked.

'No,' I said. 'She's left.'

She heard. And then she looked at me in a way that said if I wanted to I could go away on the yacht. One chance in a thousand. And it had come off.

PART TWO

I DRANK two glasses of chianti one after the other, and waited. I don't know what for, for Carla to serve dinner perhaps, or for the wine to begin to take effect. She watched me drinking and she too waited for the wine to work on me.

It did so. I felt it spreading through my arms, through my head, and I abandoned myself to it. She was made up, and wore a black dress specially for the dance. She was extremely beautiful, extremely desirable. All the newcomers who were seeing her for the first time looked at her all the time and spoke about her in whispers. She looked at me. Once I turned round to make sure it was me and not somebody else sitting behind me that I hadn't noticed. But no, I was the only person at that end of the terrasse, there wasn't even a cat sitting on the wall. I drank another glass of chianti. Eolo, sitting near the door, watched me too, sympathetically but with some anxiety. He whispered something to Carla, and she hurried to supply me with a plate of pasta.

'My father says you must eat something,' she murmured, blushing, 'and you oughtn't to drink too much chianti.'

She turned away quickly, embarrassed. The woman stopped her as she went by.

'I'm coming to the dance with you,' she said.

I ate a few mouthfuls of pasta, then had another glass of chianti. Inside my head there was a train rushing through the darkness, and I drank to cure myself of it, to forget it. My body ached, my face burned from having lain so long on the ground, in the sun. The wine was good. She watched me almost continuously. Our tables were quite close. It suddenly became imperative that we should speak.

'Very good wine, this,' I said.

'Yes,' she said softly. 'I like it too.'

95

Then she added after a moment:

'Are you going to the dance too?'

'Of course,' I said. 'He wouldn't let Carla go alone with you.'

She smiled. We had to wait until Carla was finished. She had had dinner and was only drinking wine now and smoking. Did she realize that after we'd exchanged those few words I had no more to say? She began to read a paper. I started to try not to drink too much.

Then it was time. Eolo told Carla she could go and change. Carla disappeared and came back five minutes later wearing a red dress. Eolo stood up.

'Shall we go?'

All three of us followed him. He took us over to the other side of the river. Perhaps he grumbled a bit, but not crossly.

'You'll bring her back to me in an hour?' he said to me.

I promised. Although he was grumbling he was in a very good temper and wasn't really sorry he had let her go. As soon as he'd put us down on the other bank he set off back to the trattoria – to finish off the waiting for Carla, as usual, he said. Carla laughed and said it didn't happen twice in a year.

She took Carla's arm and I walked beside her. I noticed that she was slightly taller than Carla, but not much, not so tall as me. Absurdly, this reassured me.

We sat down at a little table, the only one still free, in a corner some distance from the orchestra. Carla was invited to dance almost straight away. She and I were left alone. That evening, mechanically, I looked round at all the faces to see if he was there. It was the last time I did it. By the next day I had even forgotten that he existed, and when I saw him on the beach I hardly recognized him. He wasn't there. I saw Candida dancing. She hadn't seen me.

'Are you looking for someone?'

'Yes and no,' I said.

Carla passed quite close to us. She was laughing as she danced. Eolo was right: it didn't matter to her yet who she danced with, she danced like a child, and so gracefully and well that we smiled at one another.

'It would have been a pity not to bring her,' she said.

I tried to think of something to say, but couldn't. I hadn't anything to say to her. Candida saw me with her as she danced past. Did she look sad? I don't think so – surprised, rather. She made her partner pause for a moment by our table, and leaned towards me.

'She's gone,' I said.

Then Candida danced away, still looking at my companion as if trying to make out what we were doing together.

'Was she the one you were looking for?' she asked.

'Not exactly,' I said. 'It was a young man.'

She was intrigued. She nodded towards Candida.

'What about her then?'

'I came here yesterday evening,' I said.

I asked her to dance. We stood up. As soon as she was in my arms, her hand in mine, I realized that I wasn't going to be able to dance. I couldn't make out what they were playing, the rhythm escaped me completely, I couldn't adapt myself to it, couldn't even listen to it. I tried, but I couldn't even listen to it for more than ten seconds. I stopped.

'It's no good,' I said. 'I can't dance.'

'It doesn't matter,' she said.

Her voice was extraordinarily kind. Nobody had ever spoken to me before in such a voice. But try as I might, I couldn't manage to dance. People kept knocking into us. She laughed. It wasn't because I desired her. Oh no, I didn't know how to desire a woman any more. It was because she was making a mistake and I didn't know how to prevent it. She couldn't know what she was doing, and I was sure that from one minute to the next she would see through me and go. My hands trembled; it made me feel faint to hold her in my arms like that. I was afraid, as before certain hazardous choices, before death, before chance. Then at last I spoke to her to warn her with my voice at least, a desperate attempt to show

97

her what I was. There were a thousand things I'd have liked to say to her. All I could talk about was her yacht, the *Gibraltar*.

'Why is it called the *Gibraltar*?' I asked.

My voice was trembling too. After I'd asked the question I had the feeling of having got rid of an enormous responsibility.

'Oh,' she said, 'it would take too long to explain.'

Without looking at her I saw that she was smiling.

'I've got plenty of time,' I said.

'I know. I heard what you said to Carla.'

'I've got all the time in the world,' I said.

'All?'

'The whole of my life,' I said.

'I didn't realize,' she said. 'I thought she'd simply left a few days before you.'

'She's gone for ever,' I said.

'Were you together long?'

'Two years.'

Things were sorting themselves out. I started to dance a bit better and to tremble less. Above all, the wine I had drunk came to my aid again.

'She was very nice,' I said, 'but we didn't understand one another.'

'I saw something was wrong this morning, in the trattoria,' she said.

'We were very different,' I said. 'She was very nice.'

She smiled. For the first time we looked at each other, swiftly.

'Aren't you?' Her tone was gently ironical.

'I don't know,' I said. 'I'm very tired.'

I was dancing better and better. My hands had stopped trembling.

'You dance well,' she said.

'Why *Gibraltar*?' I asked again.

'Because,' she said. 'Do you know Gibraltar?'

Suddenly we were talking quite naturally.

'Oh no,' I said.

She didn't answer at once.

'I'm glad we met,' she said at last.

We smiled at each other again.

'Gibraltar's very beautiful,' she said. 'People always talk about it as one of the most important strategic points in the world, but they never say how beautiful it is. It's got the Mediterranean on one side and the Atlantic on the other. They're very different.'

'I see. Are they as different as all that?'

'Very. On one side you have the coast of Africa. It's very lovely. A plateau with a sheer drop into the sea.'

'Have you often been there?'

'I've passed through often.'

'How often?'

'About sixteen times, I think. The Spanish coast, on the other side, is much gentler.'

'But it wasn't because it was beautiful that . . .'

'Not only because of that,' she said.

Presumably she felt that our meeting wasn't of sufficient importance for her to tell me why.

'Was it because of her you drank so much at dinner?'

'Because of her, and – I don't know – because of life in general.'

The dance ended. All three of us met back at our table.

'Are you enjoying yourself?' she asked Carla. 'You dance very well.'

'And yet I hardly ever do,' said Carla.

She looked at Carla.

'I shall be sorry to leave here,' she said.

'You'll come back,' said Carla.

She lit a cigarette and looked absentmindedly into the distance.

'Perhaps,' she said. 'If I do it will be to see you, to see if you're happy, if you've got married.'

99

'Oh, I'm young,' said Carla. 'You musn't come back just for that.'

'Are you leaving then?' I asked.

'Tomorrow evening,' she said.

I remembered what Eolo had said: not hard to please, not a woman to make difficulties.

'Couldn't you stay one more day?'

She looked down, and said, apologetically:

'It's difficult. Are you staying long in Rocca?'

'I don't know. Probably some time.'

The music began again. Carla went off to dance.

'Well,' I said, 'we can always dance while we're waiting.'

'Waiting for what?'

'For you to go.'

She didn't answer.

'Tell me about the ship,' I said. 'About the *Gibraltar*.'

'The ship's not the most important thing.'

'No, they told me it was a man. Was he from Gibraltar?'

'No. He wasn't really from anywhere. Perhaps,' she added, 'perhaps I could stay until the day after tomorrow.'

What had I been thinking? When they're at sea, Eolo had said, she must make do with the sailors. My hand wasn't trembling now, and I didn't feel faint any longer at holding her in my arms.

'And you don't live with him any more?'

'No.'

'You've left him?'

'No, he left me.' She added in a murmur, 'Yes, the day after tomorrow would be all right.'

'What does it depend on?'

'Me.'

'Do you have a schedule then?'

'Of course,' she said, and smiled, 'if only because of the tides.'

'Yes,' I said. 'Especially in the Mediterranean.'

'Especially in the Mediterranean,' she said.

I thought about the man who had left this woman. I didn't understand. I didn't speak.

'And you, why did you leave her?' she asked, very softly.

'I've told you – no particular reason.'

'But one always has some idea,' she said.

'I didn't love her. I'd never loved her.'

The music stopped again. Carla came and sat down. She was hot.

'I'm so sorry that you're going,' she said.

She must have been thinking about it even while she was dancing; she couldn't forget it.

'I'm very fond of you,' she said to Carla.

She flashed a look at me, then turned again to Carla. But I was still thinking about the man who had left her.

'You must get married,' she said to Carla. 'Don't be like your sisters. Get married as quickly as you can, as well as you can – afterwards you can see. You mustn't get old before you've even started.'

Carla grew pensive, and blushed.

'Father says it's difficult to get married,' she said. 'So it must be even more difficult actually to choose.'

She blushed slightly too. But only I saw it. Then she said, quietly:

'The important thing is that it should be you who chooses. Afterwards, all you have to do is want it.'

'Oh,' cried Carla, 'I should never be able to.'

'Yes, you will,' she said.

'I'm thirsty,' I said. 'I'll go and get some drinks.'

I went to the bar and brought back three glasses of chianti. Carla had gone off dancing again, so I drank hers.

'Let's dance again', I said.

'Are you so fond of it?' she said.

'No,' I said, 'but let's dance anyway.'

She got up reluctantly. I think she would have liked to talk.

'Why are you laughing at me?' I asked.

'I'm not laughing at you,' she said.

She was surprised. Even just for one night, I thought. And for the first time, encouraged by the chianti, I held her a bit closer.

'You mustn't be angry with me,' she said.

The train wasn't rushing through the dark in my head any more. I desired her. It seemed to come upon me from forgotten regions of my body and my memory.

'I'd like you to tell me about him.'

She was the sort of woman who spent one night with a man and left him the next day. And that was how I desired her, just like that.

'You might say that he was a sailor,' she said. 'He was in a little boat just off Gibraltar when we saw him from the yacht. He was making distress signals. We picked him up. That was how it started.'

'Was it long ago?'

'A few years,' she said.

'And why was he making distress signals?'

She spoke rather as if she were reciting something:

'He'd deserted from the Foreign Legion three days before,' she said. 'He'd been in it three years, and didn't want to wait the two years he still had to do, so he'd escaped in a rowing-boat. He'd stolen it.'

Her voice had an inexhaustible gentleness. In the depths of her being there must be an inexhaustible gentleness.

'Why had he joined?'

'He was wanted by the police,' she said, 'for murder.'

I wasn't unduly astonished. She said it very naturally, and with what seemed like a touch of weariness.

'You like people who send out distress signals, don't you?'

She drew away and looked at me. I was even getting used to her beauty now.

'Oh no,' she said with a touch of embarrassment, 'not only that.'

'I've never killed anybody,' I said.

'It's not all that easy,' she said, smiling. 'The occasion has to arise . . .'

'I've never come anywhere near it,' I said. 'I think I shot a pigeon when I was eight, but that's all.'

She laughed aloud. How beautiful she was.

'How beautiful you are,' I said.

She smiled and didn't answer.

'And so you picked him up?' I went on, 'and gave him something to eat? And I'm sure he hadn't had anything to drink for two days, had he?'

'Everyone can kill,' she said. 'It's not just the privilege of a few.'

'The ideal distress, in short,' I said.

'If you like,' she said. 'Yes, I think it was the ideal distress too.' Then, after a pause, she added:

'May I ask what you do?'

'Colonial Ministry, registry section. I used to copy out births, marriages and deaths. After every death I went and washed my hands. In winter I always had chaps.'

She laughed a little, close to my face.

'At the end of the year we used to draw up comparative statistics of the number of birth certificates asked for. The results were very interesting. It varied from year to year – can you credit it?'

If she laughs, I thought, she'll stay another day. She laughed.

'They put the statistics up on the wall in the office. Perhaps someone might be interested, you never know.'

'And it varied from year to year?' she said, still smiling.

'Yes. No one could ever explain why. All I could make out was that more birth-certificates were needed in leap-years than in other years. I submitted a report, but it wasn't adopted.'

I held her tighter still. I found it difficult to speak.

'Why do you speak in the past tense? You're only on holiday, aren't you?'

'More than that.'

The dance was at its height. It was difficult to move about on the dance-floor, but no one minded any more. The orchestra was playing atrociously.

'What? Have you left your job?'

I thought she'd understood, but she hadn't. Even she didn't understand everything straight away.

'Put yourself in my place,' I said. 'I couldn't go on, always copying, I couldn't go on. I can't even write in my own handwriting any more.'

'When did you give it up?'

'This morning, to be exact, during lunch. When they brought in the cheese it was done.'

She didn't laugh. I was holding her very close.

'Oh,' she said. 'I didn't know.'

'You like people in distress, don't you?'

'Why not?' she said at last.

The dance ended. The audience had asked for it to be repeated several times, and we had been dancing a long while.

'I am enjoying myself,' said Carla. 'But I'm thirsty – I'd like a lemonade.'

'We'll have to go for it,' she said.

'I'll go,' I said. 'Shall I get a couple of cognacs for us?'

'If you like. But it's getting late.'

There was such a crowd I could hardly get near the bar. I had one cognac there and brought two more back with the lemonade. Carla drank hers straight off and went back to dance again. We drank our cognacs more slowly and did the same.

'You're really fond of dancing, aren't you?' she said.

'I wouldn't miss one dance.'

'Eolo said an hour,' she said, more softly. 'We've been here more than an hour now.'

'No, it can't be quite that yet.'

'The launch was supposed to come for me after an hour.'

'Well, it's not here yet, is it? We'll have to wait. We can go on dancing for a bit.'

My voice trembled, but not with fear. I kissed her hair.

'Talk to me about the sailor from Gibraltar,' I said.

'Later on,' she said. 'You're getting obsessed.'

'I'm a bit drunk.'

She gave a forced smile. The dancing was getting on her nerves. We were dancing very badly.

'I think Italy's very beautiful,' I said.

We were silent. I remembered Jacqueline again, and was again in the stifling train rushing on and on through the dark. It had come back to me several times before, but this time I couldn't get rid of it. I relaxed my grip on her. She looked at me.

'You shouldn't think about her,' she said.

'It's so hot on the trains at this time of year. That's what bothers me.'

'She was very angry at lunch-time,' she said kindly.

'I must have been making her suffer a good deal.'

'Did she understand why you were leaving her?' she asked after a moment.

'Not in the least. I must have explained it very badly.'

'Don't think about it . . . I really don't think you ought to think about it.'

'But she didn't understand,' I said.

'That happens to everyone some time.'

It was as if she were rebuking me slightly, but she was still very kind, gentler than any woman had ever been to me.

'And what are you going to do?'

'Must one always do something? Aren't there some situations in which you can avoid it?'

'I tried to do nothing. You can't. You always end up doing something.'

'And he? What did he do with himself?'

'For murderers,' she said, smiling, 'it's easier. Other people decide for them. Haven't you any idea?'

'None. It's only a couple of hours since I gave up my job.'

'True. You couldn't know yet.'

'But still,' I said.

She waited.

'What?'

'I'd like to be in the open air.'

She was surprised, then gave a little burst of laughter.

'There aren't many jobs in the open air,' she said.

The dances now followed each other in such quick succession that no one sat down any more in between, but just stood up waiting for the music to start again. But when, as now, the music stopped, we stopped talking too. The music began again.

'There's the sea,' I said.

Now it was my turn to laugh.

'That's true,' she said. 'But you have to be trained for that too.'

I took the bull by the horns and said:

'Not always. Anyone could polish the ship's brass.'

She probably saw how I felt. She didn't answer. I dared not look at her. I went on:

'Aren't there enough doorhandles on a ship to keep one man occupied?'

'I don't know.'

After a moment she added:

'I've never thought about it.'

'I'm just joking, of course.'

She didn't answer. I couldn't go on dancing.

'I'd like a cognac,' I said.

We stopped and made our way to the bar, where we had a cognac without exchanging a word. The cognac was horrible. I didn't look at her. We started dancing again.

'Was it really so awful, the Ministry?'

'One always exaggerates.'

'People ought to take a holiday now and again,' she said. 'Whatever they do.'

I began to hope again.

'No,' I said. 'I always took my holidays regularly and

respectably. To believe in holidays is like believing in God.'
Then I added: 'Forget what I said. Please.'

The dance ended. Carla came back streaming with
perspiration. The music was silent for five minutes. They
seemed interminable. I wanted her to forget about the
brass.

'You're still thirsty,' she said to Carla. 'Go and get
another lemonade.'

'I'll go,' I said.

'No,' said Carla, 'I'm used to it, and it amuses me to do it
here. I'll be quicker than you. Shall I get two cognacs as well?'

Carla went. She watched her go.

'When I was her age I served lemonade too.'

'You must go tomorrow. And the brass – that was only
because I was a bit tight. You must forget what I said.'

She looked at me, still without answering.

'Even if I was asked to look after the brass I wouldn't. I
drink too much, and then that's the sort of thing I say.'

'I've forgotten already,' she said. Then in a different voice:

'When I was Carla's age I cleaned the brass and served
lemonade.'

She was silent. Then:

'Were you in the Ministry long?'

'Eight years.'

Again she fell silent.

'Did you say you served lemonade in cafés when you were
Carla's age?'

'Yes, my father ran a café in the Pyrenees. When I was
nineteen I got a job on the yacht as barmaid or something.
The sort of mad thing a girl does. Carla might easily do something like it.'

It was the first time we'd talked sitting down. I thought
she'd forgotten about the brass.

'The same yacht?' I asked.

'Yes,' she said. She made a little gesture of apology. 'You
see where it leads you.'

Her smile of amusement must have been just the same when she was sixteen.

'Why did you stay there eight years if it was so awful?'

'What a question. Cowardice.'

'And are you sure you won't go back?'

'Certain.'

'Can one be certain of a thing like that after eight years?'

'It's rare, but it can happen. And it was on the same yacht that you met him?'

'Yes. No one quite knew what to do with him so they took him on as a member of the crew.'

The dancing began again.

'One more dance,' she said, 'and then we'll take her home.'

I didn't answer. She added, quietly:

'If you like we could go and have a drink on the ship. The launch will be waiting at the little landing-stage on the beach.'

'No. Let's go on dancing for a bit,' I said.

She laughed.

'No?'

I nearly went off with her and abandoned Carla.

A moment went by.

'Do you think I'm at so much of a loss?'

'No, not really. Anyway, it's all the same to me. No, but this morning before lunch, I don't know why . . .'

'I'm sure you like people who are at a loss.'

'Perhaps,' she said, this time with such youthful confusion that once again I nearly went off with her there and then. 'Perhaps I have got a weak spot for them.'

'I left her,' I said, 'because she was never at a loss. We're alike.'

'Who knows? Yes, perhaps we may be.'

For a whole dance we didn't speak. I couldn't remember ever having desired a woman so much.

'And is one allowed to ask what you do?' I asked.

She thought for a moment.

'I'm looking for someone,' she said. 'I travel.'

'Him?'

'Yes.'

'Don't you do anything else?'

'No. It's a full-time job.'

'And what are you doing here? Looking for him?'

'Now and again I take a holiday too.'

'I see,' I said.

Now I kissed her hair all the time. Candida was watching us. Carla noticed. I didn't care. She didn't seem to either.

'It's funny,' I said. 'You must admit it's funny.'

'Yes,' she said. 'Why don't we go?'

'Very funny,' I repeated. 'The funniest story ever.'

'Not all that funny,' she said.

'Let's go,' I said.

We stopped dancing. She went to get Carla.

Carla looked at us both with surprise and a touch of disapproval. She had seen me kissing her hair. She must have noticed.

'What's the matter?' she asked.

'Nothing,' said Carla.

'Oh, don't be silly,' she said. 'Don't be like that.'

'I'm tired,' said Carla, embarrassed.

'Whatever you do you mustn't be like that,' she said.

I hired a boat and we took Carla home. While we were crossing the river she lay in the front of the boat, away from me, a little upset by Carla's attitude. Carla noticed.

'I'm sorry – forgive me,' she said.

She kissed her without answering.

Eolo was waiting for us in front of the hotel.

'We're a bit late,' I said. 'I'm sorry.'

He said it didn't matter, and thanked us. I told him I was seeing her back to the launch. Perhaps he believed me.

We set out for the beach.

The music grew fainter in the distance. Soon we couldn't

hear it any more. The yacht came in sight. Its decks were lit up and empty. I knew what she expected of me. But I suddenly decided to leave things to her and just follow. Suddenly I wasn't angry about anything any more. When we got on to the beach I turned her round to face me and kissed her joyfully.

'You love him,' I said.

'I haven't seen him for three years.'

'So?'

'I think I'll always feel the same about him, and that when I find him . . .'

'You want to find him very much?'

'It depends,' she said slowly. 'But I can forget him for a while too.'

She hesitated, then said:

'But even when I forget him I don't forget that I'm looking for him.'

Her eyes wandered a little, as if she was inviting me to consider this mystery, and expected me to explain it.

'So your life is just a grand passion, all alone on the sea?'

I swore to myself that I'd never explain it to her, even if – one never knew – even if one day I understood her strange story better than she did.

'Possibly,' she said.

She came close to me and hid her face to say it. I raised her head and looked at her.

'This is the first time I've ever met a woman belonging to a sailor from Gibraltar,' I said.

'Well?'

'I think that's the sort of woman I needed.'

Every time my lips touched hers I nearly fainted with joy.

'I'm glad you came,' she said.

I started to laugh.

'Are there many who don't? Any?'

She laughed too, heartily, but without answering. We went on walking towards the little landing-stage where the launch was waiting. We could see its light already. I had my arm round her waist – I was carrying her, almost, so as to be able to follow her better.

'You get bored sometimes looking for him,' I said. 'Is that it?'

'Yes,' she said. She hesitated. 'Sometimes I feel a bit lonely.'

She added timidly:

'The time seems so long.'

I stopped.

'I understand,' I said.

She laughed. We both did. Then we walked on.

There was a sailor in the launch, asleep. She woke him up.

'I've kept you waiting,' she said, gently.

He said it didn't matter and asked if she'd enjoyed herself.

'Must have done,' I said, indicating myself. 'She stayed two hours instead of one.'

I was drunk. They both laughed. In fact, during that day I was never sober.

I lay down in the bottom of the launch without the slightest embarrassment. I'd finally decided to leave the comforting simplicity of moral systems to other people.

On the way to the yacht I heard her talking to the sailor about some delay in their departure, which I still thought had nothing to do with me.

I had never possessed a woman before her. That night, Jacqueline became a distant memory which never again caused me pain.

We came out of the cabin at about midday. We hadn't slept very much and we had tired one another out. But it was such a lovely day she wanted to go for a swim. We went to the beach in the little launch. It wasn't far, hardly a couple of hundred yards. Before we got there she jumped into the water.

We stayed in for a long time, but didn't swim much. We dived and floated and lay on the beach to get warm again in the sun. Then, when it got too hot, went back in the sea again. It was lunch-time and we were the only two on the beach.

At one point, when we'd just come out of the sea and I was just going to lie down beside her, I saw a man come on to the beach – not from Rocca, but from the other direction, from Marina di Carrare. I didn't recognize him until he was quite close, only about fifty yards away. I'd completely forgotten about him. He recognized me, then her – the woman he had told me about, beautiful and alone. He stopped, astounded. He looked at us for a while, then changed direction so as to go by without coming near us. I sat up.

'Hallo!' I called.

He didn't answer. She opened her eyes and saw him. I got up and went towards him. I didn't know what to say.

'Hallo,' I said again.

'What about the girl that was with you?' he asked. He didn't return my greeting.

'She's gone,' I said. 'It's all over . . .'

He looked at her again. She was lying a few yards away from us in the sun. She could hear what we said. She didn't appear to be interested.

'I don't quite understand,' he said.

I must have looked happy. I couldn't prevent myself from laughing as I spoke to him.

'There's nothing to understand,' I told him.

'What about your job?'

'That's all over too,' I said.

'And you made up your mind like that, in just a few days?'

'I had to. You said yourself that it was possible and I didn't believe you. Now that it's done I see that it was possible.'

He shook his head. He didn't understand. He looked at her again, but without saying anything. He just looked at me questioningly.

'She's leaving this evening, 'I said. 'I just met her by chance.'

We stood looking at each other for some time. Then he shook his head again, in a way that seemed curiously hostile.

'Believe me,' I said.

I couldn't have told him what it was I wanted him to believe.

'Just like that,' he said, 'in a few days?'

'It happens,' I said. 'I didn't believe it, but it happens.'

'Good,' he said at last.

'It was you who told me,' I said.

He looked ill at ease. We didn't know what to say to each other.

'Goodbye.'

'I'm staying at Rocca,' I said. 'I'll be seeing you.'

He went. But instead of continuing, he turned back the way he had come. I stood and watched him go. Then I realized that he must have been to look for me at the trattoria and come straight from old Eolo's; that he must have been here since yesterday, and must already have been to borrow the goggles from his cousin, and must have thought about and chosen the best place for us to go fishing. Another thing he had to reproach me with was forgetting that we were to have spent the day together. For a moment I felt like calling him back. But I didn't. I went and lay down beside her.

'Do you know some of the people around here?' she said. We used the familiar 'tu' to each other now.

'That was the driver of the van that brought us from Pisa to Florence,' I said. 'We were supposed to go underwater fishing together today. He didn't like to remind me, and I'd forgotten.'

She sat up and watched him as he disappeared in the distance.

'But you ought to call him back.'

'No,' I said, 'it's not worth it.'

She hesitated.

'It's not worth it,' I repeated. 'I'll see him again. I was thinking about it all day and every day for a week, and now, today, I'd forgotten all about it.'

We started to laugh.

'You told him I was leaving tonight,' she said. 'I'm not leaving till tomorrow.'

'It's going to seem a long time,' I said, still laughing.

We went back on board for lunch. Then we went to her cabin again. We stayed there a long time. She fell asleep, and I was able to look at her as she slept, in the already waning light from the sea. Then I went to sleep too. The sun was setting when we woke. We went up on deck. The sky was ablaze and the quarries of Carrara sparkled white. All the chimneys of Monte Marcello were already smoking. The beach was a long, gentle curve in front of us. There were people bathing, Eolo's guests and sailors from Gibraltar. We were alone on board.

'You're sad,' she said.

'When you go to sleep in the afternoon,' I said, and smiled at her, 'you always feel sad when you wake up.' Then I added: 'Things look very different when you see them from a ship.'

'Very different. But finally one wants to look at them from the other point of view too.'

'I expect so.'

The bathers were playing ball. We could hear their cries and laughter.

'It's late,' I said.

'What does that matter?'

The blazing sky suddenly grew a shade darker.

'It's late,' I said again. 'In twenty minutes it will be dark. I don't like this time of the day.'

'If you like,' she said very softly, 'we could go and have a drink in the bar.'

I didn't answer. I had watched her sleep for a long time. I was a little bit afraid.

'I'm going back,' I said.

'I'll have dinner with you,' she said calmly.

I didn't answer.

'Perhaps Eolo will be shocked. Are you sure you still want to?'

'I don't know.'

'Do you often have changes of mood like this?'

'Yes, often,' I said. 'But today it isn't that I've had a change of mood.'

'What then?'

'I don't know exactly. Perhaps too many things have happened to me in two days. Shall we have a drink then?'

'Nothing easier. There's everything we want in the bar.'

We went and had two whiskies. I wasn't used to drinking whisky. I didn't care for the first much, but I liked the second. In fact, it seemed necessary. She was used to it, and drank hers with great enjoyment, without speaking.

'Whisky's very dear,' I said. 'Can't afford to have it very often.'

'Very dear.'

'Do you drink a lot of it?'

'Quite a lot. I don't drink anything else – any other spirits, that is.'

'Aren't you ashamed, at three thousand francs a bottle?'

'No.'

We were forcing ourselves to talk. We were very aware again of being alone on the ship.

'But it's very good, whisky,' I said.

'You see . . .'

'Yes, it's very good. Why be ashamed about it? Did he like it?'

'I think so. We didn't drink it very much.'

She looked out through the door of the bar at the darkening beach.

'We're the only two on board,' she said.

'You're taking advantage of me,' I said, laughing. 'Some people make one want to drink and others don't. You make me want another whisky.'

'Why's that?'

'Who knows? Perhaps it depends on how seriously they take life.'

'Aren't I serious?'

'Oh yes. But there's seriousness and seriousness.'

'I don't understand.'

'Me neither,' I said, 'it must be the whisky. It doesn't matter.'

She smiled and got up, poured me a drink and came over to me. 'It's very difficult to do without it,' she said, 'once you've got into the habit.'

'Very difficult.'

She went and sat down again. We were trying hard to forget that we were so alone on board.

'How do you know?' she asked.

'I guess,' I said. She lowered her eyes.

'When I'm rich,' I said, 'I'll drink it all the time.'

She looked at me. I looked at the beach.

'It's strange,' she said, 'how glad I am to have met you.'

'Yes,' I said, 'very strange.'

'Yes.'

'It's the grand passion,' I said.

We laughed. Then we stopped and I got up and went back on deck.

'I'm hungry,' I said. 'Shall we go to Eolo's?'

'We'll have to wait for the crew,' she said. 'They've got the launch. Unless of course we swim . . .'

We leaned against the rails. She made signs to the crew and one of them came to fetch us in the launch. Before going to Eolo's we went for a short walk along the beach, away from the bathers.

'If you have time,' I said, 'you must tell me the whole story.'

'It's a long one – it would take ages.'

'I'd like to hear it just the same, even if you had to compress it a bit.'

'We'll see,' she said. 'If there's time.'

Eolo watched us coming, surprised – though really, funda-
mentally, not all that astonished – to see us together. I
hadn't been back since the dance and he knew very well that
I was with her. Carla blushed crimson when she saw us. I
didn't see any need to give them an explanation. She spoke to
Carla as she had the day before, though perhaps with a touch
of constraint. I felt no inclination to talk to anyone but her,
so I said nothing. There were the usual hotel guests, and two
visitors just passing through. She was tired, but to me she
looked even more beautiful than the day before, probably
because it was I who had made her tired. She talked indiffer-
ently to Eolo and Carla in turn; she could feel me looking at
her. We ate a good deal and drank a fair amount of wine. As
soon as we'd finished she asked me in a low voice to go back
with her to the yacht. The dance had already begun. We
could hear the same sambas as yesterday floating across the
river. As soon as we were alone on the way to the beach I
kissed her; I couldn't wait. It was she who, just before we got
to the landing-stage, spoke again for the first time about what
I intended to do in the immediate future. She laughed as she
asked the question, as if it were only a joke, but there was a
shade of insistence there.

'Do you still think you'd like to clean the brass?'

'I don't know.'

'You don't like women who belong to sailors from Gibraltar
any more,' she said, smiling.

'I must have spoken hastily, before I really knew them.'

'They're like all the others.'

'Not quite. In the first place, they're beautiful. And then,
they're never satisfied.'

'And then?'

'And then, as very likely they belong to everyone and to
no one at all, it must be very difficult to get used to them.'

'It seems to me you could say the same thing about a lot of
women.'

'Probably,' I said. 'But with them you're not deceived for a second.'

'I'd gathered you didn't set much store by . . . what shall I say? . . . by that sort of security.'

'I don't. But isn't it the same as with everything else? When you're sure there's no chance of having that sort of security, don't you begin to want it?'

She smiled, but to herself.

'Perhaps,' she said. 'But one shouldn't let that kind of fear stop one from doing what one wants to do.'

I didn't answer. Then, still with perhaps a shade too much insistence in her voice:

'If you're as free as you say,' she said, 'why don't you come?'

'I don't know,' I said. 'But, indeed, why not?'

She turned her head away and said with a trace of confusion:

'You mustn't think that you're the first.'

'I've never thought any such thing.'

She was silent, then resumed.

'I say that so you shouldn't think what you're going to do is so very extraordinary. So that you should come.'

'Have there been many?'

'Some,' she said. '. . . I've been looking for him for three years.'

'What do you do with them when you've had enough of them?'

'Throw them in the sea.'

We laughed, but not very gaily.

'If you don't mind,' I said, 'let's wait until tomorrow to decide.'

We went to her cabin again.

Again we woke late. The sun was high when we came out on deck. Everything was at once the same as before and quite different, partly because of the impending departure. We had lunch in the bar on what we could find – cheese, anchovies. We drank coffee and wine. Again we were alone on board, and again, as we ate, we couldn't forget it. She looked at her watch several times during the meal, and seemed rather anxious because clearly I didn't know what I wanted myself. It looked as if she was going to have to make my mind up for me about whether I went or not. She spoke about it again.

'If you don't come, what will you do?'

'One can always find something to do. I've decided too many things'– I laughed –'I can't decide any more.'

'What difference does one more make?'

'Who was the sailor from Gibraltar?' I asked.

'I've told you,' she said. 'A murderer. Twenty years old.'

'What else?'

'Nothing else. When you're a murderer, you're nothing else, especially if you're only twenty.'

'I'd like you to tell me about him,' I said.

'There's nothing to tell,' she said. 'When you become a murderer at twenty there isn't any more to tell. You can't go forward, you can't go back. You can't succeed, you can't fail at anything in life any more.'

'I'd still like you to tell me about him. Even briefly.'

'I'm tired,' she said, 'and there isn't anything to tell.'

She leaned her head back in her chair. She was tired. I went and got her a glass of wine.

'You won't find anything to do in Italy,' she said. 'You'll go back to France and start copying out births, marriages and deaths again at the Ministry.'

'Never.'

I didn't ask her any more. The sun was already shining on the floor of the bar. It was she who spoke first.

'You see,' she said, 'he was someone doubly threatened by death. And for men like that one always has, in addition to love, a . . . a special fidelity.'

'I understand,' I said.

'You'll go back to Paris,' she said, 'and you'll see her, and you'll go back to the Ministry, and it will all start all over again.'

'Even briefly,' I said. 'About yourself.'

'I haven't much time left,' she said. And added: 'I still think the best thing you can do is come away on the yacht. I mean, in your situation.'

'We'll see,' I said. 'Talk to me.'

'There isn't anything to tell about me, apart from him.'

'Please.'

'I've told you,' she said. 'My childhood was spent in a village on the Spanish frontier. My father ran a café. I was the eldest of five children. The people that came to the café were always the same – customs officers, smugglers, in the summer a few tourists. One night when I was nineteen I went to Paris with one of the customers in his car. I stayed there a year. I learned the sort of thing one usually learns there, how to be an assistant at the Samaritaine, hunger, dry bread for dinner one day, a blow-out the next, the price of blow-outs, the price of bread, liberty, equality, fraternity. You think you're learning a lot, but it's nothing beside what you can learn from one single other person. After a year I'd had enough of Paris and went to Marseilles. I was twenty – people are always crazy at that age – and I wanted to work on a yacht. I had an idea of the sea and travel that I associated with the whiteness of yachts. At the Yacht Club there was only one job going – as barmaid. I took it. The yacht which had taken me on was going round the world and would be away a year. It left Marseilles three days after I took the job. It was a morning in September. We headed for the Atlantic. A few hours after we'd set sail, the next day at about ten, one of the crew sighted something on the sea. The owner looked through his glasses and saw a man ahead of us in a rowing-boat. He was coming towards us. They stopped the engines and let down the gangway. One of the crew hauled him on board. He said he was thirsty and tired. I can still hear him saying it.

When I try to remember his voice it's always those words I hear. The sort of thing people say all the time, but that's more or less important according to the circumstances. He said that, then fainted. They brought him round with vinegar and by slapping his cheeks, and gave him some brandy. When he'd drunk it he went to sleep there on the deck. He slept for eight hours. I went past him often – he was just near the bar. I looked at him a lot. His face was burned and stripped by the sun and the sea; his hands were raw from rowing. He must have spent several days looking out for a boat to steal first of all, and then several more at sea waiting for someone to pick him up. He was wearing a pair of khaki trousers – the colour of crime, the colour of war. He was young, twenty. But he'd already had time to become a criminal. I'd only had time to go to the cinema. One does what one can. And I think that even before he woke up I loved him. That evening, after they'd given him something to eat, I went to see him in his cabin. I switched the light on. He was asleep. He was gone so far in terror that not only could he not imagine that a woman could want to be with him that evening, but he couldn't even wish it. But I think – yes, I'm sure – that that too was how I wanted it to be. He recognized me and sat up, and asked if they wanted him to leave the cabin. I said no. That was how it started. It lasted six months. The owner took him on. Weeks went by. He never told anyone about himself, not even me. I still don't know his name. One evening, six months later, at Shanghai, he went ashore for a game of poker and didn't come back.'

'And you still don't know who he killed?'

'One evening in Montmartre he strangled an American. I didn't know who until much later. He took his money, gambled with it at poker, and lost it. He didn't kill him for his money though, it wasn't poverty that made him do it. No, at twenty people do it for no precise reason – he'd done it almost involuntarily. The American was the ball-bearings king, Nelson Nelson.'

I started to laugh, and she laughed too.

'But even if it's only the ball-bearings king, if you kill him that makes you a murderer,' she said. 'And when you're a murderer, that's all you are, nothing else.'

'I've always thought,' I said, 'that that was a situation that must have its good side, its convenient side.'

'It relieves you of a lot of duties,' she said, 'almost all. Except the duty of not dying of hunger.'

'But what about love?' I said.

'No,' she answered, 'he didn't love me. He could have done without me, without anybody. They say one person's absence can make the world a desert, but it's not so. But if the world is absent for you, no one can people it. I never peopled the world for him, never. He was like all the others, like you – he had to have Yokohama, the boulevards, the cinema, the elections, work, everything. What was I, a woman, beside all that?'

'In short,' I said, 'he was someone who had nothing to say to anyone.'

'That's right. Someone one talks about as best one can, but who has nothing to say to anyone. There are some days when I wonder if I didn't entirely invent him – if I didn't just invent someone based on him. His silence was something quite extraordinary – I could never describe it. And his gentleness was just the same. What had happened to him didn't strike him as awful. He hadn't any opinion about it. Everything amused him. He slept like an infant. Nobody on the ship ever thought of judging him.'

She hesitated a little and then said:

'You know, when you have met innocence, when you've seen it sleep beside you, you can never quite forget it.'

'It must change one a lot,' I said.

'A great deal,' she said, smiling, 'and for ever, I think.'

'I've always thought,' I said, 'that anyone who makes someone else doubt the foundations of his morals hasn't lived in vain.'

'Yes,' she said. 'Even though he never said anything. It's because people like him don't think twice about doing themselves great harm that others are brought to question lots of their own prejudices.'

'And what about the poker?' I asked.

'You have to hazard something,' she said, 'whatever you can. One Sunday evening, all of a sudden, he felt like a game of poker. He played with some friends of his among the crew. Probably he'd been a very keen player since he was quite young. Since the murder he hadn't played any more. That evening he started again. At first he was winning. Then, in the middle of the night, he started to lose. I watched all the time the game lasted. He was transfigured, he set very high stakes, it was as if he couldn't get rid of the money fast enough. When he began to lose it didn't seem to affect him at all. He lost much more than he won, nearly a month's pay. He threw the money on the table with a sort of joy, as if after all he could still do that, people could still get that out of him. Wasn't money the one thing he still had in common with other men? That and the love of women – not of one woman, but of women, for all this time, to him, I'd been just anybody, more or less. That's how it began, that Sunday night on board the yacht – I mean, I realized that I was soon going to lose him. We'd already crossed the Atlantic and passed the West Indies, Santo Domingo. We'd been through the Panama Canal, and now we were in the Pacific. We'd passed Hawaii, New Caledonia, the Sunda Isles, Borneo, the Straits of Malacca. Then, instead of going on as we were supposed to do, we turned back towards the Pacific. Up till then we'd hardly been ashore at all. Once at Tahiti, once at Nouméa. Apart from little excursions ashore to buy shaving soap, things like that, that was all. That was all until Manila, two days after the game of poker. At Manila he wanted to see the town. He had some money, that was what it was, it was weighing him down. He'd lost one month's pay, but he still had plenty more, all those months he'd accumulated. We'd

123

gone ashore so little, there was so little to spend money on, that when we got to Shanghai he had quite a lot in his wallet.

'It was there that he told me he was going to have a game of poker and would soon be back. I waited for him all night. Then all day. Then the next day I looked for him all over the town. I know Shanghai inside out now. I didn't find him. So I went back on board, thinking perhaps he'd got there first. But he wasn't on the yacht either. I'd got so tired searching that I hadn't the strength to go ashore again: it was all I could do to wait for him on board. I went and lay down in my cabin. I could see the gangway through the porthole. I watched it, and fell asleep watching. I was only twenty, too, and I slept easily. When I woke, it was dawn and the ship was out at sea off Shanghai. He hadn't come back on board.

'I've often wondered since whether it wasn't the owner of the yacht who gave the order to sail while I was asleep. I asked him, later. He said no. I still don't really believe him. But what does it matter? If he hadn't gone ashore at Shanghai he would have gone ashore farther on.'

'You wanted to die. You thought it would be easy to open the door of the cabin and throw yourself in the sea.'

'I didn't do it. I married the owner of the yacht.'

She was silent.

'I'd like a glass of wine.'

I went and got her one. She went on:

'You see, we'd never said we loved each other. Except him, the first evening, when I went to see him in his cabin. But of course that evening he said it out of surprise, out of pleasure, just as he might have done to a whore. You might almost say it was to life that he said it. After that he had no reason to. I had every reason in the world to say it: but I didn't. The silence lasted as long as we did – six months. It made the silence that came after Shanghai all the greater. I was full of all the words of love there have ever been, and I couldn't deliver myself of one.'

She didn't say any more for a moment. I got up and went

over to the rail. She called me.

'It's very difficult,' she said, 'to do what you want to do – to start a new life, as they say. You must be very careful.'

'And afterwards?' I asked.

'What?'

'After Shanghai?'

'I told you. The owner of the yacht got a divorce in the United States. His wife agreed, on condition that he paid her a lot of alimony. Immediately after the divorce we were married. He changed the name of the yacht to mine. I became a rich woman. I went into society. I even took lessons in grammar.'

'You weren't thinking of looking for him then?'

'The idea only came to me quite a long time afterwards. I don't remember having got married for that reason – no, I didn't. But when I got the idea it did seem to me it was a good thing I had got married like that. Looking for someone as I do is a very expensive luxury.'

'Was it while you were married that you got into the habit of sleeping with . . . just anybody?'

She was silent, taken aback, then said apologetically:

'I did try sometimes to be faithful to him, but I could never succeed.'

'You shouldn't even have tried,' I said, laughing.

'I was young,' she said. 'Life on the yacht was gay. He gave dances every night to make me forget . . .'

'The sea,' I said, 'the seamen . . .'

'Yes.' She smiled. 'But dances aren't enough to make anyone forget them.'

'I believe you.'

'The more guests I saw the more I thought about the men below who could hear the celebrations that were supposed to make me forget one of them. I used to run away, into the crew's quarters, and sometimes I used to be unfaithful to him. One day . . .'

She stopped and looked at her watch.

'I haven't got time,' she said.
'You have if you want to. There's no real hurry.'
She smiled again.
'One day he did something that was really insulting. He had a wire partition put up between the upper deck and the rest of the ship. The guests had been put ashore because they'd been talking about me.'
'What did they say?'
'I think they said what's bred in the bone will come out in the flesh.'
She stopped while we laughed, then went on:
'So we were left face to face with each other on the upper deck. I promised him I wouldn't go beyond the partition. I meant to keep my promise – seeing him go to those lengths made me fear for his reason. It wouldn't have helped to have him go out of his mind. Weeks went by. Months. I spent my time reading, lying in a deck chair in the sun. When I look back on it it seems as if that time were a sort of long sleep. But it was during that sleep that I gathered strength for the rest of my life. Now and then, to please him, I'd bestir myself about the ports we were coming to, or the latitudes, or the submarine depths. Then I'd go back to my book. It was all in good faith. I believed that this really was an existence, in its own way. My husband seemed to think so too, and his suspicions were lulled.
'Then one day we had to put in to Shanghai. We had to take on more oil; as you can imagine, we wouldn't have stopped there unless we'd had to. And it was there, you might say, that I woke up for ever.
'We arrived quite early in the morning. We were already up, reading, behind our partition. I stopped reading and looked at the town where I had searched for him so desperately. I looked at it from eight o'clock till midday. He sat beside me and watched me look at it. He'd stopped reading too. At noon I asked him if he'd let me go ashore for a little while. He said: "No, you wouldn't come back." I told him he

wasn't in Shanghai any more, that there was nothing to be afraid of, and that I would have liked to walk through the town for an hour, no more than an hour. He said: "No, even if he's not there any more you wouldn't come back." I told him he could send one of the crew with me to make sure. He said: "No, I don't trust anyone." I asked him if he thought he had the right to prevent me from going ashore, if any man had the right to exercise force over any woman like that. He said yes, he was only acting "for my own good," to prevent me from doing something crazy. I didn't ask any more. He seemed to be suffering, but I could see that he would never give way. We didn't have any lunch. We just sat there in our deck chairs waiting for the ship to leave. He saw I'd have liked to kill him – it was quite natural, and all one to him. The afternoon passed, and evening came down over the city. We still sat waiting for the ship to leave, he watching me, I wanting to kill him. The lights went on in the town, and the red glow shone on the deck, where we sat looking at each other behind the partition. I can still remember my husband's face in that light. I asked him once more to let me go ashore, even with him, if he liked. He said: "No. Kill me if you like, but I can't." The ship sailed at about eleven. The town took a long time to disappear in the darkness. I don't know why I'm telling you all this. Probably because it was then that I started to have a certain amount of hope again – I mean it began to seem possible that I might leave my husband, might one day lead a different life from the one I was leading then. What sort of a life? You don't think about that kind of thing very clearly. A life that would be – what shall I say – more amusing, perhaps. So, after that awful day and the foul dusk I saw coming down over Shanghai, life with my husband gradually became bearable. It seemed so easy to leave him that the time seemed short. And yet it took me three years to do it. Cowardice, as you said. But even if one waits a long time to do what one's decided to do, that doesn't mean one's not capable of doing it. I did it, but three years later.

'One year went by, in Paris. When he talked to me about the future I smiled, in a way I probably shouldn't have been able to if I'd believed in it. I was nice to him. Did he sometimes think that I'd forgotten the sailor from Gibraltar? He may have done. But not for long – hardly a year.'

'What happened then?'

'I saw him again. Twice. Once, and then again after another four years. The second time I even lived with him.'

'And you really haven't got time to . . .'

'No,' she said, 'I haven't got time now.'

She was silent. Time seemed slow, as it always does when you come back to it after having forgotten it. The sun was going down. I smoked a cigarette. She suddenly looked at her watch, then went to the bar to fetch a drink. She handed me a glass of wine.

'Time for a drink,' she said.

'It's a strange story,' I said.

'Oh no, it's just like any other story.'

'I wasn't just talking about yours,' I said.

She was alarmed for a moment, but became reassured again almost at once.

'If you say that,' she said, 'it's because you've just . . .'

'It frightens me, I can tell you,' I said.

'It shouldn't,' she said.

'One's always more or less looking for something,' I said. 'For something to arise in the world and come towards you.'

'And then,' she said, 'when it holds out its hand to you, whether it's him or something else . . .'

'That's right,' I said. 'Him or something else. And yet if it was him, it would be all up really, and it isn't every day that . . .'

She interrupted me.

'You never can tell . . .' she began.

'Don't worry,' I said. 'Don't you worry at all.'

'What I wanted to say too,' she said slowly, 'is that you never can tell all that's going to happen.'

'No,' I said. 'But in any case don't worry.'

She looked at me doubtfully, hesitantly.

'What does it depend on?' she asked.

'The rest?'

'Yes,' she said, 'the rest, as you call it.'

'On whether one's really serious. No?'

She relaxed completely and got up, smiling.

'That's right,' she said. 'On whether one's really serious. If you want to be you are, aren't you?'

'All you have to do is want to be,' I said.

'So are you coming?'

The sound of the engines could be heard already. The sailors were unfurling the sails.

'I'm coming,' I said.

She suddenly became very different from the day before. Rather as if we were going to share a great deal of pleasure on the yacht, but nothing else. She left the bar and went to speak to the crew. I heard her gently hurrying them. Then she came back.

'We must send someone to pay Eolo,' she said, 'and collect your things.'

'I'd like to just leave them for once,' I said, laughing.

'It's a bit silly.'

'I know. If you like they could tell Eolo to keep my case for me.'

She went out again.

It was seven o'clock. I stayed alone in the bar until we sailed. Half an hour. We weighed anchor as night fell. I went out of the bar and stood for a long time by the rail. Just after we'd begun to move, Carla came running on to the beach. Her tiny dark form could be seen waving a handkerchief. Then, as we swiftly slid away, she grew dim and finally disappeared. The mouth of the Magra cut the beach in two. The marble mountains hung dazzling over all the shore for quite a long while still.

She often went by behind where I stood, but not once did

she join me at the rail. Each time she passed I thought perhaps I ought to turn round and say something, but I couldn't make up my mind to do it. Once she stood quite close and talked with a couple of the crew about times and tides.

The sea was smooth and warm. The ship cut through it like a blade through ripe fruit. It was darker than the sky.

Yes, perhaps she would have liked me to ask her where we were heading for, or to say something about my going, or the dusk, or the sea, or the motion of the ship, or perhaps about the feelings you experienced at suddenly finding yourself on that ship after eight years in the Ministry ignorant of its existence, of her existence, eight years copying birth certificates not knowing that there were women like her who spent their whole lives looking for sailors from Gibraltar. Hearing her go to and fro behind me, I might have thought she expected me to express some opinion about all these things that were so new to me. But I didn't really think so. I thought rather the opposite, that she did go to and fro behind me to find out whether I had an opinion about all these things that were so new to me, that she was watching me, so to speak, but without realizing it. But how could I have any opinion, even about the dusk, even about what sort of a sea it was? Once one had embarked on this ship, and without actually having decided to do so, one could have no opinion about anything, even about the setting sun.

Some sailors leaned against the rail and, like me, watched the Italian coast get farther and farther away. From time to time they stole a look at me too. They seemed curious, but not unduly so, and not at all maliciously, to see what sort of a person it was she'd taken on this time. One of them, a small dark man, smiled at me. Finally, as he was standing no more than a couple of yards away from me, he spoke.

'It does you good to see a sea like that,' he said with an Italian accent.

I agreed. The ship was increasing speed. The mouth of the

river was no longer visible; you could only see the indistinct shapes of the hills. Lights were going on all along the coast. Mechanically, I counted the men. There were four of them on deck. Counting those in the engine-room, the helmsman and the quartermaster, that must make seven, plus one or two for the kitchens. The normal complement must be nine. I was extra. Midway between her and them. I'd gathered there had never been more than one man between her and them.

The ship got farther away from the shore still, and night suddenly came down. You could no longer see even the vague outlines of the mountains; they were swallowed up in the mist. The coast became a continuous line of lights, a line of fire on the level of the horizon dividing the sky from the sea. It was only when this line of fire itself grew dim that she came and stood beside me. She looked at me too, but her curiosity was different from the men's. We smiled at each other at first, without saying anything. She was wearing the same black trousers and black cotton jumper as at Rocca, but now she had a beret on too. It was two days since I had first met her. I already knew the body hidden under her clothes, and I'd already had time to watch her as she slept. But the situation was different now. When she came near me I started to tremble, like the first time, at the dance. Perhaps it was going to begin all over again and I would never get used to seeing her come near me, never get used to looking at her.

She was still looking at me. She wasn't a woman who ever looked you straight in the eye, and that evening even less than usual. Probably she was wondering what I was still doing leaning there against the rail when there was nothing more to see and I'd already been standing there for an hour. She didn't ask me, however. It was I who spoke.

'You've put a beret on,' I said.

'Yes,' she said. 'The wind.'

'There isn't any wind.'

She smiled.

'What does that matter? It's a habit,' she added, her head

131

turned towards the sea. 'Sometimes I forget to take it off when I go to bed, and go to sleep with it on.'

'It suits you,' I said. 'So what does it matter?'

'Sometimes,' she said, still in the same tone, 'I sleep with all my clothes on. Sometimes I don't even do my hair, or wash.'

'It's all a matter of habit,' I said. 'One's as good as another.'

The reflection of the lights between-decks danced on the smooth dark surface of the sea. Her arm was touching mine, but her head was still turned towards the water.

'Do you eat?' I asked.

'Yes, I eat.' She laughed. 'I've got a huge appetite.'

'Always?'

'It takes a lot to stop me eating. But not to make me forget to wash.'

We looked at each other at last. We both felt the same rather nervous desire to laugh. I could see it in her eyes. But we didn't. I mustered up some remark.

'Well, here I am at sea.'

She smiled freely and sweetly.

'Oh, that's nothing much,' she said.

'No.'

We remained silent a moment. She was still turned towards me.

'Do you still feel strange?' She sounded rather apprehensive.

'It does feel a bit unusual.'

'And have you got a good appetite?' she asked after a moment.

'I have,' I said. 'As a matter of fact I was beginning to wonder...'

'Let's go and have something to eat,' she cried gaily, with the same child-like laugh as when I'd told her I would come on the yacht.

I followed her to the dining-room, the bar. I knew it well already. There didn't seem to be any trace left in the lamps, the carpets, the book-shelves, of what it had been like when the yacht was still called the *Cypris*. It was obvious at once that it was a long time since there had been guests on board. The place was more like a guard-room than a bar. It had been arranged for the general convenience, in no particular style, in fact as if purposely without any style at all. The crew's old mess near the tanks was no longer in use: they ate here with her. People ate when they felt like it, any time between seven and ten in the evening. There were two dishes for every meal, kept warm on electric hot-plates. Everyone helped himself. On a shelf over the bar there was always cheese, fruit, bottles of anchovies and so on, things that could just be eaten as they were. There was also as much wine and beer and spirits as anyone wanted. When we entered, a radio was playing quietly. For the first time I noticed a piano in the corner and a violin on the wall above it.

She sat down at a table, and I sat down facing her. At another table nearby, three of the crew were having their meal. They watched me come in without interrupting their conversation. I recognized the small dark man who had spoken to me on deck. He smiled at me again, discreetly. She got up and went over to the bar with two plates, then came back and sat down again as before. She paid no attention at all to the fact that the men were watching me. As she passed them she said:

'Everything all right?'

'Yes, fine,' said the small dark one.

There were two grilled fish on my plate, with fennel sticking out of their jaws. They too looked at me curiously.

'Is that all right for you?' she asked. 'If not there's something else.'

It was all right for me. I cut off the two heads with my fork and put them at the side of my plate. Then I put my fork down. She watched me. I could feel the men looking at me and was slightly embarrassed by it. Not that they were hostile. On the contrary. But I wasn't used to being an object

133

of curiosity of any sort, and it rather took my appetite away.
I think she pretended not to notice. She let a moment pass
after I'd put down my fork, and then said:

'You don't like it.'

'Where are we going?' I asked.

She smiled sweetly and turned to the three sailors. They
smiled too – without hostility, with friendliness even.

'To Sète,' she said to them. 'I mean, to Sète to start with,
isn't it?'

'That's what we thought,' said one of them.

'You don't like the fish,' she said. 'I'll get you something
else.'

I like fish better than anything, but I let her go. She came
back with something or other steaming on the plate.

'Why Sète?'

She didn't answer, and the sailors didn't answer for her. I
got up and went to the bar for a glass of wine as I'd just seen
one of the sailors do. I drank it, then asked again.

'Why Sète?' I asked everyone in general.

But the men still didn't answer. It was up to her, they felt.

'Why not?' she said, turning towards them.

But obviously they didn't approve of this answer. I waited.
She turned back to me and said in a low voice:

'Yesterday I had a message from Sète.'

As soon as she said it the sailors went out. We were left
alone. But only for a moment. Then another man came in and
cleared the tables and washed the glasses. As he worked he
looked at me curiously. I found it difficult to eat. She watched
me as she had two days before in the trattoria.

'You're not hungry,' she said.

'No,' I said. 'Not very, this evening.'

'Perhaps we're tired. I'm usually hungry all the time, but
not this evening.'

'Yes, we must be tired.'

'If you're not eating because of Sète,' she said, 'you're
wrong.'

'When did you get the message?'

'Just before I went to the dance.'

'After lunch?'

'Yes, an hour after you went upstairs.' She smiled, avoiding my eyes. 'It's two months since I've had a message. It seems rather as if it happened by design.'

'Who is it from?'

'A Greek sailor, Epaminondas. He's got a very lively imagination. This is the third message he's sent me in two years. I can't ignore it without hurting his feelings.'

I didn't feel a bit like eating any more. She said, pretending not to know what was the matter:

'Epaminondas is a character. You'll see.' Then added gently: 'I wish you'd eat something.'

I tried.

'Do you never look anywhere else but in ports?' I managed to ask with some difficulty.

'It's in ports that there's the best chance, not inland,' she said. 'Not in the Sahara. And in big ports, not the little ones – ports at the mouths of rivers.'

'Talk to me,' I said.

'They can take big ships. They're the wealth of the continents they serve, and the refuge of men in hiding.'

Then she added, smiling:

'Eat while I talk.'

'Go on.'

'I've thought a lot about it,' she said, 'naturally. That's all I've thought about for years. It's only in a port that he'd be able to manage, the way one has to manage when one's in hiding, trying to merge with all the others. It's a well-known fact that ports are the places for secrets.'

She spoke at once timidly and boldly – rather as if she were warning me against making some mistake.

'I've seen it in the films,' I said. 'That the best way for a man to hide is to mingle as closely as possible with the people looking for him.'

135

'That's right.' She smiled. 'In the Sahara there may not be any policemen, but there isn't so much as a dandelion to hide behind either. So . . .'

She drained her glass of wine and went on quickly:

'It's not easy being the only one there to see your own footprints on the sands of the Sahara. That's not the sort of trace people generally want to leave behind them. They're rotten hiding-places, the desert, the forest, Calabria.'

'There are lots of different kinds of Sahara in the world,' I said.

'Indeed. But the sort I'm talking about is not the sort one chooses.'

'I see.' Then I added, without thinking: 'Perhaps you are a bit mad after all.'

'No,' she said reassuringly. 'Less mad than most people.' Then she went on: 'Towns, on the other hand, are safe places. It's only on asphalt that sailors from Gibraltar can rest their weary feet at last.'

She stopped.

'I'll fetch you another glass of wine,' she said.

Every time she moved – ate, or raised her glass, or stood up – I noticed it, and with more and more intensity.

'To be hidden by the ten thousand people going to and fro along the Canebière,' she said, 'that's the only respite for sailors from Gibraltar.' She added softly: 'It's Italian wine.'

I drank it. It was excellent. She seemed pleased to see me drinking it so readily.

'What an adventure,' I said, laughing.

'Do I have to go on talking long?'

'As long as you can,' I said.

'It's only there,' she said, 'that a man in hiding feels himself come alive again to a hundred of life's possibilities. He can go on the metro, or to the cinema, sleep in a brothel or on a bench in a square, relieve himself, or go for a walk, all in a comparative peace that he can't find anywhere else.'

'Have you never done anything all your life but look for a sailor from Gibraltar?'

136

She got up without answering and went and got me another glass of wine.

Some other sailors had just come in, and they too began to look the new man over. I drank my wine. I was hot. The wine was cool and pleasant. I didn't care if they looked at me. She was still gazing at me, her eyes mocking and gentle.

'I think I've been looking for him long enough,' she said at last. Then, in an aside that must have been obvious to everyone:

'Are you often going to make me talk to you like this?'

'I find it hard to tell you to stop,' I said.

She got up again, went to the bar, and came back with a third glass of wine.

'You'd do better to take a whole bottle and have done with it,' I said.

'I never thought of it,' she said, laughing, 'but you're right.'

The beret made her look rather like a sailor. A very handsome sailor. Her hair was down on her shoulders, but she didn't notice. When I'd finished my last glass, she said in a low voice:

'You like wine, don't you?'

I didn't answer.

'I mean,' she said, 'you're always happy when you drink it?'

She leaned towards me as if it were a question of the utmost importance.

'Always,' I said. 'Go on talking.'

That may have vexed her, but she hardly showed it.

'It's only in ports like that,' she said, 'that footsteps and other actions leave none of those traces the police are so fond of. There are so many traces of all kinds in a big town, of law-abiding citizens as well as the others, that the police spend all their time running to make sure they aren't missing anything . . .'

I hardly heard what she was saying. I watched her speak,

but that's a different matter. And she saw quite clearly what was in my eyes.

'In ports, you see,' she went on, 'the police are more over-worked than anywhere else, even though there are more of them and they're tougher. All they bother about is watching the exits. They just keep an eye on the rest as best they can – they don't over-exert themselves.'

The crew were listening in some astonishment, but on the whole they agreed with what she said.

'It's true,' one of them said. 'They leave you in peace more in Toulon than in Paris.'

'And then,' she said, 'you feel better, don't you, when the sea's not far away? In certain cases, I mean?'

She was trying to get me to say something.

'When you haven't got any family,' she said, ' – no clothes, no papers, no home, because you wouldn't know what to do with all that security respectable people are so keen on, and you've got enough to do just getting yourself from place to place – then don't you feel more at ease when you're by the sea? Or on it?'

'Not only in certain cases,' I said.

I laughed, and so did she. Then the sailors joined in.

'Even,' I said in a low voice, 'when you've got so much money you don't know what to do with it.'

She laughed again.

'Even then,' she said.

'And then,' said one of the men, 'when you're in Marseilles it's rather as if you were in Diego at the same time.'

'All you have to do,' said another, 'is sign on as a bunker-hand on the first cargo-boat to leave.'

'Don't people say that these sudden departures are part of the charm of sea-ports?' she said. 'All the tourists go to see them in the summer. But what do they know about it? Only the harbour, if that.'

'And you,' I said, laughing, 'you who have such experience of crime?'

'I see what people don't usually notice, the side-streets, the alleys, the places where you can hide. But . . .' She hesitated. 'But too often I've seen shadows that have disappointed me . . .'

'So?'

'So I don't go ashore any more. The yacht's the same, only the name is different. What's the point in going ashore? You can see a yacht more easily than you can see me, can't you?'

'You couldn't miss seeing a yacht,' I said.

A sailor switched on the radio. It was jazz, badly played.

'Don't you want any cheese?'

I got up to get some. She stood up too.

'I don't want to talk any more,' she said.

'You must show me my cabin,' I said.

She stopped eating and looked at me. I went on with my cheese.

'Of course,' she said softly. 'Of course I'll show it to you.'

'I'm still hungry,' I said. 'I'll have some fruit.'

She didn't want any, but she went and fetched two glasses of wine.

'Tell me . . .'

She bent towards me again. Her beret fell off. It was late. Almost time to go to bed. Her hair was coming undone.

'What?'

'You like the sea, don't you? I mean . . . you're just as comfortable here as anywhere else?'

'I don't know much about it yet,' I said, laughing in spite of myself. 'But I think I'm going to like it.'

She laughed.

'Come on,' she said, 'I'll show you your cabin.'

We went down. The six cabins opened on to the quarter-deck. Four were occupied by members of the crew. She went into the second on the port side. It was empty, and obviously had been for a long time. It had one bunk, and was adjacent to her own cabin. The mirror needed cleaning, the wash-basin was covered with fine soot. The bed was unmade.

'It's fairly often unoccupied then,' I said.

She leaned against the door.

'Almost always,' she said.

I went over to the port-hole. It looked on to the sea and not the deck as I'd expected. I went back to the wash-basin and switched the tap on. It was stiff, and when the water did come out it was rusty at first. I washed my face. It still hurt – I'd got sunburned while I was asleep under the plane tree waiting for Jacqueline's train to go. She watched me.

'You certainly got sunburnt,' she said.

'It was waiting for that train. It was a long wait.'

'The day before yesterday you were very drunk at lunch. You kept getting up and sitting down again. You looked happy – I didn't remember ever seeing anyone look so happy.'

'I was, terribly.'

'After lunch I looked for you for a long time round about the trattoria. I wanted to see you again right away. It was obvious that you weren't in the habit of being happy. It suited you.'

'It was the wine. I'd drunk a lot. But that didn't stop me getting sunburnt.'

'You oughtn't to wash it. You should put some cream on it.'

The water was refreshing but it made the sunburn smart. I kept on rinsing my face. It felt as if it had been scratched with somebody's fingernails. I hadn't noticed it for two days.

'I'll go and get you some cream,' she said.

She went out. The cabin was quiet for a few minutes. I stopped washing my face and waited. I could hear, clearly now, the vibration of the propeller and the hiss of the sea against the side of the ship. I tried hard to feel astonished, but I couldn't. I could only be astonished that she wasn't still there in the cabin. She came back very soon. I put some cream on my face, and then finished with it. She had lain down on the bunk with her hands under her head. I turned to her.

'What an adventure,' I said, laughing.

140

'Unheard-of,' she said, laughing too.

We hadn't anything more to say.

'You're not very talkative,' she said.

'He didn't talk much either, I expect?'

'In Paris he talked to me a bit. But that's no excuse for you.'

'No. I'm not a murderer,' I said. 'One day I'll talk to you properly, for a long time. For the moment I have to unpack.'

'It was crazy to have left everything behind like that, you know.'

Suddenly she remembered something and laughed.

'There was one,' she began. Then she stopped and blushed.

'One what?'

'I'm sorry,' she said.

'One what?'

'I'm always making blunders,' she said. She lowered her eyes. She wasn't laughing now.

'One what? I want to know.'

'There was one,' she said, starting to laugh again, 'who brought a huge case on board with him. I thought, perhaps he hasn't got a smaller one. The second day he came up on deck in a pair of white shorts. The third day, in addition to the white shorts, he was wearing a peaked cap. The crew called him the station-master. Then he decided he wanted to get ashore again as soon as possible. He took the cap off, but it was too late.'

'You see,' I said. 'I cotton on quickly.'

I laughed, and so did she, stretched out on the bunk.

'And what did the others bring with them?' I asked.

She stopped laughing.

'No,' she said.

Sometimes it's not what you desire the most that you want, but the opposite – to be deprived of what you desire the most. But she couldn't stand that sort of paradox. She had her own, which were different, and I wasn't on that ship to try to alter them.

But she went back to her own cabin very late, in the middle of the night – too late perhaps, later than my rôle towards her on the yacht required.

I slept badly the rest of the night, and woke at about ten. I went to the dining-room for a coffee. There were two sailors there, and we exchanged good-mornings. I'd already seen them at dinner the previous evening, and they seemed to have got used to my being there. As soon as I'd had my coffee I went out on deck. The sun was high already. A golden wind was blowing full of some extraordinary happiness. As I came out I had to lean against the door of the bar, dazzled, probably by the blueness of the sea.

I walked round the deck. She wasn't there, she wasn't up yet. I went forward and came upon the short dark sailor who had smiled at me the evening before. He was mending ropes, and singing.

'Beautiful day,' I said.

'At home in Sicily,' he said, 'the sea's always like this.'

I sat down beside him. He asked nothing better than to have a chat. He told me she had signed him on a couple of months before, in Sicily, to replace a member of the crew who was staying on in Syracuse. Before, he'd been ship's boy on a cargo-boat that took oranges from Syracuse to Marseilles.

'It makes a change,' he said, 'to be on a yacht. There's so little to do I sometimes make work for myself.' He held up the ropes.

The ship was hugging the coast now – a narrow, inhabited plain with hills behind.

'Corsica?' I asked.

'Of course not. That's Italy still.'

He pointed to a big town with chimneys rising out of it.

'Leghorn,' he said, laughing.

'Where's Sète then?'

'Sète's on the other side,' he said, still laughing. 'But the sea is so good she probably wants to make the voyage last as long as possible.'

'I suppose we'll change course at Piombino,' I said.

'Or Naples,' he said, laughing still.

I picked up a piece of rope and wound it idly round my hand.

'I saw you at the dance the day before yesterday,' he said suddenly.

I had the feeling that this man hadn't had time to see many like me, if he'd only been there two months.

'I met her three days ago,' I said.

He threw me a rather embarrassed look and didn't reply.

'I just thought I'd come,' I explained, waiting for him to speak.

'I see,' he said.

He was a talker. He told me he knew the story of the sailor from Gibraltar too. The crew had told him. He admired him, but he couldn't understand 'why he'd killed the American', or why she was looking for him like that.

'She says she's looking for him, as if you could look for someone like that, all over the world. I think it's just talk.'

'In that case,' I asked, 'how do you explain her travelling about like this?'

'Yes, that's difficult to explain. But perhaps she just likes to travel about.'

'Was it an American he killed then?'

'Some of them say it was, others say not. They say all sorts of things.'

'Anyway, whatever it was, an American or an Englishman . . .'

'Yes,' said Bruno, smiling. 'If you ask me I just think she's bored.'

'But isn't it more boring alone on a ship than anywhere else?'

He looked amused and embarrassed at the same time.

'Alone,' he said. 'She isn't always alone. But she must fret just the same, and it must be about something else as well as him, otherwise it couldn't be like this.'

I didn't disagree, and that encouraged him.

'But sooner or later she'll have to stop. She can't go on like this all the time. No one could stand living on this ship for long. The man I replaced told me that. I didn't believe him, but now I can see it for myself.'

He told me she paid her crew three times the usual amount and was very easy to work for, never made a fuss about anything, but after a couple of months, or three, or six, they all left, especially the young ones. They always parted from her on the best of terms, though; there was no question about that.

'But you can't just go on looking for him for ever and never find him,' he added with a touch of confusion. 'You'll see what it's like yourself. You never go anywhere, you do practically nothing to earn all that money. If you go somewhere it's always just by chance, unless there's been a message, but that doesn't happen very often. When you get there you just cast anchor and wait. And what for? In theory for him to recognize the ship and come on board.'

He said he'd got so fed up with having nothing to do that he'd almost asked for his discharge at Viareggio, just because he'd seen some men really working at unloading a cargo of cheese.

'But it's different for her,' I said. 'What could she do if she left the ship?'

'You can always find something,' said Bruno. 'That's all a lot of nonsense.'

'That's true.'

'Some day or another, you'll see, she won't be able to stand travelling around like this any more.'

'And what do you think? Has she got the slightest chance?'

'What of?'

'Finding him.'

'You'd better ask her,' he said, sounding slightly vexed, 'if it interests you all that much.'

'Oh no,' I said. 'I just asked as a matter of course.'

144

We started to talk about the sailor from Gibraltar again.

'Personally,' said Bruno, 'I have no opinion on the subject. The whole story bores me stiff. They go on about it so much you could write a book. It's the same with the messages. Some of them see him everywhere. And even when there are messages it's still not really as if you were actually going anywhere.'

'Better than nothing,' I said.

'Well, it's a help. At least they don't have to think where to go.'

'And then you never know, do you?'

He gave me an encouraging look.

'That's true,' he said. 'You never know. But there are so many men in the world. Millions.'

'Still,' I said, 'there must be a good many people who know she's looking for him. It's not as if she were looking for him all on her own. She's probably got more chance of finding him than people think.'

'I think they know she's looking for him in all the big ports all over the world,' he said. 'But what good does that do as long as *he* doesn't know it? He may be in the middle of some continent somewhere making a lot of money and never wanting to hear of her at all. The funny thing is it hasn't occurred to her that perhaps *he* mightn't be so keen on finding *her*. After all, isn't she the only person who can recognize him?'

'I think it must have occurred to her,' I said.

However, Bruno was more worried about what was going to happen to him than about her. He wanted to leave the yacht already.

'After Sète,' he said, 'I'll see what I can do. They say I'll come back too – that people go, but they always come back again on this ship. Apparently all the sailors she's ever employed have come back again at some time or other. They leave – and then, it's very funny, afterwards they want to come back again. After another month or two they leave again. This is the third time for the quartermaster. And for Epaminondas, the one we're going to see in Sète, it's the third time too.'

Did she understand about their leaving?

'What doesn't she understand,' he said.

'You don't like her much,' I said.

He looked astonished.

'It's not that,' he said. 'But I think she's just having everyone on.'

'I don't get that impression,' I said.

'Well, I do,' said Bruno. 'I can't help myself. Mind you, I don't hold it against her. But I think perhaps I'll leave when we get to Sète.'

As I listened to him I was still watching for her to come.

'People always ought to do what they want to do,' I said.

'Sometimes I feel a bit . . . well, ashamed at being on this ship,' he said.

'One ought to be able to choose not to be ashamed,' I said.

I left him and went back below, and waited outside her cabin. I had no inclination to do anything but wait for her. The thought of the brass came back to me like some distant folly. I wouldn't have been able to do anything. And I'd worked long enough in the dark, all those years, to allow myself to do no more than that – just wait for a woman to come out into the sun. Lots of men would have done the same as me. I was sufficiently sure of it to feel less alone than during all those years of honest toil.

She came out of her cabin and came over to me. I must have shut my eyes as I had when I saw the sea that morning. She was happy. Her happiness was always rather childlike.

'Leghorn,' she said. 'We're making good speed.'

I learned later that it was always like that: she was always taken by surprise about the distances between ports, and had to be reminded about them. Probably they seemed to her to get shorter and shorter: she'd been sailing about for three years now.

'But what about Sète?' I asked.

She smiled, looking at the sea.

'Plenty of time,' she said.

I looked at the sea too, and at Leghorn in the distance.

'But someone's waiting for you in Sète, aren't they?' I said.

'I've let Epaminondas know . . .'

'When?'

'Yesterday, before we sailed.'

'You don't take things seriously,' I said, trying to laugh.

'Yes, I do,' she said. 'But what does it matter, for once?'

We didn't talk about it any more. She was carrying her atlas, and I asked her to show it to me. It was a plastic folding atlas that she'd had made in South America. It only showed those parts of the coast that were inhabited – she pointed out the tiny dot that was Rocca, among a thousand others on the Italian coast. It also showed depths and currents. The continents were mostly as white and empty as the seas. It was the atlas of a topsy-turvy universe, a negative of the world. She claimed to know it by heart.

'I think I know it as well as someone who lives there,' she said.

We sat down in a couple of deck-chairs facing the bar. All the men were working, more or less. I was the only one doing nothing. From time to time this occurred to me.

'If you like,' she said, 'we could go ashore together at the next port of call.'

She was wearing sunglasses now, and smoking as she looked at the sea. She was very good at that – sitting looking at the sea and smoking, reading or not reading, doing nothing.

'Tell me about the others,' I said.

'Are you going to start making me talk again?'

'In the evening,' I said, hesitating, 'you never want to.'

'Why should you be interested in the others?'

'What a question. Do you dislike talking about them?'

'No,' she said, 'but I'd like you to tell me why you want me to – you never say anything.'

'Because I'm curious, and so that I shan't be tempted to think I'm the only one.'

We laughed.

'They were just anyone, more or less. I'm always making blunders.'

'I'd like to know about them, the blunders you made.'

'The most obvious,' she said, 'the most ridiculous. But sometimes I wonder if they really are mistakes, or if it isn't really that I . . .'

'Because of never seeing anybody?'

'Probably. Then there was a time when I would have taken just anybody, as you said.'

'I said that, but there isn't such a thing as just anybody.'

'I mean people who didn't suit me at all.'

'Do some suit you better than others?'

She didn't laugh.

'Who knows?' she said.

'Begin,' I said. 'There was one who . . .'

'There was one who made himself at home the very first day. When I went to his cabin a few hours after we'd sailed, he was already installed. He'd arranged his books on the shelf. The complete works of Balzac. His toilet things were all in a row over the basin. Unfortunately there were several bottles of Yardley's lavender water. When he saw the way I was looking at them he said he couldn't do without them – one never knew what one was going to be able to get and what one wasn't going to be able to get when one was travelling, so he'd brought some stocks with him.'

She started to laugh.

'That's the sort of mistake,' she said.

'What about the others?'

'Oh, if I'm going to tell you all of them I'm going to need a drink.'

'Just a minute then . . .'

I ran to the bar and came back with two whiskies. She drank hers.

'Usually,' she said, a little embarrassed, 'I asked them to help me look for him. They'd agree. They all used to agree to begin with. I'd leave them in peace for three days to get accustomed to the idea. Then I'd see that they hadn't understood at all.'

I drank my whisky.

'Still,' I said, 'it must be possible to understand, even if you're not left in peace for three days.'

We laughed, she more heartily than I.

'They used to ask: "What do I have to do? Just say, I'll do anything to help you." But if you told them they had to mend the crew's boots, they refused. They used to say: "That's not what I was asked to do. What's that got to do with what I was asked to do?"'

'Let's have another whisky,' I said.

I went to the bar and came back once again with a couple of whiskies.

'Go on.'

'There was another one who drew up a timetable as soon as he came on board. He said health depended on regularity. He did physical jerks every morning on the foredeck.'

I drank my whisky.

'One day,' I said, 'I'll write an American novel about you.'

'Why American?'

'Because of the whiskies. That's what Americans drink. Go on.'

'There was one who stayed three weeks. That was the longest. He was young, and poor, and good-looking. He had hardly any belongings – no white trunks, and no eau de Cologne. But he never looked at the sea, he hardly ever came out of his cabin. He was reading Hegel. One day I asked him if it was interesting, and he said it was philosophy and of the utmost importance. He said that if I'd been able to read it it would have thrown a great deal of light on my own situation. That struck me as – I don't know – rather tactless. He read all the time, because he said he'd never have another oppor-

149

tunity like that in his life, he must make the most of it because he'd never have so much spare time ever again. I gave him enough money to be able to read Hegel for a year without having to work.' Then she added: 'Actually, I might have kept that one.'

She drank her whisky.

'We'll be tight,' she said.

'A bit more, a bit less,' I said. 'What does it matter?'

'You know,' she said, 'I've never taken on a drunkard.'

'Never?'

'I meant it was a mistake I hadn't made until now,' she said, laughing.

'Well ' I said, laughing too, 'now you'll have made them all.'

'You can build a whole career out of mistakes.'

'Go on.'

'There were lots of them. I'll only tell you about the ones that were amusing. There was one who said to me the first evening: "And now, tell me frankly, what is this crazy story?" I said: "What story?" And he said, "You know, all that about the sailor from Gibraltar." . . . We still hadn't left the port where we met.'

She laughed so much that she cried, and had to take off her sunglasses to wipe her eyes.

'Another one,' she said – she couldn't stop now –'produced a camera on the third day. "It's a Leica," he told me, "but I've got a Rolleiflex too and a little Zeiss – that's the one that I prefer, even though it's not very up-to-date." And he used to trot round the deck with either his Rolleiflex or his Leica or his Zeiss, on the look-out, he said, for unusual marine effects. He was going to publish a book about the secrets of the sea.'

I said as little as I could so that she should go on talking.

'The most awful one,' she said, 'was the one that believed in God. Sometimes that sort of thing can go unnoticed on land, and even on the sea it can be quite difficult to spot. I suspected it with him because he hadn't made friends with any of the crew, and he asked them questions all the time about their private lives. But I think Laurent noticed something before I did. One evening I got him tight. He started to talk and talk, and I led him on, and finally he said that the sailor from Gibraltar had killed a man, that he was an unfortunate who deserved to be pitied, and it might be a good thing to pray for him.'

'So what did you do?'

'Never mind. I wasn't very nice that time.'

'And are you sure that sort of thing isn't noticed on land?'

'Not always.' She hesitated. 'I used to think then that it would be wrong for me to choose too carefully.'

I drank my second whisky. My heart was beating loudly, but probably that was partly because of the whisky and because we were lying in the sun. Suddenly she burst out laughing at something vividly remembered.

'There was one,' she said, 'who said to me the first evening, "Let's go away together, my darling. Forget that man. You're ruining your life for him." '

She went on, shaking with laughter.

'Another one was always hungry. He was always ready for something to eat even while he was still ashore, but on board it was incredible. He thought we didn't eat enough on the ship, and between meals he used to go into the kitchen and gulp down bananas. He was afflicted with fantastically good health. He liked good living, and wanted to keep it up while he was at sea.'

'You were quite a collector,' I said.

'Another one, he was quite nice too, said, as soon as we'd set sail: "Look, there are shoals of fish following us." There *were* shoals of herrings. I explained that it was quite usual, and that sometimes schools of sharks would follow us for a week together. The only thing he thought about after that was the herrings. He never looked any farther out to sea than them. What he'd have liked would have been to stop the ship and catch a few with a fishing-rod.'

151

She stopped.

'Go on,' I said.

'No. There aren't any more that were amusing.'

'Say something about one that wasn't, then,' I said, laughing, in such a way that she understood what I meant.

'Ah yes,' she said. 'There's one that I was forgetting. This one had always wanted to polish the door-handles on a ship. The open air and brass door-knobs. What he'd been waiting for all his life was . . .'

She took off her sunglasses and looked at me.

'What?' I asked.

'I don't know what you were waiting for.'

'Nor do I. What does everyone wait for?'

'The sailor from Gibraltar,' she said, laughing.

'That's it,' I said. 'I'd never have thought of it by myself.'

We were silent. Then I suddenly remembered the one who'd said 'Let's go away together, my darling. Forget that man', and I burst out laughing.

'What were you thinking about?' she asked.

'The one who said let's go away together.'

'What about the one who thought about the herrings!'

'What did you expect them to do? Spend their time scouring the horizon through a pair of binoculars?'

She took off her sunglasses again and looked at the sea. Then, with complete sincerity, she said:

'I really don't know.'

'They weren't really serious,' I said.

'Ah,' she said smiling, 'I like that word. And you say it very well.'

'But you can see straight away,' I said.

'What?'

'That you can't bring cameras or eau de Cologne on board this ship, or the works of Balzac, or Hegel either. Not even a stamp collection, or a ring with initials engraved on it, or the merest shoehorn, if it was only made of tin, or an appetite, or a liking for roast mutton, or concern for one's nearest and dearest ashore, or concern about one's future, or one's pitiful past, or a passion for herring-fishing, or a timetable, or a half-finished novel, or an essay, or sea-sickness, or the habit of talking too much, or too little, or of sleeping for too long.'

She listened to me with eyes like a child's.

'Is that all?'

'I expect I've forgotten something,' I said. 'Especially if, aware of all these impossibilities, of which I quote only a small selection, one doesn't know that one can't stay on this ship anyway, then one can't really stay on it.'

'All that's not very clear,' she said, laughing. 'If you put things like that in your American novel no one will be able to understand it.'

'As long as the people on this ship understand it a bit,' I said, 'I shall be satisfied. You can't make everybody understand everything.'

'I'd never supposed,' she said, 'that the people on this ship were particularly discerning.'

'They are extraordinarily discerning,' I said.

I'd had two whiskies, and I wasn't used to it.

'In short,' I said, 'you're a splendid whore.'

She wasn't in the least shocked.

'If you like,' she said. 'Is that what a whore is?'

'I think so.'

'Very well,' she said. She smiled.

'And can't you really do without these . . . these mistakes?'

She was confused, lowered her eyes, didn't answer.

'And . . . was it he who left you with the need for them?'

'I think so,' she said.

'And then you're hard to please into the bargain,' I said, laughing.

'But if one never made any mistakes it would be dreadful,' she said.

'You talk like a book,' I said.

That afternoon I stayed for a long time lying on my bunk

in my cabin, dazed with all the whisky we'd drunk. I'd have liked to sleep, but as soon as I lay down I didn't feel tired any more. Again I couldn't get to sleep. I tried to read. But I couldn't do that either. There was probably only one story I could have read, but that story wasn't yet written. So I threw the book on the floor. Then I started to look at it and laugh. No doubt the whisky had something to do with it, but I found it funny. Half the pages were turned back, and if you tried hard enough you could see it as someone who had fallen flat on his face. She must be asleep. She was a woman who after two whiskies went to sleep and forgot everything. The one who wanted to fish for herring, and the one who said 'Let's go away together, darling', and perhaps even the one who read Hegel hadn't been able to take such offhandedness. I laughed to myself, a thing I didn't often do. Then time went by, and the whisky withdrew, and with it the desire to laugh. And then, naturally, the question of my future presented itself again. What was going to become of me, sooner or later? I had the common habit of worrying about my future. But that was the last time, after I started to share her travels, that I did it: suddenly it started to bore me. It wasn't long before my brother, the one who was obsessed with the idea of catching a herring, interested me more. I should have liked to know him, I liked that sort of person. Could you be afraid at finding yourself alone with a woman and the horizon, with only an occasional albatross in the shrouds? Probably, in the middle of the Pacific, a week's voyage from the nearest port, you could be subject to unimagined fears. But I wasn't very frightened. I lay there for a long while, doing nothing, thinking about all this. Then I heard her footstep in the corridor. She knocked and came in. I'd never really stopped waiting for her. She noticed the book on the floor at once.

'I've been asleep,' she said.

She pointed to the book.

'You threw your book away?' she said.

I didn't answer. She added anxiously:

154

'Perhaps you're going to be rather bored.'

'Oh no. There's absolutely no need for you to worry about that.'

'If you don't like reading,' she said, 'you're practically certain to get bored.'

'Perhaps I might try Hegel.'

She didn't laugh or say anything. Then she went on:

'Are you sure you're not bored?'

'Quite. Go back to your cabin.'

She wasn't too astonished. But she didn't go straight away. I looked at her without saying a word or making any movement, for a long time. Words and gestures were unnecessary. Then again I asked her to go.

'Off with you.'

This time she went. I went out almost immediately after. I went straight to find Bruno, who was still mending his ropes. I was exhausted. I lay down on the deck beside him. He wasn't alone, there was another sailor with him painting the winch. I promised myself to sleep on deck some nights, because it was a thing I'd always dreamed of doing, sleeping on the deck of a ship. And also so as to be alone. So as not to keep on waiting for her.

'You're tired,' said Bruno.

I laughed, but he didn't smile.

'A tiring woman,' I said.

The other sailor didn't smile either.

'And then I've always had to work,' I said. 'This is the first time I've done nothing. That's tiring too.'

'I told you she was tiring,' said Bruno.

'Everyone's tiring,' said the other sailor.

I recognized him from lunch-time and the day before in the dining-room. He was about thirty-five, as brown as a gipsy. He'd struck me as the least talkative of them all. She'd told me that he'd been on the ship over a year, and still showed no sign of wanting to leave. Bruno went off somewhere and I was left alone with him. The sun went down. He went on painting the winch. He was the one she called Laurent. I remembered that he was the only one, the evening before in the dining-room, who'd seemed to feel more sympathy for me than curiosity.

'You're tired,' he said.

He didn't say it in the same way as Bruno. It wasn't a question. I said yes I was.

'The novelty is tiring,' he said. 'That's what it is.'

A moment went by. He was still painting his winch. The dusk was beginning, lovely and interminable.

'I like it very much on this ship,' I said.

'What did you do before?'

'I was in the Colonial Ministry. Registry section. I stayed there eight years.'

'What sort of work was it?'

'Copying out births and deaths. All day.'

'Awful,' he said.

'You can't imagine.'

'This makes a change then,' he said.

'You can say that again.' I laughed. 'What about you?'

'A bit of everything. I never stuck at one job long.'

'You had the right idea.'

'Yes. I like it on this ship too.'

He had fine, laughing eyes.

'It's very funny,' I said. 'If you told this story in a book no one would believe you.'

'Her story, you mean?'

'Yes.'

'She's a very romantic woman.' He laughed too.

'Yes, that's it, romantic,' I said. We laughed together. We understood each other.

The dusk grew deeper. We were very close to the Italian coast. I pointed to a luminous blur over the sea. A fairly large town.

'Leghorn?'

'No. I don't know. But we've passed Leghorn,' he said.

Then he added, jokingly:

'What a way to go to Sète.'

'Yes,' I said. Then: 'She's rich.'

He stopped laughing and didn't answer.

'It's true,' I said again. 'She's rich.'

He stopped painting and said quite roughly:

'What do you want her to do with it, give it away to the starving orphans?'

'No, of course not. But all the same, this yacht . . .'

He interrupted me.

'If you ask me it was the best thing for her to do. Why not?'

And then he went on, sententiously almost:

'It's one of the last great fortunes in the world. Perhaps it's the last time anyone will ever be able to afford to do what she's doing.'

'A historic moment, in fact,' I said, laughing.

'Yes, if you like to look at it that way – a historic moment.'

The sun on the horizon grew enormous, and suddenly turned crimson. A slight breeze sprang up. We hadn't got any more to say. He put his brush in a pot of turpentine, put the lid on his paint, and lit a cigarette. We watched the coast going past, and all the lights coming on.

'Usually she goes straight there when she gets a message,' he said.

He looked at me.

'This is only a small détour,' I said.

'I'm all for détours,' he answered.

I changed the subject.

'Leghorn isn't very far from Pisa, is it?' I said.

'Twenty kilometres. Do you know it?'

'I was in Pisa a week ago. It was bombed. But fortunately the main square wasn't hit. It was very hot.'

'You had a woman with you at Rocca,' he said. 'I saw you at Eolo's.'

'Yes,' I said. 'She's gone back to Paris.'

'You were right to come on the yacht,' he said.

'What's the next place after Leghorn?'

'Piombino. We're bound to stop there.'

'I shall have to have a look at a map,' I said.

He kept looking at me.

'It's funny,' he said, 'but I think you'll stay.'

'I think so too,' I said.

We laughed, as if it were a good joke.

Then he went too. The dusk grew deeper still. I'd known her for four days and three nights. I didn't go to sleep straight away. I had time to see several little ports go by, and night fall. Darkness covered the deck and the sea. It spread over me too, and ate at my heart. The sky remained light for some time. I must have gone to sleep just before it grew dark as well. I woke up what must have been about an hour later. I was hungry. I went to the dining-room. She was there. She smiled at me and I sat down facing her. Laurent was there too, and gave a friendly nod.

'You look strange,' she said.

'I've been asleep on the deck. I've never done that before.'

'Did you forget all about everything?'

'Yes, everything,' I said. 'When I woke up I couldn't understand anything any more.'

'Nothing?'

'Nothing.'

'And now?'

'Now I'm hungry,' I said.

She took my plate and stood up. I followed her to the bar. There was still some grilled fish and some stewed lamb. I chose the lamb.

'There's no reason why you should eat fish every day just because you're on a ship,' I said.

She laughed. She watched me as I ate, but without appearing to do so.

'The open air gives you an appetite,' I said.

She laughed again. She was in a very good humour. We

talked and joked about this and that with the sailors. Some of them would have preferred to keep on as far as Sicily before heading for Sète. Others said that it was very hot already and it was better to change course before, off Piombino. No one said anything about what we should do after Sète. When dinner was over I went back on deck to watch the Italian coast go by. She came and joined me.

'It could make you keep wanting to go ashore,' I said, 'seeing the coast go by right under your nose all the time like that.'

'I looked for you,' she said, 'and I found you by the winch. I let you go on sleeping.'

I pointed to a bright light on the coast.

'Quercianella,' she said.

'Let's stretch out in some deck-chairs. I'll go and get you a whisky.'

'I don't feel much like talking,' she said, pleadingly.

'Make something up, anything,' I said. 'But you must talk to me.'

I put two chairs side by side. She lowered herself into one reluctantly. I went and fetched her a whisky.

'It lasted six months?'

'I can't talk about it,' she said.

'You married the owner of the yacht, you were rich, years went by.'

'Three years,' she said.

'Then you met him again.'

'I met him. It's always the same. I met him at a moment when I might have thought at last, not that I was forgetting him, but that I might perhaps one day be able to live on something other than the memory of him.'

She turned her head sharply towards me and was silent.

'Which means one must never despair,' I said.

She drank her whisky. Then she watched the Italian coast for some time without speaking. I waited for her to speak. She knew it, and there was no point in reminding her. At last

159

she turned to me and said with gentle irony:

'If you say anything about that meeting in your American novel, you must say that it was very, very important for me. It enabled me to see, to understand, a little, what the whole thing meant – that is, the meaning it had for him, at least, and perhaps the one it had had for me too . . . And that it's since that meeting that I've believed it to be within the bounds of possibility to meet him again, to meet someone, no matter whom, no matter when. And it's since then that I've believed I'm bound to look for him, as others are bound to . . .'

'To what?'

'I don't know,' she said. 'That, I don't know.'

'I'll say it,' I said.

'It's not just literature,' she said after a moment. 'Or if it is, it's because sometimes that's the only means of understanding certain things.'

'I'll say that too,' I said.

'If it is just literature,' she said again, 'then I came to literature through that.' She smiled.

'It's possible,' I said. 'I'll put that too.'

'It was in winter, in Marseilles. We'd come to the south for a holiday and we'd stopped at Marseilles. It was during the night, it must have been almost five o'clock. The nights were very long and deep. It must have been on a night very like that that he'd committed the murder, six years before. At that time I didn't know much about it except, as I've told you, that it was an American he'd killed.

'There were four of us – my husband, two friends of his, and me. We'd spent the night in a restaurant in a side-street leading into the Canebière. We'd never have met if we hadn't had to park the cars in the Canebière itself because there wasn't enough room in the side-street. It was when we were walking back to the cars that we met him.

'Well, we came out of the restaurant, all four of us. It was five o'clock in the morning. I remember how long and deep the night had seemed. But I could go over all these details a thousand times.

'They closed the restaurant as we came out. We were the last to leave, as usual. We were always the last customers everywhere; probably we were the ones with the least to do. I'd become one of those people who sleep till midday every day.

'Marseilles was deserted. We started to walk down the side-street towards where we'd left the cars.

'Our friends were in front – they were cold, and walked more quickly than we did. Before we'd gone fifty yards someone entered the street from the Canebière, and came towards us.

'It was a man. He was walking fast, and carrying a little case that looked very light. He swung it in his hand as he went along. He hadn't got an overcoat.

'I stopped. As soon as he'd come in sight, just from the way he walked, I'd recognized him. My husband couldn't make it out. He asked me what was the matter. I couldn't answer. I stood rooted to the spot and watched him come nearer. I remember my husband turning and looking at him too. He just saw a man coming towards us, he didn't recognize him. And yet he'd been of some importance in his life too. But probably he hadn't studied him closely enough to recognize him from so far away. He thought it must be something else that was preventing his wife, as he called me, from walking on and from answering his question. He didn't know what. He was very perplexed. Our friends were still walking along in front. They hadn't noticed that we'd stopped following.

'He stood still for a moment on his side of the street, looked up and round, then suddenly crossed quickly over to the couple in front, and stopped facing them. They stood still too in surprise. He spoke to them. He could only have been about ten yards away from me. I couldn't hear anything he said but the first word: "English?" He asked the question quite loudly, but the rest he said in a low voice I couldn't make

161

out. He held the case in one hand, and in the other some small object that looked like an envelope. His face was expressionless. A couple of seconds went by, the time it took for the people to realize what he meant. Then there was an indignant cry that I could hear perfectly clearly: our friend in front shouted, "Clear off, and quick!" My husband heard too, and recognized him. He, the other, smiled pleasantly and made no answer. He started to walk on, and came face to face with us. And suddenly he recognized me. He stopped.

'It was three years since we'd seen each other. I was in evening dress. I saw him look. I had a fur coat on, magnificent and expensive. He looked at the man I was with, and then recognized him too. He looked surprised, but only for a moment. He turned to me again and smiled. I wasn't able to smile back at him yet. I was too occupied looking at him. He was wearing a light summer suit that was old and didn't fit him. He wasn't wearing an overcoat – he never had before, either. Yet even in this winter dawn he didn't seem to be cold. It was as if – yes, as if he took summer about with him wherever he went. I remembered how handsome he was, and he looked as handsome to me then as the first day, when he went to sleep on the deck of the yacht. Sometimes, since Shanghai, I'd wondered whether he was really as good-looking as I'd thought. But no, I was wrong to doubt it. The look in his eyes was still the same – still bold, still full of lurking preoccupations. Since I'd seen it, every other look had always seemed uninteresting. He hadn't been to the barber's for a long time. His hair was badly cut and too long, just as it used to be. He couldn't go to the barber's except at the risk of his life. The only thing that was new was that he was almost as thin again now as when we'd picked him up in the yacht. But he was a man to whom hunger was as natural as to the stray cats that prowl by night. I knew him in spite of his thinness; I would have recognized him just by his eyes. And when he smiled at me slightly apologetically, because of that evening at Shanghai when he hadn't come back on board, I understood, and recognized him so intensely that I almost cried out. There was no shame in that smile, and not a trace of bitterness either, only a sort of unconquerable freshness. He had forgotten his case, and what was in it, and his reason for being there at that hour of the night, in the street, in the cold, hungry. He was glad to see me.

'Neither he nor I was the first to speak. It was my husband. For him alone the long silence of those first few moments was unbearable, he alone wanted to break it. And yet, since he'd married me, it must have occurred to him that this meeting might one day take place. People do think about such eventualities and what they would do if they arose, don't they? But probably the more one thinks about them the less one is able to deal with them when they do arise. He must have thought about it too much. Though a thousand times forewarned, he was strangely taken aback.

' "Have you given up the sea, then?" he asked.

'And then he walked off from us a little way, and stood in a doorway. He leaned against the wall, and I think he felt ill, though not enough to need to lie down. Once he'd left us we spoke to each other.

' "How are you?" he asked.

'I said I was all right.

' "So I see," he said.

'I smiled at him. Sometimes, on my bad days – and I had plenty of those – I'd thought they must have caught him and killed him. But of course, that couldn't really happen to a man like him. No, the world still bore him, and with pride. He did it honour – of all its inhabitants he was one of those most fit for it, he was a connoisseur of its depths. Ah, how it suited him, living! And from what adventure had he emerged now? From what real voyages had he just returned? What maelstrom of rovings, of networks, of nights and suns and hungers and women, of poker and of fate had been necessary to bring him back there at last, before me? My own story seemed rather shameful. He had smiled when he said "So I see."

Didn't he really mean "I might have guessed"? I didn't want us to talk about it. I said:

' "I'll take the lot," pointing to the postcards.

'Our former boss was still leaning against the wall, suffering horribly from jealousy. So he said to me quietly:

' "Hello."

'That was his way of letting me know that he remembered everything. I must have . . . yes, I must have shut my eyes, as I did the other time. And then he must have understood that it was the same for me too, that I remembered everything too. It lasted a few seconds. But it was enough for us to meet again that dawn with as deep an emotion as before, in my cabin after the day's work. When I opened my eyes he was still looking at me. I tried to pull myself together, and said again:

' "I'll take the lot."

'At that moment my husband came back. But he didn't seem to notice. He bent one knee and balanced his case on it. It was all warped by the rain, and probably as old as his clothes were. He must have been trailing it about with him him for ages. He opened it. There were about a dozen envelopes inside it like the one he had in his hand. And with them was a bit of bread. There was nothing else in the case except the envelopes and the bread. He collected up all the envelopes one by one and held them out to me.

' "I'll give them to you."

'I took them and put them in my muff. They were icy. I thought that the bread must be frozen too, and that it was because of the envelopes that he'd been able to buy it. In short, he was giving me his bread. But I took it. Suddenly we heard a voice:

' "How much?"

'Hearing him, he noticed that my husband was there again.

' "Nothing," he said, "seeing it's for her."

'But my husband was of a different opinion. He took a

bundle of thousand-franc notes out of his pocket and threw it into the case. As it was so small the notes fell on top of the bread, and half hid it. There were a lot of them. He looked at them for a minute, then collected them up one by one, as he had the envelopes, only a little more slowly. Then I said:

' "It was for less than that, I expect – much less than that – that you killed the American?"

'I felt my husband take my arm and try to pull me away. I snatched myself free.

' "Much less," he said, laughing. "Less than half, even."

'He'd collected up all the notes, and with his free hand – the other still held the envelopes – he held them out to my husband. There was nothing left in the case except the bread. I said to him:

' "No, you must take them."

' "You're joking," he said lightly.

'I told him he must, he must.

' "What's the matter with you?" he asked.

'He was still holding out the wad of notes.

' "At least he didn't count them," I said.

' "Why did you do that?" he asked my husband. He wasn't angry.

' "So that you'd leave her alone," said my husband faintly.

'He still looked at him.

' "You shouldn't have done it," he said.

'My husband didn't answer. He regretted his rather facile gesture already.

' "It's a habit," I said. "So that he can say you didn't give them to me. They consider themselves dishonoured other-wise."

' "She's my wife," said my husband, I remember his voice – sincere, pleading.

' "No," he said, "you shouldn't have done it."

'I was still looking at the bread. I cried out:

' "Since he threw it in your case there's no need to give it back."

' "It's impossible," he said. He was very calm; a bit surprised.

' "It's me that's giving it to you."

' "It's impossible. I can't. You know very well."

' "I don't want you to give it back to him."

' "But don't you see, I can't," he said.

'He was still astonished, still very mild. I said:

' "Well, what else could he have done, I ask you?"

' "But I can't."

' "But I'm married to him, aren't I?"

'He looked at me. He must have understood, then, a lot of things that he hadn't bothered to understand before.

' "Anna," he said, "I can't."

' "It isn't entirely his fault, he did what he could."

'The bread was still there alone in the case. Now my husband was looking at it too. He didn't take the money.

' "Please," said my husband, "take it."

' "Impossible. As you say, one does what one can. I can't."

'Then I said it for the first time, I shouted it – the thing I'd never said. That I loved him.

'He looked up sharply. This time he didn't say he couldn't take the money. I explained.

' "It's because I love you that you must take it."

'Then I ran away. My husband followed me. The first time I turned round I saw that he hadn't tried to stop me. He watched me go. I could just make out the wad of notes still held out in his hand. The second time I turned round, at the end of the street, I couldn't see him any more – he'd gone. I didn't see him again for another four years.'

She was silent.

'And afterwards?'

'Oh! afterwards, everything was much less important. We caught up with our friends. All they'd been able to hear of our conversation was the words I'd cried out, but they hadn't understood them. But they'd seen us buy what they had refused, and they were very surprised.

' "Do you mean to say you bought that filth from him?"
said the man.
' "It's just encouraging vice," said his wife.
'I asked what vice, but no one could tell me. I felt alone
with him against the whole world. In my muff, pressed
against me, I held the bundle of envelopes. I think I loved
him then as I did the very first day.
' "We knew him," said my husband.
' "Ah," said the man, "if you knew him it's another
matter."
'I asked him what, but no one could tell me.
' "He was a sailor," said my husband. "He worked for six
months on the *Anna*."
'I couldn't help smiling at the aptness of his expression.
' "No," I said, "you're wrong: on the *Cypris*."
' "That's right," said my husband, "it was still called the
Cypris then."
'He said offhandedly that he came from Gibraltar. I said
he didn't come from Gibraltar any more than from Shanghai
– no one knew where he came from.
' "Funny sort of cove," said the friend knowingly.
'Then I told them who he was. Sometimes I do things like
that, for no reason at all. I didn't think I was taking any risk
because neither they nor I knew his real identity. As for why
I talked to them about him rather than to anybody else,
there was nothing to choose – I knew the rest of my
husband's friends just as little as I knew them. Besides, quite
simply, that night I couldn't have prevented myself from
speaking, couldn't have gone on being silent. So I said what I
knew and what my husband didn't up till then: that he'd
committed a crime, in Paris, when he was twenty, against an
American whose name I didn't know. I told them the little I
did know.
'Then the friend remembered something. He asked me how
long ago it was since the murder was committed. I said five or
six years. He said there was a murder in Paris about then that

there was a lot of talk about, in which the criminal was very young and the victim a prominent American industrialist.

' "I remember," the friend suddenly cried. "It was Nelson Nelson, the ball-bearings king."

' "Ball-bearings? – Really?" I asked him.

'I laughed and laughed. I hadn't laughed so much for three years. I thought, he'll never stop astounding me.

' "But that's marvellous," I said.

' "What?" asked my husband.

' "I don't know – that it should have been the ball-bearings king."

'My husband said he didn't see why.

'I didn't see why either, but it didn't matter. I was laughing so much I couldn't walk.

' "They never found out much about it," the friend went on. "It was one night in Montmartre. Nelson Nelson had knocked a young man over in his Rolls Royce. The street was dark and badly lit, and the car was going very fast. The young man didn't have time to jump out of the way, and so he was knocked down. One of the mudguards cut his head a bit. The American made him get in the car and told the chauffeur to drive to the nearest hospital, but when they got to the hospital all they found in the car was the corpse of the American. He'd been strangled. He hadn't even had time to let out a cry. The chauffeur didn't notice anything. Nelson Nelson's wallet had disappeared. Apparently it had contained a great deal of money. It was supposed that he'd taken it out to compensate the young man for the accident, and that the young man had lost his head at the sight of so much money."

'I questioned the friend to try to find out more, but that was all he could remember. We went back to our hotel.

'It was as we were driving back that I remembered something too – a scar he'd had on his head, underneath the hair. When I discovered it, one night while he was sleeping, I was surprised to see that there was a sort of black splinter in the middle of it (a sliver of paintwork from the Rolls), which stood out against the whiteness of the skin. I'd thought it strange, but hadn't supposed it to be of any importance, and hadn't even asked him what it was.

'The journey back was an uncomfortable one. My husband said he'd been expecting it for a long time, that he couldn't have stayed in Shanghai. I told him to remember that I'd always made life difficult for him. For the first time it seemed useless to console him with empty promises.

'I remember it well. Once I was alone in my room I didn't hurry. I undressed and drew the curtains and lay down on the bed. Not until then did I take the envelopes and open them one after the other. There were ten. There were ten photographs and two postcards in each; they were all held together by a thin elastic band of the kind you get round pots of yoghourt. Each envelope contained the same ten photographs and the same two postcards. In his eagerness he had given me ten that were all alike. It's only flowers that are given like that, all alike and in a bunch. But it was flowers that I was holding. Only the photographs might have been called obscene. The postcards were of the Eiffel Tower and the grotto at Lourdes filled with pilgrims. The photographs were thin, obviously cut out of books, and the postcards were there just to add thickness.

'We went back to Paris the next day.

'For three days and three nights I waited for him to telephone. It wasn't foolishness on my part. He could telephone me quite easily – I was in all the directories, alas. All he had to do was open one and look for the name of the former owner of the *Cypris*. I had no means of getting in touch with him. I waited three days and three nights. But he didn't 'phone.

'After a few weeks I told myself it was probably better like that. That with a hundred times the money he took in a day, he couldn't have resisted. I still think now he must have gone off to play poker. He was a man who had never been able to calculate about anything, and this time, again, he hadn't calculated about me. If he'd stayed with me he would still have hankered after his poker. I preferred that he should have his poker and hanker after me. I even got to the stage of seeing in this apparent infidelity a desire to be truly faithful. He knew as well as I did what it was all about.

'The war came. Time went by. That time I didn't see him for another four years.'

She stopped.

'I'd like another whisky,' she said.

I went to fetch her another glass. Laurent was still in the bar, playing cards with another of the sailors, and so absorbed in the game that he didn't see me come in. When I came back on deck she was standing up by the rail and looking at the coast. I gave her the drink. We were passing a small port; the jetties were deserted and dimly lit.

'Castiglioncello,' she said, 'unless it's Rosignano already.'

I could hardly make her out in the faint light on deck, and I felt a great desire to see her clearly. But it was still bearable.

'I suppose you tell that story often,' I said. I smiled.

'No,' she said, 'but of course'– she hesitated, a little shame-facedly –'I've thought about it a lot.'

'Do you tell it whenever anyone asks you to?'

'Sometimes I talk about something else,' she said.

'But you tell it to those you bring on the yacht?'

'No,' she said, 'not that. I just tell them what comes into my head. You can't tell everything to everyone. Sometimes I tell them I'm just on a cruise.'

My desire to see her better suddenly became very hard to bear.

'Come,' I said.

We went to my cabin. She lay down on the bunk, tired and preoccupied. I sat down beside her.

'It makes me very tired to talk,' she said.

'But I think it's a sort of tiredness that does you good.'

170

She was surprised, but let it pass.

'Hadn't you ever told him before?'

'All he could afford,' she said, 'was a temporary love, and I always acted so that ours might seem like that.'

'Did you think he might be worried otherwise?'

'I still think so, and perhaps even a bit repelled, because he would have thought I expected the usual sort of assurances, or at least considerations. And that would have scared him away even sooner.'

'Is that very different from most other loves?'

I couldn't help smiling.

'I don't know,' she said.

She looked at me intently, waiting for me to speak. I went and opened the port-hole and came back.

'You were happy,' I said, 'even if it was only for six months . . .'

'That's a long time ago now,' she said. 'What were you saying?'

'I can't remember. And will the ship stop one day?'

I could see she was gradually emerging from the story.

'Tomorrow,' she said, 'at Piombino, we can go ashore if you like.'

'There or somewhere else, it's all the same.'

'I like going ashore more and more,' she said. 'But I couldn't do without the ship.'

'There's no reason now why you shouldn't go ashore.'

'And you,' she said. 'Have you been happy?'

'I must have been once, but I can't remember exactly.'

She waited for me to explain.

'I took an interest in politics,' I said, 'the first two years I was in the Ministry. I think it must have been then. But only then.'

'And afterwards?'

'I didn't take an interest in politics any more. I didn't do anything much.'

'And you've never been happy . . . in any other way.'

'As I said, I must have been, sometimes, now and again. It's always possible, even in the most hopeless cases.'

I laughed; but she didn't.

'And with her?'

'No,' I said. 'Never for a single day.'

She looked at me, and I could see that she emerged now from the story altogether.

'You're not very talkative,' she said very gently.

I got up, and went over and rinsed my face, as I had the day before. It didn't hurt nearly so much now.

'We can't both talk at once,' I said. 'But one day I'll talk to you, you'll see. Everyone has things to tell.'

'What?'

'My life. You'll see, it's fascinating.'

'Is your face better?'

'It doesn't hurt at all any more.'

Again, inevitably, we had no more to say to each other. I smoked a cigarette, still standing.

'What was the matter with you this afternoon?' she said, with a little hesitation.

'It was the whisky. I'm not used to it.'

She got up.

'Do you want me to go back to my cabin again?'

'I don't think so,' I said.

The next morning we were in sight of Piombino. Again I'd gone to sleep late and slept badly, but I woke up very early. It was still fine. When I came out on deck we were just entering the Piombino channel. I picked up a guide to Italy that was lying on a table in the bar. The only thing it mentioned about Piombino was its big iron-foundries, I chatted for a moment with Bruno, about the heat. It was cloudy. Bruno said it was the first storms gathering, but another sailor who was there didn't agree, he said it was too soon for that. She came up at about eleven, when we'd already got in. She reminded me that we were going to have lunch ashore

together, then she went off somewhere, to her cabin, I
suppose.

I stayed on deck for an hour. The arrival of the yacht had
attracted all the poor children of the port. Laurent and two
other sailors were walking up and down the quay waiting
for the oil tanker. Every now and again Laurent would say
something to me about nothing in particular. When the
tanker arrived all the children swarmed round it. While we
were filling up, or at least to begin with, every single one of
them crowded round and stared religiously. Before we'd
finished she came and stood beside me. She'd put a dress on.

'I've been reading,' she said.

'My word,' I answered.

She said, with a sort of reluctant insistence:

'You ought to read sometimes too.'

'I don't feel like it,' I said. I looked at the children.

She dropped the subject.

'Shall we go ashore?'

'Yes.'

We went ashore. We walked about looking for a restaurant,
but it was difficult and took a long time. It was a big port, but
not many tourists came there. The streets were new and
depressing, built at right angles to each other, without any
trees, and with big identical blocks of flats on either side.
Most of the roads hadn't been tarred, and were very dusty.
There were very few shops, just an occasional greengrocer's
or butcher's. We walked for a long way without seeing a
restaurant. It was still cloudy and oppressive. There were
lots of children about still. They came up close to look at us,
then fled to enormous grandmothers dressed in black and
weatherbeaten by the sea air, who stared suspiciously at this
strange woman. It was lunch-time, and there was a smell of
fish and garlic. Finally we found a little restaurant on a
corner, without a terrasse. It was cool inside. There were two
workmen eating at a table. At the bar three better-dressed
customers were drinking black coffees. The tables were made

of grey marble. 'I can't offer you much,' the proprietor said: 'Minestra, salami, or a fried egg. If you have the time we could cook you some pasta.' We said that would do. She ordered some wine. It was poor stuff, mauve and heavy, but it came straight from the cellar and was pleasantly cool to drink. We'd been walking a long time, and we both had a couple of glasses one after the other.

'Not that it's all that good,' I said, 'but it's the right temperature.'

'I like this kind of wine.'

'It's not good for you though,' I said.

'It's treacherous, you mean?' she said, laughing.

'That's right.'

We started to talk earnestly about wine. I kept on refilling her glass. Then the man brought the minestra. We hardly touched it.

She blushed slightly and said, 'When it's so hot you can't eat.'

I felt the same. The wine was making me tired again – I'd really not had much sleep since I'd met her. But it was a strange, abstract fatigue that didn't make me drowsy. I found it difficult to eat, rather as I had four days earlier, after I'd been swimming, under the trellis at the trattoria. Her face looked as it did then, when I'd seen her again for the first time, in the greenish light of the grapes. She ate just slightly more than I did. I was probably getting all the strength I needed from my fatigue, or possibly from the wine. I ordered another carafe.

'Sometimes there are days when I can't stop drinking wine,' I said.

'I know,' she said. 'But we'll be drunk.'

'That's what we need,' I said.

The proprietor brought the salami, and we ate a little, just taking the slices straight from the dish. Then he brought a tomato salad. It was warm – the tomatoes must have just come from the greengrocer's window nearby. We ate very

174

little, and the man came to speak to us. 'You're not eating anything,' he said in Italian. 'Isn't it all right for you?'

'Yes, it's fine,' I said. 'But we haven't got much appetite in this heat.'

He asked if we'd like him to do some eggs for us, but she said it wasn't worth putting him to the trouble. I ordered another carafe of wine.

'Have you finished then?' he asked.

'Yes, thank you,' I said.

We talked for a bit, about the proprietor, who was a nice man, and about his wife who sat knitting in a corner and was rather good-looking. Then, of course, I asked her to talk to me again. But she was expecting it.

'I'd like to know the end of that story,' I said, 'about the woman who loved the sailor from Gibraltar.'

I didn't have to insist. We weren't eating any more, only drinking. It seemed as if the heat had taken away our conversation too, so she was quite willing to tell me about their life in London. How boring it was there, and how then, after the meeting in Marseilles, she couldn't forget him. No doubt the boredom of London had something to do with it. Then the end of the war, the discovery of the concentration camps, and then the Sunday – nothing special had happened in the preceding days to lead up to it – when she decided to return to Paris. How she went one afternoon when her husband was out, leaving him a letter. Then she stopped talking.

'I'm drunk,' she said. 'All this wine.'

'Me too,' I said. 'What does it matter? What did you say in the letter?'

'I don't remember very well now, something about the friendship I felt for him. And I said I knew how awful it was to suffer for love, but that I couldn't go on devoting my whole life to just sparing him. And that I might have loved him if fate – yes, I said fate – hadn't bound me so strangely to the sailor from Gibraltar.'

She grimaced.

'It's a horrible story,' she said.

'Go on.'

'I got to Paris, and for three days I just walked about. I hadn't walked so much since Shanghai, five years before. One morning, after three days, in a café, I caught sight of my husband's name in a newspaper lying on a table. He'd killed himself. A hero puts an end to himself in London – that was the headline. That sort of thing made news in the circles my husband moved in. But it was terrible – the first thing I thought of when I read it was that if it was in the papers, *he* might see it. I saw it as a means of getting in touch with him. My husband's house in Paris was occupied by the Free French, except for the first floor, where my room was. I'd been to see them and asked them to let me occupy the room for three days. They agreed, and even let me have a telephone. For three days after the item had appeared in the paper I stayed in my room. The concierge brought me my meals. She cried, because she'd seen the paper. She said she knew how unhappy I must be. The paper had said he killed himself because his nerves were bad and the war had got him down. I allowed three days for the sailor from Gibraltar to get to Paris if he wasn't already there, and to come and find me. In short to make sure that he was still alive. I read; I don't remember what. If he hadn't telephoned I would have killed myself. I promised myself that – it was the only thing that stopped me from thinking too much about what I'd done by coming away from London. I called upon fate to give him back to me, and I gave it three days to do it. On the evening of the second day he telephoned.'

Again she stopped speaking.

'And afterwards?'

'We lived together for five weeks, then he went away.'

'Was it . . .was it the same as before?'

'It couldn't have been. We were quite free.'

'Tell me.'

'We talked to each other more. One day he told me he

loved me. Oh yes, and another day I talked to him again about Nelson Nelson. We'd just mentioned it as a joke when we'd met, but we hadn't talked about it properly. That evening I'm speaking of I told him I knew that when he was younger he'd been knocked down by a car, that he'd been taken into the car to be driven to hospital, that the owner of the car was fat and old and had asked him if he was in pain, and that he'd said no. He made no objection. He told me the rest of the story. He said the American had said, "Your head's still bleeding a lot," and he thought he was looking at him rather strangely. It was the first time he'd been in a car like that and he asked what make it was, and the American laughed and said it was a Rolls Royce. Immediately after that he undid his overcoat and took a big wallet out of his inside pocket. He opened it. It was quite light in the car because of the street lamps. The American took out a wad of thousand-franc notes, and he saw there were at least four more still left in the wallet. He took the pin out of the wad he was holding and started to count them, slowly. He was bleeding quite a lot and couldn't see quite clearly, but he could see him counting them well enough. A thousand francs. He told me he could still remember the fat white fingers. Two thousand. He looked at him again. He hesitated, then took the third note. Then the fourth, hesitating even longer. Then he stopped and folded up the rest of the wad of notes and put them back in his wallet. It was then that he killed him. We never spoke of it again.'

She was silent once more, and looked at me rather mockingly but kindly still.

'You don't like this story very much,' she said.

'That's neither here nor there,' I said. 'I'd like to know about it just the same.'

'Is it him you don't like?'

'I think so. I mean, sailors from Gibraltar in general.'

She waited, smiling, for me to speak. There was no reproach in her glance.

'I'm always a bit suspicious about people whose lives are exceptional,' I said. 'I don't want you to misunderstand me . . . Even when they're exceptional in the way his is,' I added.

'It isn't his fault,' she said gently. 'He doesn't even know I'm looking for him.'

'It's yours,' I said. 'You want yours to be the greatest love ever.'

I laughed. We were both rather tight.

'Who doesn't?' she asked.

'Of course,' I said. 'But it's only possible with them, with people like him.'

'It's not their fault,' she said, 'if the others love them for the wrong reasons.'

'No, it's not their fault. And what are "the wrong reasons"? I think you can love people for the wrongest possible reasons, I don't think that's got anything to do with it.'

'But if you don't like people whose lives are exceptional, why do you want to hear about them?'

'Because those are the sort of stories I like best.'

'Untrue ones?'

'No, interminable ones, if you like. Bottomless pits.'

'Me too,' she said.

'So I see,' I said, laughing.

She laughed too, then asked:

'If it's not that then, what is it?'

'While he was pursuing his dazzling career,' I said, 'I was sitting on my backside in the Ministry. Perhaps that's it.'

'I don't think it's that,' she said.

'He'd probably dazzle me,' I said.

'Oh no,' she said. 'But he, who's supposed to be a disgrace to mankind, and yet who looks at it with the eyes of a child – it seems to me that everyone ought to be able to love him . . .'

'Everyone does,' I said. 'They love what you've made of him . . .'

She was listening intently.

'What he's become because of you.'

'What's that?'

'An instrument of justice,' I said.

She didn't answer, but grew serious again.

'But you,' I said, 'you wouldn't be able to understand that.'

'So,' she said slowly, 'a murderer must always be alone, lost? People ought not to look for him, ever?'

'But of course not,' I said. 'And even when it's possible, even then . . .'

'If he is an instrument of justice,' she said after a moment, 'it's without knowing it.'

'But you know it,' I said. 'It's entirely because of you. Go on with the story.'

She did so, but rather reluctantly.

'Nothing very much more had happened. For years he hadn't had any other women but chance encounters. But he said that went back longer than the war, to our meeting in Marseilles. He also said that since that night he'd wanted more and more to see me again. He couldn't understand why.

'When I was there he found life worth living again. I mean that straight away he wanted ships to start leaving so that he could go away. It was I that made him want to go away, but I'd chosen that rôle a long time ago. He'd been shut up in France for four years. He'd been in the Resistance during the war, and a bit in the black market too. When I came he started to eat regularly again, and he talked about going away. He said that the police would still be on the look-out for him for at least another two years, but that was better than the life he had been leading. He couldn't get used to the idea of all the ports being closed and all the ships at a standstill. In short, as soon as I found him I knew I should lose him again. Frontiers irked him as prison bars do others, and that's not just a figure of speech. Since he'd left the *Cypris* he'd been round the world three times. I pulled his leg about it, I said that if he went on like that the world would soon seem too small for him. He used to laugh. He said no, the littleness of the world hadn't bothered him too much yet, and that its roundness delighted him. He liked the way it was made because like that when you went away from one place you necessarily got nearer to another, and when you had no home a round earth was the best kind you could have. He never said where he might come to rest one day, when time had made him immune from the law. He only talked about the journeys he would make.

'We didn't live under the same roof. As a precaution, just as if the war was still on, I rented a room by the week. I dressed very quietly. I didn't tell him my husband had left me all his money.'

Suddenly rain started to lash against the windows of the café. She lit a cigarette and watched it.

'You were certain, then, I suppose, that you'd never touch it,' I said.

'Yes,' she said. 'I even looked for a job.'

'And didn't you find one?'

'I can't type. There was a vacancy for a hostess in a night-club. I didn't take it.'

'Naturally,' I said.

'I didn't mind what I did,' she said, 'so long as it wasn't at night.'

'You can't forget it if you've got a yacht,' I said, 'and a lot of money. One day you're bound to remember . . .'

'In certain cases you can forget it,' she said. 'But not in mine.'

She turned towards the rain again and smiled at it.

'I'm not a heroine,' she said. 'If I'd given up the yacht it would only have been to salve my conscience, as they say. You can't be a hero in your own cause.'

Then she added, quietly, almost penitently:

'I know very well that everybody, everywhere, thinks the same about yachts, as a rule. They're objects of scandal. But there was this yacht doing nothing on the one hand, and on the other hand me not knowing what to do with myself . . .'

'In my American novel,' I said, 'you'll make lots of enemies with your yacht. People will say, that woman on that yacht of hers. A nice thing. That woman, that . . .'

'What?'

'That useless, idle creature . . .'

'And what else?'

'That chatterbox . . .'

'Oh.' She blushed.

'Anna,' I said.

She leaned towards me, her eyes lowered.

'You looked for a job,' I said.

'I've had enough of this story,' she said.

'All the more reason to hurry up and finish it and get it out of the way,' I said.

'I looked for a job. But I didn't have time to find one. Before I did, he'd gone. What can I tell you about what passed between us? It lasted five weeks. I would never have thought it possible. Five weeks with him. He went out every day. Where to? Oh, he walked about Paris. But he came back every evening, and every night it was the same. And there was something ready for him to eat always when he came in. I know it would have been cleverer of me to let him starve a bit, but I didn't have the heart. He'd been hungry too often already. One day he started to play poker again. He told me. I pinned my hopes on the poker. It lasted five weeks. I did the shopping and the housework and the cooking. I went for walks with him along the boulevards. I waited for him. Several times, when I was on my own, I met some of my husband's old friends. They asked me to go and see them. My grief was a good excuse for not accepting. One day I even met the only two of them who knew of his existence, the two we were with when we met him in Marseilles. They asked me what had become of him, and I told them I didn't know. No one suspected I was happy.

'He looked for work too. Once. He got taken on in an insurance company. I'd had false papers made for him. He was a salesman. After two days he didn't eat any more. His life hadn't accustomed him to the hell of the usual daily round. I persuaded him to give it up, it was a farce. Then he started going out again and playing poker, and I began to hope again.

'Sometimes we used to get tight together, and he'd say, "I'll take you to Hong Kong, Sydney. We'll go there together on a ship." And sometimes I believed him, sometimes I believed that it was possible, that perhaps it might be possible that we wouldn't be parted any more. I'd never thought that one day I might have what's called a real life, and it frightened me rather; but I let him go on talking about it. I let him believe things about himself that I knew weren't true; I loved even his mistakes, his illusions, his foolishness. Sometimes I could hardly believe that we were really living together, and when he was more than usually late back and I was anxious, alone in the room, in a way that reassured me.

'Five weeks. One day it was announced in the papers that a cargo ship belonging to the *Chargeurs Réunis* was sailing from Marseilles. I remember it was called the *Musketeer*. It was going to pick up a cargo of coffee in Madagascar. Then a second, and a tenth and then twenty ships sailed from all the ports of France that hadn't been destroyed. He stopped playing poker. He lay on the bed smoking, and he drank more and more. Suddenly I wanted him to die. One morning he told me he was going to Marseilles "just to see what was going on". He asked me to go with him. I refused. I didn't want any more of him, I wanted him to die, I wanted some peace. He didn't try to persuade me. He said he'd come back for me or write to me to join him. I agreed. He went.'

She stopped talking once more. I poured her a glass of wine. The rain was not so heavy now. The little café was so quiet you could hear yourself breathe.

'But are you sure,' I asked, 'during all those five weeks . . . are you sure you weren't . . . well, a bit bored?'

'I don't know.'

182

She added, as if surprised:
'I don't think the question arises.'
I said nothing. She went on.
'And even if I was bored, it wouldn't have mattered much.'
'After all,' I said to her, smiling, 'it's the common lot.'
'I don't understand.'
'I mean I'd have liked to see you fighting against the common lot.'
Her expression was childlike again. She frowned.
'I think that when I find him,' she said, 'it can always last five weeks.'
She thought for a moment, and resumed in a different tone:
'It seems to me,' she said, 'that like that I could live with him for five weeks every three or four years.'
'He telephoned?'
'Yes.'
'He said: "Can I see you?"'
'You can't talk about that sort of thing,' she said.
'You want to talk about it,' I said as gently as I could, 'and I want to hear you. Well then? He said: "Can I see you?"'
'Yes. He made an appointment with me to meet him an hour later in a café in the avenue d'Orléans. I took my case and left my room. I sat in the little inner room facing a mirror that reflected the bar and the door. I remember seeing myself in the glass. It was odd – I didn't recognize myself, the person I saw was...'
'...the woman who loved the sailor from Gibraltar,' I said.
'I ordered a cognac. He arrived a little while after me, about a quarter of an hour. I saw him come in in the glass, stop and look round for me. I was able to watch him find me, still in the mirror, and smile at me shyly, perhaps with a touch of anxiety. As soon as he came in through the revolving door I felt a pain in my heart. I recognized that pain. I'd had it often on the *Cypris*, when he came up on deck black with oil and dazzled by the sun. But this time I fainted. It couldn't have lasted longer than the time it took him to come from the

door over to my table. It was his voice that brought me to. I heard that he was saying something I'd never heard him say before. His voice was slightly broken, perhaps something to do with the war. I'd never fainted before in my life. When I opened my eyes and saw him bending over me I didn't believe it. I remember I touched his hand. Then for the second time he said to me: "my love". What was this strange way of talking? I looked at him and saw that he had changed a little. He was better dressed this time, in a ready-made suit that was still quite new. He wasn't wearing an overcoat, but he had a scarf. He still couldn't be eating enough – he was as thin as ever. He said, "Say something." I tried, but couldn't think of anything. I suddenly felt very tired. I remembered that in order to see him again I'd more or less killed my husband. That was the first time I realized it, even. It astounded me, I was astounded at loving him so much. He said roughly, "You must talk to me." He got hold of my hand so that it hurt. I said, "You're hurting me." Those were the first words I said to him. I don't think I could have found any that were more appropriate. He smiled and let go. Then we looked at each other closely, and we saw that there was nothing to be afraid of. That we'd make short work even of the death that was now between us, that everything was the same, it would just be easily swallowed up in our story. He asked me: "Had you left him?" I said yes. He looked at me curiously, perhaps more curiously than ever before. I remember that the neon lighting in the café was very strong and it was as if we were facing each other in the glare of projectors. His question surprised me. Then he asked: "Why now?" I said it was because of London, I couldn't bear living in London any longer. He took my hand again and squeezed it. I didn't object this time. He looked away. His hand was cold because he'd just come in and he hadn't any gloves. He said: "Ages since we met." With his hand in mine I realized that there was nothing to be done, that my happiness would always come to me through him, and everything else too, sorrow too. I said to him: "I would have done it anyway sooner or later." He picked up his cognac and drank it straight off. I went on: "He'd got so much in the habit of being depressed, and so much time on his hands to make it worse. . ." He interrupted me. "Don't." He said it was strange how much he'd wanted to see me again. We weren't looking at each other any more. We leaned against the back of the seat, staring into the glass opposite. There were a lot of people in the café. The radio was playing patriotic songs. The war was over. I said: "He was quite nice, it was the marriage that was all wrong." He said he'd been in Toulouse the day before when he saw the paper, and that he wasn't sure whether I was in Paris, but came anyway. I said: "But I don't see what else I could have done but marry him." But he went on talking about something else: "When I got back the *Cypris* had sailed half an hour before." What with the war and everything, he must have thought about me since Marseilles. "Did you lose everything?" He said: "No, I was winning. I was still winning when I left." He laughed, slightly embarrassed. I said, "Good God" . . . and I laughed too. He said: "Don't you believe me?" It wasn't that, but I hadn't known he would ever be capable of it. Neither had he. One of the other players had said what the time was, and he'd thrown down his cards and run. I said: "You're terrible." And he: "But even if I'd arrived in time, what could we have done?" I didn't answer. I remembered something and started to laugh. I said: "Do you know, his name was Nelson Nelson and he was the ball-bearings king?" His eyes widened, he was struck motionless with surprise, and he burst out laughing. "No," he kept saying, "the ball-bearings king," several times. I said he would have known if he read the papers. He said, "But I was running away, how could I?" He started to laugh again, not looking at me now, and I laughed too. He asked: "Are you sure?" I said I couldn't be absolutely sure, but who could invent a thing like the ball-bearings king? He kept repeating, delightedly: "Nelson Nelson." He gave a long burst of laughter. I liked watching him laugh . . . "If I was on the scaffold," he said, "I still couldn't help splitting my sides – the ball-bearings king." I said he was lucky it wasn't the king of billiard balls. Ah, I loved to see him laugh. He said that was true; or it might have been the king of mugs. He said in one breath, as if reciting it: "Life imprisonment for the murder of the king of mugs – if only I'd known." I asked him what he would have done. He didn't know very well, he'd have let him get away, you couldn't murder the king of billiard balls, it was ridiculous. When he'd stopped laughing a bit, I said it was those respectable friends who had turned up their noses at his envelopes that had told me. Then he remembered again: "Even if I'd got there in time, what could we have done?" I explained that I'd never aimed at being happy, as people called it, with a fixed salary coming in and the cinema every Saturday and all that. He said he knew, but just the same we'd have lost each other suddenly, at the turning of a street. Then I said it's not the same when you're expecting it to happen. He explained to me slowly that it was only after Shanghai that he realized . . . He groped for the word. I interrupted him. He wasn't surprised. He said he'd had lots of other women since we parted but it had never been any use to him. I interrupted him, and asked: "And after you gave me the photographs, did you go and play poker again?" He said no; that he'd waited outside a post-office for it to open the next morning, that he'd put in a call to Paris and had to wait a long time to get through. When they connected him, he hung up. That was all. Wasn't it rather that he decided not to go through with it? He said no, it was just that he was tired, he was sleeping in a common lodging-house, there are certain situations in which a man has to do without a woman. I didn't ask for any other explanations. I waited a bit, and then asked: "And now?" He said he had a room in a hotel. I blushed still when he looked at me. He said: "Knowing you, I can't tell whether you're all that beautiful or not. Are you?" I said yes. He added that he'd been tired in Marseilles, but that he wanted to see me again so much that when Paris came through on the 'phone he didn't know what he was doing. So that's how it happened.

'Suddenly he came close to me and undid my coat and looked at me. Then he said, "My God." And so it all started all over again.'

'And what about you?'

'I said we'd had rotten luck. And it started all over again.'

'So,' I said, 'you found your youth again, and the bewitching scent of oil-tanks, and the magic seas that flowed beneath your desire. And the neon lighting of the café, that had seemed so harsh a moment before, became a sweltering sun.'

I asked the proprietor to bring another carafe of wine.

'Forgive me,' I said, 'you like talking about these things.'

'What else can I talk about?' she said.

I didn't answer. She said, rather sadly, softly:

'Yes, it's true – I did want to talk to you about them.'

'And afterwards?'

'I told you. We lived together for five weeks and then he went.'

'And after he went?'

'That's not so amusing,' she said, trying to smile. 'I left Paris and took a room somewhere in the country. I was so depressed that it was three weeks before I came back to Paris to see if there was a letter from him. While I was still away I started to tell myself there was no point, there wouldn't be any letter. I was trying to make myself be reasonable. But just the same I did go back to Paris. No letter had come to our little furnished room. I only stayed in Paris two days, and then went back to the country. I thought I should be able to stay there for a long time, but I only stayed for a week. Then I went from one town to another towards the south, towards the Spanish frontier, and without quite meaning to, near to the village where I was born. When I got there I went to a hotel and stayed in my room until the evening. I remembered my brothers and sisters; some of them had still been quite small when I went away. Perhaps I felt some remorse. I walked through the dark to the little bistro. France had been liberated by now and the windows weren't blacked out any more. I could see right in. There were four people there: my father and mother, and a brother and sister. My father was asleep in his chair. My mother was knitting a stocking. My sister was doing the washing-up. My brother was sitting behind the counter waiting for some customers and reading the *Parisien libéré*. My sister had got older; my brother was tall and sturdy and yawned as he read the paper. I didn't go in. As soon as I saw them it was as if I'd just that moment gone away. I didn't feel any desire to talk to them, get to know them again, tell them about myself. I left again the next morning, and went back to Paris once more. My husband's place was empty. The concierge wept again when she saw me; she was a very sensitive woman. She said: "When you think of our poor gentleman." There wasn't a letter there either. The garden was neglected, and there were several panes of glass missing from the windows in my room. I paid the concierge, and told her that I was going away from Paris but would be back. Then I went back to the little room. I'd kept it on. And when I was there, in the evening, I did a thing I shouldn't have believed myself capable of. I telephoned some old friends of my husband's and asked if I could spend the evening with them. Not just anybody; the ones that had been with us when we met him in Marseilles. They invited me round. Already, on the telephone, the sound of their voices was horrible and disgusting, but just the same I went. They were very polite, and assumed the appropriate tone to ask: "We know these things are painful to talk about, but do you think you could tell us what happened?" I didn't tell them; I just left. The next day I left Paris for the third time and went to the Côte d'Azur. I rented another room, but this time overlooking the sea. It was still warm enough to bathe. I went in every day, sometimes several times. And for the first time I didn't feel an overpowering desire to go away again. I didn't have any idea what I was going to be able to do with myself. A month went by. Then, gradually, I began to regret what I'd done, to regret not having gone with him to Marseilles and even further. And then one day I remembered the yacht, and I had the idea that I might start to look for him. And to try once more, either with or without him, to make what people call a life.

'I didn't come to that decision when my desire to see him again was at its strongest. On the contrary, I think. But even so that was the thing I most wanted to do.

'I went to America, claimed the money my husband had left me, had the yacht seen to, and came away again.

'I've been looking for him now for three years. I still haven't found a clue to where he is.'

I divided the wine that was left in the carafe between us. We drank it without speaking, and then slowly smoked a cigarette.

'And now,' she said, 'now there's no more to tell.'

I called the proprietor and asked for the bill. Then I suggested we went for a walk round the town before going back on the yacht.

She neither agreed nor refused. She got up when I did and we went out of the restaurant. The weather had cleared, and it wasn't so hot. It must have been quite a heavy downpour – the streets were still wet and there were puddles where the surface was bad. Whether it was because it was later in the afternoon, or because of the storm, the town seemed almost cheerful now. There were a lot more people in the streets than when we first came. All the children were out of doors, splashing about barefoot in the puddles. It seemed to me she paid more attention to them than she had in the morning. Perhaps she was rather surprised at my saying nothing; every so often she stole a glance at me. But that didn't stop us from enjoying our walk. We walked easily, at the same pace, and in spite of our fatigue and the wine we could have gone on for hours. In spite of the times she'd fixed with Laurent before we left, too. It was already past one, but we didn't mention it, and walked farther into the town away from the port. After half an hour we came out by chance into a very busy street with shops all along either side and crowded trams running right down the middle. I spoke a few words then.

'It reminds me of that little place – Sarzana – near Rocca.'

'I went there once with Carla,' she said.

'This is the sort of place I like best. I like everything that's deprived.'

'How do you mean?'

'One-horse towns, awkward situations. I don't like privileged towns, or privileged situations, or anything at all that's privileged.'

I smiled.

'I think you may be exaggerating,' she said.

'Oh no,' I said. 'I'm sure of it.'

She hesitated a moment, then asked:

'And could you say why?'

'It's a question of character,' I said. 'You feel more comfortable in places like this. But there must be some other explanation too.'

'And you don't know what it is?'

'I'm trying to find out.'

She didn't pursue it. I pressed her arm and said:

'I think I'm glad I came.'

She looked rather suspicious, probably because of the tone in which I said it, and didn't answer. I went on:

'If you like we'll come ashore again the next time.'

'If you like.'

She relaxed, and added smiling:

'But I shan't have anything more to tell you.'

'We can always talk about something else,' I said.

She smiled frankly.

'Do you think so?'

'I'm sure. Everyone's got something to say, everyone's got his story, hasn't he?'

'You know, don't you,' she said slowly, 'that everything's always possible? I mean it's always possible that he might be at the corner of the next street?'

'I know,' I said. 'He might even be back on board waiting for us.'

'Yes,' she said, only half laughing. 'That's what it's like when you look for someone.'

'I know. But I'm sure the sailor from Gibraltar is a very understanding sort of chap.'

She walked on for a moment without speaking.

'It's strange,' she said, 'but I never ask myself what I'd do if I found him.'

'Never?'

'Hardly ever.'

'There's a time for everything,' I said. We laughed.

'I can't think any further than the moment when I see him again,' she said. 'The moment when he's standing there in front of me.'

'It must be beyond the time limit now,' I said, 'they can't arrest him now. It's a free man you're looking for, isn't it?'

'Yes. Another man, almost.'

'And yet you still look for him in ports, the places where criminals go.'

I laughed rather like Bruno when he said she was having everyone on. She took it very well.

'You can't look everywhere at once,' she said.

We'd left the shopping street and come to the edge of the town. We could see it gradually petering out among the fields of maize.

'There's no help for it,' I said. 'We shall have to go back.'

We walked right back across the town. It didn't take long – hardly twenty minutes all the way to the harbour. Just before we got there she said:

'When you talk to me, what will you say?'

'Everything you expect me to,' I said. 'I shan't stop.'

We got to the harbour. The crew were annoyed.

'You do go a bit far,' said Laurent. 'I wonder why you bother to draw up schedules at all.'

But he wasn't really cross. She apologized:

'I don't know either,' she said. 'I suppose it's because it looks more serious.'

She went off with Laurent and I saw them go into the bar. Sometimes they had things to talk about that didn't concern me. I went out on the deck, over by the winch, and lay down in my usual place. It was late, and none of the men was on this part of the deck. The ship sailed almost at once. It moved slowly away from the quay towards the mouth of the harbour, but there, instead of turning south, it turned right about. So in a few minutes I had turned right round too, and suddenly found myself looking ahead at the island of Elba. She hadn't said anything to me, and the surprise made me laugh. She must have just given the order to head north for Sète, where Epaminondas and the sailor from Gibraltar were waiting. It did just occur to me that she might at least tell people. The ship gathered speed. Elba gradually faded in the distance on the port side, as we left the south behind us. The ship was still increasing speed. I think it must have been going at full steam, or at any rate faster than at any other time since we'd left Rocca. She wanted to make up the time she'd lost telling me the story of the sailor from Gibraltar. The sea was perfect – fantastically beautiful. The sun set. But this time I didn't see darkness fall. The sky was still light when I fell asleep, though we must already have left Italy far behind.

When I woke up she was sitting beside me. It was quite dark.

'I slept too,' she said. 'Do you feel like coming and having something to eat?'

I must have slept very deeply, and for a long time.

While I slept I had forgotten that she existed. Now I suddenly remembered, I recognized her by her voice. We could hardly see each other. I sat up and put my arms round her and pulled her down on the deck beside me. I clasped her tight, suddenly, as one sometimes does on waking. I don't remember much of what happened or for how long I held her close, pressed against me in the dark.

'What's happening to us?' she whispered.

'Nothing.' I suddenly let her go.

'Yes, there is.'

'Nothing,' I said. 'I slept too long.'

I stood up and took her to the dining-room. The light was dazzling after the darkness outside. Her eyes were wide, and more astonished than I'd have thought they needed to be. I'd thought she already understood what was happening. Laurent and another sailor were in the dining-room. They'd finished their meal and were talking.

'At this rate we'll soon be at Sète,' said the other man.

Laurent didn't answer. She talked to them a bit about Epaminondas, her mind obviously on something else. The other sailor, whose name was Albert, advised her to take Epaminondas on the yacht. Neither he nor Laurent mentioned the message he'd sent. The other sailor said there wasn't anybody like Epaminondas. She agreed and promised to take him on, and then quite suddenly stopped talking to them. When our eyes met we looked down. We couldn't speak to each other. It was so obvious I think Laurent must have noticed it. He quickly went out. Two other sailors came in just afterwards. One switched on the radio. Someone was talking about the reconstruction in Italy. She took a pencil out of the pocket of her trousers and wrote 'Come' on the paper table-cloth. I laughed, and said softly, no, not every night, it wasn't possible. She neither laughed nor asked again. She said goodnight to the two sailors and went out.

I left the bar immediately afterwards and went to my cabin. I didn't even have the strength to lie down. In the mirror I could see someone gnawing at his handkerchief to stop himself from calling. She came almost immediately after I entered the cabin.

'Why not every night?' she said.

I didn't answer.

'Why?' she said. 'Even if . . .' She smiled. 'Why can't you be with me every night, the same as if I was anyone else?'

'In a few days' time,' I said.

Perhaps it was still looking at her that I enjoyed more than anything.

'If I'd known,' she said, 'I'd have told *you* I was on a cruise as well.'

The idea of this made us laugh. She sat on the edge of my bunk, her arms round her knees.

'It's just a story like any other,' she said. 'You must have misunderstood.'

'It's not that,' I said. 'The story itself is rather conventional.'

She smiled, rather mockingly. She wasn't properly balanced on the edge of the bunk and her sandals fell off on to the floor.

'What is it then?'

'It's not the story. It's just that it's very tiring.'

She looked down and gazed, like me, at her bare feet. She stayed like that for some time, then, in quite a different tone, quite conversationally, she asked again:

'Tell me, then, what's happening to us?'

'Nothing's happening to us.'

Probably I spoke rather harshly. She still smiled.

'I said I'd been asleep just now,' she said. 'But it wasn't true. I couldn't sleep.'

'Well,' I said, 'that's one good reason for going to bed early tonight.'

She ignored this.

'You know,' she said, 'there's a great difference between saying things and not saying them.'

'So you told me. But I didn't know the difference was all that great.'

'I did.' Then she added, sensibly: 'You must find yourself something to do on board.'

'I'm going to fish for herring.'

She didn't even smile.

'Go back to your cabin.' I must have almost shouted. But I might not have spoken as far as she was concerned. She put her head in her hands and kept it there as if she never intended to move again.

'It's true,' she said in a low voice. 'There's a great difference. One's always learning something one thought one already knew.'

'You're crazy.'

She looked up and said with tranquil irony:

'But you do know, don't you, that we shall be able to talk to one another in the end?'

'Oh yes, we'll talk to one another,' I said. 'We'll be a nice little happy family, illegal and temporary of course. Go back to your cabin.'

'I'm going,' she said. 'Don't worry.'

'One day,' I said, 'when you're a bit less crazy, I'll tell you a nice long story that'll make you laugh. Endless, it is.'

'What's it about?'

'What do you think?'

She lowered her eyes. I stayed by the door so as not to go to her. She could see this quite well.

'Now,' she said. 'Tell it now.'

'It's much too soon – how can I? But before long I'll tell you the main features. And I'll teach you the art of hunting him. It will be endless.'

'The art of hunting him,' she said, in some surprise. 'No one in the world can teach me anything about that.'

'I think I can,' I said. 'About the art of hunting him together. Go back to your cabin.'

She got up, put on her sandals meekly, and went back to her cabin. I took a blanket and went out to sleep on deck.

It was the cold that woke me again. We had just rounded Cape Corsica; it must have been a little while after five. You could smell the scent of the maquis in the wind. I stayed on deck until sunrise. I saw Corsica disappear on the horizon; the scent of the maquis grew fainter and fainter and died away. Then I went to my cabin. I stayed there, half asleep, for most of the morning. Then I went back up on deck. I didn't see her until midday, at lunch. She looked quite calm; cheerful, even. We avoided talking to each other or being left alone together in the bar. I was sorry we'd established the habit of always eating at the same table. But now it was impossible to do anything else, if only because the sailors were there and could see us. I left her straight after lunch and went to see Laurent, who was on duty that day in the wheel-house. We talked about this and that. Not about her. About the sailor from Gibraltar. About Nelson Nelson. I'd been there half an hour when she came along. She seemed a little surprised to find me there but didn't show it much. For the first time since I'd met her she gave the impression of not quite knowing what to do with herself. She sat down at Laurent's feet and joined in our conversation. We were just talking about Nelson Nelson and laughing.

'They say he used to give his victims a pension for life, a handsome one,' said Laurent. 'So he got a reputation for generosity. The arrangement had two advantages. He had to drive fast on business sometimes, and he'd worked it out that it was cheaper to run someone over now and again than to go slowly.'

'You've got plenty of imagination,' she laughed.

'I read it somewhere,' said Laurent. 'He had twenty-five victims to his credit. With all that practice he couldn't have been far out in his reckoning with your sailor from Gibraltar.'

'Far enough,' I said. 'What a dilemma to be in, though, when you come to think of it. Wouldn't anyone have done what Nelson Nelson did?'

We all laughed, especially she and I. But it was evident

that we wouldn't have felt like laughing in the least if Laurent hadn't been there.

'The whole point was that he got him out of the dilemma,' she said.

'But could anybody say what poor old Nelson ought to have done if he'd had another chance?'

'That's no excuse,' she said. 'I think – and I've thought about it a lot – that the only thing left for him to do was to die. He'd made plenty of ball-bearings already – he was the king of them. All the cars in the world ran about on Nelson ball-bearings, didn't they? Well, as there was no chance of the earth itself ever needing them to help it turn on its axis, his imagination could only go round in circles, so to speak. That's why he died – lack of imagination.'

'You're in good form,' said Laurent.

'Why didn't he say, for example: "Between you and me I've had about enough of ball-bearings. I'm going to take this opportunity and turn over a new leaf, give generously, just out of the kindness of my heart." He'd have run like a hare.'

She stopped and lit a cigarette.

'Or else,' she went on, 'if he'd just said: "It hurts me to see that young head bleeding." That wouldn't have cost him a penny, and he'd still have been as good as new today.'

'Not like you,' said Laurent.

'No,' she said. 'In fact it all hung on a word . . .'

'You'd have thought of something else,' said Laurent. 'I've no doubt about that.'

'It wasn't only the ball-bearings,' I said.

No one answered.

'It couldn't have been,' I said. 'What else was it?'

'Steel,' she said. 'Always steel. The steel ball-bearings are made of, or yachts . . .'

She saw I wanted to hear more.

'He was the only son of a very rich family who'd made their money all out of steel.'

'But he wasn't a man of steel,' said Laurent. 'He was ashamed of it.'

'He'd run away from home,' she said. 'Gone to sea. In that sort of family, you know . . .' She smiled. 'But as we've seen, steel still bound them together . . .'

'Even if only the steel the yacht was made of,' I said.

'Not a man of steel, an innocent of steel,' said Laurent. 'But it's in good hands now, anyway,' he added, laughing.

She laughed heartily, still not looking at me.

'Still,' she said, 'it's not every day people take such a lot of trouble over murderers.'

'Oh,' said Laurent again, 'I've no doubt you'd have thought of something else, even without a murderer . . .'

'All you need is a nice obsession,' I said. 'Nothing like it.'

'What for?'

She leaned towards me.

'A good excuse,' I said.

'What for?'

'Travelling,' I laughed.

Laurent began to sing to himself. We didn't talk any more. Then, suddenly, she went away, and I stayed with Laurent. For an hour, practically without speaking. Then I went away too. I didn't go to my cabin, but back to the part of the deck by the winch. I didn't sleep. When I went into the dining-room she was just going out. She didn't even glance at me.

Again that night I slept on deck, so as not to have to wait for her in my cabin. As on the day before, and the day before that, it was the dawn that woke me. It was a whole day since I'd seen her alone. But I was as tired as if we'd slept together. I went and leaned on the rail. We'd reached the French coast, and were sailing along quite close to the shore. The little ports went by one after another, the strings of lamps in the boulevards lighting up the sea. I didn't look. I leaned my head against the rail and closed my eyes. I felt then as if I wasn't thinking about anything at all, but was full of her image, right down to the tips of my fingers. She was asleep in her cabin, and I couldn't think of anything else but her sleeping. The towns going by were nothing else but objects near which she slept. I began to think that I wasn't going to be able to hold out much longer against such violent desire, that soon I would have to speak to her. I stayed there a long while with my head on the rail. And then the sun rose. I went down to my cabin almost without meaning to, drunk with imagining her asleep. She was there. She must have waited for me a long time and finally gone to sleep. On the bedside table stood a bottle of whisky. An outrageous woman. She was asleep with all her clothes on, the sheet wrapped round her, her sandals fallen on the floor, her legs uncovered. She couldn't have drunk much whisky; the bottle had hardly been touched. But she was sleeping very deeply. I lay down on the floor, on the mat; I didn't want her to wake, and I avoided looking at her for too long. It was important to me, her rest.

Once I was there, knowing she was there too, I managed to sleep a little. I woke before she did. I was fully dressed as well. I crept out of the cabin and went to the dining-room, where I drank a lot of coffee. All the crew were on deck. It was nine o'clock. We were getting to Toulon. I'd been asleep hardly four hours. When I went out on deck I was dazzled as I had been the day before, every day. I was probably still not used to the light from the sea.

I went ashore at Toulon for as long as the yacht was there – an hour. I didn't ask her to come. I didn't know whether I was going to come back on board. But I did. In spite of our putting in to Toulon the day seemed endless. I spent the whole time in my cabin. She didn't come to find me. I saw her at dinner. She looked as calm as she had the day before, but in her eyes there was a sort of painful fatigue I'd never seen in her before. Someone, one of the sailors, asked her if she was ill.

She said no. That night too she went quickly to her cabin. I followed her immediately.

'I was expecting you,' she said.

'I don't quite know what I want,' I said.

'You must sleep on deck,' she said slowly.

I stood near her as she lay on the bunk. I think I was trembling.

'Talk to me,' she said.

'I can't.'

I tried to laugh.

'I've never really talked to anyone. I don't know how to.'

'That doesn't matter,' she said.

'We're crazy. I'm getting to be crazy too.'

This time it was she who asked me to go.

I didn't sleep very much, but that night I did sleep in my cabin. And I woke up just as early as the day before. Scalding hot coffee always after sleepless nights – on that ship they knew there must always be coffee ready for those who'd slept badly. Bruno came over to me. He was wearing a peculiar expression.

'You're not well,' he said.

I reassured him, leaning against the door of the bar.

'It's the light,' I said. 'I'm not used to it.'

He pointed to the coast, laughing.

'Sète. We'll be there in half an hour. We'll have to wake her up.'

I asked him why he was looking so cheerful.

'I'm beginning to see the funny side of it,' he said.

Laurent came up and heard what he said.

'About time too,' said Laurent. 'The face he's been pulling ever since Sicily.'

'Do you still mean to leave the ship at Sète?'

'Well,' said Bruno, 'I don't know, if you can see the funny side of it, perhaps it's possible to stay on a bit. It's a question of how you look at things.'

She came on deck soon after I did, and called me from the

door of the bar. We said good morning quite pleasantly, and for the first time she asked me how I was. She was dressed as usual in her black jumper and slacks, but she hadn't done her hair yet and it hung down on her shoulders. I said I was well but hadn't slept much. She didn't ask any more questions. She drank two cups of coffee standing by the door, then went out on deck and looked at the town. She said good morning to Bruno, who was also watching the town and still laughing. I knew she'd been anxious about Bruno, and she was pleased to see him laughing. She joined in. It looked as if they were laughing at the town; it was very strange.

'Aren't you leaving us at Sète then?'

'Perhaps not yet,' said Bruno. 'Ever since I've heard about Epaminondas I've been wanting to get to know him a bit.'

'I'd be glad,' she said, 'if you stayed on for a while.'

We were about a hundred yards from a dock. A man came on to the quay and made signs at the ship. She answered him, laughing. I came over to her.

'You'll see,' she said, 'there's no one like Epaminondas.'

'Or like you,' said Bruno, laughing still. You'd have said he'd been drinking all night.

She left us to go and do her hair. By the time the boat drew in, she was back.

Epaminondas was young and handsome and of Greek origin. I could see from the look he gave her that he still remembered his time on the yacht very well. The first thing I noticed about him was not so much his face as a strange tattoo-mark that showed through his open shirt, over the heart. It was in the shape of a heart itself, placed exactly over his and pierced right through by a dagger. Under the blade, in a frozen shower of blood, a name was written. It began with the letter A. I couldn't see the rest. As he was excited at seeing her again, the tattooed heart beat rapidly with his own, and the dagger leapt spasmodically in the wound. It must have been a great passion of his youth. I shook his hand warmly, too warmly perhaps. She noticed my attempts to see the tattoo-mark better, and she smiled, looking at me for the first time since Piombino. She smiled almost as if she wanted to reassure me, as if she knew we would eventually overcome our difficulties. As if it was just a question of patience and goodwill – yes, just a question of goodwill. We had a drink in the bar after Epaminondas had exchanged profuse greetings with the crew, especially Laurent, whom he'd been particularly friendly with. No doubt Epaminondas would have preferred to be alone with her, but she insisted on my staying with them. We opened a bottle of champagne. Epaminondas looked at me too, but his curiosity was less avid than mine. He must have seen several others before me, and this sort of thing no longer surprised him. In any case I didn't at all mind being regarded as one of the things necessary to a woman's existence. Anyway, Epaminondas's curiosity was soon satisfied. He began his account of what had happened.

Epaminondas had changed his job and become a lorry-driver between Sète and Montpellier. It was in the course of his work that he had come across the sailor from Gibraltar. The sailor from Gibraltar could also be said to have changed his job. He kept a service station on the motorway between Sète and Montpellier. She smiled when she heard this, and so did I. As soon as Epaminondas started to speak I was seized with an irresistible cheerfulness. He told his story very well. He apologized for having to tell her about the service station, but, he said, sailors from Gibraltar did what they could and not always exactly what they wanted – it wasn't quite the same for them as for other men. The service station was an ultra-modern one with a good trade and must bring in a fair amount. According to what people said, the sailor from Gibraltar was manager and even part-owner.

He was known as Pierrot this time. Everyone in the *département* knew Pierrot, but no one knew where he came from. It was only three years since he'd arrived in Hérault – just after the Liberation, in fact. Pierrot probably wasn't his real name, but as no one, even you, he said to her, knows the sailor from Gibraltar's real name, what did it matter? What was more relative than names, proper or otherwise? Wasn't he, Epaminondas himself, known as Heracles to everyone in Sète? – and, he said ironically, he had never been able to find out why. She agreed. Pierrot had a lot of customers, he went on. What else? He was French, and as far as he'd been able to tell from his accent he must have spent some time in Montmartre. Pierrot was exceptionally good with his hands. On Sundays you saw him go by in an American car that he'd picked up for a song and patched up so that it did a hundred and twenty kilometres an hour without turning a hair. Another peculiarity was that Pierrot wasn't known to have any regular girls. He had plenty of irregular ones – and plenty of lady customers, the rich, idle, unsatisfied wives of Hérault wine-growers. But he wasn't married, and lived alone. One day Epaminondas had asked him why, and Pierrot had said something that Epaminondas would rather not have had to tell Anna.

'I had one once,' Pierrot had said – Epaminondas blushed and guffawed –'but she took it out of me so much I don't feel like starting all over again.'

All three of us laughed. Epaminondas apologized again – but he had to tell the whole truth, hadn't he?

Epaminondas had been struck the very first time he saw Pierrot. Although at that time there was no connection as far as he knew, although the idea never so much as entered his head, he was struck by him. Why? He couldn't really say. Was it his distant, even melancholy manner, like the hero of a film? His dashing way of driving? His success with women? His solitude and the mystery that surrounded him? How is it that you sometimes seem to recognize someone you've never seen before? Where do such convictions come from? Can you explain them without damaging them for ever?

Every day Epaminondas passed Pierrot's service station on his way to pick up his vegetables in the market at Montpellier (he transported vegetables in his lorry). He went by at about eleven o'clock at night, and Pierrot didn't shut till midnight. Epaminondas often stopped for a chat. But Pierrot was a man of so few words – that was another striking thing, wasn't it? – that it took him weeks to start to get to know him.

But even though he'd only started, that meant that Epaminondas knew more about Pierrot than the rest of the *département*, who didn't know anything about him at all. For six months he'd been stopping four times a week – that was the best he could manage – at the service station. The first thing he found out was that Pierrot used to be at sea. Once he knew that, things had begun to move a bit faster. They got into the habit, every time Epaminondas dropped in, of talking about the various places they'd both been to on their travels. At this point Epaminondas explained that he'd thought it . . . what should he say? . . . more tactful not to tell Pierrot the circumstances in which he'd made his voyages. That was right, wasn't it? Yes, that was right, she said. Naturally, one day they came to talk about Gibraltar.

Epaminondas asked Pierrot if he knew it.

'What sailor doesn't,' Pierrot had replied.

Epaminondas agreed.

'It's in a good position,' Pierrot had continued. To Epaminondas his smile had seemed significant.

That was as far as it went that evening; Epaminondas hadn't pressed the matter. He hadn't like to raise it again for another week. Perhaps he might have waited longer, but he couldn't contain his curiosity.

'A nice spot, Gibraltar,' Epaminondas had said.

'Maybe,' Pierrot had answered. 'It depends how you look at it. Anyhow, strategically it's better than anything anyone could ever have invented.'

'It's a strange place too,' Epaminondas had continued.

'I don't quite understand what you're getting at,' Pierrot had answered. 'I don't see what you mean.'

As he said it he wore a strange smile, stranger than before. How can I describe it? How could I describe your smile? Epaminondas asked her. Those are things you can't describe.

One thing was certain and that was that Gibraltar appealed to Pierrot's imagination, and Epaminondas had found him more communicative about those straits than on any other subject.

'If you look at that rock on the map, right at the entrance to the Mediterranean,' he'd said, 'then you believe in God – or in the devil, according to how you're made.'

Wasn't it a rare thing to find someone with such strong personal opinions about a strait? Anna got up and kissed Epaminondas.

And that wasn't all, went on Epaminondas, encouraged. First of all one evening he'd heard Pierrot whistling one of the songs they sing in the Foreign Legion, and although of course a lot of old sailors knew these songs it did corroborate the rest. Then, another evening, Epaminondas's dynamo broke down and he'd had a very interesting conversation with Pierrot on the subject. Epaminondas, in order not to waste such an opportunity, had pretended that the breakdown, which had really happened the day before, had only just occurred, and that he couldn't go any further without having it seen to.

'If it's only the ball-bearings,' Pierrot had said, 'I might be able to fix it. I know something about them.'

He'd set to work rather nervously, Epaminondas thought. He dismantled the dynamo. The bearings were completely worn, and he replaced them. As soon as he'd finished Epaminondas tried to get him to talk.

'Jolly useful invention, ball-bearings, when you come to think of it,' said Epaminondas. 'I don't know anything about them, though.'

'It's the same as everything else,' Pierrot replied. 'Unless it's your job . . .'

He'd said 'job' rather strangely. Epaminondas saw some

205

connection between this and the idea of the murder, or rather execution of Nelson Nelson. Perhaps this was a bit far fetched, but still . . .

'Whoever invented ball-bearings,' Epaminondas went on, 'he was no mug.'

'Perhaps not,' Pierrot had said, 'but I'm ready for bed.'

Epaminondas apologized for keeping him up so late, but pressed the matter just a bit farther.

'You've got to admit it's ingenious,' he'd said.

'You're a bit late in the day with your admiration,' said Pierrot. 'They were invented twenty years ago. Besides, it's ten past twelve.'

It didn't seem important, but Epaminondas saw this refusal to continue the conversation as a vague proof that it meant something to him.

He ended his account. That was all he'd been able to do, he said, as if he were under some inescapable obligation, wherever he was, to send her a message, to recognize, to find again at all costs, a sailor from Gibraltar. He apologized for not having been able to do any better this time, to bring her other evidence than this, which, he admitted, was more a matter of intuition than of fact. But, he added, he didn't think what he'd been able to tell her was negligible, for all that. I remembered her having told me that this was the third message Epaminondas had sent her in two years. I'd looked and listened closely while he spoke, and laughed a good deal too. But I'm sure I believed him. And now that he'd finished, and hardly believed in his story any more himself, and suddenly suspected himself of having made it up so that she should come and see him in Sète, because he'd had enough of the journey between Sète and Montpellier and would like to go to sea again, I still believed in his sincerity. She did too, I think. It was unmistakable. If he seemed a bit crestfallen mightn't it also have been that he found it impossible to communicate this sense of recognition that he had felt, impossible to give an account of it, even to her?

He waited for her to speak, his eyes on the ground. She asked the usual questions.

'What colour is his hair – brown?'

'Yes. Slightly curly.'

'And his eyes?'

'Very blue.'

'Very very blue?'

'If they'd just been blue I wouldn't have noticed. Yes, very very blue.'

'Well, well.' She thought for a moment.

'Really so blue that you notice them right away?'

'Right away. As soon as you see them you say to yourself, well, you don't often see a pair of eyes as blue as that.'

'What sort of blue? Like your shirt? Like the sea?'

'Like the sea.'

'And what sort of height?'

'Difficult to say. A bit taller than me.'

'Stand up.'

She got up too. They stood side by side. Anna's hair came to the top of Epaminondas's ear.

'I come up to the same height on him as you do on me,' said Epaminondas.

She put her hand up to that height, above Epaminondas's head, and considered it for some time.

'It would be strange,' she said, 'if you could be as mistaken as that.'

She thought again.

'And his voice?'

'Rather as if he always had a cold.'

I laughed, and so did Epaminondas, and so did she, but less.

'Is that noticeable right away too?'

'I noticed it right away.'

She put her hand to her forehead.

'You're not just having me on?'

Epaminondas didn't reply. Suddenly, like me, he saw that

she'd grown very pale. It had happened all at once after he had spoken of his voice. No one laughed now.

'Why not a service station?' she said in a low voice.

She stood up and said she was going there. She went down into the hold through the hatch by the door of the bar. The two cars belonging to the yacht were kept there. I went after her. Epaminondas seemed to hesitate, then he went down on to the quay to tell Laurent to wind down the door of the hold. It was very dark down there. She didn't switch on the lights. She turned suddenly towards me and threw herself into my arms. She was trembling so much I thought she was crying, but when I lifted up her chin I saw that it was laughter. We'd only drunk one bottle of champagne and it usually took much more than that to make her drunk. A deafening noise started up – Laurent winding down the door. She couldn't tear herself away from me, and it was very hard for me to let her go. The door began to open. The hold got a little lighter. We were still in one another's arms, she laughing, I unable to let her go. As she'd got her eyes shut she didn't see that the hold was opening up and that we should soon be in full view. I tried to push her away, but still I couldn't. I'd been sleeping alone, away from her, for two days. Suddenly Epaminondas's head appeared, as if cut off by the upper edge of the door. I thrust her away. Epaminondas looked at us, then turned his head and went away. She went over to the car nearest the door of the hold. To reach it she had to go round the other one. She knocked into it and fell full length against the mud-guard. Then, instead of getting up, she lay there with her arm round the car. Laurent and Bruno looked at her through the open door, and Epaminondas came back and looked too. At first I didn't think of helping her up. She lay flat on the wing of the car, her hands gripping the edge, and I had the feeling that she was resting, and that it was necessary that she should be left. Then Bruno shouted something, and only then, alarmed, I ran to her and lifted her up. I asked her if she'd hurt herself, and she said no. She got into the car and started the engine; her face was concentrated and calm. And then I was afraid. I shouted to her, but, perhaps because of the sound of the engine, she seemed not to hear. I called to her again. She drove across the door, which now lay between the floor of the hold and the quay, and then away. I ran to the entrance to the hold and shouted her name a last time. She didn't turn round. She disappeared behind the railings of the quay. I got into the other car and started it up. Laurent came running up, followed by Epaminondas and Bruno. They'd heard me calling her.

'What's the matter?' said Laurent.

'I'm going for a drive.'

'Do you want me to come?'

I didn't. Epaminondas was pale. He looked as if he'd just woken out of a long sleep. He was standing in front of the car.

'What?' said Bruno. 'Is it . . .?'

'Ask him,' said Epaminondas, pointing to me with an expression at once terrified and proud.

I shouted to him to let me pass. Laurent dragged him away by the arm. I saw Bruno still shrugging his shoulders. He told Epaminondas they'd have to let us sort it out for ourselves. I think Laurent went for him.

I caught her up on the way out of Sète, in a narrow street where a market slowed down the traffic. I followed her. She couldn't see me because she had to concentrate going through the market. She drove well – easily and accurately. At one point I was only about ten yards behind her. We got on to the road to Montpellier. She accelerated. Her car was probably more powerful than mine, but I managed to keep up with her, within about a couple of hundred yards. It must have been a lovely day. I don't know why I was following her – probably because I just couldn't have stayed on the ship waiting for her. I could see her quite plainly. Sometimes I almost overtook her; I was only keeping fifty yards between us. She had a green scarf over her hair. Between the scarf and the black jumper there would be room to kill her. Just before she got there she started to drive very fast, and she kept up the same speed all the way to the service station. I had difficulty then keeping up with her. But it didn't last long: a quarter of an hour after we'd left Sète, at a seventeen kilometre post that Epaminondas had told us about, Pierrot's marvellous red petrol pumps appeared. There were three cars already standing in the covered forecourt. She slowed down, turned neatly, and fell in line behind them. I also slowed down, turned, and fell in line a few yards behind her. She still hadn't seen me; at least I didn't think so. She had her back to me and I could still see only the back of her neck between the green scarf and the black jumper. She switched off her engine. The man stood a few yards away, serving petrol, his eyes on the gauge of a pump. She propped herself up on her seat, looked at him for a couple of seconds, and fell back again rather abruptly. The first car in the queue moved off. The man moved to the second, and saw her. He looked at her too. All that happened was that he went on looking. He showed no sign of recognition. I hadn't been able to see her expression. His seemed to be directed towards a beautiful woman travelling alone, but whom he didn't know. He filled the tank of the second car quite calmly, looking at her from time to time. He couldn't have been all that young. But I couldn't see him very well. She was between us, and her presence filled the air with flame. I could only see a blur of a face, as if it was decomposed by fire.

Then it was her turn. She didn't seem to notice. As far as I could judge it looked as if she'd gone to sleep. The man came over and said, smiling:

'Move along, please.'

He was a few yards away from me, right in the sun. And suddenly, at last, I could look at him, I saw him. I recognized him, recognized the sailor from Gibraltar. Of course she hadn't got a photograph of him and I'd never imagined what his face was like at all, but I had no need of such aids. I recognized him as, without knowing them, you recognize the sea

. . . or innocence. It lasted a few seconds, then it was over. I recognized nobody. It wasn't his expression, it was anybody's. Soon it was entirely covered by the shadow of the common resignation. You could only be mistaken about it for a few seconds. But that was enough – as she told me later – for her almost to have fainted again when she saw him. She moved slowly up to the pump keeping close to the kerb. A car drew up behind me. I followed her to make room for it.

She was still clutching the wheel.

'Twenty litres,' she said.

I recognized her voice although I could hardly hear it. The man's face was entirely his own again by now. He was looking at her with a sort of coarse boldness made up of cynicism, confidence, and curiosity. How had it been possible for that wild resemblance to be born – or, who knows, reborn – in his face, even for a couple of seconds?

When it was really time for her to drive off, she got out of the car. She turned her head and saw me, but she must have known I was there, for she showed no surprise. She was smiling in a way I'd never seen her smile ever since I'd known her – drawn, insistent. She was telling me that she hadn't been able to forget my existence for a second, even while she still thought she had found him again, and she was apologizing to me for having to admit that this was so. I made a great effort not to call out to her. She turned quickly towards the man. From behind she seemed to me very curiously dressed, in her black slacks and black cotton jumper. Wouldn't her face frighten the man away now? But he didn't appear at all inclined to run away.

'I'd like you to check my tyres,' she said.

I couldn't understand why she wanted to stay. I had to make an effort to remind myself that for years she had only had chance encounters with men, and that it was a sort of duty for her to preserve this habit, a sort of fidelity. The man looked at her with avid curiosity. But he was losing some of his assurance. Perhaps he suddenly felt that there was something going on between her and me.

'Pull over to the side,' he said. 'I'll have to serve the others first.'

He nodded towards the other customers, me among them. She got back in the car and parked it on one side, clumsily.

'I've got plenty of time,' she said.

It was my turn to move forward. I was very close to the man. He had nothing in common now with the man I'd seen a few minutes before. He seemed childish to me in his ignorance of what he had almost become a moment before, both for her and for me.

'Ten litres,' I said.

He scarcely looked at me. No, he hadn't begun to understand what was going on. He served me absent-mindedly. He was in a hurry to get rid of his other customers so that he could attend to the woman.

I drove off towards Montpellier, leaving her alone with him.

I still had thirty kilometres to go to Montpellier. The car was going well. The speedometer rose to a hundred, a hundred and ten, a hundred and twenty. I did my best to keep it at a hundred and twenty. I'd never driven so fast before in my life, and the road was bad, so I had to concentrate hard. It was only when I passed or overtook another car, or slowed down for a bend, that I remembered that she must still be there alone with the man, and her smile when she turned and looked at me.

When I was halfway there I stopped. I had nothing to do, and I didn't want to go back yet. I lit a cigarette. Her smile came back to me, I saw it as clearly as if she was smiling at me then. My forehead was suddenly covered with sweat. I saw her again, and again. Then I tried not to see her any more, to think about something else, to deny myself that happiness, to remember for instance that she was alone with the man inside the service station, that she had nothing on under her black jumper, and made very little of taking it off. But her smile prevailed. It kept shining on me, sweeping everything I could think of away with its strength.

I started up again towards Montpellier. On the outskirts of the town I stopped again, then drove on into the suburbs. There I left the car by the side of the road and went into the first bistro I saw. I had one, two, three cognacs. Then I spoke to the proprietor.

'Marvellous day.'

I'd just noticed it, thanks to the brandies and the cool inside the bistro.

'Yes indeed. A wonderful September we're having.'

He didn't speak with the local accent, but in a very polished way, quite unexpected. My desire to talk evaporated. I had a fourth cognac, paid, and went off down a narrow path that led to the right just past the bistro. I didn't know what to do with myself. My desire to see her again was as strong as the first time on the beach, but I had to wait until she'd finished with the man at the service station. Because of the brandies I thought even more forcibly than before that she was perhaps just taking off her black jumper, but it was bearable. I walked on. There were paving stones strewn all along the path, which must have been brought there to make proper pavements, and then just abandoned because of the war. Seeing them there I sat down on one of them after I'd gone about five hundred yards. I sat and waited. A factory hooter went off in the distance. Noon. No cars came down this way, only an occasional bicycle. The path led to a group of small houses surrounded by garden plots, very poor, with a few sparse and already withering acacias growing round them. Most of the houses were made of wood with tarpaulin roofs. Lines of washing hanging up on wires vaguely indicated the boundaries between them. The clatter of saucepans and crockery mingled with the sound of chiding voices. The people who lived in the houses were having their lunch.

Suddenly I realized I wasn't the only one on the path. Two

children were going to and fro in front of me. The elder looked about ten, and was walking his brother up and down in a push-chair between the turning I had come down and a rubbish dump about thirty yards farther on, with nettles and bits of old iron sprouting out of it. Beyond there was a short line of hedge, and then a field with two football posts without nets, stretching as far as the motor-way and its stream of cars. There was a smell of decomposition in the air.

Since my arrival the little boy had shortened his route so as to go past me as often as possible. I intrigued him. The little one was asleep, his head flopping to and fro. A transparent thread ran from his nose to where it was arrested by the curve of his upper lip. His hair, wiry and unkempt, fell in his eyes; some of it had actually been caught between his eyelashes. Late summer flies buzzed round his face persistently without waking him up. The elder child stopped from time to time and looked at me. He was barefoot and thin, with dull, tousled hair. He was wearing a little girl's overall. His head was small and compact. They were the most forgotten objects you could imagine. My stillness made the elder brother bolder. He left the little one a few yards away, and came towards me step by step, almost without realizing it, reassured by my immobility. This went on for some time. He examined me rather as he would have done some terrifying but irresistibly novel object. I looked up and smiled at him. I must have done it too abruptly, for he fell back a step. He was extraordinarily shy. I stayed still again so as not to frighten him away.

'Hello,' I said very gently.

'Hello,' he said.

He grew a little more confident. He spotted a stone about ten yards away from me and sat down on it. I took out a cigarette and smoked it. The shade of the acacia was scanty, and it was hot. I saw that the child had forgotten his brother. The push-chair was right in the sun, and the baby was still asleep with his face tilted up right towards it.

'Don't leave him right in the sun like that,' I said.

He got up as if he'd been caught doing something wrong, and gave the push-chair a shove on to the other side of the stones, into the shade of the acacia. The baby didn't wake. Then he came and sat down again on the same stone as before and resumed his silent contemplation of me.

'Is that your little brother?'

He nodded without speaking. The smell of the cigarette wasn't strong enough to drive away the odour of decomposition. The two children must have been born and grown up in it.

'I live on a ship,' I said.

His eyes widened. He got up and came nearer.

'It's as big as from here to that house,' I went on.

I showed him the distance with my hand, and he followed it with his eyes. He wasn't in the least shy now.

'Are you the captain?'

I couldn't help laughing.

'No, not me.'

I could have done with another brandy, but I couldn't bring myself to leave the little boy.

'I like aeroplanes best,' he said.

There was a sort of insatiability in his eyes that was almost painful. For just a moment he forgot about me and thought about aeroplanes. Then I saw him emerge from his dream and come over quite close and examine me again.

'Is it true?'

'What?'

'That you live on a ship?'

'Yes. It's called the *Gibraltar*.'

'What do you do if you're not the captain?'

'Nothing. I'm a passenger.'

Just in front of me there was a splendid nettle in flower. Time seemed to be passing unendurably slowly. I leaned forward and on a sudden impulse broke off the nettle and crushed it in my hand. Why? To wring the neck, as it were, of this endless stretch of time. It worked. It hurt my hand. I heard the boy laughing. I stood up, and he suddenly stopped laughing and fled.

'Come back,' I said.

He came, very slowly. He expected me to explain.

'That'll teach me,' I said, laughing. He looked at me intently.

'Didn't you know it would sting?'

'I'd forgotten,' I said.

He was reassured. He'd have liked me to stay on a little.

'I must go. I'd have liked to buy you an aeroplane, but I haven't got time now. One day I'll come back and buy you one.'

'Is your ship sailing then?'

'Yes, right away. I must go.'

'Have you got a car as well?'

'Yes, I've got a car as well. Do you like cars?'

'Not so much as aeroplanes.'

'I must be off. Goodbye.'

'Will you come again?'

'I'll come back to buy you the aeroplane.'

'When?'

'I don't know.'

'It isn't true. You won't come back.'

'Goodbye.'

I went. I turned round for a last look at the boy. He'd completely forgotten me. He was running round in big circles with his arms spread out like wings, playing at being an aeroplane. The baby was still asleep.

When I passed the seventeen kilometre post I saw that all was quiet. The car had gone. The man was sitting on a stool facing the road, waiting for customers and reading a paper. I stopped a bit farther on and smoked a cigarette. Then I drove very fast back to the ship. We'd been gone almost two hours. Epaminondas was waiting for us, talking to Bruno. He ran over to me. As we'd been away such a long time and she still hadn't come back he was full of hope. So was Bruno, it seemed to me.

'Well?' cried Epaminondas.

I told him as tactfully as I could that I didn't think it was exactly the man. Bruno shrugged his shoulders and immediately lost interest. He went off.

'As she's staying so long,' said Epaminondas, 'mustn't it be to make absolutely sure?'

'Perhaps,' I said, trying to console him, 'perhaps she wants to make absolutely certain that it's not him.'

'I don't quite understand,' said Epaminondas. 'You know about that sort of thing at once. You know straight away if you've known somebody before or not.'

'That's what I thought.'

I haven't the faintest idea what expression I must have been wearing. Epaminondas poured me out a cognac, and took the opportunity to have one himself.

'She carries it a bit far,' he said. 'There aren't two men on earth who are so alike that you could confuse them once you'd spoken to them. It's impossible.'

I didn't answer. Epaminondas ruminated.

'Unless,' he said, 'there really were two people who were so alike that they were interchangeable. If you made up your mind not to look too closely, I mean.'

He must have drunk a fair amount while he was waiting for us, and he had ideas on every aspect of the matter.

'You see,' he said, 'if she likes, Pierrot *is* the sailor from Gibraltar. All she has to do is want it to be so. People get fed up in the end. One day she will too. She'll say that's it, and that will be it, and who'll be able to deny it, eh?'

'That's true enough,' I said. 'No one will be able to deny it.'

I offered him a cigarette.

'Aren't I unique too, in my own way? People get fed up in the end.'

'We're all unique,' I said, 'in our own way. That's what makes it so complicated.'

His thoughts took another direction.

'Supposing,' he said suddenly, 'supposing she asked him about Nelson Nelson?'

'That's what I mean,' I said. 'It's complicated.'

'We shall see what we shall see,' he grinned. 'If Pierrot's not him he'll say he doesn't know anything about Nelson Nelson.'

He could see I wasn't following him, but what did it matter?

'But still,' he went on, 'what reason could a man have for refusing to recognize a woman like her?'

'Don't let's exaggerate,' I said.

Epaminondas supplied his own answer.

'The service station! Suppose it really is him. There he is, owner of an ultra-modern service station, making money, left in peace by the police, and perfectly happy. Then she comes along and says drop it all and come with me!'

'True,' I said. 'I never thought of that.'

'It's quite possible he'd hang back, isn't it? Who knows?' he said after a pause, 'perhaps they've been discussing that all these two hours.'

'Who knows?' I said.

'He'd be ashamed, too, wouldn't he, at having given up his wanderings, as you might say, the sea and all that, and just settled down like anybody else, like one of his own petrol pumps?'

'There's something in what you say,' I answered.

As we talked we watched the quays. She didn't come.

'It's true that I left the sea for the road too,' said Epaminondas. 'But you see I don't have to account for myself to anyone. I don't possess anything under the sun. Even the lorry doesn't belong to me. So I can always go whenever I like.'

He stopped talking for a moment, probably thinking about his own lot.

'What I think is,' he said, 'that it's only if Pierrot isn't

Pierrot that he'll tell her all she wants to know, Nelson and everything else. I don't need to tell you what for?'

'No,' I said.

But he still had some doubts. He was growing very impatient at not seeing her arrive on the quay.

'The more handsome men are,' he said, 'the more difficult it is to recognize them. It's much the same with women. It's a good thing he's got that scar on his head.'

'Yes,' I said.

'But you need time before you can start rummaging about in a man's hair,' he said. 'You can't start rummaging about in a man's hair from the word go. . .'

Suddenly he started to roar with laughter.

'Though of course she's a fast worker!' he said. 'Excuse me for saying so, but she's a fast worker!'

'A record-breaker,' I said. 'No getting away from it.'

'But supposing he has got the scar?' he said, serious again. 'He couldn't deny it.'

I laughed.

'I should think not,' I said, without thinking.

Epaminondas was hurt.

'Are you laughing at me?' he said.

'Excuse me,' I said. 'It's true enough that if he really . . . I think I'll go and lie down for a bit.'

I left him and went down to my cabin. I hadn't been there for ten minutes when I heard the sound of her engine on the quay. Epaminondas yelled for me at the top of his voice, and then called to her from the deck.

'Well?'

'Alas,' she said, 'no go, my poor Epaminondas.'

'What the hell have you been up to for two hours then?'

'Wandering about,' she said. 'Alas, my poor Epaminondas.'

I went up to the bar. They were both sitting at a table with a couple of whiskies in front of them. She avoided my glance.

'But still,' groaned Epaminondas, 'you did have doubts?'

'Well,' she said, 'I'm beginning to think you can have doubts about anything.'

I sat down beside them. Her hair had come undone a bit in the wind, and wisps of it were escaping.

'So I've sent you out of your way again for nothing,' lamented Epaminondas.

'It's never quite for nothing,' she said.

She went and fetched a bottle of champagne to soothe her friend's qualms. She looked happy. Epaminondas watched her, shattered. I uncorked the champagne. Yes, she looked happy, like someone coming out of a dark room where he's been shut up for a long time.

'In any case,' said Epaminondas, 'it doesn't appear to have affected you much.'

'You get used to anything,' she said.

She was still avoiding looking at me. It was quite obvious. Had Epaminondas noticed?

'It's always one to add to the number that can't be him,' I said.

'If you look at it that way,' said Epaminondas,' we've got our work cut out for us.'

She and I both started to laugh.

'I suppose you think that's funny?' Epaminondas said to her.

'What isn't?' she said. 'Aren't I too?'

'Not always,' said Epaminondas. 'Not today.'

'You think yourself strong,' she said, 'and all the time you're as weak as water.'

'Now you're depressed,' said Epaminondas. 'It's all my fault.'

'You don't know what you do want,' said Anna. 'When I laugh you don't like that either.'

'And you?' said Epaminondas. 'Are you quite sure you know what you want?'

She looked at me and smiled at last, but so boldly that I blushed. This time Epaminondas did notice, and was silent.

'Do people always know what they want?' she asked me.
'Yes, always,' I said.

She was still smiling. I went on quickly, to change the subject and to keep Epaminondas, who looked as if he was about to get up and go.

'Even if there was only one man left on earth, you'd still have to hope that it would be him. When you're serious you have to carry it right through.'

She laughed at the word 'serious'. Then she poured more champagne into our glasses. She made Epaminondas drink some more.

'It's never quite him,' he said. 'There's always something not quite right.'

'This was the third time,' she said in an ordinary, peaceful conversational tone, 'that Epaminondas told me he'd found him.'

I drank my champagne.

'We are up against the impenetrable mysteries of human identity,' I said severely.

Epaminondas looked at me in horror. Anna reassured him.

'He means,' she said, 'that it's very difficult to find exactly the person you're looking for. Do you remember? Once he was keeping a brothel in Constantinople. Another time it was Port Said. What was it he was doing at Port Said?'

'He was a barber,' said Epaminondas. 'Either it's the story that doesn't fit, or the voice, or the scar . . . It's always something.'

'What it comes to in the end,' she said, looking at me, 'is that you mustn't see too many of them, too many men. It's the same as with everything else – you have to keep within bounds.'

'We'll never do it,' declared Epaminondas, losing heart again.

'It's not easy,' she said. 'What would you say, Epaminondas, if I told you that sometimes there's something in your eyes that resembles his?'

She laughed, but Epaminondas did not. He lowered his eyes as if remembering that they had cost him dear. He was silent for a little, and then said:

'What'll really make me laugh is when you really do find him and you try to see if he looks like Pierrot. Then I'll know you really are round the bend.'

We burst out laughing. Epaminondas began to get over his depression.

'Sometimes,' he said, 'when the ship comes in, you think you see him on the quay. Then, when you get ashore, it isn't him any more. Sometimes even ashore you still have doubts, and you go a bit closer. And sometimes you have to get very close indeed to make sure it's not really him . . .'

'Oh yes,' laughed Anna.

'But still it's a marvellous life,' I said, 'looking for a sailor from Gibraltar.'

'Sometimes though,' she said calmly, 'I really do wonder what can have become of him.'

'So do I,' said Epaminondas sadly.

We were on our second bottle of champagne.

'Epaminondas,' Anna explained to me, 'was very much struck by the story of the sailor from Gibraltar.'

'I don't know whether it was that that struck me,' said Epaminondas in a childish voice, 'or whether it was something else.'

I burst out laughing.

'It's always the sailor from Gibraltar,' I said, 'who starts it off.'

He nodded sadly. We were all three drunk by now. We were never very far off it on that ship.

'In Constantinople,' said Epaminondas,' it was touch and go. You ought to put a bit more goodwill into it.'

'If there's one thing I've got too much of,' she said, 'it's goodwill. I sometimes ask myself if it's any use.'

'You can say what you like,' said Epaminondas, who was beginning to get into a groove, 'but in Constantinople it was touch and go.' He was getting worked up.

'Is it as important to you as all that that she should find him?' I asked.

'I shall have some peace,' he said. 'I was quite young, and she came and took me away from my family and took me on the yacht before you could look round, and ever since...'

'Touch and go,' said Anna, who wasn't inclined to pursue that discussion. 'As if after three years I'd make difficulties about nothing. Let's get this question of Constantinople straight. If you hadn't been there, I'd be whoring somewhere else than on the sea . . .'

'Until she finds him,' Epaminondas told me, 'I shall never have any peace.'

'I wouldn't have minded the brothel so much,' she said. 'It was more the lack of air . . .'

Epaminondas's face lit up.

'Yes,' he said. 'As soon as I told him the story he said straight away that's me, tell her to come. To tell you the truth I thought that was a bit much, and the way he earned a living made me suspicious too. I didn't tell you at the time, but when you went back on board I punched his face in for him. Left him a nice scar, in fact.'

'That makes it even more complicated,' she said, laughing.

'Now I shan't say any more,' said Epaminondas. Then he added in a tone of disillusion:

'Anyway, you can always wait until I send you some more messages.'

'Oh no,' she said. 'That's the very thing, the one thing not to do.'

But clearly Epaminondas had some idea in his head. He was holding it back so as to bring it off better.

'If you ask me,' I said, 'I think that Pierrot of kilometre seventeen was well worth the trouble.'

She looked at me and laughed softly, as if she had played a good joke on me.

'At any rate,' said Epaminondas, 'it was the best I could

do in this lousy *département*.' Then, in a low voice: 'No one could have done any better with petrol the price it is.'

Anna leaned towards him and said, very affectionately:

'You sound as if you don't like your job much. You must say what's worrying you.'

'Yes, you must,' I said. 'If you can't tell her, who can you tell?'

'I'm depressed,' said Epaminondas. 'I shan't say anything.'

But immediately afterwards he said – you had to admire him:

'Seeing he's the sort of man he is, what I think is that you ought to look for him in Africa.'

A great silence formed, as it was right that it should, around this pronouncement.

'Africa's a big place,' said Anna. 'You'll have to be more precise.'

He was. It lasted half an hour. We hardly heard what he said, she and I, because we were thinking about something else. The idea was that we should go to Dahomey to see a certain Louis, from Marseilles, who'd once been a sailor on the yacht. She remembered him. Louis had written to Epaminondas only last week to ask his opinion about someone called Gégé who lived among the Eoués in the Abomey district. According to Louis there was no doubt that he was the sailor from Gibraltar. Epaminondas hadn't replied to Louis yet. He'd thought it more sensible to speak to Anna about it first. He talked to us about the Eoués. He'd read them up. They were a farming, nomadic tribe who lived for part of the year on the plateaus of the Atakora. It was a beautiful country, with lakes and kudus – only little ones, but still. These considerations apart, he didn't know whether Louis really had sufficient reason for getting her to go as far out of her way as that. That was for her to judge. It was true it was a long way away . . . What he said was, after all . . . He went on for a long time, mingling the charms of the kudus with those of the sailor from Gibraltar. He went on too long. We looked at each other too long. Absorbed in his Eoués, he didn't notice anything.

'Why not?' she said at last. 'You could come with us.'

'I don't know about that,' said Epaminondas bashfully.

'Is it your lorry that prevents you?' I asked.

'It isn't even mine,' he said. 'I've nothing except the clothes I stand up in.'

I could understand perfectly well, and with reason, what Epaminondas wanted. But suddenly she said we must let her think about it, and left us. This astonished Epaminondas, but I left him to it, and went and lay down in my cabin. The die had been cast in some way, I couldn't quite say how. We were leaving for central Africa. I went to sleep in a green savannah swarming with kudus.

I slept for a long while. I must have woken up just before dinner-time. I went straight up to the bar. She wasn't there. Only Epaminondas, sleeping deeply stretched out on two chairs. There was nobody else on board. I switched on the lights. Epaminondas groaned but didn't wake up. The hot-plates were cold; no one had prepared dinner. I ran down to the hold and saw that both cars were still there. I went slowly back up to the bar, woke Epaminondas, and asked him where she was. He told me what I already knew – that she was in her cabin.

'She's thinking it over,' he said. 'If she's trying to work out whether we should go to Dahomey or not, she's got her work cut out. As if you needed to think about a thing like that.'

He told me she'd come up again from her cabin just after I'd gone down to mine and given all the crew leave until midnight. She'd said that we'd be sailing again during the night, but had omitted to say where to.

'I'm waiting until she's thought it over long enough,' said Epaminondas, 'to find out whether I've got to let my boss know.'

I left Epaminondas and went down to her cabin. For the

225

first time I went in without knocking. I switched on the light. She was lying fully dressed, her hands under her head, in an attitude that reminded me of the way she had lain beside the reeds. I sat down beside her. She must have been crying.

'Let's go and have dinner in a restaurant,' I said. 'Come on.'

'I'm not hungry.'

'You're always ready to eat.'

'Not always.'

'Epaminondas is up there eating his heart out. He's waiting for you to decide to go and see the Eoués, so that he can let his boss know.'

'But you can tell him – we're going, we're leaving tonight.'

She tried to remember.

'Where is it we're going?'

'You're the limit,' I said. 'To see the Eoués of Dahomey, in the Abomey district.'

'Oh yes. It's a long way.'

'How long will it take? Ten days?'

'Yes, if there's a calm sea. A fortnight if it's rough.'

'Don't you want to go hunting kudu, like in Hemingway?'

'No,' she said. 'This is the twenty-third message I've had since I started looking for him.'

Then she added softly:

'We're hunting something other than kudus.'

'But as he's so rare, this sailor, we could spend a few days hunting something else. Every so often you need some little animal to stow in the bag. We'll hunt the kudu.'

'Supposing he's there among the Eoués?'

'Then you'll hunt the kudu with him.'

She was silent. I didn't like to look at her too much.

'And is hunting kudus dangerous?'

'A little. Just dangerous enough. And then, since people think that one kudu is as good as another, it's . . . what shall I say? . . . easier.'

'Do you speak while you're hunting the kudu?'

'When you're hunting you mustn't make the slightest noise, you mustn't speak. Everyone knows that.'

'Can't you speak very softly, whisper? You can whisper, can't you?'

'I expect so,' I said. 'But you only talk about what you're hunting. You can't think about anything else.'

'I never dreamed I'd taken on such an expert hunter. But the kudu is a very difficult thing to catch.'

'But the most beautiful in the world.'

'And they really don't talk to each other about anything else but kudus?'

'Sometimes, in the evening, after the day's hunting, they talk about literature. But first and foremost they are kudu-hunters.'

'And never anything else? Never?'

'You can never be quite definite about anything. Perhaps, sometimes, they might be something else.'

'You ought to see the town,' she said. 'It's beautiful.'

I got up. She put out her hand and stopped me.

'Did you talk as much as that to that girl? Did you?'

'I was saving it up for better days. I never talked to her at all. I wasn't happy.'

'I think I was,' she said, slowly.

'That's what people think,' I said.

I went out and rejoined Epaminondas in the bar. He was awaiting me impatiently, with a glass of wine in front of him.

'What did she say?'

'Nothing.'

'But' – he drank and made a clicking sound with his tongue – 'but this time it's really it. So it must be that she doesn't want him any more.'

I remembered the errand she'd given me to do.

'She told me to tell you we're going to see the Eoués.'

He didn't show any pleasure. On the contrary, he flopped into a chair with his glass still in his hand.

'When?'

'Tonight. You know that.'

He began to moan and groan.

'There I am, off again. I shall never get anywhere.'

'You'd better make up your mind what it is you want,' I said.

'She came and hunted me out at Majunga, at my poor old mother's,' he said. 'For all she wanted from me, she might just as well have left me where I was.' Then he added, more quietly: 'I still wonder what she saw in me . . .'

'We're all more or less in the same boat. There's no point in moaning about it.'

He wasn't listening.

'My mother's always writing to me telling me to go back. My father's old. We had a good business in oranges, but it's all going to rack and ruin . . .'

'All you have to do is go back to Majunga.'

He got angry.

'You'll see – you'll see what it's like to go back to Majunga after she's lugged you round to Tampico and New York and Manila. It'd kill me in Majunga. You don't know what you're talking about.'

'There's no reason why you should ever go back there,' I said.

'When she's found him, then I'll go back. Not before.'

'I don't understand.'

'When she's found him I won't be able to bear myself anywhere, so I might as well go back to Majunga.'

'You've got plenty of time then,' I said.

He gazed at me for a minute.

'It's not quite the same thing for you. She's gone on you.'

Because I didn't answer, he thought I didn't believe what he said.

'I know what I'm talking about. You can see. I've never known her to think so long about anything. I hardly know her.'

'Are there really kudus in the Eoué country?'

He was transfigured.

'A few. But on the Zambesi there are thousands. In the Ouellé country too – but there they're quite big. You can catch them like flies. It's hardly worth the trouble.'

He waited, but I didn't answer.

'Why are you asking all this? Do you want to go hunting kudus?'

'I don't know. I just ask out of curiosity.'

He seemed disappointed. Suddenly he remembered something.

'My boss! I haven't let him know!'

'Well, go on, then.'

'I can't. It's twenty kilometres away. You'll have to take me in the car.'

'You're a hell of a nuisance.'

He pretended to be in the depths of despair.

'Well, that's all there is to it, if you won't, I shall have to stay behind.'

'I don't know how to open the door of the hold.'

'I do,' he said. 'You bet I do.'

I could have told him to go alone, but if I'd stayed I'd have gone straight down to her cabin. I didn't want to do that. He didn't suggest going without me because he didn't like the idea of making the journey alone. In less than five minutes he'd gone down and opened the door of the hold.

We were away two hours, explaining matters to his boss and collecting his things from a little rooming-house in Sète. As we were driving back he talked to me a bit about Louis.

'He's my pal,' he said. 'He's a scream. You'll see.'

'Do you often lead her this sort of dance?'

'Dance? Do you think it amuses me to drag all the way to Dahomey?'

'Sorry. It amuses me.'

'I'd never have thought so.'

When we got back the crew had returned too. The lights

were on in the bar. Laurent was slightly tight, and Bruno considerably so.

'It's really funny,' bawled Bruno. 'The first bastard that comes along could tell her he's living in a tent on the top of the Himalayas and she'd go straight off there. I'm going to stay on. I wouldn't want to miss that.'

Epaminondas hurled himself on him.

'Take that back or I'll punch you on the nose.'

'If you can't make a joke any more, I quit, then,' said Bruno. 'I'm not taking back anything.'

'He's right,' said Laurent.

Epaminondas stalked away.

'What I can't make out,' he said, 'is why she takes on mugs like that who don't know anything about anything.'

I left them, and went down to her cabin. She'd switched out the light again. I switched it on. She was lying in exactly the same position as before. This time I had the impression that she'd been waiting for me. I told her about my drive with Epaminondas, and some of the things he'd told me about Louis in Dahomey. I talked for quite a long time. I could see she was growing impatient. Then suddenly I had no more to say, not even about the pleasantries of Epaminondas.

'Perhaps it would be better if you went ashore here,' she said.

Then she added:

'Like all the others.'

I sat on the floor, my head resting against her bunk.

'I don't want to.'

'A bit sooner, a bit later – what's the difference?'

'Not yet. I shall go ashore, but not yet.'

'What do you think you'll have to wait for before you go ashore?'

'The sailor from Gibraltar.'

She did not laugh.

'I'm sorry,' I said. 'But I don't know.'

Suddenly, quite harshly, she said:

'But where did you come from?'

'I told you. The Ministry. I used to copy out . . .'

'Are you such a fool that you can't see what's happening?'

'I'm not a fool. I can see what's happening.'

'And you still don't want to leave?'

'Not yet. It's the only thing I know how to wish for. There's no reason why I should leave.'

'But I,' she said slowly, 'you know I have every reason for making you go.'

'I don't give a damn for your reasons.'

She grew calm again. And rather as if she were talking to a child, with a sort of gentle perfidy, she said:

'So you're going just to stay and say nothing – keep on saying nothing?'

'I'll do what I can.'

'And do you think one can keep on saying nothing?'

'I think one ought to say nothing as long as one can. But not . . . not always.'

I lay down beside her.

'I can't say nothing any longer,' I said.

For a moment it was as if we had spoken. But the moment passed, and soon it was no longer enough. She put her face against mine and lay there a long time without moving.

'Say something to me – anything.'

'Anna.'

The watch on the table said two o'clock. But we weren't sleepy.

'Something else,' she said.

'I like it on this ship.'

She lay down and didn't ask anything more. She switched out the light. Through the porthole you could see the quay crudely lit by a street-lamp. We might have thought that all desire between us was dead.

'We must go to sleep,' she said. 'We haven't slept for ages. We're a couple of very tired people.'

'No, you're wrong.'

231

'I like you just as you are, really. Adamant.'

'Ssh . . .'

'The greatest love in the world – what does that mean?'

I could just make out her face, lit by the street-lamp out-side. She was smiling. I got up to go. She tried to keep me.

'Silly girl,' I said.

I disengaged myself, and she let me go, made no attempt to keep me.

'Don't worry,' she said, 'in my own way I keep silent too.'

The ship sailed during the night. I hardly slept at all. The vibration of the propeller woke me and for a long time I couldn't get back to sleep. Then, just as I'd given up hope, just as the sun was rising, I went to sleep. I came out of my cabin at about noon. She was on deck, calm and cheerful, as she was every morning. She was talking to Bruno. He wasn't drunk now, but in a very bad temper, claiming that he'd been carried off against his will, saying that he didn't want to hear anything about going to Dahomey, and so on. She tried to console him by telling him we were going to hunt for kudus. I heard her saying:

'It's a thing one ought to have done, and now you'll have done it . . .'

He looked at her suspiciously. He was the youngest of the crew. He badly missed the precariousness of the world. We all had a lot of trouble trying to make him understand the necessity of our travels. But everyone was very patient with him.

We had lunch together. Epaminondas joined us at our table. From then on he sat at our table every day. He was never in our way. That morning he was in great spirits. It was a marvellous day, he had forgotten Majunga and his scruples and perhaps even the reason why we were going to Dahomey.

'So we're on our way,' he said, clapping me on the shoulder.

'We're on our way. No need to get excited.'

232

'You might say you got your own way with me,' she said, rather too easily.

Epaminondas was the picture of indignation.

'If anyone gets his own way with you it isn't me,' he said.

She agreed, laughing.

'And whether you're here or anywhere else,' said Epaminondas, 'isn't it a case of out of the frying pan into the fire?'

'I should hope so,' I said, 'or else . . .'

'What would be best,' she said, 'would be if he were a milkman in Dijon while I still go on whoring round the seven seas looking for my hero.'

'The seven seas and elsewhere,' laughed Epaminondas.

Everyone laughed, even the sailors at the other tables. No one took offence.

'In Dijon, or nowhere,' I said.

She laughed. Epaminondas didn't understand, and a sort of fear appeared in his face, as it did every time this happened.

'It's just a manner of speaking,' she explained.

'Do you allow that sort of joke now?'

'Just as a joke,' said Anna.

'I think I'll leave the ship at Tangier,' said Epaminondas, suddenly sad again.

'I was only joking,' she said. 'You're getting too sensitive.'

'All the same, if he is there among the Eoués you'll laugh on the other side of your face,' he said.

'She won't be the only one,' I said.

The thought of that meeting made me laugh and laugh.

'You might explain,' said Epaminondas, who was easily hurt and thought perhaps that I had doubts about the outcome of our journey.

'I was thinking,' I explained, 'of the possibility of a very rapid discharge.'

They laughed too.

'Yes,' laughed Epaminondas, 'he must be pretty quick on the draw.'

'It wouldn't be long before we joined Nelson Nelson and his ball-bearings.'

'You're forgetting about me,' she said.

'Not likely,' I said.

'You used not to be like this,' said Epaminondas. 'You're changing, and I don't mean for the better.'

He nearly choked with laughter.

'No more journeys,' he cried triumphantly. 'Just stay at home like everybody else . . . I'll stay on at Cotonou, though, to hunt the kudu.'

He turned to me as if he'd just remembered me, and so did she. He looked slightly embarrassed. I looked at her.

'And what about you?' Epaminondas asked me timidly. 'What will you . . .?'

'How should I know?' I said.

No one said anything. She had the most beautiful eyes. They waited for me to speak. But I said nothing.

'Anyway, what I shall do,' said Epaminondas almost in a whisper, 'is stay on at Cotonou to hunt for kudus. I'll try to capture them alive and sell them to zoos.'

'There aren't any kudus in Cotonou,' I just managed to say.

'But on the Zambesi,' he said, 'there are swarms of them.'

'But if you don't capture them alive what do you do with them?' she asked.

'You ought to know,' I said.

'How should she?' said Epaminondas, nonplussed.

'Don't try to understand everything,' she said. 'He means because I'm hunting for the sailor from Gibraltar. It's an allusion.'

Then she went on, pleasantly:

'What do you do with them? Eat them?'

'Of course,' said Epaminondas. 'You eat them. Then there's the horns, and the skin, and . . . I don't know, only a person who doesn't know the first thing about hunting would ask such questions.'

234

'The kudu,' I explained to her, 'is a very rare animal. Hunting for a rare animal is real hunting.'

'The rarer the better,' laughed Epaminondas, who had understood.

Anna always laughed at Epaminondas's jokes. She laughed now, but was grave again almost at once.

'I enjoy laughing more and more all the time,' she said. 'I must be getting old.'

'It's not because you're getting old,' said Epaminondas knowingly.

'It's because the light has dawned,' I said.

Anna laughed for some time at that.

'You could have told me before that I was in your way,' said Epaminondas.

'If anyone's in our way, as you put it,' said Anna, 'don't worry, it's not you.'

Epaminondas understood and was vexed, but only slightly.

'No point in going on about it,' he said. 'But you've certainly changed.'

I spent the whole day trying to read, without success. At the end of the afternoon I went up to the bar to look for Epaminondas. He was reading too, slumped in a chair. She was talking to the crew about the sort of weather we were likely to have in the Atlantic. Everyone noticed when I came into the bar. Some, Bruno among them perhaps, probably thought that the crucial moment of my stay on the ship had arrived, and that I wouldn't go as far as Dahomey. I could see from her manner that the ambiguity that surrounded our relationship didn't bother her – on the contrary, she, like me, took a certain pleasure in prolonging it. I walked across the bar and went out on deck. Epaminondas soon joined me. This was what I wanted. We got on well, and I needed someone to talk to.

'So,' I said, 'you don't do a hand's turn either?'

'I had a vague idea I might tidy up the bookshelves,' he said. 'But it's only a vague idea.'

'Who's ever going to need tidy bookshelves on this ship?'

'You never know,' he said. 'She might take on a philosopher at the next port of call.'

We laughed.

'I haven't got anything to do,' said Epaminondas. 'There's no work for me. Besides, I never much cared for work.'

'Me neither. Still, some day . . .'

'You keep yourself busy just the same, though,' he laughed.

'We're approaching Gibraltar,' I said.

'Tomorrow at dawn . . . Yes, it made me feel queer too the first time.'

'What do you think?'

'What about – Gibraltar?'

'Do you think she has a chance?'

'What the hell would we all be doing here if she hadn't?' he cried.

'True. I just wanted to know what you thought.'

'You ask some funny questions.'

'There's one thing I wanted to say to you. Nelson Nelson seems a very funny sort of name to me.'

'Again, what would we all be doing here . . .'

'Yes, but we could be here just the same even if it was someone else.'

'I suppose you're right,' said Epaminondas. 'It could be the ball-bearings king or the king of mugs, so long as he killed him.'

'Sometimes I get the impression there are ten stories of the sailor from Gibraltar.'

'That's quite possible. But the sailor from Gibraltar himself – there's only one of him. And he's solid enough.'

He was silent, eyeing me with some suspicion.

'You ask a lot of questions,' he said. 'I can't say I like it.'

'No harm in talking. Why not?'

Then I added:

'Anyway, I don't need to ask questions. She's a woman who talks a lot. I just speak about that the same as I would about anything else.'

'No. She may not always quite know what she wants, but she's not a talker.'

'But we're going to see your Eoués, aren't we?'

'She has no choice. If she had . . .'

'That's true. She has no choice.'

'She's got herself into such a fix, how do you expect her to draw back? That's what it is.'

'Are you very keen on finding him?'

'I'm the only one who believes it's possible.'

'She might as well do that as anything else,' I said.

'Well,' he said, 'not quite.'

'No,' I answered.

I liked him. I think he liked me too, but rather against his will.

'You ought to get some rest,' he said. 'You look like nothing on earth.'

'I can't sleep. Is she really not a talker?'

'No.' Then he added, as if it were his duty to tell me this, 'Of course, even I only know what other people have told me, what I've heard. But of course, a person can become talkative quite suddenly.'

'I expect they can,' I said, laughing.

He scrutinized me again.

'What was your job?'

'Colonial Ministry,' I said. 'Registry section.'

'What sort of work was it?'

'I copied out birth and death certificates of people born in the colonies. I stayed there eight years.'

'Christ,' said Epaminondas, with a certain respect. 'This must make a change for you.'

'I'm happy,' I said to him.

He didn't answer. He took out a packet of cigarettes and we smoked.

'Did you drop everything?'

'The lot.'

'And you haven't finished yet,' he said, amicably.

For some time I'd been trying to see the name that was written underneath his tattoo-mark. Suddenly he stretched and I saw it. It was Athena. I was very glad for him.

'So it's Athena that you've got written on your chest,' I said. I spoke amicably too.

'What did you think? Of course, I hesitated, then one day I thought to myself, I shall only look a mug, and so ...'

We laughed. We understood each other perfectly. Then he went back to the bar and I to my cabin. I met her as I was going down the hatchway. She stopped me and told me in a whisper – very quickly, looking down – that we'd be going through the Straits of Gibraltar the next morning about six-thirty.

I spent the rest of the day and part of the night waiting for her. But I didn't even see her at dinner.

We arrived at Gibraltar a bit earlier than she'd said – just before six.

I got up and went on deck. She was already there. The whole ship was asleep, even Epaminondas. She was in her dressing-gown, with her hair down. Probably she hadn't slept either. We didn't say anything. We hadn't any more to say to each other, or rather we couldn't say any more to each other, not even good morning. I went forward and stood beside her, we watched the straits approaching, leaning on the rail, very close to each other.

We passed right by the Rock. Two planes were flying over it, sparkling, circling above it in ever-decreasing circles, like vultures. In white villas perched on dynamite, huddled together in stifling but eminently patriotic promiscuity, England slept, true to herself as ever on the reeking soil of Spain.

We left the Rock behind, and with it the disturbing and

vertiginous reality of the world. The straits drew near, and with them its no less disturbing, no less vertiginous non-reality. The water imperceptibly changed colour. The coast of Africa rose up, bare and stark as a plateau of salt, its implacable outline interrupted by Ceuta. The Spanish coast, darker and more sheltered, gazed across at it, clothed in the last pine-lands of the Latin world.

We entered the straits. Soon we saw Tarifa, minute, burned up by the sun, crowned with smoke. At its innocent feet was hatched the most miraculous metamorphosis of waters in the world. The wind blew stronger. The Atlantic appeared. She turned at last and looked at me.

'Suppose I'd invented it all?' she said.

'All of it?'

'Yes.'

What was to be between us was becoming inevitable. It was as if she were telling me so.

'It wouldn't make much difference,' I said.

The ship changed course. The water was growing green and frothy. The straits widened out, and a complete change came over the colour of the sea and the sky and of her eyes. She was still waiting, looking ahead.

'So we've got to that point, have we?' I said.

'Yes,' she said. 'We've got to that point.'

I went over and took her by the arm and led her down. We had been in Tangier an hour when she fell asleep. We hadn't exchanged a single word.

I left her in the cabin, had a cup of coffee in the dining-room, and went ashore. I don't think I even glanced at the town from the deck. I hurried ashore and started to walk. It must have been eleven o'clock, and it was hot already. But the wind from the sea blew through the town and made it quite bearable. I took the first side-street I came to and after a quarter of an hour's walk, without having actually intended it, I came to the town – a noisy boulevard with dwarf palms growing along it. I'd had very little sleep, not only the night before, but every other night since Rocca, and I was at my last gasp. The boulevard was very long. It must have been the town's main commercial thoroughfare. It led to the harbour at one end and at the other to a square too far away to be distinguished. Huge lorries loaded with coal were coming down it, and others laden with packing-cases, machines, or iron filings were climbing up it painfully in the other direction. From where I was I could see right along it from the port to the square. It was almost entirely covered with two long streams of vehicles, mostly lorries, halted at regular intervals by traffic lights at pedestrian crossings. They all seemed to be going at the same speed, stopping and moving off again with the regularity of a long, slow swell. The boulevard looked enormous to me, practically endless, moving and sparkling like the sea. I had to sit down on a bench to help me to bear the sight of it. A squad of international police marched across it, led by a band, just near where I was sitting. They strutted proudly, rhythmically across under the amused eyes of the lorry drivers. When they'd gone by I got up and walked up towards the square. It looked as if there might be other trees there besides the dwarf palms, which didn't give any shade, and above all there would probably be some cafés with chairs outside. I walked very slowly. I think I must have been as tired as I'd been in Florence when I went to look for the driver of the van. But this time the town didn't close round me. On the contrary, it seemed to keep opening out before me. It was as if I would never get to the end of it, and once I'd reached the cafés in the square would stay there for the rest of my life. I was desperately happy. I sat down on nearly every bench and listened. The whole town was feverishly at work. If you listened hard – and that took a certain amount of concentration – you could distinguish, through the enormous racket of the lorries climbing up the boulevard, the dim and distant hum that rose from the harbour. I got up and went on walk-

240

ing. It must have taken me about half an hour to reach the square. Freshly watered terrasses lay in the shadow of the plane trees. I stopped at the first one I came to. It was there, probably because I was so tired, that suddenly I no longer understood what had happened to me, and felt I would never have the strength to go through with it. But it didn't last. It was over in the time it took to close my eyes and open them again. A waiter dressed in white with a napkin in his hand asked me what I'd like to drink. I said coffee. I hadn't died of love for the woman who loved the sailor from Gibraltar.

'Iced?'

'I don't know.'

'Aren't you well?'

'Very well. But I'm tired.'

'Hot would probably be better then.'

'All right, hot,' I said.

He went away. The square was the highest part of the town, overlooking the sea. There was a view of the trading port, and, a little farther to the right, of the yachting harbour. The *Gibraltar* was there, the biggest yacht of all, you could pick her out at once. Perhaps she was still asleep, or perhaps she was awake, wondering where I'd got to. Perhaps, who knew, the sailor from Gibraltar was on board. The waiter brought the coffee.

'Would you like something to eat?'

I didn't want anything. He noticed that I was looking over at the yachting harbour. It was lunch time, he hadn't many customers, so he could chat if he wanted to.

'The *Gibraltar* came in this morning,' he said.

I must have started slightly, but he didn't notice, he was looking over at the port. The ships interested him.

'Do you know her?'

'There aren't many thirty-six metres left, she's one of the last. You can't help knowing them.'

I swallowed the coffee scalding hot. It was quite good. I liked coffee, and drank a lot of it in the mornings. The street round the square was one-way, and an endless stream of lorries drove through. The iron filings glittered in the sun. An Arab street-vendor stopped in front of me. He was selling postcards, innocent ones, views of the town. I bought one. I took a pencil out of my pocket and wrote Jacqueline's address – my own, that is – on the right hand side. I'd promised myself I'd do this before I left Europe. As I wrote I saw my hands. Since Rocca I hadn't changed, as I hadn't any clothes to change into, nor had I had time or need to wash much. The waiter was still standing beside me looking at the harbour. He was quite indifferent to me, but it was the time of day when waiters don't know what to do with themselves and enjoy doing nothing.

'It's a woman who lives on the *Gibraltar*,' he said. 'She's going round the world.'

'Just like that – round and round without stopping?'

'They say she's looking for someone. But of course people say anything.'

'Yes, anything.'

'What's certain is that she's as rich as Croesus. So she has to find something to do.'

A customer came in alone and called him over. I tried to think of what to write to Jacqueline. But I couldn't think of anything. My hands were dirty. I wrote: 'Thinking about you,' then tore it up. The yachts danced at their moorings. Occasionally women walked past the terrasse, whores with nothing to do, looking at the men alone and idle. They all reminded me of her who must still be asleep in my cabin. I remembered how she slept, the careless boldness. When I imagined it too clearly I felt a physical pain.

The waiter returned and stood beside me again. I asked him for an iced *crème de menthe*. I wanted to chill myself to the marrow, to freeze away the pain. I drank it straight off. But the drink as well only reminded me of her. I tried to remember the iced *crèmes de menthe* in Florence, which had completely occupied my thoughts and which I'd sweated out alone. But in vain. This one was different, it tasted so strong it exhausted me. I couldn't recall either the heat or my solitude during the five days it had lasted. I'd become someone without memories. I had as much difficulty in recalling Jacqueline as I had in remembering the *crèmes de menthe*: I could hardly summon up her face, or even her voice. It was six days since I'd left her.

I must have stayed in the café quite a long while. It gradually filled with people just come from lunch. The waiter was soon too busy to talk to me any more. There was no room left on the terrasse, and he came and indicated politely that it was time I went.

'Excuse me,' he said. 'That will be a hundred francs.'

I took out my wallet. All I possessed was in it – the savings of the last eight years about which I'd forgotten everything. I put a hundred-franc note on the table and said I'd like to stay a bit longer.

'You'll have to order something else then.'

I ordered another coffee. He brought it right away and said it would be a hundred and thirty-five francs. I gave him a thousand-franc note, and he went off to get change. I gained ten minutes like that. I drank the coffee, which exploded in my mouth like the scent of her hair. The waiter came back with the change, and I managed to leave at last. I started to stroll about the town again. I was slightly less tired, but the coffee made my heart pound and I could still only walk quite slowly. The restaurants were emptying. The wind had fallen and it was much hotter than in the morning. I went on walking. Soon I heard it strike two. I must have been hungry, but the idea of eating never entered my head. I had other things to think about. I didn't know whether I was going to go back on to the ship or let it sail without me. I came to a square. An empty seat in the shade of a plane tree. I sat down and fell asleep. I must have slept for half an hour. When I woke up I was still terrified of happiness and no nearer to knowing whether I was going back or not. Even so I stood up and started to look for the boulevard I'd come by in the morning. It took me some time, but when I found it it was still the same, just as exhausting as ever, interrupted by the traffic lights at the pedestrian crossings, covered with the swell of lorries climbing up from the harbour. I went slowly back towards the quay, the way I had come that morning. The *Gibraltar* lay there in the sun, her decks empty. They were filling up with oil. Bruno, who was on duty, came over to speak to me.

'You should get back on board,' he said.

'Aren't you leaving the ship at Tangier?'

'You'll know soon enough when I leave. You should get back on board.'

So I went back on board, with Bruno standing watching me from the quay. I went straight to the bar. She was there with a glass of whisky. She'd seen me come along the quay and back on board. Epaminondas was with her. She'd been afraid. As soon as she saw me she told me, without shame.

'I was afraid.'

I saw straight away she must have drunk quite a few whiskies. Epaminondas looked pleased to see me.

'I looked for you,' he laughed. 'Always looking for people – what a life. If we've got to start looking for you as well...'

'I was in a café,' I said.

'You've been drinking,' she said.

'Coffee and iced *crème de menthe.*'

'You look as if you're tight.'

'I am.'

'He hasn't had anything to eat,' said Epaminondas.

She got up and fetched a piece of bread and cheese, handed it to me, and then, as if after all the whiskies she'd had it was the last thing she could do, she collapsed into a chair beside me.

'I'd have preferred you to go to a brothel,' she said.

'As if he had any need to do that,' said Epaminondas.

She watched me eat, without speaking, dazed, following

all my movements mechanically as if she were seeing me for the first time. When I'd finished she stood up and went and got three glasses of whisky. Epaminondas helped her bring them back. She was staggering.

'Don't drink any more,' I said. 'We're going for a walk in the town.'

'I'm a bit tight,' she said, smiling.

'She can't stand,' said Epaminondas.

'I haven't been drinking,' I said. 'I'll help you along. I'm very keen that you should come.'

'What's the point?' she said.

'No point,' I said. 'There isn't any point in anything.'

Epaminondas left us. Perhaps he was slightly annoyed at my not having asked him to come with us. I went down to her cabin with her and helped her to dress. For the first time since the dance she wore a dress, a summer dress. I can remember it – green and red cotton. She put on a hat too, right on top of her head, a bit too small to hold in all her hair. Under it her face seemed to waver, like that of a woman asleep with her eyes open. She tried to go down the gangway alone, but she couldn't manage it. She got frightened halfway down, and stopped. I took her by the arm. I don't know how many whiskies she'd had, but she was very drunk. Whenever she was alone with Epaminondas she drank without stopping. As soon as we were ashore she wanted to go into a café and have another. But there wasn't a café, as I told her, and made her start to walk. We went up the same side-street and came out on to the boulevard. There she stopped and wanted to go into a café again. But still there wasn't one. So she said she wanted to sit down on a bench. I didn't want her to because I was afraid that as soon as she sat down she'd go to sleep. She resisted. She tried to sit down, and I pulled her away, so energetically that her hat fell off and her hair came undone. She scarcely noticed. I picked up the hat and she walked on with her hair down. People stopped to look at us. She didn't see them. Sometimes she was so tired that she shut her eyes. I'd never seen her in such a state. The sweat was pouring off me. But I was feeling much stronger now, and managed to drag her along. It must have taken us about thirty minutes to get halfway along the boulevard. The slope was gentler now. It was four o'clock. The wind had risen again and blew her hair about all over her bosom. I was dragging her along as if I was hauling her to the police station, or as if she'd gone mad. She looked beautiful to me beyond all possible expression. I was as drunk as she was just from looking at her. She kept on telling me to leave her alone.

'Leave me alone.'

She didn't shout. She just kept repeating it gently, sometimes with a touch of surprise because I wouldn't take any notice.

'You must keep walking,' I said.

I kept telling her she must keep walking, but I didn't say why. I'm not sure I knew myself. All I knew was that she had to. For a while she would believe me and put one foot in front of the other for a few minutes. Then her drunkenness would prevail again and she'd begin to hold back and tell me to leave her alone. So I would start to persuade her again that she must go on. I never once abandoned hope of reaching the square, and finally we got there. She sat down automatically on the first terrasse we came to, as I had; the same terrasse as I had sat at before. She threw her head back and sat there like that with her eyes closed. The waiter came up, the same one. He stood in front of us, and he and I both looked at her. He understood, and smiled kindly.

'Just a minute,' I said.

He went away. I spoke to her softly.

'Anna.'

She opened her eyes and I put her hair back. She let me. She was very hot; her hair clung to her forehead.

'We'll have an ice,' I said.

I called the waiter, who'd been watching us curiously from a few yards off. I ordered two ices.

'What flavour?'

The question made me laugh. He understood.

'The vanilla ones are the best,' he said.

'No,' she said. 'No ices.'

The waiter looked at me inquiringly.

'Two vanillas,' I said.

She didn't say anything. She was watching the passers-by. There were quite a lot of them now. It was almost the end of the afternoon. But the lorries still went by, and there were buses too, now. The waiter came back with the ices. They weren't very good. She took a spoonful, pulled a face, and left it. Then she watched me eat mine with a sort of vague interest. I ate it all. There was a traffic jam in the boulevard and the square was full of lorries and buses that were held up. Two buses stopped outside the café, one full of little girls and the other full of little boys. All the cars were hooting. The little boys were singing *'Auprès de ma blonde,'* and at the same time the little girls were singing a song in English. In front of the bus with the little boys there was a third, full of old ladies, Americans, who gazed at them wistfully. The noise was terrific. She didn't like it and screwed up her eyes. She didn't understand anything of what was going on, but just resigned herself to it rather as if I'd brought her from the yacht to this terrasse in her sleep. Her face was still sad. But she wasn't quite so drunk.

'You're not eating your ice.'

'It isn't very nice.' She pulled a face, trying to smile.

'You can't leave it,' I said, 'because of the waiter.'

She tried again, but no, she couldn't.

'I can't.'

A good many soldiers and sailors of all nationalities were going by, two by two. As they passed the café they would walk more slowly and stare with a sort of startled stupidity at this woman with her hair all over the place.

'Have a nice cup of coffee,' I said.

'Why coffee?'

247

'A nice coffee will do you good.'

The waiter stood a few yards away, still looking towards the port but keeping his eye on us all the time. I ordered coffee.

'But why?' she asked again.

When the waiter brought the coffee it wasn't very good, hardly lukewarm. She just tasted it and said, in great distress, as if she was about to burst into tears:

'Everything is awful in this café. The ice was terrible.'

I took her hand and explained:

'They're the same everywhere here. If the ices are terrible in one café they're terrible all over the town. They all get them from the same place.'

'What about the coffee then?'

'The coffee's different,' I said. 'If you like we'll order a *filtre*.'

'Oh no,' she said.

She lit a cigarette. But her lighter wouldn't work. She gave a long groan. I took the cigarette out of her mouth and lit it for her. Ordinarily she never got impatient at that sort of thing, never complained about anything. She smoked the cigarette, her lips tense with disgust.

'We'd have done better to stay on board,' she said. 'It's always the same, going ashore.'

I felt my face start to crumple with irresistible laughter, but she didn't see.

The street streamed past us. Coaches, cars and lorries drove by the terrasse in serried files, making a deafening racket.

'I'll never go ashore again,' she said.

'You'll have to at Dahomey,' I said, 'when you get to where Epaminondas's Eoués live.'

She smiled as politely as she could.

'I'm sure it's going to be a success,' I said, 'I'm sure we're going to hunt the kudu and enjoy ourselves. The mistake most people make is that they don't enjoy themselves enough. We'll dress up – I'll wear a tropical helmet and dark glasses and riding breeches, and I'll give you a little game-bag that will come in very useful if we ever have a breakdown.'

'No,' she said.

'I'll talk to you at night in the tent,' I said, 'with the lions roaring outside. Shall we take Epaminondas?'

'No.'

'I'll talk to you,' I said.

'No,' she said. 'There aren't any kudus left.'

'The world's full of them,' I said. 'You don't know anything about it.'

'It isn't him I'm waiting for any more,' she said, 'now.'

'One's always waiting for something,' I said. 'If it takes too long you change and wait for something else that comes more quickly. Kudus are especially for that – for little waits. You must get used to it.'

She didn't answer. It was difficult to speak, you practically had to shout. At regular intervals, when the lights changed, a cataclysm of noise burst on us. The houses trembled, conversations ceased.

'I'd like to go now,' I said, 'but you won't be able to walk yet. You must have a proper cup of coffee.'

'No,' she said, 'no coffee.'

I called the waiter again, and explained that she needed a good cup of coffee.

'It's her,' I said to him confidentially, 'the woman from the *Gibraltar*.'

He looked dumbfounded. He believed me right away, without a moment's hesitation. And as if what I said was a quite sufficient explanation, he said he'd get her a *filtre*. It would only take about ten minutes. I said we'd wait, though she didn't want to.

'I want to go back to the ship,' she said.

I pretended not to have heard. During the next ten minutes, while we were waiting for the coffee, she fretted at the noise in the square.

249

'It's not worth waiting,' she said. 'I'm sure the coffee will be awful.'

She'd have liked everything to be as bad as possible, to go from bad to worse. I thought she was going to shout, and I took her hand and pressed it so as to prevent her. The waiter noticed how impatient she was. He came over to us, and I told him again I was relying on him to make sure the coffee was good. He said he was making it himself, the water was on, he was doing all he could. She smiled at the waiter, but rather as if it were all my fault and nothing to do with her, and as if she wanted to let him know she didn't blame him.

'It should be ready by now,' he said, 'I'll go and fetch it.'

He disappeared, and came practically running back with the *filtre*. Then we had to wait for the water to drip through. I tapped the filter to hurry it up.

'You'll spoil it,' she said.

I tasted it, and it was all right. She took it out of my hand and drank it down at a gulp. It was hot and burned her and she let out another moan.

'It was very good,' I said.

'I don't know. I want to go.'

I told her she'd have to do something to her hair. She tied her scarf round it.

'Where do you want to go?'

She stood up straight with her eyes full of tears.

'Oh I don't know, I don't know.'

'Let's go to the cinema then.'

I took her arm, she picked up her hat, and we set off down an avenue leading to the beach, in the opposite direction from the harbour. There weren't any cinemas this way, only banks and offices, but she didn't notice, didn't look at anything. The avenue was a quiet one, ending in a park that you could see in the distance. It made you want to go back to the boulevard. We walked for ten minutes, then I turned round.

'You don't know what you do want,' she said.

250

'I do know. A film. You need to see a film every so often.'

I could hardly have said then whether I hadn't just begun to love her. Yes, I could have believed that it was only just beginning. I held her arm very tight, and she made little faces, but as if she had to accept this pain I was causing her just like the noise from the lorries and everything else, like something inevitable. I would have liked not to have known her yet, and I tried to imagine her there in front of me for the first time with that face and those eyes. But of course I couldn't. But I found her more beautiful than ever and more astonishing even than the day when I'd seen her beyond the reeds.

'Why the cinema?' she asked softly.

'Why not?'

'Do you know which one we're going to?'

'Of course I know,' I said.

She turned and looked at me as if she suspected me of some ulterior motive.

'I want to tell you something,' I said.

'What's that got to do with the cinema?'

'Who knows?'

We reached the boulevard that ran from the square to the harbour, and saw again the long streams of lorries with iron fillings and coal. I stopped by a crossing. There was no need for us to cross over, and I think she realized this, but she didn't say anything.

'We're going to cross over,' I said.

Yes, I think she must have understood, because there was obviously no cinema on the other side of the street, and she was hardly drunk at all now. A policeman dressed in white and perched up in a sort of raised white crow's-nest was controlling with pontifical gestures the movements of the huge iron filing lorries. They would pull up with a deafening screech of brakes at a mere movement of his gloved hand.

'Look at the policeman,' I said.

She looked at him and smiled. I let two of his signals go by.

Each interval lasted three minutes – three minutes for the pedestrians to cross and three for the lorries. There were a lot of people about.

'What a long time it takes,' she said.

'Very.'

The interval for the pedestrians was over. It was the lorries' turn to go ahead. A lorry laden with packing-cases started up noisily. There was no one left on the crossing. The policeman swung round and opened his arms like someone crucified. I put my arm round her and dragged her forward. She saw everything – the lorry starting up, the empty crossing. But she didn't resist. For the first time I didn't feel as if I was having to drag her along against her will. We flew across. The wing of the lorry brushed my leg. A woman screamed. Just before we got to the island, just after the woman screamed, in the midst of the yells of the policeman, I told her I loved her.

She stood still by the island. I held her very close so that she shouldn't fall against the lorries. It wasn't anything much that I'd just said to her – a few words among a thousand others that I might have said. But I think that this was the first time since she'd lost the sailor from Gibraltar that she'd needed to hear someone say them. She stood by the island, still and pale.

'Papers!' shouted the policeman.

Still holding her to me I got out my identity card and held it out to him. He wasn't very cross. Seeing her like that he thought she'd been frightened that I was going to be knocked down. She smiled at him just as if it were him she was thinking about, and when he saw it he smiled back. He gave me back my identity card and swung round again to stop the lorries and let us pass. We crossed over.

'I don't feel much like going to the cinema,' she said.

She laughed, and so did I. The street was spinning about us like a merry-go-round. I was dizzy from having told her. We turned round and crossed back, this time at the proper signal.

252

The policeman looked surprised, but smiled again. We found a cinema in a little street that led out of the boulevard. We arrived back on the ship just before dinner. Once more Laurent was waiting for us, to set sail.

The voyage lasted ten days.

It was peaceful and gay.

I became a serious person. It started after Tangier, and lasted. She became serious too. For her also it started after Tangier and lasted. I don't mean to say that we were perfectly serious when we arrived at Cotonou. No. But much more than we had been at the beginning. It takes a lot of time and effort to become serious, as everyone knows. You can't do it in a day, or even in ten. You can only make a beginning.

So the passage was peaceful and gay.

At Casablanca I bought three shirts and started to wash and keep myself clean again. That too was a bit difficult, of course. But by Grand Bassam I was practically perfectly clean again. Sleeping took a bit longer. Still, I slept every night – sometimes more, sometimes less, but every night. Little by little, making a bit more progress each day, I gradually came to occupy my proper place on the ship. And each day she gradually left me more opportunity to do so, each day she saw more clearly that it was better for both of us. This place soon became very precious to me. Getting used to such a life probably seems quite easy if you look at it from a distance, but I don't think many men would have got used to it as well as I did. Looking for someone is like everything else: to do it well you must do nothing else, you mustn't even regret giving up any other activity, you must never doubt for a moment that it's worthwhile for one man to devote his whole life to looking for another. In other words you have to be convinced that you haven't anything better to do. For me, this was true. I hadn't anything better to do. Than to look for him, I mean. And although it was a very delicate and difficult business, which could assume the most contradictory appearances, including for example that of total idleness, and although I was still far from understanding all its aspects and all its difficulties, I think I may say without boasting unduly that during that voyage I began to have the makings of quite a good searcher for the sailor from Gibraltar.

We stopped at Casablanca, Mogador, Dakar, Freetown, Edina, and lastly Grand Bassam. She only went ashore twice, at Dakar and Freetown, and I went with her. But I went ashore at all the other places too – Casablanca, Mogador, Edina and Grand Bassam – and there I went with Epaminondas. Going ashore like that, with her, and even with Epaminondas, I quickly acquired a taste for a certain kind of geography, human geography. When you're travelling like that, in search of someone, you take quite a different sort of pleasure from the one you get from ordinary travelling. We weren't tourists, we couldn't possibly have been. For people who are looking for someone all ports of call are the same, not so much places of natural interest as the haunts of certain kinds of men. Probably he was the magnet that set up this strongest of all bonds between us and the world. Of course we were going to Cotonou to look for him, but we couldn't forget that we might find him at any port of call before. When we happened to look at the plastic atlas, even on the way to Cotonou, the whole world shown there seemed to us to be inhabited by him and him alone. And going through the avenues of Dakar or the alleys of Freetown or the docks of Grand Bassam, we sought him mechanically in every white man that we met. Nature seemed insipid in comparison. I always came back tired from these excursions. I drank whisky to restore myself. I was drinking more and more of it. So was she. We both drank more and more as the voyage went on. First of all in the evening. Then in the afternoon as well. Then in the morning. Every day we started a bit earlier. There was always some whisky on board. She'd been drinking it for a long time, of course, ever since she'd been looking for him, but during this voyage I think she drank it with more pleasure than before. I soon got into her rhythm of drinking, and completely gave up trying to restrain her when we were together. Probably it was because we were becoming serious. We drank whisky mostly, but also wine and pernod. But of course we liked whisky best. Apart from being a favourite with Americans, it's also the finest possible drink for long sea quests.

We hugged the coast of Africa, never losing sight of it after Tangier. Rocky and chaotic until we got to Senegal, after that it became flat and grey. It stayed like that the rest of the way. Sometimes, partly as a result of the whisky, no doubt, we detected some variety in it.

Once, even, through her, I discovered a comic aspect to my situation. Seeing her going round sempiternally like that, it suddenly seemed irresistibly funny for me to be bound to the ship as I was, to the point of not even batting an eyelid at being hauled off to Africa, when all the time I might be chucked off at any moment. She laughed and said it was the same for a lot of people, but of course they didn't realize, because not everybody had the coast of Africa to bring it home to them; my situation was not as unusual as I thought.

Just before Cotonou, three days before, there was a fairly heavy storm. The doors and portholes were shut and no one was allowed on deck. Epaminondas was seasick and was sorry he'd 'let himself be persuaded'. It lasted two days. The ship rose up like a sperm-whale and then fell back inert into terrifying troughs. Each time you wondered whether it would ever emerge again. Bruno often wondered about it, and so did Epaminondas sometimes. It was different for us. The ship's movement, continual but unavailing, never advancing yet enduring as best it could, might have seemed a symbol of our own efforts. But the next day our efforts, like the ship's, like everyone's, went on. And the day after that the storm was still not over, but we saw the sun. Through the portholes of the bar we watched the sea raging in the sun. It was very beautiful. Often the propellers rose right out of the water and the whole ship shrieked with fear. But the idea that it could possibly sink before Epaminondas's appointment only made us laugh.

So the sky cleared the day after that, two days before our arrival. We made good speed then, making up for lost time, towards the sailor from Gibraltar.

Arriving in Africa is always very sudden, without an island, without a bay where the swell breaks gently, without those archipelagos that usually dance on the sea, heralding new continents.

It was a beautiful day. Schools of porpoises came out to meet us, leaping all silver through the warm waves and trying every device to lure one of us in as a sacrifice. She threw them some bread. There was a slight swell and we entered the Gulf of Guinea in waters of three thousand fathoms, surrounded by horizons perfect and unbroken, save, towards the end of the afternoon, by the funnel of a cargo-ship, and later still by the yellow sails of a few local cotton-boats. We landed at Porto Novo at six o'clock in the evening.

The exchange of greetings between Louis and Epaminondas took some time. They'd known each other very well two years before, first at Marseilles, then on the ship, and they were great friends. They settled down in the bar and told each other all that had happened to them since they last met, forgetting all about us for half an hour. We drank whisky and waited discreetly for them to finish. Louis had tried various jobs, but now he ran bananas between Cotonou and Abidjan in an old cutter he'd bought from a company that had gone bankrupt. He told Epaminondas he spent all he earned patching up the cutter, and never had a penny to bless himself with. So we learned in the very first few minutes that Louis needed fifty thousand francs to buy a new cutter because apart from the fact that the present one cost him all he earned, he risked going down with her every time he went to sea. This reminded him, in perfectly good faith, of Anna. I may as well say straight away that two days later he asked her for the fifty thousand francs. Of course she gave them to him at once, with pleasure even. Her pleasure was increased rather than lessened by the fact that Louis had sent her the message as much to give her the opportunity of coming and doing him this small service as because he thought he'd found the sailor from Gibraltar.

Louis, small, thin and sunbaked, was striking for his breeziness and energy. Like Epaminondas, like all the sailors who sent her messages and 'recognized' him no doubt rather easily, he had a very special sort of grace. Probably, in him, because of his life under the African sun, this grace was a shade immoderate. I think – because even I, the first day, before I was used to him, was tempted to wonder – I think a lot of people would have thought he was mad. But he wasn't. He mixed only with black men. The white inhabitants of Porto Novo wouldn't have anything to do with him; he made them feel tired. They said he was unstable, a chatterbox, a good-for-nothing, who damaged the white man's reputation. Only the negroes liked Louis. The extravagance of his character didn't bother them in the least, and the life he led, precarious and hand-to-mouth, didn't upset them. On the contrary.

We soon grew very fond of this precariousness. And his extravagance didn't frighten Anna. She knew, from years of experience, that not only could the slightest, vaguest clues, clues that novices would laugh at, sometimes conceal a seed of truth, but also that sometimes one has to trust to anyone, to liars, fools, and even madmen. Everyone may be mistaken, she said. She trusted Louis to the point of going on his advice into the deepest regions of Central Africa, into the green savannahs of Ouellé.

Louis lived in a dilapidated little two-roomed bungalow

overlooking the port. He was the only white man in that part of the native quarter. He'd been living for two years with a young Peul woman, in a state of instability which seemed to suit her as well as it did him. Louis invited Anna and Epaminodas to dinner the first evening. I went with them, and when we got there Louis, informed no doubt by Epaminondas, though a bit late, of my rôle on the ship, apologized for having forgotten to ask me. He said he was very glad I'd come, and treated me in a friendly, natural manner, as one more of the men she took with her to make it easier to wait for the sailor from Gibraltar, and who in fact also helped her to look for him. Moreover the attention I paid to the story we were told that evening completely confirmed him in his ideas about my relationship to her. There was a fourth guest at dinner – Louis's best friend, a black teacher at the boys' school in Cotonou, whom Louis introduced to us as the man who knew the sailor from Gibraltar better than anyone else in Dahomey, and the author of a book, written in French and six hundred pages long, published by the propaganda service of the Colonial Ministry, relating the saga of Domicigui, queen of Dahomey and ancestor of king Behanzin. There was a good deal of talk about Domicigui during dinner. Especially as, like all the clerks in the Ministry, I'd seen a copy of this demonstration of the benefits of colonialism – this book written in French by a black citizen of the Republic. Louis explained at great length how he had helped to compile and correct it. He thought it was masterly. I congratulated the author warmly on having written it, omitting to mention, of course, that I hadn't read a single word of it. Thus it was that for Louis and his friend I became the only white man, besides the sailor from Gibraltar, they told us, who'd read and liked Domicigui. It doubled their pleasure, and because of this coincidence our meeting and our visit to Dahomey seemed to them all the more justified, so to speak. It was very natural. And if Louis's friend's account of his meetings with the sailor from

Gibraltar was interspersed with allusions to the history of Dahomey, it didn't seem to bother Anna. As for me, who was ready for anything, why should it have bothered me?

The dinner was simple but excellent. Louis's young Peul woman waited at table very gracefully, but took no part at at all in the conversation. However glorious the history of Dahomey it obviously left her cold, and as for the sailor from Gibraltar, she probably knew his story so well that she had nothing to learn from the teacher. When dinner was over she went out on the porch and sang pastoral chants from the high plateau of Atokara. Anna had brought enough bottles of Italian wine to keep the party going well into the night, and to prevent anyone being unduly astonished at the story Louis's friend had to tell us.

Here it is. He told us it at about two in the morning, in a whisper – for the police, he said, are everywhere – in epic and mysterious tones, more than a little drunk, and accompanied by the sad, heroic accents of the sagas of Akatora.

'There lives in Abomey, capital of Dahomey and former seat of the so-called savage kings of our land, of whom the greatest, as you doubtless remember, was alas the last – I mean Behanzin, eye of the world, whose history and rehabilitation so urgently require to be undertaken at last – there lives in Abomey, as I was saying, a certain white gentleman. According to what Louis tells me, according to the story he has been dinning into me for the last two years, this white gentleman corresponds as exactly as possible in his person with another white gentleman in whom you, Madame, are interested, and to the search for whom you devote your life. The other white men in the colony usually refer to him as a scoundrel, a pimp or a ponce – I don't know whether this last term, which is new to me, is as insulting as the others. Louis says it's worse. The whites also say he is a disgrace to the colony, but I personally don't see why one out of all the whites in this stew, as Louis calls it, excuse me please, should have to take all the blame. One thing that distinguishes this

259

gentleman is that he is wanted by the white police of Porto Novo and Cotonou and all the towns where they have them – with the exception of Abomey, where, I repeat, this white gentleman lives, and where as Louis says, the police are in a blue funk, excuse me please – all the towns where they have them, white police that is, the black police not being entitled, on account of their colour, to hunt out white criminals. I tell you straight away that this gentleman is wanted by the white police, because I gathered, with my alas so modest intelligence, that this was one of the most remarkable characteristics of the other gentleman the search for whom has been so long your favourite pastime. I mean, excuse me please, the sailor from Gibraltar.

'The charges made against this gentleman, the sailor from Gibraltar, are many and various. Murder, theft, smuggling, and – excuse me please, Madame, if I so express myself, but I have to tell you the whole truth – rape also. I must add at once that these last charges, of rape, and it's a little failing of white people that they don't seem to be able to understand it, are comparatively minor offences in Dahomey. Especially when the person concerned is this gentleman, the sailor from Gibraltar, who is so very highly thought of amongst us, and in consequence amongst our wives and daughters, who always hanker, alas, after the good old days in Dahomey, when people made love as easily as they breathed, at every age, at any hour of the day, and in any position, without justice coming and poking its nose in.

'For my own part, I tell you straight away that I have had the great honour of approaching this gentleman, the sailor from Gibraltar. I am, you must know, a native of Abomey, and my wife lives there most of the time. I often go there so that we may both partake of conjugal delights. These journeys do not interfere with my professional duties as a teacher, which allow me a certain amount of leisure. It was thus that I had the great pleasure and honour of meeting the sailor from Gibraltar and of sometimes exchanging friendly greetings.

'We, the people of Dahomey, do not refer to this gentleman as the sailor from Gibraltar. The reason for this is that apart from Louis and myself, whom Louis has let into the secret, no one knows that that is his real designation, or rather yours, your designation of him who is dearer to you than all worldly honours and necklaces of gold, as they say. We, the people of Dahomey, know him under the humble name of Gégé. Please note that I say Gégé and not – excuse me please, but you might confuse the two – not Glé-Glé, the illustrious sire of Behanzin, eye of the shark.

'I should find it somewhat difficult to describe Gégé – I'm sorry, the sailor from Gibraltar. Being myself, as you may easily judge, black, I suffer from a sort of racial incapacity to distinguish the physiognomical differences of white men. They all look so much alike to me that one day I greeted our respected Governor General with the words, "Hello, boy, how goes it?"– thinking it was Louis here. This was at the beginning of our friendship, and I don't mind telling you the consequences for me might have been grave. However, I think that possibly I might just venture to suggest, without being at all categorical about it, that this gentleman, the sailor from Gibraltar, might just be said to bear a slight resemblance to Mr. Epaminondas. My difficulty in giving you an idea of what he looks like is increased by the fact that the sailor from Gibraltar wears a tropical helmet and dark glasses, and I have never encountered him in the streets of Abomey save with these preservatives indispensable to every white man in our colony, which as you know is so close to the Equator. Nevertheless I can tell you that the ladies – forgive me, Madame, for putting such a strain upon your feelings – the ladies say that his eyes are blue. Some say – I have been obliged to inform myself on the subject, in order to be able to inform you – some say they are the colour of the blue sky in the morning, others that they are the blue of the lakes on the plateaus of Akotara in the mists of twilight. But as dark glasses are of course opaque, I cannot give you an opinion derived from my personal experience. Your visit here will give you an opportunity, if you wish, of judging these subtle and poetic differences for yourself. For my part I could see that around his dark glasses, themselves extremely symmetrical, his features were very regularly disposed about his face, and his hair – though you must forgive me, for what I say here is, because of the tropical helmet, somewhat arbitrary – his hair seems still to cover his head in its entirety. I have only seen the tips of it, but I can tell you that the tips of his hair are black.

'The resources of the sailor from Gibraltar are many and various. They are mostly concerned with what the white men here call "the trade". I believe that by this word they denote a commercial activity that is at once new, original and as they say, very personal. It is concerned with articles of local manufacture, and also with gold. This gentleman does not work alone. They say that the sailor from Gibraltar has his representatives all over Africa, especially on the Ivory Coast, in Nigeria, and the eastern Sudan, but also in Fouta Djallon, Labbé, and even in the basin of the Ouellé, among the Montboutou tribes, which as you know are called cannibals.

'As to the activities of the sailor from Gibraltar, although our conversations have always been brief and confined mostly to the exchange of personal news, I know by hearsay that these activities concern alcoholic beverages, in particular the one known as whisky, which according to Louis is that which is most appropriate when one has a disagreeable past and heavy burdens on one's conscience. He hunts too, all the kinds of animals there are in the colony, and even, when there's nothing else, the crows in the streets of Abomey. He lives like us, the poor blacks, whom he calls his brothers, and he shares his house with a dozen Peuls that he calls his brothers too, and whom people say he has raised up against his false white brothers of the colonial administration. A detail that I personally find very endearing is that he is extremely well up in the history of Dahomey, and holds our beloved Behanzin in the highest possible esteem.

'The sailor from Gibraltar is regarded in our country as a fine fellow. Among the simple folk, the shepherds of the high plateau, he passes for something even more, for a man who is invulnerable and protected by the gods. They compare him to the great kudu who flies like the wind in the rising sun, and some fertile imaginations see him as one of the avenging reincarnations of our illustrious Behanzin. He likes these comparisons. And the tobacco he gives these shepherds of the high plateau! But I won't dwell on what the sailor from Gibraltar represents for us. Your mythology is so different from ours that it wouldn't mean anything to you. What I will tell you is that the sailor from Gibraltar has changed his ways, as they say. Now he's armed not only with his fists but with a Mauser as well. And every man that lives with him has a Mauser too. Which means, if I'm not mistaken, that the sailor from Gibraltar has ten Mausers. He buys them in British Nigeria; he has friends there too. His Mausers hold six bullets and are very deadly. The sailor from Gibraltar is never seen without his Mauser, and makes no attempt to conceal his activities or even, up to a point, his past. We too know that once upon a time he committed a crime in the great capital of Paris. He speaks of it with great simplicity and humility, and says that if it were still to do he'd do it again, and even that he's sorry sometimes that it's done and not still to do. But, whether from prudence or not I couldn't say, he has never told of the circumstances in which his crime was committed, or said who the victim was. And you will readily understand that I for my part have never questioned him about it. In view of the liveliness of his character I couldn't, without the risk, as Louis says, of getting myself peppered, tell him to his face that I knew that he was the instrument of justice in the case of the American king of car bearings, Mr. Nelson Nelson. I was just going to let him know I knew from a distance, by correspondence that is to say, explaining myself in such a manner that he could judge of my good intentions, when alas the sailor from Gibraltar was obliged to fly from Dahomey.

'Believe me, it is with regret that I appraise you of this sad news. This gentleman, the sailor from Gibraltar, suddenly made himself answerable for two new crimes here in Dahomey, and he is no longer among us. He slew with a single Mauser shot, just one, a policeman in Abomey who was new to the colony and had the effrontery to ask him for his papers in the street there, and he also killed a white settler who'd been bothering him for some time by competing in the gold business. He committed both these imprudences in the course of a single day. What could be the explanation of such irritability? It had been very hot recently in Abomey. But the white settlers were not interested in any explanations. They were horrified by this sudden recrudescence of the sailor from Gibraltar's activity, and presented a petition to the Governor General. So the Governor General set all the police forces of the colony on to the sailor from Gibraltar. It was your humble servant who had the honour to communicate this news, by means of an intermediary, to the sailor from Gibraltar. While the whole of the police were moving up from Porto Novo to Cotonou, the sailor from Gibraltar came down from Cotonou to Porto Novo. It was quite easy, there wasn't a single white policeman left in Porto Novo, so he was able to get away in peace.

'He went first into the bush, and then, with the help of friends, into the Belgian Congo. Once there – and you will probably recognize this characteristic device – the sailor from Gibraltar let it be known that he had been reduced to the last extremity because the Belgian authorities proposed to exercise their rights of extradition against him, and so he got his cannibal friends, the Montboutous, to eat him on the occasion of their annual tribal feast. He'd been turning this trick over in his mind for a long time, Madame, and you needn't feel in the least uneasy about it. In fact during one of our encounters the sailor from Gibraltar told me himself that if the worst came to the worst he would go along the coast to the Belgian Congo, and if they still wouldn't leave him in peace when he got there he would adopt the extreme solution, that is he would spread the rumour that he had been devoured by the Montboutous. "Gégé will never fall into the hands of the police, never," he told me. By the way, I should point out to whom it may concern that the sailor from Gibraltar never refers to himself except in the third person. He'll say: "Gégé's hungry," or: "Gégé's fine," or: "Gégé's got a pain in the neck," and so on. In the course of the aforementioned conversation, the longest I've had the honour of holding with this gentleman, he explained that seeing that his life had been what it was, that is the kind of life he would have chosen if he'd been asked to choose, he had no regrets about it and wouldn't wish to change it for another – no doubt he meant for a life in prison – so he'd just as soon die among the Montboutous. Strange to say, he told me that that was even the sort of death he had always wanted. "It would be a pity for Gégé to die in all his health and strength to no purpose, and for all that strength to rot away uselessly and for ever in the soil of Africa. Especially when it would give his pals the Montboutous of the Ouellé so much pleasure to make a friendly meal out of him. If Gégé were sick or rotten or poxy, the soil of Africa would do, but since he's what he is, it would be a pity to waste such a juicy morsel!" Stuck up on the sailor of Gibraltar's house the police found a cardboard notice he'd left, which confirms what I've just said: "Don't waste your time looking for Gégé. Gégé is no more. Don't even bother to look for his corpse. There's no trace of Gégé's corpse in the soil of Africa for the good reason that, as anyone in Abomey can tell you, Gégé has been eaten by his friends the Montboutous of the Ouellé. Put that in your pipe and smoke it. P.S.: Gégé has no regrets, either for the colonial or for the copper."

'When they questioned the population of Abomey they all of course confirmed what their lord had said. The police could do nothing, so they went back to Porto Novo.

'If I thought it worthwhile to send a message to Mr. Epaminondas it was because we now know where to find the sailor from Gibraltar. A month ago he wrote to us from Leopoldville. The letter was addressed to me – not that I was his best friend, but because I am the only one who can read French. We destroyed the letter, of course, but we can remember it perfectly. "Dear Behanzin," he called me as a joke, "Gégé is in Leopoldville, amusing himself as best he can. It's a big place, one of the marvels of lousy colonialism. You'd have to have killed your father and mother to be able to stick it. But he's met some friends, and he gets a game of cards. Bury his Mausers. So long. Yours, Gégé."

'When this letter came Louis decided to write to the sailor from Gibraltar by means of a third person. We hadn't got much time. You were already on the way to Sète; we knew Epaminondas had sent for you to go there. So we were caught short, as they say, and we decided finally, taking advantage of the distance, to speak to him about his past, about you, Madame, and about the way you pass your time. We asked him if he was not the instrument of justice in the case of Mr. Nelson Nelson, the king of American car bearings, and if he was, to let us know. We also told him that a lady called Anna was looking for him everywhere all over the world on a ship called the *Gibraltar*.

'Were we too explicit? Too indiscreet? In our haste we may have phrased it without enough thought. For the day before yesterday we had a rather irritable reply from the sailor from Gibraltar. This is what it said: "If Gégé was the murderer of Nelson Nelson he wouldn't be very likely to say so, especially on paper. You'd have to be either mad or weak in the head to think so. As for this Anna, you can always direct her to Gégé, and we'll see what we can do for her. Tell her to ask for Gégé in Leo, in the first bistro on the left bank of the Congo."

'Please forgive me, Madame, for having taken up so much

of your time. I don't think I have anything more to tell you, except that I have the greatest sympathy for your undertaking.'

It was quite late when we got back on board. We were tired from having to hold back the laughter inspired by this new version of the story of the sailor from Gibraltar. We all three went to the bar, of course, to have a whisky and sum up our evening. Besides, Epaminondas looked so downcast that we couldn't do otherwise.

'I don't think this can be it,' he said.

She reassured him as well as she could.

'He might have altered,' she said. 'Why shouldn't this be it? Hasn't he got the right to change like anybody else?'

But when she suddenly burst out laughing, after the first whisky, even Epaminondas couldn't resist.

'Well,' he said, 'you can certainly say I've got you into a fine old fix this time.'

'I shall end up by believing that he exists,' I said, 'And in no uncertain fashion.'

Epaminondas put on his horrified expression.

'He means,' explained Anna, 'that with all those Mausers perhaps we ought to be a bit more careful than with the others.'

'When people who get irritated easily carry guns about with them everywhere they're apt to make use of them . . . what shall I say? . . . without undue reflection.'

'I haven't done anything,' said Epaminondas. 'I don't run any risk.'

'I don't suppose he's interested in such fine distinctions,' I said.

Epaminondas's thoughts took a new direction.

'Well? Are you going to the banks of the Congo then?'

'People change,' she said suavely. 'Sometimes they change a lot.'

Then she suddenly looked at me, absently.

'If he's changed as much as that,' said Epaminondas, 'do you really think it's worth going and getting a bullet through you on the banks of the Congo?'

'The banks of the Congo,' I said, 'and above all the banks of the Ouellé, are swarming with kudus.'

'If that's all we're after,' said Epaminondas, 'why don't we go and hunt them somewhere else than on his doorstep?'

'He could have changed a lot,' went on Anna. 'Completely, even. Why shouldn't he be allowed to get older like everyone else? There's nothing to prove it's not him. Him, changed.'

'That's true,' I said. 'Why shouldn't sailors from Gibraltar get old too, the same as everybody else?'

'I'd never thought about it,' said Anna.

'Everyone gets old,' said Epaminondas, summing it up. 'But if he's got as old as all that do you think it's worth going looking for him on the banks of the Congo?'

'I've never seen you so reluctant,' laughed Anna.

'I've done quite enough for you already,' said Epaminondas, 'to have the right to think twice about getting a bullet through me. And if he's so changed you don't recognize him, what's the point of going to look for him?'

'Older or not,' I said, 'supposing he is the one who killed the American king of car bearings?'

'Where does that get you,' snapped Epaminondas, 'if he's taken to killing everybody right, left and centre?

'Can one give up the whole goal of one's existence so lightly?' asked Anna timidly.

'Lightly!" said Epaminondas. 'That's a good one.'

'Anyway,' I said, 'until she sees him with her own eyes how can she know? Who says he's changed all that much?'

'It won't do her much good if he shoots her as soon as she recognizes him,' said Epaminondas.

'Well,' said Anna, 'do you think I could give him up, knowing there's just a chance that it might be him, and then go and start looking for him again somewhere else?'

'You two make a fine pair, that's all I can say,' answered Epaminondas.

'If you don't follow up that chance,' I said, 'you might as well give up right away.'

'Well,' said Epaminondas to me, 'you certainly seem to be in a great hurry this time.' Then, after a moment, 'You know, I've got the feeling that it's not only him that attracts you to the banks of the Congo. I think there must be something else too.'

'The kudus,' I said. 'Just a little.'

'Don't you laugh at me,' said Epaminondas. 'I know very well it's not the kudus.'

'What is it then?' asked Anna.

'I don't know,' said Epaminondas, looking from one to the other of us. 'All I know is it's not only him and the kudus. And that you know very well there's only one chance in a thousand . . .'

'That's not so bad,' said Anna, 'one chance in a thousand.'

'Even if there was only one chance in ten thousand,' I said, 'it still shouldn't be neglected. Our images will be reflected in the waters of the Congo.'

'I'm not sure mine will,' said Epaminondas.

'I adore you,' said Anna.

'Maybe,' said Epaminondas, 'but the way he is now you're going to have a job getting him to give up his Mausers.'

'I have no objection to guns,' she said.

'And I suppose you've no objection to cannibals either?'

'They're fine fellows,' I said. 'We'll give them some kudus. And if they won't be persuaded I promise you I'll offer myself for the grill in your place.'

'Come to think of it,' he said, starting to laugh, 'what have you got to lose? . . .'

'I don't think we shall be reduced to that,' she said. 'Gégé will intercede for us. He must be very persuasive.'

We stayed in Dahomey for three days to see to some slight damage the ship had sustained during the storm we'd run into just before we arrived. Those three days brought us very close to Louis and his friend the schoolteacher. Epaminondas and Bruno, accompanied by Louis, had a try at hunting kudus in the Tchabé district. Epaminondas wasn't used to hunting and didn't get anything, but he missed enough different kinds of animals to come back full of enthusiasm. All his qualms had disappeared as if by magic, and he couldn't set out soon enough for the basin of the Ouellé. Bruno turned out to be a good shot and brought back a young stag. He too was changed when he came back, transfigured, even, and admitted at last that he was glad he'd agreed to come on board at Sète. Louis had the tact to bring nothing back with him. Laurent took advantage of the two days they were away to spend two consecutive nights with the little Peul girl, who was getting very bored with Cotonou. To make things easier for him Anna and I fell in with the teacher's suggestion to go for a drive as far as Abomey. The next day we went as far as Lagos in Nigeria. We didn't regret it. By the time we got back we had another friend. The other members of the crew spent the time in the brothels of Cotonou and Porto Novo. In short, everyone enjoyed themselves, and talked about the visit to Porto Novo for a long time afterwards.

The evening before we left, when everyone was back from hunting and the brothels and Lagos, Anna decided to give a dinner-party in honour of our two friends. It was a gay evening, memorable on various accounts. The dinner itself was nothing out of the way, but it was washed down with such lavish draughts of Italian wine that everyone enjoyed it. When it came down to it we were all delighted at the prospect of going to the Ouellé country. And we were all as light-hearted as if we'd really tracked down the sailor from Gibraltar. No one doubted our success any more; by the time the dinner was over everyone, except perhaps Laurent, Anna and me, were sure of it. Bruno sang Sicilian songs, Epaminondas talked about kudus, the teacher about

Dahomey and its glorious past, Louis about his new cutter and the huge and rapid fortune he was going to make carrying ten times as many bananas as before between Abidjan and Cotonou. Laurent had a long conversation with Anna of which I didn't hear a single word. The other sailors told each other more and more frankly as the dinner wore on about their respective exploits in the brothels of Porto Novo. The little Peul girl, who was sitting next to me, talked to me about travelling, Cotonou and the monotonous life she led there. In short everyone talked at once about whatever interested them, and didn't bother whether anyone listened or not, a state of affairs both rare and agreeable. From time to time, no doubt in order to restore a spirit of unanimity in constant danger of breaking down, Louis and his friend the teacher – both of them much too humble to suppose that the party was in their honour – would propose toasts, either to Behanzin whom no one really understood, or to Gégé, called the sailor from Gibraltar, who had taken refuge by the Ouellé from the idiotic rigours of respectability. That's what they're like, good seekers of sailors from Gibraltar. By the time dinner was over the minds of a lot of those present were so confused by the Italian wine that we found it difficult to distinguish between the respective merits of the two heroes, and in the end, to simplify matters, the names were left out and we merely drank to the unhappy fate of innocence in general. She was sitting opposite me and if it hurt me rather not to be beside her, I'd got so used by now to this kind of discomfort that I could adapt myself to it and behave as cheerfully as everyone else.

Suddenly, towards two o'clock in the morning, Louis got up from the table and informed us that he'd written two sketches, one about the sailor from Gibraltar and the other about Behanzin. He said he wouldn't like to miss the opportunity of celebrating the virtues of one or other of these two heroes before such a large and sympathetic audience. He asked us to choose which sketch we would like. Everyone voted for the sketch about Behanzin, no doubt by way of a change.

He asked us to push back the tables so that he would have room to act what he called 'the incident of the 1890 treaty'. We did as he said and everyone sat around anyhow in a large circle. Again she was quite a long way away from me, but it was probably better like that. Louis asked us to excuse him and disappeared for a moment on deck, together with the schoolmaster. He returned in such a curious get-up that the sailors all roared with laughter: he wore a paper hat that looked like a shower cap but which he said represented the head-dress of the kings of Abomey, and was swathed down to the ankles in a white waist-cloth, the normal dress, he told us, of these same monarchs. In his hand he held a sheet of white paper which was to serve as the 1890 treaty. He asked us to stop laughing. It took us a long time, but finally, with the aid of Laurent, Anna and myself he got everybody quiet.

The performance began with a long silence during which Behanzin looked at the treaty which he was supposed to have just signed, this dreadful deed he'd just committed, just been made to commit before he realized what it implied. After he'd been sufficiently appalled, unable to pronounce a single word, Behanzin began to speak.

'A treaty,' he began, 'what is a treaty? What is it? To begin with, what is paper? And then what does it mean, to sign? They shoved a pen in my hand, they held my hand, and "Sign, sign!" they told me. What? The handing over of Dahomey? Don't make me laugh! They guided my hand to make me cut my own throat!'

The schoolteacher, much moved, explained the ins and outs of Behanzin's uncertainties.

'As he didn't understand what a treaty was, how could he realize what he was doing? It takes a long while and a lot of effort to get such relative matters into someone's head.'

'Us country of great customs,' went on Louis, 'but that

one we not know. Paper, we not know. Sign, don't make me laugh. We'll blow out your brains if you don't sign, they said. And how I supposed to sign, and how I supposed to make you promises, don't make me laugh!'

'As innocent as a newborn babe,' said the schoolteacher, 'Behanzin signed his own death warrant.'

We had drunk so much that Behanzin's fate left us unmoved. Louis fascinated us. The crew were splitting their sides, but this was of no consequence to our two friends. Anna was laughing too, she hid her face in her handkerchief so as not to show it too much. Only Louis and the little Peul girl remained quite serious. She, after a childhood passed on the high plateaux of Akotara, must have spent a little while in a brothel in Cotonou. She'd forgotten Laurent and was making eyes at Epaminondas and me with a studiousness that was quite touching, as if to show us that she knew how to behave in society. It couldn't have been the first time she had seen the tragedy of Behanzin performed.

Louis, in despair, wept, tore at his hair – really tore it out – and rolled on the floor, holding the 1890 treaty between his teeth for convenience as he did so.

Anna watched him, helpless with laughter. She'd complately forgotten me.

'They've made me sell my people,' he cried, 'my little people of Abomey, my Peuls, my Haoussas, my Ecoués, my Baibas. Sign, they said, sign why don't you? I signed. What does that mean, sign ? I ask you. To be or not to be, to sign or not to sign, what difference does it make to me, the eye of the world? How innocent I was! Oh, Glé-Glé, my noble father, your curse is upon me! I am no more the Eye of the Shark, the eye of the world, the great king of Abomey! I am no one! I am the innocence of the world, that suffers!'

The schoolteacher had tears in his eyes. Louis didn't leave him much respite.

'No,' moaned the schoolteacher, 'no, you are not accursed. Other generations will arise and proclaim your innocence!'

'Meanwhile,' groaned Louis, 'they shoved a Mauser in my back and said sign! Fart or sign, what's the difference, I ask you? And is it like this I must sell my Baibas, my Ecoués, my Haoussas? Like this, at a blow, that I must give all my daughters to the brothel? Enslave all my sons to these palefaces? Why? What for?'

We were all torn between sympathy and laughter. Laughter usually won.

'To think we came three thousand miles to see this,' moaned Epaminondas, slapping his sides with glee. The little Peul didn't give him much respite. She was becoming insistent. She was still making eyes at all of us like a school-girl. 'What's your name?' I asked her. 'Mahaoussia, sheep's udder,' she replied, taking her breasts in both hands by way of illustration. This shook us slightly, Epaminondas and me. Anna noticed it. 'What do you do?' asked Epaminondas.

'I princess,' she said, 'also whore in Porto Novo.'

Louis was no longer in doubt. He understood at last what he had done. Seized with terrific rage, he lay on the ground and spat spasmodically on the 1890 treaty, wiped his behind with it, calling his subjects to revolt.

'Come, my children, and show these white men that our customs are as good as theirs. We'll run them through with our spears, we'll roast them, we'll feast on them. Come and show them that our customs are as good as theirs and better!'

He gnawed ravenously at an imaginary biceps. The betrayal was complete. The paper had been crumpled up in a ball and thrown away.

'He'll make himself ill,' said Anna.

The sailors were laughing so loud Louis had to yell to make himself heard.

'Patience, Behanzin,' cried the schoolteacher.

'The day of the great massacre is come,' cried Louis. 'To arms, my sons! Come hither, you battalions of black Africa, and drive out the oppressor! Awake, blood of our ancestors!

Let our soil be cleansed of all these soldiers! Let's roast all these generals and colonels!'

The little Peul was getting very insistent.

'We could go outside,' she said. 'There's time.'

'That might interest me, perhaps,' said Epaminondas.

'After the story of General Dodds,' she said, 'deporting of Behanzin. Long sufferings. There's plenty of time.'

We'd never heard of this Dodds, and she explained that he was a French general, the hero of the conquest of Dahomey.

'Does he perform like this often?' I asked.

'Nearly every night. No theatre at Cotonou.'

'Does he always do the 1890 treaty?'

'Sometimes the story of the sailor from Gibraltar.'

Louis was still on the call to arms. There was no stopping him now. His friend accompanied his appeals to his subjects with rhythmical handclaps.

'No more of this abomination on our soil. Eat their colonels! Eat their generals, even! That might teach them to stay at home!'

'Patience, patience,' cried the schoolteacher.

Suddenly Louis relapsed into despair. He must have been tired.

'Ah, in the hands of the palefaces I am as light as the empty calabashes with which our shepherdesses cover their breasts!'

'No, Behanzin, you are heavy on the conscience of mankind!'

But Louis was inconsolable.

'Alas,' he cried still, 'innocence has no voice to make itself heard! Those who don't understand it now will never understand it!'

'Patience, patience, everyone will understand. Those who haven't yet understood will understand. The hour of the sailor from Gibraltar will come!'

At these words Louis let go of his imaginary biceps, which in theory he'd still been holding on to, and rose to face his friend with the nobility of an archangel. He seemed even drunker now than when he had begun his performance. He was beautiful. Anna grew slightly pale. He seemed to be thinking what to say, then, unable to think of anything, he advanced very slowly towards his friend, hands outstretched. No one laughed any more.

'It hasn't come yet, the hour of the sailor from Gibraltar,' yelled his friend falling back a pace. 'You must still be patient, Behanzin.'

Louis stood still, and suddenly the fright his friend was in made him laugh. Everyone laughed with him, even the friend. Louis abandoned the appeal to General Dodds.

'Some other time,' he said, worn out.

'Did he say another time?' said Epaminodas in astonishment.

But no one answered. Everyone clapped Louis enthusiastically. The drinking began again. Three sailors went on with the tragedy of Behanzin, splitting their sides. Louis and his friend split their sides watching them. The little Peul sidled up to me. Epaminondas, engrossed in Behanzin, didn't mind. Neither did Louis – he probably never did mind much. Anna watched us from a distance, smiling. The little Peul's dream was quite simple – to meet a sailor, an officer, who would take her to Paris, the 'great metropolis'. What for? To make a 'career', she said, but try as I might I couldn't get out of her what career. I tried to advise her against it just the same. As I spoke to her I looked at Anna. She was tired with so much laughing, but she kept smiling at me. She looked very beautiful. As discreetly as I could, and also to calm her down a bit, I gave the little Peul all the money I had on me. But she was so dazzled by this she immediately asked to be allowed to stay on the ship. I told her it was impossible, that there was only room for one woman on this ship. I showed her which. They looked at each other. I described the life we led on board, I told her it was uncomfortable, difficult, entirely given up to the search for the sailor from Gibraltar. I told her that this evening was quite exceptional and contrary to our usual habits. She was sure we should find the sailor from Gibraltar in the basin of the Ouellé. She'd seen him once when he came down to Cotonou. Like all the black women in Dahomey, she dreamed about him and would even have given up her career in the great metropolis for him. The women of the Ouellé were said to be very beautiful, and so civilized that even in the unlikely event of our not finding him, Dahomey would never see Gégé again. I left her grieving over this sad prospect and went across to Anna. The sailors were still laughing among themselves. They were reminding each other of all the most comical incidents in their various quests for the sailor from Gibraltar. I thought as I came near her that I was tired out with being serious. She saw, and grew uneasy. Her eyes grew wide and pale. In them I saw a special kind of fear, a fear that I alone could share with her, which was in fact the only thing I could share with her entirely, the only thing we possessed. I put my arm round her and drew her on to my lap. I told her not to be afraid, and she grew calm again.

'It's beginning well,' she said, 'our kudu hunt.'

'You haven't seen anything yet,' I said.

'No?' she laughed.

Laurent was sitting beside us. But it never bothered us to have anyone there, especially not Laurent. She added, child-like:

'Ah, you're a great one for hunting kudus,' and turned towards Laurent.

'Don't you think so?' she said.

'Yes, I think so too,' said Laurent, looking from one to the other of us. 'And I think that hunting kudus can be a very useful thing when it's done with enough . . . what shall I say? . . . enough passion.'

We all three laughed.

'You're right,' she said. 'I shall end by believing that wisdom consists in only taking on great poker players and great kudu hunters.'

'And the great drinkers,' I said, 'what about them?'

'The great drinkers,' she said, throwing herself back in her chair and starting to laugh, 'they must be incomparably reassuring too.'

'I should like to be the very greatest drunk of all the southern seas,' I announced.

'Why?' she said, laughing.

'Why indeed?' I said.

'I don't know,' she answered. 'How should I know?'

'How indeed?' I said. 'What are you laughing for?'

'What do you ask me what I'm laughing for?'

She turned to Laurent. They were very fond of each other.

'Have you ever seen any great loves,' she said, 'apart from mine?'

'On land,' said Laurent after a moment, 'I've seen a few. It's rather a depressing sight.'

'You're talking of the sort of loves,' she said, 'that are never threatened in any way? Those that apparently there's nothing to prevent from going on for ever.'

'All set for eternity,' said Laurent. 'That's right.'

'Eternity's a long time,' I said.

'Don't they say,' said Anna, 'that nothing gives you such a sense of eternity as a great love? In short, that nothing else resembles it so much?'

'Little loves that take every day as it comes have other advantages,' I said.

'Those aren't a depressing sight,' said Laurent, laughing.

'They wouldn't know what to do with eternity, those people,' I said. 'Life is enough for them.'

'Tell me,' she said, 'what is the sign that heralds the end of a great love?'

'One of those that, apparently, there's nothing to prevent from going on for ever?' I said.

'And what about those,' laughed Laurent, 'that everything prevents from going on for ever?'

'Ah,' I said, 'you can't expect us to know about those yet.'

'I'd never have thought,' said Anna,' that hunting kudus was so amusing.'

I was quite drunk myself and kept kissing her. The sailors were used to our behaviour, and Louis and his friend were too tight and too happy to take offence at anything whatever. Besides, surely everyone could understand that someone had to kiss her while she was waiting for the sailor from Gibraltar? Wasn't that what I was there for? I think it was only the little Peul that took umbrage. She wanted to go. Anna asked me to see her home, so I went with her as far as Louis' bungalow. When I got back the party was still going on, the sailors were still laughing. They were competing to see who could invent the most ridiculous places for the sailor from Gibraltar to be. Laurent had joined in and was laughing too. She was waiting for me. We joined in the conversation too, and it went on for some time. Then, on the suggestion of Bruno, who was beginning to take an interest in life again in no uncertain manner, everyone decided to pay another visit to the brothels in the town. Only she and I were left on board.

We got to Leopoldville three days after leaving Cotonou. It was the hottest time of the year. A low grey fog covered the town. Several times each day a storm would burst through and disperse it for half an hour, and then it would re-form again. It was hard to breathe. Over and over again the grey cloud re-formed and the storms shattered it. Tepid waterspouts hurtled down on the town. People breathed for a moment, then the grey cloud re-formed, and they waited for the storm again. It's a rich town with big wide streets. There are buildings thirty storeys high, banks, a big police force. There are quite a lot of diamonds in the subsoil of the colony. Thousands of blacks dig it, break it up, sift it in deep underground galleries so that the widow of the late Nelson Nelson may deck her fingers. Africa encircles the town closely. The city shines with the implacable glint of steel in the midst of the black night that surrounds it, but treats that darkness

279

with respect. Otherwise, it would soon be all up, Africa would close again over the city and crush its skyscrapers in swarming lianas. But when we came there Leopoldville was still in command: Mrs. Nelson Nelson could still sleep safe.

We anchored the yacht, and Anna, Epaminondas and I reconnoitred the cafés along the Congo, as arranged. We drank a lot of beer under the electric fans, listening to what the other customers were saying. We diluted the whisky a bit so as to listen as lucidly as we needed to. Epaminondas stayed with us all the time. When we spoke, we talked of nothing else but hunting kudus. We were still sufficiently doubtful about Gégé's identity to talk only about kudus.

This went on for three days. We drank a great deal of beer in those three days. Fortunately the kudus came in unexpectedly handy. Epaminondas, who had become uneasy again when we arrived, recovered sufficiently to start worrying once more about whether we were going to get the chance to go hunting them.

Then at the end of three days, after dinner, when Epaminondas had entirely given up hope both of hunting kudus and of ever getting out of that heat alive, we overheard a remarkable conversation.

It was in a fashionable bar on the outskirts of the town. We'd been there twice before because of the barman, a tall, middle-aged disillusioned barman who talked to us about Africa when he wasn't too busy. We'd been there about half an hour when two men came in. They were dressed in white with leather gaiters and carried guns slung over their shoulders. One was tall, the other short. They were very hot and splashed to the knees with mud. The Congo sun had bronzed them deeply. They'd come a long way and were glad to have got here. They weren't regular customers. They ordered two whiskies.

'Phew, what a journey,' began the first.

'You said it,' said the second.

'It sounds as if you gentlemen have come a long way,' said

the barman politely.

'From the Ouellé country,' said the first.

'Did you you hear that?' whispered Epaminondas.

'What a journey,' said the second. 'Same again.'

'It looks as if the heat has set in earlier this year,' said the barman politely.

'Yes, curse it,' said the first. 'Our tyres practically melted. But you were all right, Henri. He's the driver,' he explained to the barman. 'He's terrific.'

'Glad to know you,' said the barman, yawning.

'You exaggerate, Legrand,' said Henri.

'No, I don't,' said Legrand, 'you're terrific.'

'Get some good hunting?' asked the barman.

'A small lynx,' said Legrand, 'and an antelope. But we didn't do much shooting.'

'No,' said Henri, 'we wanted to get along. And of course we made clouds of dust, and those animals, there's no flies on them . . .'

'Naturally,' said the barman.

'Four hundred kilometres we did,' said Legrand. 'Henri, you were terrific. The worst thing of all is trying to be patient. Forty kilometres an hour for four hundred kilometres is enough to try the patience of a saint.'

'What isn't?' said Anna, who was beginning to get interested.

'What?' said Henri, eyeing her.

'What isn't enough to try the patience of a saint?' said Anna.

'Is the lady disillusioned?' asked Legrand urbanely.

'That's the last thing!' laughed Epaminondas, who after all was on his third whisky.

'Take your mind off for a second,' said Henri, 'and you get swallowed up in the mud and there you are stuck until someone happens to come along . . .'

'I can't bear to think of it,' said Anna.

'What?' said Legrand suspiciously.

'That you might not be here drinking your whiskies.'

Legrand was beginning to scowl at her, but Henri signed to him not to get cross. Anna smiled sweetly.

'I expect you're a Parisian,' he said. 'The ladies there are always very quick, you can pick them out straight away.'

'Meanwhile,' said Epaminondas, who was also starting to get a bit worked up, 'it's quite true that life is enough to try anyone's patience.'

'Do you think so?' I asked Anna.

'That's what they say,' she said in a low voice.

'When I had a pee,' said Henri, 'it sent up a cloud of dust. Same again,' he said to the barman.

'I've been here eight years,' said the barman. 'What I wouldn't give to pee on some ice for once.'

'Me too,' said Henri. 'A nice thick lump of ice, nothing like it. But here – forty-three degrees at Touatana. Not much hope of any ice.'

'Personally,' said Legrand, 'I always liked the heat better than the cold. But the amount you have to drink here! But I still prefer it.'

'It's funny, isn't it?' said the barman.

'Not me,' said Henri, 'never in your life. I used to think the drink would make me change my mind. But not any more.'

'God,' said the barman, 'what wouldn't I give to have a pee on the ice.'

'People say that,' said Epaminondas, 'and then it's just the same as everything else. It's only natural – once you've got what you want . . .'

'You can say what you like,' said Henri. 'You can't tell me the ice age could have been much fun.'

'There wasn't anybody there to see,' said the barman, yawning, 'so . . .'

'Are you sure?' asked Epaminondas, with interest.

'There must have been some animals at least,' said Anna.

'And aren't animals anyone?' demanded Henri.

'I don't think there were any,' I said.

'There must have been,' said Anna. 'At least just some teeny weeny ones.'

'I don't think so,' I said.

'Did you ever see the Sea of Ice?' said Henri to Legrand.

'I should think I did,' said Legrand. 'In 1936. That was the best time to see it. The funny thing was there were waves, just as if it had all been frozen over at once, quite suddenly.'

'Are you sure there wasn't anything?' Anna said to me. 'Not even any kudus?'

'Well,' said Henri, 'in the ice age the whole world was like the Sea of Ice.'

'There must have been some tiny little animals underneath the ice,' said Anna, 'waiting for it to melt.'

'If you like,' I said. 'After all, who knows? Perhaps everything existed then already.'

'It's impossible that there could have been nothing at all,' said Epaminondas with some heat. 'If so, how would you explain all those millions of animals afterwards?'

'It's funny,' said the barman. 'Whenever it reaches forty in the shade people always start to talk about the ice age.'

'That's right,' said Anna. 'How would you explain all the animals there are now?' She smiled at me.

'That's enough,' I whispered to her. 'Do you always keep on like this?'

'If you haven't noticed that yet . . .' laughed Epaminondas.

'It's difficult to bear,' said Anna. 'Don't you think so?'

'Everybody manages to bear it,' I said. 'And a good deal more besides. You can't imagine what I'm having to bear at this moment . . .'

'If that's how you go about it,' said Epaminondas indignantly.

'Is something the matter?' said Henri to Legrand, who had his eyes closed and wore an expression of ecstasy.

'Wait,' said Legrand.

'I don't like the look of him,' said the barman.

'Well?' said Henri uneasily. 'Come on, spit it out.'

'Wait, wait,' said his pal.

'If he's going to fall down dead,' said Anna, 'you'd better take his glass away from him.'

'Saumurians!' cried Legrand. 'That's the word I was looking for.'

'Does he often get taken like this?' asked Anna.

'In the ice age there were saumurians,' said Legrand, delighted with himself.

'He's like that,' said Henri, for the benefit of everyone in general. 'He looks quite nice and ordinary and all that, but really he's an intellectual. There are no flies on him.'

'What made me think of it was sauce, and then saumure, the brine they use for pickling,' explained Legrand.

'If you knew he was like that,' said Anna to Henri, 'you might have warned us.'

'I can't bear not being able to remember a word,' said Legrand. 'In the ice age,' he declaimed, 'the world was inhabited by saumurians.'

'You see,' said Anna to me, 'there was something.'

'I think it was saurians,' I said.

'That's what I thought,' said the barman. 'It was the saumure that led us astray. Personally I've no objection.'

'Saurians then, if you like,' said Legrand, slightly mortified.

'Well?' said Anna. 'Were there any or not?'

'I can't remember,' I told her softly.

'I'm sure the saurians came before,' said Epaminondas suddenly.

'There's no reason why we should take your word for it,' said Legrand with dignity. 'Did you know?' he asked Henri.

'Well,' said Henri, 'if there wasn't anything else but ice, I was wondering what these saurians found to eat . . .'

'Are they big animals, saurians?' Anna asked me.

'Huge,' I said. 'They're like crocodiles.'

284

'You can eat anything if you must,' said Legrand. 'It's a well known fact. If there isn't anything else but ice you eat ice, that's all there is to it.'

'If saurians were as big as all that,' said Anna, 'well, perhaps there weren't any of them. But I think there must have been some little tiny animals just the same.'

'And a fat lot of good that does us,' said the barman. 'What I'd like would be just one little pee on the ice.'

'Tiny little animals,' said Anna, 'as minute as you like. But there must have been some. Little insects. What do they eat? Hardly anything, and they hardly breathe either, so they could stay under the ice for ages . . .'

'Haven't you nearly done working him up like that, you and your little animals?' Epaminondas asked her.

'If only it was just them,' I said.

Epaminondas guffawed.

'To begin with,' said Henri, 'how can they tell there was nothing?'

'They just know,' I said. 'Are you really so set on your little animals?' I asked Anna.

'I shan't lose any sleep over them,' she said.

'What do you lose any sleep over?' I said.

'If you're going to keep this up,' said Epaminondas, 'I'm off.'

'I shan't lose any sleep over it,' said Anna, 'but just the same it's hard to bear.'

'Everyone manages to bear it,' I said. 'No one can explain it, no one at all. Relax.'

'There must have been a fine old slush when the ice melted,' said Henri.

'I should think so,' said the barman. 'But as there was no one there to see . . .'

'And even if there had been,' said Anna.

'Marvellous when you come to think of it,' said Henri, seriously. 'Same again, André.'

'No water? I see they take it neat in the Ouellé country.

285

But I agree with you – it must have made a fine old mess when it melted.'

'And then,' said Anna, 'the oceans filled up and all the little animals that were under the ice crept out.'

'It's a good thing people don't think about things like that all the time,' said the intellectual's pal. 'A good thing they forget about them, like everything else.'

'Yes, it's very fortunate,' said Anna.

'Very,' guffawed Epaminondas.

'Very fortunate indeed,' said the barman.

'I should think so,' said Epaminondas. 'It's bad enough as it is.'

At this point another customer came in. He was about thirty, very nattily turned out.

'Here's Jojo,' said the barman. 'Now we're going to enjoy ourselves.'

'Good evening,' said Jojo.

'Good evening,' said everyone.

Jojo went and sat down beside Henri and immediately cast a connoisseur's eye at Anna.

'So when did the saurians come, then?' she asked me.

'Have some saurians come?' said Jojo.

'Yes, two days ago,' I said.

'Three,' said Epaminondas.

'Hark at them,' said the barman.

'What are saurians like?' said Jojo.

'Just men like everybody else,' I said. 'Only they've got such enormous appetites they devour everything they come across.'

There was no reaction to this. Everyone listened, but no one understood. It was too hot to understand anything.

'I think we've had it for this evening,' said Anna quietly.

'Next time we'll draw them a picture,' said Epaminondas.

'What the hell are saurians doing here?' said Jojo at last.

'That's enough,' said Henri.

'I'll tell you,' said the barman. 'Don't get excited.'

286

'They don't do a thing,' said Anna, laughing. 'It's a perfect disgrace . . .'

'They were very big and very ugly,' said the barman. 'And they hunted everything there was, on sea and on land . . .'

'That's putting it in a nutshell,' said Epaminondas, convulsed.

'Never heard of that,' said Jojo.

'Christ, you're the only one then,' cried Epaminondas.

'What about birds?' asked Henri.

'Yes,' said Anna, 'I think we've had it for this evening.'

'Birds are like love,' I said. 'They've existed always. All other species disappear, but not birds. Like love.'

'We get you,' said Epaminondas. 'When you've got wings,' he explained, 'you can escape from the earthquakes.'

'Marvellous,' said Henri. 'Same again,' he told the barman.

'Seems we're going to disappear too,' said Henri. 'Can we offer you a drink?' he said to me, 'and Madame? Five then, André. Your name is André, isn't it? Yes? Yes, neat, please.'

'Let's hope we shan't disappear though,' said Epaminondas.

'But are there any saurians still left?' asked Jojo.

'Who knows?' I said.

'Some fun we're having,' said Epaminondas.

'We came here for some fun,' explained Henri. 'Ouellé's very pretty, but you couldn't call it amusing . . .'

'No?' said Epaminondas, waiting for more details, which were not forthcoming.

'Well,' said André, 'it looks as if you're going to give yourselves a treat now.'

'Look,' said Anna, pointing to Legrand. 'He's at it again.'

'You do look a bit funny,' said Henri. 'What's the matter? Trying to remember another word?'

'No,' said Legrand. 'I'm thinking, if you don't mind.'

'About time,' I said under my breath.

'Have some saurians come to Leo, then?' asked Jojo.

No one answered him.

'I find this conversation very interesting,' said Legrand mischievously. 'It doesn't bore me in the least.'

'Where were we then?' asked Epaminondas.

'The quaternary era,' said the barman.

'I thought we'd got past that,' said Legrand, mischievously still and looking at Anna.

'So did I,' said she.

'What happens after that?' said Jojo.

'Nothing,' said the barman. 'Man in his turn will vanish off the face of the earth.'

'How I love a good mug,' said Epaminondas, enchanted by Jojo.

'Are saurians a kind of bomber, then?' asked Jojo.

'Hark at him,' said Legrand, still looking at Anna, his face lit up.

'But are they coming, or are they already here, these saurians?' insisted Jojo.

'They can't be long now,' I said.

'Here we go again,' said Henri to the barman. 'I'm beginning to get a bit fed up with it.'

'Man isn't a saurian,' said Legrand suddenly. 'You mustn't get them confused. Man is a very cunning creature. When it doesn't suit him any more in one place, he goes off and plants his tent somewhere else. He isn't just a silly old saurian . . .'

'Don't they plant anything then?' said Jojo.

'No,' said André. 'Haven't you heard what they've been saying?'

'Yes, it's going to start all over again,' groaned Henri.

'People have got to talk about something, haven't they?' said Legrand to Anna. 'It's better than speaking ill of your neighbour.'

'Why has man got to vanish off the face of the earth,' said Jojo, 'if he replants everything he eats?'

'Because the earth is like everything else,' said the barman. 'Like patience. It gets worn out. I read in the paper the other day that in thirty million years man uses up seventy-five centimetres of soil, so in the end, even if we do replant everything we eat, the earth gets fed up.'

'Christ, we haven't got long to go,' said Jojo.

'That's how it is,' said the barman.

'I see,' said Jojo. 'So if the saurians don't replant anything, it's because they're bastards.'

'Got it in one,' said the barman.

'At the rate we're going,' said Henri, 'seventy-five centimetres . . . makes you wonder that we're still here at all . . .'

'Did you see about the Germans? All the kids they're having?' said his pal.

'They're within their rights,' said Henri.

'People ought to be warned about things like that.'

'Same again,' said Henri. 'Last round.'

'Why the last round?' said Legrand. 'We don't come to Leo every day.'

'That's true enough,' said Henri wistfully. 'And we are enjoying ourselves.'

'Don't be sad,' said Anna to Epaminondas. 'It's not certain that we shall all disappear.'

'I'm not sad,' said Epaminondas. 'On the contrary, I adore Jojo.'

'You're fantastically pretty,' said Legrand to Anna.

'Why fantastically?'

'Just a manner of speaking. I'd never have believed it possible.'

'We shall be wiped out long before with that atomic bomb of theirs,' said Henri, who had obviously lost the thread.

'Before what?' said Jojo.

'Before the earth gets fed up,' Epaminondas hissed at him.

'Six hundred of them they've got,' said Henri. 'Enough to blow us all up ten times over.'

'It's a funny thing,' said the barman, 'but even when they start off talking about the ice age people always get back to atomic bombs. There seems to be some law.'

289

'You know, I only come here because of André,' said Jojo. 'He is clever.'

'Well, do you like it here?' said Legrand to Anna.

'It's not bad,' said Anna.

'As if there weren't enough natural catastrophes,' went on Henri, 'without going looking for atomic bombs.'

'You're just having me on,' said Jojo. 'I bet saurians are really a new kind of jet bomber.'

'Oh Christ,' bawled Henri, 'you and your bloody saurians!'

'How I love real mugs,' laughed Epaminondas.

'Well, all you've got to do is just tell me what a saurian is once and for all,' said Jojo piteously, 'and then I won't ask any more questions.'

'It's a sort of crocodile,' said André. 'See?'

'No, you're just having me on still, aren't you?' said Jojo indignantly. 'Don't try to tell me they've got atomic crocodiles now!'

'That's right, atomic crocodiles,' cried Henri. 'Now do you understand? Yes or no? If a person can't just say what he has to say in peace . . .'

'Man is a very cunning creature,' intoned Legrand, delighted with the turn things were taking. 'He's not just a silly old saurian.'

'Why do you talk to him like that?' said Henri. Then, turning to Jojo again, 'Saurians are just animals pure and simple, get that into your head once and for all. Of course it's only the fifth time you've been told.'

'If you start that,' said André, 'you'll never have done. He's not a man, he's a trap, a nightmare.'

'What sort of animals?' asked Jojo.

'Crocodiles!' yelled Henri. 'Croc-o-diles! Reptiles, if you prefer it.' With his hands he imitated a crocodile crawling over the bar. 'And now that's enough – understand?'

'You want to be careful about introducing new words,' said André. 'They bother Jojo, they do. He likes to understand everything. One day someone came in here and was foolish enough to start talking to him about cattle-rearing in the Charolais – remember, Jojo? – and I swear it went on till two in the morning. The chap broke half a dozen glasses, he got so wild. Mind you, Jojo, I'm not blaming you. You're different, people just have to know how to take you. You've got a one-track mind, that's all. But you've got a right to a place in the sun just like anyone else, don't you worry.'

'I should think so,' said Anna.

'I'm interested in everything,' said Jojo. 'That's why I'm like this. But nobody's interested in me.'

'Oh no,' said Legrand absent-mindedly, 'you mustn't say that.'

'You do look a bit queer though, Jojo,' said André.

'My dinner's just going down,' said Jojo. 'That must be it.'

'Mine hasn't had the chance,' said André. 'I haven't had time to eat.'

'You're always so romantic,' said Jojo.

'He's not the only one,' I said.

'I'll say,' said Epaminondas.

'Of course,' said Henri, 'atomic energy has its good side. In twenty years' time everything will be run on atomic energy.'

'I'll believe that when I see it,' said André.

'Aeroplanes do already,' said Henri.

'I thought as much,' said Jojo. 'They *were* jet bombers after all.'

'No, of course not,' said Anna. 'They were crocodiles. But they were huge, and they ate up everything they could. There haven't been any left for . . .'

She turned to Legrand.

'Three hundred thousand years,' said Legrand, laughing.

'Crocodiles aren't reptiles,' said Jojo, 'I'm as sure of that as I'm sitting here. Anyway what have they got to do with it?'

'To do with what?'

'With the bombers?'

'Oh my God,' moaned Henri. 'Has he finished or hasn't he?'

'I warned you,' said André. 'You have to treat him as a sort of curiosity.'

'They haven't got anything to do with the bombers,' said Anna soothingly.

'What about the things you were talking about when I came in?'

'They've got everything to do with those,' said Anna.

'Yes indeed,' I said.

'I should just think so,' said Epaminondas, who was crying with laughter.

'I may not know much,' cried Jojo, 'but what I know I know. What the hell's the use of talking about them if they don't exist any more?'

'Hell's flaming bells,' groaned Henri.

'I've never enjoyed myself so much,' said Epaminondas. 'I think I'll stay in Leo.'

'Just for something to talk about,' said Anna. 'We just happened to talk about that, as we might have done about anything else. You've got to talk about something, haven't you?' she said to Legrand.

'Of course,' said Legrand.

'The fact that they don't exist any more isn't any reason why people shouldn't talk about them, is it?' I said.

'What's wrong with him,' said André, 'is that he sees connections between everything, don't you, Jojo? A saurian is a crocodile, Jojo, and an aeroplane's an aeroplane.'

'I don't understand,' said Jojo.

'What?' asked Anna.

'Anything,' said Jojo.

'Don't shout,' said Epaminondas, 'and tell me what it is you don't understand.'

'I'm not going to say anything,' said Jojo.

'What he's got inside his skull isn't a brain,' groaned Henri, 'it's boiled cottonwool.'

'I don't know about that,' said Epaminondas, 'but he certainly is a curiosity.'

'André, give me a glass of the best Napoleon brandy you've got,' said Jojo loftily.

'He knows plenty about that subject anyhow,' said André.

'There we all were having a peaceful conversation,' said Henri, 'and now everybody's all gathered round his lordship trying to make him understand something that doesn't need any understanding at all.'

'True enough,' I said.

'Don't you care,' said André to Jojo. 'Always look on the bright side.'

'What about moving on somewhere . . . ?' said Legrand to Anna confidentially.

'No hurry,' said Epaminondas. 'Jojo amuses me.'

'That's right, there's no hurry,' said Anna.

'We've got the rest of our lives in front of us,' I said.

'I am saurian,' said Jojo. 'I bet that means something in English.'

Epaminondas laughed.

'I am very saurian!' he said.

'And you're from . . . ?' asked Legrand.

'Cotonou,' said Anna, writhing with laughter.

'And you?' said Legrand to me.

'Cotonou,' I said, laughing too.

Legrand put on a totally blank expression. Then he said:

'Life can be very funny,' he said. 'And there we were talking to you about saurians and all that – the lot.'

'Yes,' I said. 'We even talked about the ice age.'

'I don't understand,' said Jojo.

'In a sense he's right,' said André. 'I'm beginning to get a bit lost myself.'

'Are the saurians at Cotonou then?' said Jojo. 'What's it got to do with Cotonou?'

'It has got to do with it,' said Legrand. 'Only you have to know what we're talking about. Eh?'

'Exactly,' I said.

'If it's about crocodiles,' said Jojo, 'what's it got to do with it?'

'It's got to do with it what it's got to do with it,' cried Henri. 'Do I keep on asking questions?'

Legrand turned to me and said very politely:

'And I hope you'll forgive me for just now when I doubted what you were saying.'

'What did you doubt?' asked Jojo.

'What the gentleman was saying about the ice age,' said Legrand impatiently. 'As I didn't know then who the gentleman was I doubted what he was saying. And now if you want to know what was the colour of the engine-driver's whiskers . . .'

'I know what I'm saying,' said Jojo. 'You don't know this gentleman any more now than you did before, and nor do we know any more than we did about those saurians of yours.'

'Shall we chuck him out?' cried Henri.

'Oh no,' said Epaminondas, 'of course not.'

'Keep your hair on,' said Legrand to Henri. 'You're quite right,' he said to Jojo. 'No one knows what you're saying, but you're quite right.'

'If I'm in the way,' said Jojo crossly, 'all you've got to do is say so.'

'Don't get angry,' said Henri. 'Same again, André. What we say to you,' he said to Jojo, 'is for your own good, we're doing you a service. You're impossible, you know, you'll have to change.'

'Oh no,' said Anna, 'he mustn't change.'

'The man who'll change me,' said Jojo loftily, 'hasn't yet been born.'

'It's nothing to boast about,' said Henri.

'Well,' said Epaminondas, 'I am saurian in my own way.'

'Are you keen on saurians, then?' said Legrand to Anna.

'Don't say that word,' said the barman. 'It's beginning to come out of my ears.'

'I wouldn't say that,' said Anna. 'Not just any.'

'I am not very reassaurian,' said Epaminondas.

'Who is Jojo?' said Anna, very politely.

'He's my best customer, aren't you, Jojo?' said André. 'And as rich as Croesus, eh?'

'Cafés belong to everybody,' said Jojo. 'If I want to I can stay until it closes.'

'In that case,' said Legrand, 'there won't be many others there.'

'Why?' said Anna. 'There's no hurry.'

'I like people who come when you're not expecting them,' I said.

'Don't talk too fast,' said Epaminondas. 'I am not very reassaurian.'

'If he went,' said Henri, 'we'd be bored to screams.'

'It's quite simple,' said Legrand. 'People can hardly bear him, but they run after him. It's queer that he shouldn't understand it.'

'Shouldn't understand what?' said Jojo.

'That between you and us,' I said, 'it's a matter of life and death.'

'You're just making fun of me,' said Jojo. 'But I don't give a damn, any more than I did about the saurians.'

'Phew,' said André.

'It takes all sorts to make a world,' said Henri. 'Never a truer word. Two beers,' he said to André. 'We've had enough brandy to be going on with.'

'Make it three,' said Epaminondas.

'Four,' said Jojo.

'Seven?' I asked Anna.

'Seven,' she said.

'I'd like to give them to you,' said André, 'but after all the brandies that have gone down the hatch they'd produce a carbonic mixture to end all carbonic mixtures. In my opinion, and I've been a barman for twenty-seven years now, you'd do better to go on with the brandy.'

'You're a real father to us all,' said Anna.

'So unless you want to study the effects of carbonic mixtures on saurians,' said André, 'I shan't give you any beer.'

'There aren't many barmen like this one,' said Henri. 'Equal to every occasion.'

'Still,' said his pal, 'a nice cool beer . . .'

'I don't understand, André,' said Jojo. 'What does carbonic mixture do?'

'Explodes,' I said.

'As if you'd swallowed dynamite,' said Anna.

'First I've heard of it,' said Jojo. 'I think you're all having me on.'

'I am not very reassaurian,' said Epaminondas.

'It doesn't always explode,' said Anna, 'only one time in a thousand.'

'What's it to be then?' asked André. 'Brandy?'

'Brandy, but with water,' said Henri.

'All round?'

'All round.'

'It's not every evening,' said André, 'that I have such reasonable customers.'

'Not me,' said Jojo. 'I want some beer.'

'You'll have brandy just like everyone else,' said André.

'I don't take orders from you,' said Jojo. 'I tell you I want beer, not brandy.'

'Well, you'll get brandy anyway,' said André. 'My treat if you like.'

'In other words,' said Jojo, 'you won't let me have any beer?'

'That's right,' said André. 'For your own good.'

'For the last time, André,' said Jojo, 'give me a beer.'

'You want to explode, Jojo, is that it?' said Anna. 'Is that what you want?'

'No need of a beer for that,' said Jojo.

'We're having brandies,' said Henri. 'Why don't you have

one too, eh? A brandy and water quenches your thirst just as well as a beer.'

'That's not the point,' said Jojo. 'What I want is a beer.'

'Much as I love you,' said André, 'you're not getting a beer.'

'Right,' said Jojo. 'I'll remember this, André.'

'I'd give anything to know,' said Henri, 'what a bloke like him can do with himself in life.'

'If I'm in the way,' said Jojo, 'just say so.'

'It's not that,' said Henri, 'but I can't help wondering what sort of a job you must do.'

'I do what I do,' said Jojo.

'That's not saying much,' said Henri. 'Everyone does the best he can.'

'If you're going to take it like that,' said Jojo, 'I'm going back where I came from. Goodbye.'

'Goodbye,' said Anna.

Jojo went out.

'Where does he come from?' I asked.

'Indo-China,' said André, 'or somewhere round there in the Pacific. I've known him for ten years, and he hasn't changed in the slightest.'

'So,' said Legrand, 'you're Anna?'

'Yes. And you?'

'Nothing,' said Legrand.

'I thought as much,' said Anna in a low voice.

The barman and Henri preserved a discreet silence.

'What about them?' said Legrand, indicating us.

'They're they,' said Anna.

'I don't understand,' said Legrand.

'I've got lots of friends,' Anna explained.

Legrand's brow clouded.

'Are they coming too?' he asked.

'Of course,' said Anna.

'I don't think I quite understand,' said Legrand.

'What does it matter,' said Epaminondas. 'If people tried to understand everything . . .'

297

'A whole lifetime wouldn't be long enough,' I said.

'Is it far?' asked Anna.

'Two days' drive,' said Legrand, still very gloomy.

'It's a small world,' said Epaminondas.

'Couldn't you go alone?' said Legrand artlessly.

'One does what one can,' said Anna. 'No, I couldn't.'

'We shan't be in the way,' said Epaminondas. 'We're never in the way.'

'Never,' I said. 'Ask anybody.'

'Well,' said Legrand, shrugging his shoulders, 'if you ask me . . .'

He left us, still gloomy, having arranged to meet us the next morning. We went back on board the ship. Epaminondas was a bit uneasy again.

'One thing or the other,' he said. 'Either it's him or it isn't.'

'You're tired,' said Anna. 'Go to bed.'

'If it's him it's him,' went on Epaminondas.

'Maybe,' I said, 'but you know very well. . .'

'But if it isn't him,' he went on doggedly, 'why are they letting you go?'

Epaminondas got up early to buy two Mausers and a rifle. We'd need them, he said, if we were going to cross the Ouellé basin, and, you never knew, we might see some kudus.

We had an appointment to meet Legrand just before lunch, in the bar where we'd met him the previous evening. Epaminondas was very keen that we should take the Mausers and the rifle with us. He was quite cheerful again now. But when Legrand saw us come in, he didn't smile at all. On the contrary.

'What's all this?' he asked.

'Two Mausers and a rifle,' explained Epaminondas politely.

The joke didn't amuse Legrand at all.

He was a person who took things seriously. He immediately asked us, quite politely however, to give him some proof of our identities and of that of the ship.

'Either one does things properly or one doesn't do them at all,' he said.

We were in complete agreement with him. He was a man of principles, he told us, and of experience, and he'd have us know that this wasn't the first time he'd carried out missions as tricky as this one. We were quite ready to believe him. His devotion to Gégé was extreme, and his cautiousness maddening. But he was shy too. We didn't learn anything about him during the journey except that he'd known Gégé for two years, that he'd come from Abomey too and that Gégé and he had worked together ever since they'd known each other. He wasn't really interested in Anna, and he never showed any sort of curiosity. He acted towards her – and towards us too, for that matter – with a reserve that seemed to aim at being almost military, and which in his view he couldn't depart from without compromising the seriousness of his mission. We must put our trust in him, he told us before we left. And we did, completely. He drove us wherever he liked, and he drove very well. The only difficulty that arose was due to Epaminondas, and that was soon smoothed out. Epaminondas had an unconquerable aversion to people who took themselves with such messianic seriousness, however much justification there might be for it. Moreover Legrand made him feel uneasy, at least the first day. But next day, with the aid of the kudu, he forgot about him. But by no means the least of the pleasures of that journey was watching Epaminondas scrutinize him for a whole evening with the vigilance of a little kudu. Ah, we never loved Epaminondas more than we did during those few days!

We left the next morning towards eight o'clock. Anna went in her car, and Legrand fortunately went in his, a jeep, leading the way. Only he knew where we were going, and where we were to sleep that night.

That day we crossed the great flat humid levels of the Upper Congo. The roads were good, the cars bowled along. In

Africa, in those latitudes, the weather presents no problem. It was very hot, of course, but whether it was because we were all so intent on our object or for some other reason, no one complained. It rains all the year round in the Congo basin, with only equinoctial variations, apparently. It rained that day too. The forest was interminable. But it's never monotonous – on the contrary, it's always different to anyone who will take the trouble to look at it properly. The hooters of the cars echoed in it as in a cathedral. The sky above it was always covered with low clouds. They emptied themselves into the forest almost hourly, you got used to it, piercing it to the depths, piercing the earth to its depths also. Tons of water came crashing down. We stopped the cars. The noise of the rain was almost frightening. She watched it falling in astonishment. It was strange watching her: her eyes went now dark green like the forest, now transparent like the rain. She was hot too, and her brow was always covered in sweat, which she kept wiping off with the back of her arm in a mechanical, absent-minded gesture that pierced my heart. We couldn't speak for the noise of the rain. So I just watched her looking at the rain and wiping her forehead with the back of her arm. But that wasn't all. Even the blinking of her eyelids pierced my heart. And once, looking at her, I suddenly seemed to see something else of her that I couldn't name and that perhaps I ought not to have seen, and I let out a cry. Epaminondas jumped and went for me. It was soon clear that a tropical climate didn't agree with him either. She turned rather pale, but she didn't ask me what was the matter. Every now and then we saw the Congo, sometimes calm, sometimes not. It coursed through the forest like a mad thing, in an immense curve which the road didn't always follow. The noise of the rapids could be heard ten kilometres away, loud enough to have drowned the trumpeting of a hundred thousand elephants. There were guided tours to them every so often, but Legrand didn't give us time to go and see them. We didn't go through many villages. Those we did go through were usually very tiny, swallowed up in the depths of the forest. Only kudus and elephants – the biggest in the world – can get used to the forest and find their way about in it. They die of old age on its inviolable earth, and it consumes them, as it has consumed itself perpetually, over and over again, since the beginning of the world. It is shot through with strange colours. Currents, veins, rivers of colour. Sometimes it grows red as murder. Sometimes grey, and then again it will completely fade into insipidity. We could hardly breathe. The constant storms filled the air with heavy oily vapours. It was not, after all, an air for men, but for elephants and kudus. But no one complained. We didn't see any flowers to remind us of the ones we knew. Probably they were only visible to the kudus too.

Legrand didn't consider it necessary for us to stop for lunch, and in the afternoon we came to a town with the curious name of Coquilhatville. Epaminondas had high hopes of it, but it turned out to be of little interest. We left the river here, but rejoined it again towards six that evening at a much smaller town called, if I remember rightly, Dodo. There we left the river for good, and struck straight north towards the valley of the Ouellé. The road began to change. First it became not too good, then bad, then it had no surface at all and we had to take great care not to sink into great quagmires of clay. Towards eight we came to the end of the plain, and began to climb gently among the savannahs of the Ouellé. It grew cooler. We stopped at a post with a few white men's bungalows and a small hotel also run by a white man that Legrand knew. Epaminondas noticed, not without some qualms, that they looked rather alike, and that we appeared to be expected. We took long showers. We were very hungry in spite of the heat, even Epaminondas. The bungalow might have seemed depressing. It was dirty, with bare walls and only an acetylene lamp. But we were told there was some Dutch whisky, and Anna ordered some right away. We had dinner. Epaminondas ate with his Mauser slung over his shoulder. He only put it down on a chair beside him after three Dutch whiskies. Legrand refused to touch any whisky, but we drank ours in spite of him. He didn't trust us. I still don't quite know what he suspected us of. But he continually suspected us of something, he even thought there must be something wrong with our appetites that evening. However, we had to talk to him a bit somehow. And what was there for us to talk to him about?

'Do you hunt kudus?' Anna asked him.

'Never set eyes on one,' he said. 'Can't tell you anything about them.'

'What a shame,' said Anna. 'I'd have liked to listen to some nice stories about kudus this evening.'

'There was once,' I said, 'and still is, in Somalia, a little kudu. The smallest one in all Africa. It lives on the slopes of great mount Kilimanjaro. It's as swift as the wind, and on its neck it has a little mane like a foal's. It is extremely timid and shy. Intelligent too. It has learned once and for all that it is a rare and difficult quarry.'

'Has it always been rare and difficult?'

'Not always,' I said. 'Once there was a kudu who saw a huntsman in a motorcar. He liked the look of the huntsman and found his car intriguing. He came up and licked the tyres gently by way of greeting. He liked the taste of the rubber. But the huntsman said to himself, this kudu's making fun of me. Huntsmen like their quarry to be rare and difficult. He made the impudent kudu realize this. Now he is far away, on the virgin slopes of Kilimanjaro.'

Legrand looked at me suspiciously.

'Are you really talking about kudus?'

Anna reassured him.

'They're what we like to hunt best,' she said.

'In any case, whether they are or not,' said Epaminondas, 'what else can we talk about?'

'And this is their country we're in, isn't it?' I said.

We were thirsty, and drank whisky and beer alternately.

It wasn't long before this produced a certain effect. Legrand watched us drinking with a disapproving expression.

'And what about Gégé?' Epaminondas asked. 'Has he killed any kudus?'

For the first time Legrand gave a meaning laugh.

'Oh, him!' he said.

He didn't finish. We all laughed knowingly, and this baffled Legrand again.

'The man who hunts kudus,' I said, 'is a being apart. He has lots of patience. He takes his time.'

'Let's hope so,' laughed Epaminondas.

'You can go without sleep hunting the kudu,' I said, 'sometimes without food too. It's a matter of temperament. Some can and some can't.'

Legrand looked at me blankly. Unlike Epaminondas, he had a countenance that became vague and unlovely when he didn't understand something.

'You might as well smile,' Anna told him. 'I'm sure no one would hold it against you. Besides, we shan't tell anyone.'

She looked so pretty I thought he'd give in at last and look on her kindly. But no.

'People can't just make me laugh when they think they will,' he said.

'Too true,' said Epaminondas.

Anna put her feet on the table, as she often did on the ship when we were chatting alone in the bar. Her ankles were as slim as a kudu's.

'You've got ankles like a kudu,' I said.

'Perhaps we shall see one tomorrow?' she said. 'I'm longing to see one like the one you said, a small one with a long mane and ringed horns standing up like flames above his stubborn little brow.'

'If we were allowed to stop for an hour,' said Epaminondas, 'we might see one perhaps.'

He glared at Legrand. But Legrand took no notice. He went on listening to me in astonishment.

'And now tell me,' said Anna, 'how they became a rare and difficult quarry after they'd licked the huntsmen's tyres.'

I began to stroke her kudu's ankles. This obviously troubled Legrand, who averted his eyes, but still went on listening to me. He must have had a very boring life.

'It wasn't that the huntsmen wished him any harm,' I said. 'They didn't. But they'd come after a rare and difficult quarry, and so they were annoyed. And then they had their rifles all ready, oiled and loaded, and they wanted to make use of them. So they did. The kudu didn't die straight away. He wept for a long time. Nobody ought to have to see a kudu weeping. Lying by the side of the road with its face bathed in blood, the kudu wept at the sadness of having to die. He wept for the grassy slopes of Kilimanjaro, for the fords across the Ouellé, the silent dawns in the clearings in the savannahs. The huntsman finished him off, loaded him on the luggage rack, and went back to his camp. He didn't tell anyone what had happened. It was only one kudu, and the world was full of them; but who can ever redeem the innocence of one kudu? The next morning seemed bitter to the huntsman. He hadn't the heart to get up, and stayed in his tent till noon.'

'Of all the daft stories . . .' said Legrand.

'It's obvious,' said Anna, 'that you never get up at noon. What happened next?'

'Kudus became very difficult to hunt. They are still.'

'And what about the huntsman?' said Epaminondas.

'They say he only got up in order to leave Africa, and that he has never returned . . .'

'He wasn't a real hunter,' said Anna. 'Oh, how I'd love to kill a kudu tomorrow.'

'And what wouldn't I give . . .' said Epaminondas.

'But when you kill one as it ought to be killed, after days and days, weeks even, of waiting, then you're very happy. You put it up on the roof of the car with its horns pointing forward, and when you get back you hoot in a special way to announce its arrival. Life is suddenly good. You look at

the kudu for a long time in the light of the acetylene lamps –
this thing in search of which you completely forgot yourself.'

'And as you look at it, do you begin to wish for other
kudus?' asked Anna.

'I should think so,' said Epaminondas.

'Ah,' I said, 'you never lose the desire for them. But it so
rarely happens that you kill one after another that while
you wait for the others you drive yourself mad with desire.'

'But can't you occupy yourself with other things?' she
said.

'Of course,' I said, 'you can go back to your usual occupa-
tions, but you're no longer the same person. You are changed
for ever.'

She smiled, slightly drunk with whisky and the longing to
kill kudus. I stroked her ankles more and more intensely.
The heat was overpowering. Now and then she would half-
close her eyes. We were very tired. Legrand went to sleep
and snored gently. Epaminondas grew thoughtful. Anna
looked at Legrand and smiled.

'A martyr to devotion,' she said. 'Gégé can't be very difficult to please. In your American novel, will you say anything
about kudus? As Mr Hemingway has already written about
them, mightn't it be considered in bad taste?'

'If it wasn't for Mr Hemingway,' I said, 'we shouldn't be
talking about them at all. Do you think it would be better to
lie and say we were talking about something else?'

'No,' she said. 'It's better to tell the truth and hope for
the best.'

She folded her arms on the table and leaned her head on
them. Her hair came undone and her comb fell on the floor.

'What else will you say,' she asked softly, 'in your
American novel?'

'I'll talk about all our voyages,' I said. 'It's bound to be a
very maritime sort of novel.'

'Will you tell about the colour of the sea?'

'Of course.'

'What else?'

'The drowsiness of the African nights. The moonlight. The Montboutou tomtoms in the savannah.'

'What else?'

'Who knows? Perhaps a cannibal feast. But the colour of the sea at every hour of the day – that certainly.'

'I should like people to take it for a travel book.'

'They will, since we *are* travelling.'

'All of them?'

'Perhaps not quite all. A dozen may not, perhaps not so many.'

'And what will they think?'

'What they like, anything they like. Really, anything they like.'

She was silent, her head still resting on her arms.

'Go on talking to me for a bit,' she said.

'When you're asleep,' I said, 'and you know the kudu is there outside your tent, you think that anything more than that kudu would be too much, that you will never have another, that this will be the only one. That's more or less what happiness is.'

'Ah,' she said gently, 'how terrible it would be if kudus didn't exist.'

I think I must have called out her name again then, as I had done that morning. Epaminondas started again. Legrand woke up, and asked me what was the matter. I reassured him. Nothing, I said. We went to bed. Epaminondas had to share a room with Legrand. I heard Legrand asking him whether we were making fun of him and if he thought this play-acting was going to go on much longer.

'Who knows? It might end tomorrow,' answered Epaminondas judiciously.

Legrand gave a loud laugh. He had understood.

We set out next morning at four o'clock, like real hunters. Legrand had a strict schedule and stuck to it. We drove through the dark for a little over an hour. The roads were bad and it was difficult going. Then the sun rose over the savannahs of the Ouellé. It was very beautiful country. There were valleys, springs, a clearer sky. Sometimes the forest returned, but much less dense than in the Congo basin. The whole place was covered with tall thick grass. This was real kudu country. Every so often black rocks cropped out of the ground in strange shapes that reminded Epaminondas of our favourite animal. It was much cooler than it had been the previous day. Ouellé is a high plateau from five hundred to a thousand metres above sea-level, rising gently towards Kilimanjaro. The wind always blows there. There were still occasional storms, but not so heavy as before. The roads got worse and worse, and we were having some difficulty in following Legrand's jeep.

Towards noon we came to a little village. There was no white man's bungalow here. Legrand told us that it wasn't possible to drive any farther, but that we were only about three hours' march from our destination. We'd been so good he seemed reassured, and we on our side had begun to get used to his ways. Even Epaminondas admitted in the end that we might have done worse.

We stayed for quite a while in this little village. Legrand told us to get out of the car and wait for him in the square. He said he had to make some enquiries before we left. He disappeared, leaving us alone. All the village had come out on our arrival. We went to sit in the square. We'd grown so obedient that we didn't move the whole of the hour that Legrand was away. The village was round like a circus, grouped about the central clearing, which was also circular. The huts were made of mud, all alike, with the same little reed-thatched verandah supported on posts before each. All the inhabitants without exception came to look at us, both the men, who didn't seem to be very occupied, and the women, who were weaving on their verandahs when we arrived. They looked very closely at Anna, and at us because we were with her. They were the first Montboutous we'd met. They were taller and more handsome than the people we'd seen before in the Congo valley. Most of them had Berber blood and were lighter in colour. Many had their cheeks and foreheads decorated with deep tattooing. Their faces were mostly very gentle-looking. The women were naked to the waist. Infants came up like little goats to feed at their breasts as they watched us. Epaminondas observed that none of these people looked particularly given to cannibalism. However, he did ask for a drop of the Dutch whisky Anna had brought with her, and we had a drink too, enough to make us share his opinion. We let them look at us as much as they liked. Strangely enough, though we kept smiling at them, they didn't smile back. They commented on us at great length – only on our physical appearance, necessarily – in very loud voices, as if they were a long way away from each other. These voices would have been terrifying if they hadn't been in such contrast with the gentleness of their aspect, and if we hadn't been in a mood in which there was little that could frighten us.

Legrand came back at last, followed by two men wearing European shorts and smoking cigars in enormous cigarette-holders. He wasn't at all happy with the results of his enquiries. He said the police had raided this village the evening before. It was probably our coming that had alerted them, and it was likely that they'd come back again today, and this time to the village where we were supposed to be meeting Gégé. He hadn't been able to find out whether Gégé had been warned. If he had, we were going to have great difficulty in finding out where he'd gone and getting to see him.

'You think it will be very difficult?' said Anna.

'Perhaps even impossible,' said Legrand.

'Oh no,' said Anna.

'Well, rather than get caught,' said Legrand.

'I'm rich,' said Anna.

'The price on his head is high,' said Legrand.

'But I'm very rich,' said Anna.

'As rich as that?' said Legrand, brightening up.

'Yes,' said Anna. 'Disgracefully rich.'

'Well then,' said Legrand, 'if it's not too late we may be able to fix it . . .'

Then as if suddenly remembering something:

'But what if it isn't him . . .?'

'It is him – enough,' said Anna.

'I don't understand,' said Legrand after a moment.

'I mean,' said Anna, 'that even if it isn't . . .'

Legrand decided that the best thing would be to get to the village, three hours' march away, where Gégé had still been in hiding the previous day. Even if we didn't find him there, it was the only place where we could find out in which direction to look next. He seemed full of drive now, and pleased with himself, especially since Anna had made her suggestion. For the first time since we'd left Leopoldville he agreed to have a drop of Dutch whisky with us.

We set out at once so as not to lose the slightest chance of finding Gégé. He might leave at any moment so we had to hurry. After a long consultation with Legrand, the two Montboutous he had consulted earlier came with us, as he wasn't sure he could remember the way.

As soon as we left the village we came to trodden mud paths, so narrow that we could only go along in single file. Anna walked in front of me, preceded by Legrand and the two Montboutous. Epaminondas brought up the rear. It was hot, but the savannah wind was still blowing and walking was quite bearable. Every now and then Anna would turn and smile at me, and we would look at each other without speaking. What, at that moment, could we have said? She looked paler, I thought, than usual, but we'd had so little sleep she must be tired. After half an hour's march Legrand handed round sandwiches and biscuits he'd got at the hotel where we spent the night. We were touched. But none of us, even Epaminondas, was in the least hungry. Nothing happened during our long march, except that every so often Epaminondas would let out a curious cry – rather like those of the Montboutous – because he thought he'd seen a kudu. He thought he'd seen one so often he put us half an hour behind schedule. Also, every now and again, the two Montboutous would talk to each other, in such loud strange voices that it made us jump every time. The ground undulated, sometimes quite steeply. When we came to a very deep hollow we dropped out of the wind and it became difficult to walk, but usually we soon climbed out again on to the plateau and the warm wind that howled through the savannah.

After two hours' march the path rose sharply and then descended into a deep valley cool with bombax and mahogany trees. Legrand turned and told Anna that we hadn't far to go now. We climbed up the other side of the valley and came out on the plateau again, very sparsely sprinkled with trees now and covered still with the dense grass, shoulder-high, through which the wind sang. Other paths, just as narrow and well-trodden, kept crossing ours. They ran like veins all through the Ouellé basin. Towards three o'clock there was a short storm, and we had to shelter under a tree until it was over. We took the opportunity to have a smoke and a drop of Dutch whisky. But no one felt like talking, not even Legrand. It was while we were waiting there that Epaminondas took a shot at a bird that had taken shelter in the same tree. He missed. Legrand was angry. We were so close now, he said, we couldn't have found a better way of frightening the sailor from Gibraltar off. However, before we started again, he fired two shots into the air with his Mauser. But this was the signal, he said. The sound of the shots made a long echo over the savannah; the air was so pure after the rain that it rang like crystal. Half an hour afterwards, his watch in his hand, Legrand fired another shot into the air, a single one only this time. Then he told us to stop and not make any noise. A minute of absolute silence went by. Then the sound of a tomtom, muffled and sad, rose out of the savannah. Legrand told us we were only half an hour away now. After that I didn't look at Anna any more, and she didn't turn round to look at me. Even Epaminondas didn't see any more kudus.

Half an hour later, just as Legrand had said, round a sharp turn in the path there came into view a little village, dark and low-built, lost like an ant-hill among the grass. I got in front of Anna and followed Legrand, but leaving some distance between us. He reached the village square first. He stopped, and I came up to him. There was no other white man there.

The village was like the one we had just left, but seemed smaller, and its central clearing was rectangular instead of round. There were the same mud huts and reed-thatched verandahs. All was quiet. Anna and Epaminondas came up and joined us. The women were weaving under their verandahs; naked copper-coloured children played with one another. A smith was making some tool and sending up showers of blue sparks into the sunlight. Some men crouched down sifting millet. The smith looked up as we arrived, then went on with his work. The women applied themselves to their weaving, the men to sorting their millet. Only the children flocked over to us uttering cries like birds. No one else bothered. Legrand grimaced. It was clear that we were not only expected but also unwelcome. Legrand scratched his head for a while and said it all looked very queer to him. He pointed to an empty verandah and told us to go and sit there. When we'd arrived the two Montboutous had gone straight over to a hut on the right of the square about ten yards from where we were, and Legrand now joined them. As he went over we saw that on the verandah, sitting on a mat, there was a woman, looking at us. The two Montboutous were talking to her, but she wasn't listening. Unlike the others, she was doing nothing. She looked at Anna. She was beautiful. We got the impression that Legrand knew her. He greeted her, thrust the two Montboutous aside, and spoke to her. She must have been very young. She must have been from another village, for her wrap was different from those of the other women, both in colour and in style. It was of fine grey stuff with a pattern of red birds over it, and she wore it fastened on the shoulder instead of round the waist. Only one of her breasts was left uncovered; it was extremely beautiful. She didn't look very tall, but she was taller than most of the Montboutou women we had seen so far. The skin of her arms and shoulders was of the same copper colour as the children's. Her smooth round cheeks were like theirs too. No, she wasn't from this village, she must have come from far away, from a town. There was rouge on her full wide lips.

There was a strange smell in the air here.

Legrand went on talking to her for about three minutes. Then he waited. She waited too, and then replied, very briefly, still looking at Anna. Her teeth lit up the darkness of her face with a barbaric gleam.

Hung up on the posts of her verandah were two dancers' masks of painted wood, black and white, surmounted by ringed horns that rose like flames. Anna looked at her too. Legrand began to talk to her again, but she didn't answer. Legrand thought, scratched his head again, and turned towards us.

'She won't say where he is,' he said.

Anna got up and went over to the hut. Epaminondas and I followed. To tell the truth, we could hardly have waited any longer. From near-to her beauty was just as perfect. Anna, very much moved, went up to her and smiled. The woman looked back at her, her eyes wide with a strange and painful curiosity, and did not smile back.

The strange smell that was in the air grew stronger, and a thin column of acrid smoke rose up behind us. But no one paid any attention to it yet except me, and I only just noticed it.

Anna stood facing the woman and looked at her. The woman gazed back, but she was still unable to smile. Anna took a packet of cigarettes out of the pocket of her shorts and held it out to her. She did it humbly, smiling, in a way I'd never seen her smile before, just for the woman herself, forgetting what she had come to ask her. The woman started when she saw the packet of cigarettes. She lowered her eyes, took a cigarette, and put it in her mouth. Her hand was a flower with blue petals. She was trembling. I leaned forward and lit her cigarette, but her hand was trembling so much that she dropped it. Epaminondas picked it up for her. She took it mechanically, put it in her mouth, and took a long pull at it. You could see she liked smoking, and derived strength and patience from it. She took her eyes off Anna for the first time, and looked searchingly at Epaminondas and me, still with the same pained curiosity. She tried to understand, failed, resigned herself.

'Tell her,' said Anna in a very low voice, 'tell her it's very probable that we're mistaken.'

Legrand translated, with some difficulty. The woman listened impassively. She didn't reply.

The evening breeze blew a great swirl of smoke over us. But no one took any notice of it, except me. And still I didn't pay it any attention, although it was strangely acrid and evil-smelling.

'Extremely probable,' said Anna.

Legrand, again with difficulty, translated. He got slightly impatient. For a moment the woman looked as if she was going to answer, but no, again she said nothing.

'Tell her,' said Anna, 'that I've been looking for him for three years.'

Legrand translated. The woman gazed at Anna, thought again, longer than before, then looked down again and made no answer.

313

'Perhaps the others'll tell us something,' said Legrand, turning round and looking towards the square.

Anna stood up.

'No,' she said, 'I don't want to speak to anyone but her.'

She still waited for some time before speaking. She was calm again now. The woman had finished her cigarette, and she offered her another. It was then that the smell of smoke suddenly became so strong that you couldn't help noticing it. Anna turned, and grew very pale. She looked into the distance, to where it was coming from. It was coming from beyond the square, not far away. Anna made as if to run away, but in the opposite direction, the direction we'd come from. Then she stopped, unable to muster the strength. Legrand obviously hadn't the least idea what was happening. I ran towards the smoke, followed by Epaminondas. In a tiny round clearing two men were roasting a kudu. Its hooves were tied together over a branch that they turned like a spit. Its head was still intact, and its nostrils brushed the ground, but the long neck that had borne its freedom through the farthest forests of the earth was already gnawed at and withered by the flames. It was its hooves that had filled the village with the smell that had alarmed us. Its horns had been cut off. They lay on the ground like swords fallen from the warrior's hand. I went back to Anna.

'A kudu,' I said. 'A big kudu.'

The woman had also watched us without understanding what it was all about. And Legrand, who had a very narrow conception of the human imagination, was no wiser than she. Anna recovered quite quickly. She leaned against one of the posts of the verandah for a minute, then turned again to the woman. At that moment the woman spoke. She had a soft, guttural voice.

'He killed the kudu for you,' translated Legrand, 'yesterday morning.'

She was silent again. Anna sat down beside her on the mat. The woman grew a little more reassured.

'I won't ask where he is any more,' said Anna slowly. 'There's no point. Tell her that he has a very . . . what shall I say? . . . a very special sort of scar, that you can't see just by looking at him in the ordinary way, but that only women, like her . . . and like me, have been able to see. Say to her that she and I could both easily recognize him by this scar.'

Legrand translated as well as he could, rather cursorily, it seemed to us. The woman thought for a moment and then answered.

'She asks what the scar is like,' he said.

Anna couldn't help smiling.

'She must understand why I don't tell her that,' she said.

Legrand translated. The woman wrinkled her eyes slightly by way of a smile. She said she understood. Then she said something quite lengthy.

'She says all men have scars,' translated Legrand.

'Of course,' said Anna. 'But this one is part of his life story. More, much more, than they usually are.'

He translated. She thought again. Our chances were dwindling. It was clear that she didn't understand. 'It's no good,' said Epaminondas. He was dancing with impatience. He could only think of kudus now, and would have liked to go as quickly as possible so as to try to get one before night-fall. Legrand was getting impatient too. When he translated now his voice sounded vulgar and coarse. Only Anna and I bore this trial of patience well. Yes, our chances were dwindling and dwindling, when suddenly the woman said something quite long again, and in a firmer tone than before.

'She says,' translated Legrand, 'that every man that is strong and brave has scars like that.'

Then he added, tapping his foot nervously:

'As if that was the point. She's going to keep you on a piece of string until the cows come home.'

'I'm used to it,' said Anna.

The woman spoke again, at even more length. Legrand's impatience had no effect on her.

'She says,' he told me, 'that there are strong, brave men everywhere, not only here.'

'Where is this scar?' said Anna.

I held my breath. Anna had gone up close to the woman and was no longer speaking to Legrand, but directly to her. I could only see her indistinctly, like the time at Sète when she turned towards me outside the service station. The woman was not lying. She left out certain things, but her expression was not that of someone who dissimulates.

'Where is it?' asked Anna again. I don't think she would have had the strength to say any more. The woman had obviously decided to give in. She didn't answer. She looked at Anna with the eyes of someone condemned to death, then lifted a finger blue as fate. I shut my eyes. When I opened them again the blue finger had come to rest on her neck, under the left ear. She cried out something. Legrand at once translated.

'A knife wound. Twenty years ago.'

Anna wasn't listening. She had leaned against the post again, her face still blank from the strain. She lit a cigarette.

'No, that's not it,' she said.

Legrand didn't translate. He was very disappointed.

'That's not it,' Anna said to the woman. She made a negative gesture with her hand. Her eyes were full of tears. The woman saw it too. She took her hand and started to laugh. Anna laughed too. I walked away.

'She's lying,' said Legrand.

'Oh no,' said Anna.

I went over towards the kudu. Epaminondas followed. Its head was in the flames now. The men had moved the fire, and were cutting long golden slices off its sides. I felt Epaminondas's hand on my shoulder. I looked at him, and he laughed. I tried to too, but I couldn't yet. I felt as if the kudu was wringing my heart. Anna came up with the woman, who was laughing all the time now like a child. Anna came

316

and stood near me and looked at the kudu. The woman said something to Legrand.

'She said you ought to eat a little piece,' he translated.

She herself cut three pieces from the kudu's dripping flank and held them out to us. Only then did I lift my eyes and look at Anna.

'It's marvellous,' she said, 'kudu.'

Her face had become the face I knew again. The flames of the brazier were dancing in her eyes.

'The best thing in the world,' I said.

I think only the woman realized that we loved each other.

They insisted on our sleeping in the village. It was too late to leave. We accepted. Epaminondas suggested we should go for a walk before it got dark. The two guides came with us. Legrand said he was exhausted, expressed his admiration of our toughness, but stayed behind. As soon as we were out of the village we stopped for a drop of Dutch whisky. It was then that she was seized with a fit of laughter. Watching her, the two Montboutous, and then Epaminondas and I, started to laugh too.

'When you write your American novel,' she said, when she'd begun to recover, 'you must tell how we ate that kudu . . .'

'That kudu or another,' I said. 'How terrible our lives would have been if . . .'

'But then who would ever have known?' she said.

Epaminondas thought he saw the grass move not far away from us.

'Be quiet,' he said to Anna. 'You'll frighten the kudu away with all your nonsense.'

We left next morning. Legrand stayed on in the village to wait for Gégé. He gave Anna an address in Leopoldville where she could send the money for the ransom. We parted on the best of terms. Anna kissed the woman goodbye.

317

We spent a bit longer than we'd intended in Leopold-ville. While we were away there'd been a fire on the yacht. Bruno had been careless and thrown a live cigarette-end too near the tank while they were filling up with oil. When we arrived the *Gibraltar* was still smoking. Only the bar and the upper deck had escaped.

Anna was in no mood to worry about it after our visit to the Montboutous.

'One thirty-six metre yacht the fewer,' she said. Then, gently: 'That'll lighten your American novel, won't it?'she said.

The important thing was that afterwards Bruno became serious too. He was perfectly cheerful from that time on. We were told that when the firemen arrived he was laughing so much people thought he'd gone mad. But Laurent had explained to them as best he could that certain people react rather strangely to fires.

We considered for a whole evening whether we should leave on a passenger steamer like ordinary people or buy another ship. In the end, so as not to have to separate and to give ourselves something to do, we decided to buy another ship. All we could find in Leopoldville was an old yacht, smaller than the *Gibraltar* and much less comfortable. But we all felt like a change, so it didn't bother anyone. Parti-cularly not Anna. To tell the truth, she'd had about enough of the old *Gibraltar*, ex-*Anna*, ex-*Cypris*.

We had a radio receiver installed, and sailed from Leopoldville. Two days afterwards we received a message from Havana. So we set our course for the Caribbean.

Laurent left us at Porto Rico, Epaminondas a bit further on, at Port-au-Prince. Bruno stayed on longer. Other old friends joined us while we waited for them to come back.

The sea grew very beautiful as we approached the Caribbean. But I can't talk about it yet.

ABOUT THE AUTHOR

One of the most important literary figures in France, Marguerite Duras is best known in this country for her novel *The Lover.* She is the author of several screenplays, including *Hiroshima, Mon Amour,* and many novels. Her memoir *The War* is about to be published by Pantheon Books.

PANTHEON MODERN WRITERS SERIES

THE SAILOR FROM GIBRALTAR
by Marguerite Duras, translated from the French by Barbara Bray

By the author of *The Lover*, "a haunting tale of strange and random passion."—*The New York Times Book Review*
0-394-74451-9 $8.95

THE RAVISHING OF LOL STEIN
by Marguerite Duras, translated from the French by Richard Seaver

"Brilliant...[Duras] shoots vertical shafts down into the dark morass of human love."—*The New York Times Book Review*

"The drama proceeds savagely, erotically, and...the Duras language and writing shine like crystal."—Janet Flanner, *The New Yorker*
0-394-74304-0 $6.95

THE ASSAULT
by Harry Mulisch, translated from the Dutch by Claire Nicolas White

The story of a Nazi atrocity in Occupied Holland and its impact on the life of one survivor.

"A powerful and beautiful work...among the finest European fiction of our time."—Elizabeth Hardwick

"A cool, brilliant modern horror story."—Mary McCarthy
0-394-74420-9 $6.95

THE WAR DIARIES: NOVEMBER 1939–MARCH 1940
by Jean-Paul Sartre, translated from the French by Quintin Hoare

Sartre's only surviving diaries: an intimate look at his life and thought at the beginning of World War II.

"An extraordinary book."—Alfred Kazin, *The Philadelphia Inquirer*

"These *War Diaries*...breach Sartre's intimacy for the first time."
—*The Washington Post Book World*
0-394-74422-5 $10.95

YOUNG TÖRLESS
by Robert Musil, translated from the German by Eithne Williams and Ernst Kaiser

A classic novel by the author of *The Man Without Qualities*, about four students at an Austrian military academy and their discovery and abuse of power—physical, emotional, and sexual.

"An illumination of the dark places of the heart."—*The Washington Post*

"A chilling foreshadowing of the coming of Nazism."
—*The New York Times Book Review*
0-394-71015-0 $6.95

ADIEUX: A FAREWELL TO SARTRE
by Simone de Beauvoir, translated by Patrick O'Brian

Simone de Beauvoir's moving farewell to Jean-Paul Sartre, her lifelong companion, in two parts: an account of his last ten years and an interview with him about his life and work.

"An intimate, personal, and honest portrait of a relationship unlike any other in literary history."—Deirdre Bair
0-394-72898-X $8.95

A VERY EASY DEATH
by Simone de Beauvoir, translated by Patrick O'Brian

The profoundly moving, day-by-day account of the death of the author's mother, at once intimate and universal.

"A beautiful book, sincere and sensitive."—Pierre-Henri Simon
0-394-72899-8 $4.95

WHEN THINGS OF THE SPIRIT COME FIRST:
FIVE EARLY TALES
by Simone de Beauvoir, translated by Patrick O'Brian

The first paperback edition of the marvelous early fiction of Simone de Beauvoir.

"An event for celebration."—*The New York Times Book Review*
0-394-72235-3 $6.95

THE BLOOD OF OTHERS
*by Simone de Beauvoir, translated by Roger Senhouse
and Yvonne Moyse*

A brilliant existentialist novel about the French resistance.

"A novel with a remarkably sustained note of suspense and mounting excitement due to the sheer vitality and force of de Beauvoir's ideas."
—*Saturday Review*
0-394-72411-9 $7.95

NAPLES '44
by Norman Lewis

A young British intelligence officer's powerful journal of his year in Allied-occupied Naples.

"An immensely gripping experience…a marvelous book…his compassion and humor are just plain terrific."—S. J. Perelman
0-394-72300-7 $7.95

PANTHEON MODERN WRITERS SERIES

BLOW-UP AND OTHER STORIES
by Julio Cortázar, translated by Paul Blackburn

A celebrated masterpiece: fifteen eerie and brilliant short stories by the
great Latin American writer.

"A splendid collection."—*The New Yorker*

"Unforgettable."—*Saturday Review*
0-394-72881-5 $6.95

THE WINNERS
by Julio Cortázar, translated by Elaine Kerrigan

Julio Cortázar's superb first novel about life—and death—on a South
American luxury cruise.

"This formidable novel...introduces a dazzling writer....[*The Winners*] is
irresistibly readable."—*The New York Times Book Review*
0-394-72301-5 $8.95

THE OGRE
by Michel Tournier, translated by Barbara Bray

The story of a gentle giant's extraordinary experiences in World War II—
a gripping tale of innocence, perversion, and obsession.

"The most important novel to come out of France since Proust."
—Janet Flanner

"Quite simply, a great novel."—*The New Yorker*
0-394-72407-0 $8.95

FRIDAY
by Michel Tournier, translated by Norman Denny

A sly, enchanting retelling of the story of Robinson Crusoe,
in which Friday teaches Crusoe that there are better things in life
than civilization.

"A literary pleasure not to miss."—Janet Flanner

"A fascinating, unusual novel...a remarkably heady French wine in the
old English bottle."—*The New York Times Book Review*
0-394-72880-7 $7.95

THE WALL JUMPER
by Peter Schneider, translated by Leigh Hafrey

A powerful, witty novel of life in modern Berlin.

"Marvelous...creates, in very few words, the unreal reality of Berlin."
—Salman Rushdie, *The New York Times Book Review*

"A document of our time, in which fiction has the force of an eyewitness
account."—*The* [London] *Times Literary Supplement*
0-394-72882-3 $6.95